THE UNRAVELING

OF DAVID MONK

a Novel

HENRY D. TERRELL

RIVER GROVE
BOOKS

Published by River Grove Books
Austin, TX
www.rivergrovebooks.com

Distributed by River Grove Books

Design and composition by Henry D. Terrell
Cover design by Greenleaf Book Group
Chapter heading art design by Greenleaf Book Group
Author photo by Sarah S. Terrell

Publisher's Cataloging-in-Publication data is available.

Print ISBN: 978-1-63299-914-6

eBook ISBN: 978-1-63299-915-3

First Edition

For Felix Scardino

David Forgets His Bible

CALLS AFTER 9:30 AT NIGHT ALWAYS BRING BAD NEWS. David Monk was not really asleep, just dozing in a state of pre-sleep, when the phone rang.

His bedtime was still nine o'clock, which wasn't fair. Not pajamas and toothbrushing time, but in bed, under the covers, in the dark. To achieve this strict timetable, enforced by his mother and more grudgingly by his dad, he had to be in his pajamas by 8:45, mouth full of foaming minty freshness by 8:55, followed at close quarters by kisses and lights out. In winter, this time fell long after deep dark, so it didn't feel so wrong. In the summer months, when school was out, it was torment. There was no seasonal adjustment, no leeway, no allowance for the fact that it was still light outside, that he wasn't expected anywhere in the morning.

Once, a couple of years ago, Dad had gone outside to get something out of his car, leaving the front door open, and David, in his pajamas, had wandered to the door and saw, through the screen, two of his friends, Randy and Walter, playing outside in the red light of dusk. They both crouched behind a car across the street, each armed with a plastic toy pistol, fighting imaginary Japanese troops. *Look out for snipers!* Randy had called out to Walter and their imaginary comrades in arms. David had slipped away in shame to bedroom exile as his friends fought heroically against great odds in the twilight.

When he was still small, prayers were said aloud and supervised by his mother, but later, she let him say his prayers, or rather prayer, on the honor system in his own room with the door closed. He went through the short ritual, a habit enforced by superstition and guilt.

Tonight, teeth and prayer were done, and the only light came from under the crack of the sliding door to his bedroom. The big black telephone had its own little alcove just outside the door, centrally located for the small house, but quite a few steps from Mom and Dad's bedroom at the other end of the hall and even farther from the den where the TV was, so if it went off in the night, David was forced to endure three or four harsh rings before Mom or Dad picked up.

On this night, the phone intruded loudly as David's thoughts drifted by like a Shrine circus parade of colorful floats, the initial stage of sleep. With the first penetrating ring, he was instantly alert, heart pounding. Blessedly, Mom was quick to answer, expecting-a-call-quick, and it only rang once. He then lay in bed, both ears uncovered, trying to make out what she said. She was being extra-quiet, and she mostly listened to someone else talk. David thought he made out, "Have you talked to Uncle Maury?" and "No, I'll go ahead and come on now." Then she said, "Thank you, Gretchen, you're a sweetheart. See you in a while," and hung the phone back on its cradle gently, presumably to not wake David.

Twenty minutes later, he heard Mom and Dad talking quietly in the living room, but he couldn't understand what they were saying. The front door opened, and then the car door banged, and the engine started. David had no idea what time it was—his only clock was a windup with no illumination at all—but it had to be very late. The sound of the car backing out of the driveway and pulling away, the front door closing. Water running in the kitchen. The television, switched off for the night, came on again in the den, and David heard it through the wall. Dad was watching Jack Paar, a show he watched every night before bed, but he usually turned it off after the first half hour. There was tinny big-band music and laughter, and Jack's wisecracks, more laughter, but David couldn't make out the words. After a while, he slept.

Very, very late, and in deep sleep, he heard the phone ring again. It took Dad four excruciating cycles to answer it. David sat up in bed. What awful thing had happened? Dad's voice was deeper and more penetrating than Mom's, and David heard every word.

"Okay, love. I understand. I'll bring him in the morning."

What? thought David. *Does he mean me?*

"It's almost two o'clock," Dad said "We can come first thing."

Come where?

"I know …I know, but …Okay, love …Okay, I can wake him up, but it will take us a while to get going."

David held his breath and listened. *But it's the middle of the night! I don't want to go anywhere.*

"I know, love," said Dad, sighing. "Okay, love. I'll see you after a while."

Dad hung up the phone. David waited for the bedroom door to slide open, but Dad's footsteps went away. Two o'clock ... in the morning. Was there a more terrible time for anything? Several minutes passed, but Dad didn't come back. David lay back down, very much awake. He allowed himself to hope that whatever had happened didn't involve him. But he knew better. When Dad's footsteps returned up the hall, David sat up again. His bedroom door slid open.

"Davie?" said Dad.

"I'm awake," David said.

"You need to get up, son. Get dressed. We have to go see Gammy."

"Right now?"

"Yes. I'm sorry. You should get dressed."

Dad never said he was sorry for anything. It wasn't in his vocabulary. So, this was serious.

"Okay." The bedroom door rolled shut. *Shunk.* David switched on his bedside lamp, which was so dim you could barely read by it, but at two o'clock in the morning, it was brilliant and glaring. Getting dressed was something he did automatically every morning without thought, but now the process was difficult. The easiest thing to do was put on the same pants and shirt he wore yesterday, which were on the floor by the dresser, not yet consigned to the laundry hamper. There was yesterday's underwear, too, but he wouldn't put those on. He wanted fresh socks as well. He retrieved them from the drawer. It took way longer than usual to get started, but once he began, he felt chilled and hurried through getting dressed, leaving the pajamas folded up and under his pillow like he was supposed to, but not making the bed. It seemed wrong to make a bed in the middle of the night.

Dad was in the front hall putting on his suede jacket.

"Put on a coat, Davie. It's cold."

David opened and poked through the overstuffed front closet and selected a yellowed cloth coat that was probably warmer than he needed—it was not a bitterly cold night—but he couldn't quite shake the chill.

"Bring a pillow."

"Why?"

"You can sleep in the back seat."

"Where are we going?" asked David. "Is Gammy at her house?"

"Yes," said Dad. "It's gonna be a couple of hours. You can sleep. In the morning, I'll take you to a café, and we can get some breakfast."

"Why are we going to see Gammy? Is she still sick?"

"Yes, Davie. She's feeling worse. Your mother says she needs to see you."

David fetched the pillow from off his bed, leaving his wadded-folded pajamas exposed and unsightly.

Dad opened the front door and waited for David to step out on the porch before he turned off the porch light and locked the door. The sky was dark, but streetlights and porch lights made pools of yellow on the street and sidewalk.

"Are we going in your company car?" asked David.

"Yes," said Dad. "It's against the rules, but your mother has the car." Dad was not supposed to use his company car except for business. Something to do with "insurance," but David didn't understand that. Randy's dad had a company car, too, and he used it every day as a second family car. But Dad's company was stingy and would get mad if he used it to drive anywhere except the office and "out in the field," wherever that was. The company car was a Buick, newer and nicer than the family Ford. It also smelled different, like car wax and tobacco, although Dad didn't smoke anymore.

David opened the rear car door and tossed in his pillow, then climbed in. Dad pulled the driver's door shut with a *thunk,* which hurt David's ears from pressure shock. *Ouch.* Only the Buick did that, not the Ford. David rode in the Buick so seldom that he never remembered to put his fingers in his ears.

As they drove, David watched the sleeping town go by, the streetlights parading shadows across the back seat until the car sped up and the lights were left behind. Looking back, David saw the city lights strung out across the horizon, gradually receding. When even those disappeared, he lay down on the seat. He pulled his coat tightly around him, scrunched his pillow beneath his head, and tried to sleep. He never did, though the roll of the road was comforting. After some time, Dad switched on the radio to a low volume. It was Paul Harvey, speaking of things David didn't understand, but that precise, resonant voice was comforting.

After a long time, David remembered something. "Dad, I forgot to bring the Bible."

"It's all right," said Dad. "I'm sure Gammy has Bibles."

David didn't try to explain, but the point of the Bible was not the document per se, but that particular Bible, a small one with the black leather cover worn smooth. He never tried to read it. It made little sense, anyway. The point was that the Bible gave him something to do with his left hand and provided authority. It was just a prop.

They rode some more in silence. David shut his eyes.

Dad spoke. "Davie, I want you to understand that Gammy is really sick. Very old and sick. She's seventy-eight." David opened his eyes and watched a light go by, a single, lonely light attached to a pole in front of a metal shed. A yellow shaft panned across the back seat, and then it was dark again. "Nobody expects a miracle," said Dad. "Your mother wants a miracle. She really doesn't want Gammy to go away because it's her mom, and she loves her. Mother just wants you to try and do what you can do."

"I know," said David, because he did know. There was a difference between what was expected of him and what he could make happen.

"Page two," said Paul Harvey.

THE SKY HAD GONE FROM BLACK TO INKY BLUE as the company car turned onto Gammy's street in Gammy's town. It was not the town where Mom or Dad had grown up, and neither had Gammy. She had just ended up here when she married for the second time, in her sixties, to a man named Gary. Grandad had been dead and gone since before David could remember. Mom had never liked Gary. Gammy's just lonely, Mom had explained. Gary was a man who had lost his wife and was just lonely, too. Gammy had moved with Gary to the house he had lived in for decades. He lasted three years before diabetes killed him.

When they arrived at Gammy's little house, their family Ford was parked in the driveway, and a couple of other cars were out front.

David was hungry. "Dad, what time is it?" he asked.

"It's almost six," said Dad.

"Can we go have breakfast?"

"After a while, Davie. I think we better see what's going on with Gammy."

David zipped up his cloth coat and climbed out into the cold predawn. The neighborhood was quiet and still, and most houses were dark. Gammy's house had lights, however. Dad just tapped on the door, then went right in without waiting for somebody to answer, and David followed.

Inside, it smelled like sickness. The house always smelled this way to David, but now the smell was stronger, a pungent mull of disinfectant, alcohol, and bathroom spray, and there was nothing else like it. For many years, even after he was much older, whenever he caught a slight whiff of any similar odor, David would flash to the little two-bedroom house with its lumpy chairs, low ceilings, and grimy knick-knack shelves.

A man David had never seen was sitting on one of the chairs in the little living room. He had black slicked-back hair that was perfectly gray on the temples. He stood up and smiled as they came in.

"Mr. Monk?" he said. "Hi, I'm Pastor Shotten." The two grownups shook hands. "It's good that you could come. I wish we were meeting under better circumstances." He turned his attention to David. "And you must be young David," he said. David offered his hand, and the pastor's enormous hand gripped his for a moment. "I've heard about you."

"Is she awake?" asked Dad.

Pastor Shotten shrugged. "Sometimes, she seems to be awake. She hasn't said anything we could understand since yesterday."

He led them into the sick room, which was the locus of the smell. Mom was sitting in a chair on one side of the bed, and a much younger woman was on the other. David didn't know it yet, but she was Gary's daughter, Gretchen, who had no stake in Gammy's life but was a caring person by nature. Mom looked tired and defeated—her face pale and puffy in the dim light. She stood up without a word and hugged David, pushing him against her thick thighs. From the other side of the bed, Gretchen smiled and waved.

"Hi, Davie," she said.

"Hi."

"Honey, did you bring your Bible?" Mom asked.

"No, I forgot it," said David. "But I don't need it."

"I'm pretty sure there's a Bible in the living room."

"No, I really don't need it."

She let David go and turned him toward the bed, where there was a shrunken version of Gammy. Her eyes were closed, but David imagined he could see her eyes through the thin blue lids and that she could see him. Her lips were tight. Her hair, which had never lost all its brown color, was held back from her face by bobby pins. She breathed in little shallow puffs.

"See what you can do, Davie," said Mom. She didn't have to say that. He knew what was expected of him.

David placed his right hand over Gammy's forehead at the right distance, close but not touching, and waited for the feeling to come, the little buzz he felt in his tummy and rib cage that meant his body was connecting to another body. He closed his eyes and tried to find the place where Gammy's soul was. For most people, it stayed just to the left or right of the centerline between the eyes, an inch or so out. On someone who was very sick or dying, sometimes it lived closer to the skin or even right on it. David tried to find it, but Gammy's soul was quiet, like a radio between stations. Suddenly, David was overcome by a fierce yawn. He shook his head and put his hand back down.

"I'm sorry, Mommy."

"It's all right, honey. Just try again."

The hand went back, and this time, he felt a dim presence, like an old TV when it was first turned on, and the picture wasn't there yet. Gammy's eyes opened halfway, and she turned her head toward him.

"Honey," she seemed to say, barely audible. The corners of her mouth moved as if she were trying to smile.

Mom's voice came from behind him, louder than the circumstances required. "Mama, Davie's come to try and help you."

Gammy's lips moved. "Davie," she said, a little clearer than before, and the mouth corners pulled upward a little bit.

"Where do you hurt, Gammy?" David said.

Gammy licked her lips, just a tiny flick of the tongue. "I don't hurt, Sweetie-pie," she said very softly.

"Mama, doesn't your stomach hurt?" asked Mom, too loud.

Lips licked again. "No," she breathed. "I'm fine."

Gretchen whispered to David's mother. "Is Davie cold? He's shaking."

"No," Mom whispered back. "He just shakes a little bit when he's working."

David tried to hold his hand steadier. He kept it just above Gammy's face and mouth, very close, then slowly moved his hand down until it hovered over her midsection, where they said the cancer lived. It was there—he could feel it—but even the cancer was resting as if it knew it had won the day. Gammy breathed deeper, and her eyelids closed again.

David realized he had been opening and closing his useless left hand and wished he had something to hold, but he didn't want to stop what he was doing. He wanted to get it done. David's right hand returned to Gammy's forehead. He closed his eyes again and tried to see her illness, but even as he found it, he saw that her internal colors were fading.

"Davie, can you help her?" asked Mom.

David said nothing and kept his hand hovering for a couple more minutes, trying not to shake.

"She doesn't hurt," said David at last.

"That's a blessing," said Pastor Shotten.

David put his hand down. "I'm really sorry, Mommy." He lowered his hand and took a little step back.

"It's okay," said Dad.

"She feels better knowing you're here," said Gretchen.

Mom put her cold hand on David's shoulder and gently turned him around, leaned over, and spoke very quietly as if she didn't want Gammy to overhear. "Honey, do you want to try the Bible? I'm sure Gammy has one in the living room."

"Please, Cathy," said Dad.

"I just want him to *try*," said Mom, her voice breaking.

"He tried," said Dad.

From the bed, Gammy's breathing quickened, and Mom pushed past David to grip her bony hand. On the other side of the bed, Aunt Gretchen stood up and took Gammy's other hand.

Dad's hand, much warmer and fatter than Mom's, came down gently on David's back. He was overtaken by another broad, inappropriate yawn. He put his hand over his mouth, trying to hold it in.

"Davie, why don't you go sit in the living room?" said Dad. "You can rest. In a little while, we'll go get breakfast. I saw a little café by the highway. I'll bet they have pancakes."

David sat on the puffy divan in the dark little living room and scooted back, nestling into the corner between the back and the puffy arms. He relaxed and shut his eyes.

He must have fallen asleep, because when he opened his eyes yellow sunlight was sneaking in through the living room curtains. A sound had woken him. It was the pastor, whose resonant voice carried easily from the other room. "… may the Lord make his face to shine upon you, and be gracious unto you …" He also heard his mother sobbing quietly.

David's stomach growled and made a draining noise.

Our Secret Identities

BОТН DAVID AND HIS YOUNGER FRIEND Randy Rafferty took setbacks and disappointments pretty well. They both hated to lose, like every kid in the world, but if they did lose, they got over it. Their friend Walter Edelstein, one year older, most definitely did not.

Randy sat on the grass in the backyard at David's house, casual as could be, grinning with a cinnamon toothpick sticking out of the corner of his mouth. You'd never guess that the three neighborhood pals had just been embarrassed, clobbered, shellacked, outplayed, and humiliated by the three Tisdale brothers at a "friendly" game of football. Four touchdowns to one, and even that one they had to argue about, insisting that Rory Tisdale, the middle brother, hadn't gotten his second hand onto David's hip, and since the game was called "Two-Below" and not "One-Below," the tackle didn't count. David's touchdown, which was between the metal posts of the swing set, did count. The Tisdales howled that David, Randy, and Walter were cheaters and sore losers, but since they were already up by three touchdowns and were having fun, they didn't let the argument go on too long. They all went back to playing Two-Below, and within a minute and a half, Bobby Tisdale, the oldest, tossed an easy floater to Rory, who ran between their goalposts (two metal trash cans set about ten feet apart) for yet another touchdown.

They played a few minutes longer, and then Pete Tisdale said he wanted to do something else, so all three Tisdales left through the back gate and returned across the alley to their regular turf on the next block.

Randy and David sat on the grass discussing what they should do next while Walter thrust both hands into his pockets and brooded. The other two boys knew it did no good to push him, but Randy, who was less tactful, said, "Oh come on, Walter, who cares? It's just a stupid game," but that never worked. Walter stood up and walked away from them, kicking the football a couple of feet at a time, meandering it around the backyard, head down, staring at the ground.

Of their three backyards on Hackberry Street, David's was the only one where a kid could sit, wrestle, roll around, or play Two-Below because the other two yards were completely infested with stickleburrs, a regional curse. David's mother spent many tedious hours, a significant percentage of her life, fighting the stickleburrs like they were Satan's minions, which they kind of were. Neither Walter's nor Randy's parents cared whether their yards were overrun with the deadly little stickers. Walter's mom, at least, watered their lawn, and his dad paid a man to mow it weekly in the warm months, which made it look deceptively green and inviting. However, any kid unfortunate enough to roll around on its manicured surface would acquire dozens of the nasty, poisonous, painful little burrs embedded in their skin and clothing.

David's yard was a haven from stickleburr agony, and all sports, real and invented, were played there.

School was starting again in one week, and a summer's-end melancholy was setting in. As the grim date approached, the boys played harder and harder to try and keep the awful thought at bay.

David and Randy idled on the grass, waiting for Walter to get over their meaningless loss of a silly game to the Tisdales.

"You wanna spend the night tonight?" asked Randy.

Unfortunately, spending the night wasn't an option for David tonight.

"I can't do it," said David. "My mom's making me go somewhere."

"Aw, man," said Randy. "You can't get out of it?"

"No," said David. Of course, he couldn't get out of it. He never got out or anything.

"Hey, Walter!" Randy called. "You wanna come over and spend the night tonight?"

Walter was still moping across the yard, but he wandered back, holding the football.

"I guess," he said. "I have to ask."

"Okay," said Randy, glum. Walter's parents had been saying 'no' much of the time lately.

The boys had taken to having sleepovers at each other's houses on Friday nights. At least David and Randy's families were agreeable to these regular stag nights. Walter was sometimes allowed to go along, too, but his family was weird about it, especially his dad. Sleepovers at the Edelstein house weren't much fun anyway because lights-out was strictly enforced by eleven o'clock, and they had to be quiet in their sleeping bags.

If they stayed at David's house, there was also a curfew, though not quite as early. David's parents would let them stay up as late as 11:30, but they weren't allowed to watch the coolest Friday night TV show, *Strange Theater*, because David's mom thought it was bad for youthful minds. The show was a local production and featured B-grade horror and suspense movies from the '40s and '50s. It was hosted by a tall guy in a Dracula suit and makeup who called himself Count Robert. The count would introduce the movies in a lame Transylvanian accent and, in the middle of the movie, would come back on to read letters from the show's fans and also plug the sponsor, Lyndon's Milk. The films themselves were often terrible, with bad monster makeup and ridiculous stories, but they held the thrill of the forbidden.

At Randy's house, however, there were no rules or bedtimes as long as they confined themselves to the den, which was as physically far away from Randy's parents' bedroom as it could be. If the boys were quiet and nobody got hurt, they could get away with just about anything. Even *Strange Theater* was allowed, and they usually watched it to the bitter end after midnight.

Tired of moping, Walter plopped down on the grass with the other two. The impending stress of school was bringing them all down. Randy and David were both starting fifth grade, which was kind of cool, at least at the top of the elementary totem pole. Walter, a year older, would be starting sixth grade, which was hardly imaginable to the others. There would be a new school filled with tough older kids and new teachers, some of them even men. The novelty should have made going to school a little bit interesting for Walter, but he was as depressed as the other two.

"Sucks that school is starting," said Randy.

The other two silently agreed that it did, indeed, suck.

"I got Miss Warton," said Randy. "I heard she's horrible. Even on the last day of school, she makes you do work. And if you get caught with a comic book, she steals it."

"Yeah," said David. "I got Miss Dunlap. A guy at my church said she has cancer and missed a lot of school last year. Maybe we'll at least get substitutes sometimes."

A chronically ill teacher could turn out to be a good thing. Substitute teachers made the day better because they had no idea what the class was supposed to do, and you could get away with stuff.

"Walter, you're gonna have a bunch of teachers at Burleson," said Randy. "And you'll have to walk from class to class. That'll be weird. Are they gonna put you in honors classes?" Walter was a genius and was good at everything, so they put him in advanced everything. In junior high, every subject had smart-kid versions except Social Studies and PhysEd.

"I'm not going to Burleson," said Walter.

Both Randy and David did a doubletake.

"What? Why not?" said Randy. "Where are you gonna go?"

"Shepherd Academy."

"Where's that?"

"I don't know. Somewhere way up on the north side. My parents signed me up, so I have to go."

"But it's a junior high, right?" asked David.

"No. Well, sort of. It's just a school school, except for advanced kids," said Walter. "They have classes with, like, ten kids in them, and everybody sits around tables instead of desks. It's not just a junior high. It goes all the way to the twelfth grade."

David and Randy were stunned. Walter had never mentioned this. He'd talked about going to Burleson all summer, where his big sister Patty was still attending. She was about to start ninth grade, which in their town was the last year of junior high rather than the first year of high school. But then Patty wasn't a genius like her little brother Walter.

"Wow," said Randy. "But do you still go from class to class?"

"Not really," said Walter. "You stay in one classroom, and the teachers go from room to room. Plus, you have the same kids in your class from the beginning to when you graduate, so you never get to meet any new kids."

"So it's a genius school?" asked Randy.

"I guess," said Walter.

Then David asked the most relevant question. "Do they have football?"

"No," said Walter. "I think they do basketball. No football. I don't know why."

Walter's general depression was more understandable now. He loved playing fifth-grade football and had the size and athletic ability. He had talked about going out for football at Burleson, maybe getting on the junior varsity, which they let a few sixth graders do if they were big enough. The lack of football at the genius school should have been a deal-killer for Walter. But then, attendance was obviously not his choice.

"That sucks," said Randy.

The boys sat in mournful silence.

"Ask your mom if you can spend the night," said Randy. An evening of junk food and *Strange Theater* might help. It was all Randy had to offer.

The back door to David's house opened, and his mom stuck her head out.

"Davie, we have to leave in fifteen minutes," she called. "Come inside and change, and brush your teeth."

"Okay." David stood up and brushed off his jeans, getting the worst bits of embedded grass off the grass-stain places. The other two boys rose on cue and left the backyard by the side gate.

"See ya."

"See ya."

David had to visit a sick person. It was something he'd been forced to do every few weeks since he was six years old. He wished he could be a regular kid like Randy, who was only an average athlete and got okay grades, but nothing extraordinary was expected of him. In some ways, David was more like Walter, who was a genius. Walter didn't like being a genius any more than David liked being what he was. Walter's genius meant that parents and teachers put extra pressure on him to be good at everything. He wasn't just really, really smart. He was also the fastest kid on the track team, with agility and finesse on the football field and the basketball court. And, as if that weren't enough, he was a musical genius, too. A prodigy, that's what David's parents called it. Walter never played music for his friends, but sometimes, the teachers made him play piano for the other kids at school. He played as well as the music teacher, and some people said he even wrote his own music on sheets of staff paper, which he played in student music competitions. For the first four weeks of every summer, he went to a genius camp in another state. Nobody had any idea what happened there because Walter never talked about it.

David was different from Walter in one important aspect. David's abilities had to remain a secret. From the day they found out David could make sick people better, Mom and Dad told him he shouldn't tell anybody. It was just a talent that God had given him and should be used sparingly, like young Clark Kent with his superpowers. Everybody knew Walter was a genius, but very few people, not even his friends, knew what David could do. He preferred it that way.

His mother had arthritis in her wrist from an accident when she was a little girl, she said, when she had fallen from a bike, and another bike had run over her arm. After she grew up, her wrist started swelling up and hurting badly every day, especially in the morning. She took aspirin by the handful until it made her stomach bleed, and the doctor told her she shouldn't take it anymore. They gave her stronger pills, but these made her stupid in the head, she said.

One morning, when David was very young, his mother was trying to sew on a button, wincing from the pain until she finally put everything down, closed her eyes, and sighed, rubbing her wrist and rocking back and forth. David hated to see his mother hurt, so he had come over to comfort her. He moved to touch her wrist, but as he put his right hand close, suddenly, he could feel the pain himself. It didn't hurt exactly, but he could feel the presence of the pain, which in his mind looked like a dancing reddish light inside her arm. When he actually touched her, the feeling diminished, but when he kept his hand very close to her wrist without touching, just an inch or so away, he discovered he could sort of suck the pain up, like soda through a straw. He pulled his hand up quickly, and when he did, he felt the red pain move through his own body and out into space somewhere.

His mother had looked at him, surprised, then rubbed her wrist some more and flexed it back and forth.

"Davie, did you do that?" she asked, wonder on her face.

David shrugged, but he knew he had done that, taken Mom's pain away. He didn't know how.

"Do it again, okay? That felt good." She rested her wrist on the cushioned arm of the chair, and David tried again, moving his hand back and forth, finding the pain, seeing the red light, letting it flow toward his hand and sweeping it up and away from his mother like he was batting away an insect.

It was not a cure, not yet, because a few days later, Mom asked David to do the same thing he had done before, and so he did, passing his right hand over her afflicted wrist, finding the red light of the pain, and allowing it to discharge through his own body like an electric charge. It was quicker this time. The pain stayed away longer, and when a little discomfort came back in a couple of weeks, the same brief treatment took it away again.

It turned out that what David did was more than just palliative. When his mother had gone for her regular visit to the arthritis doctor, he had taken X-rays, felt and squeezed her wrist, then remarked, "Cathy, I do believe our treatment is working—better than I had even hoped. The inflammation is way down, and your mobility is much, much better. Let's keep it up."

The doctor was proud of himself because he thought the latest pill he had prescribed was effecting a cure. He re-upped her prescription and told her to keep taking it, but when she got home, she tossed the prescription into the trash and never took arthritis medicine again. At first, she only discussed what had happened with her husband. But after a time, when it was clear that the arthritis was gone for good and a miracle had happened, she confided in the pastor at the First Christian Church.

He was less skeptical than she thought he might be, and one Sunday night, when they were at an "unction" service, which meant a service to help sick people, the pastor asked David to come to the front where a large middle-aged man named Mr. Hector was kneeling on a cushion. The man suffered from unrelenting pain in his back from an accident he had in the Navy years ago, the pastor said. Could David help him? It was strange doing this in front of twenty or thirty people, but he did as he was told. He stood behind the corpulent man, who smelled of pipe tobacco and body sweat and passed his right hand across his back several times. However, he couldn't see the pain color, couldn't locate its presence in the man's large back, and was self-conscious about being the center of everybody's attention.

The pastor then said, "Here, David," and handed him a small Bible, which he clutched in his left hand while he tried again to find the pain in Mr. Hector's back. He moved his hand farther away and swept it back and forth between the man's shoulder blades, down toward his lower spine, and up to his neck. Unexpectedly, he did find the pain, which he perceived as a glowing dull yellow, but it wasn't in his back at all. The pain clustered just below the back of his head where fat furrows met the hairy neck, and when he was close to the right spot, he was able to gather the pain and make it discharge into the room. Mr. Hector felt it go and turned around to look at David in amazement. "It doesn't hurt anymore. Oh, my Lord, it doesn't hurt a bit," he said. "Young boy, you are a miracle worker."

"Miracles come from the Holy Spirit," said the pastor. "Young David is God's chosen vessel. Let us thank Him for this gift," said the pastor. Everyone beamed at David while his ears turned crimson.

At the second unction, a month later, there were more healings. This time, it was three people, all middle-aged women. Two suffered from lower back pain, and one had debilitating headaches. David realized that each person was different, that he had to hold his hand in different places at various distances from the body to find the problem. But the gathering and discharging was almost the same every time and always ended with David turning his hand and sweeping up and away as if he were shooing away a fly.

Again, everyone at church was effusively pleased with him, but it left David feeling shaky and spent. At the end of the service, the pastor stood in front of the congregation and told them that they must keep young David's special gift a secret, or else he might become a public spectacle and not be allowed to have a normal childhood. Because the church was small and close-knit, people mostly complied. The unctions continued monthly, but they came to be better attended. David noticed that women sought out healing more often than men. He didn't know why. He assumed that sickness was democratic. Maybe men were ashamed to admit they hurt. His own father often returned from long days of making sales calls to farms and dairies, complaining about what hours in the car was doing to his back, but he never asked his son for help.

From then on, he was known as Young David. After a couple of years, he rebelled against doing his secret tricks at church, so his healing interventions became rarer and were done privately. Today was one of those.

"Let's go," said Mom. David slipped into the front seat. Dad wasn't home from work yet. David didn't ask who they were going to see. It was almost always old people who smelled musty. Mom told him anyway. "Today, we're going to visit the Feishmans," she said. "I think you might have known their daughter Linda. You and she are in the same grade, but she goes to a different school now. Or she did. She's been sick."

That was different. A girl his age was an unusual case. It might be weird.

"Linda got sick a couple of years ago," said Mom. "Her kidneys stopped working. Those are the organs in your back that keep your blood clean. She had to go in the hospital, and they did an operation where they gave her one of her big sister's kidneys."

"Wouldn't that make her sister sick too?"

"No, it's funny, but when you have only one kidney, it turns out that one is all you need, so her sister is fine. I guess God gave us an extra because you can't live without kidneys."

"So why don't we have two hearts, then?" said David. "In case one gets an attack."

Mom chuckled and kept driving, lost in thought. It had been a serious question, but she thought he was joking. He didn't follow up.

The Feishman's residence smelled like dirty laundry and cats. As they walked toward the back of the house, there was the aroma of flowers and a hint of disinfectant, and unbidden memories came in waves. His mother and Linda's mother whispered together for a few minutes. Then Linda's mother, a woman with deep lines on her face that made her look a lot older than Mom, said, "I'll tell her you're here." She disappeared through a door.

David heard the mother speaking, and then a girl's voice came through, whining. "No! I said no! I don't want him here. I don't want to see anybody. Tell them to leave me alone."

The mother's voice answered more quietly, so they couldn't hear what she said, then the girl's voice came again. "Mama, I don't want to. I just don't want to." More quiet voices, then acquiescence, "Okay! Okay!"

A very blonde girl with an ashen, puffy face lay on the bed. Off to the side were tall stands, the kind doctors attach bags of liquid to. There was a bandage on her right arm at the elbow. At that moment, he remembered Linda. She had been like a normal kid in third grade, though very white-complexioned. Then, after Christmas break, she didn't come back, and the teacher never explained where she was until he started hearing about a big fundraiser at the school to help Linda's family pay the doctor's bills. He never heard how it all worked out, but he didn't see Linda again, not until now. She didn't look much like the girl he remembered. Also, she didn't look happy to see him.

"How long is this going to take?" she demanded, not of David, but of her mother.

"I don't know," the mother said. "But you need to roll over onto your stomach."

"I don't want to," Linda said. "It hurts!"

"I know, I know. But you need to do it so he can get close to your kidney. I'll help you."

"I don't need help!" she said. She scooted to one side, then, squinching her face, rotated her body and came down into a prone position with the side of her head on a pillow.

This is so unfair, thought David. *It's Friday.* But the only way to be finished was to start, so he walked over to the bed. Linda glared at him sideways.

David's mother had come in with him. "He really works best if he's alone," she said, and David was grateful, though he really could work with people in the room as long as they were quiet. It was better if he could just focus and get done so he could go home.

"What are you gonna do?" Linda asked. "Are you gonna touch my back? It just makes it hurt more."

"I won't touch your back. I just put my hand close."

"Okay."

With this tacit permission, he raised his right hand and started sweeping from side to side. His left hand hung uselessly. He no longer carried a Bible—that was stupid and pointless—but he wished he could hold something.

Linda's energy field was quite high off her body. There was the color of pain, not sharp and localized but moving, spread across her back and buttocks. There was also another color, a dark gray, centered on the left side of her lower back. This part of her body seemed asleep, quiet. He wondered if he could wake it up. David closed his eyes and focused on the gray, placing his hand very close. It was not dead, but it wasn't very alive, either. It wasn't a presence of something but more an absence. There was nothing for him to take away. He nudged the area with his thoughts, but it was like poking a sick cat that just wanted to be left alone to pass away in peace. He reached up to just above the top of her spine, slowly moved his hand down, and easily gathered the pain and swept it up. Though it was strong, it wasn't hanging on to Linda very hard. He took a deep breath and discharged the colors into space. It made his scalp and feet tingle. He did it twice more, moving down her spine, then stopped because his arm ached.

"Okay," he said. "Does that feel better?"

Linda looked at him curiously, then raised on her elbows. She rocked her body from side to side, testing, then rolled over and sat up.

"Yeah," she said. "It does. It does feel better." She didn't smile, but she did look him right in the eyes. "Thanks."

"Okay."

David turned and walked back out of the room. Linda's mother was standing just outside the door and swooshed past him to the bed.

"Oh, my goodness!" she said. "You're sitting up. Does it feel better?"

"Yes. It's a lot better," said Linda. Her mother kissed her on the head, then turned to David to embrace him in a soft hug. "Thank you," she said, her voice choking up. "Oh, thank you."

David and his mother left. Including the drive, it had taken less than an hour. Maybe there was still time to arrange a sleepover.

"Can I spend the night at Randy's?" he asked.

"May I spend the night," said Mom.

"May I spend the night at Randy's?"

"Maybe. I have to talk to his parents," she said, by which she meant Randy's mother. Mothers made the sleepover decisions. But David was owed one, and she would probably allow it. "I'll call them," said Mom.

She drove for a little while in silence. She seemed to be thinking hard thoughts a lot these days. Then she spoke again. "Davie, I really appreciate what you did for that girl. I know it's not fair to make you help. We've tried hard to limit what people can ask of you. It's just that the Feishmans have had it so rough. It's been two years since Linda got sick. You are a very good person to help her."

"I helped her pain," said David. "But I couldn't help her kidney. It's dying. I can't save her."

The Hataali

THE CHINLE SAVE-U MARKET on Arizona Highway 191 was a shorter driving distance from home, but its quality had been going downhill for the past couple of years. These days, the staff didn't even bother gathering and securing the shopping carts at closing time—the rusty cages with wobbly wheels were left scattered across the vast, potholed parking lot every evening after the manager locked up and everybody went home. An employee would reluctantly gather them when they opened in the morning.

"How do they not all get stolen?" said Mama Pender as she drove past the building and gave a wince of disgust. Theft was a major problem in Chinle and everywhere on the reservation. Maybe nobody bothered stealing the old shopping carts because they just weren't worth the trouble.

Mama preferred shopping at El Rey Grocery, which was a longer drive but a much better store, with well-stocked aisles, a functioning air conditioner, and a staff that wasn't sullen. Fruits and vegetables cost a few cents more. Soft drinks and snacks cost quite a bit more, but Mama never bought such luxuries anyway. The tourists who drove up from the National Monument to resupply their camping trips bought the chips and sodas at inflated prices and kept El Rey in business.

It was a nice morning, not yet hot. The sky was deep early-autumn blue, and the breeze held a hint of mountain snow. Mama pulled into the El Rey parking lot and found a spot a couple of rows back from the front of the building. Young Carol, whom everybody called Callie, didn't understand why because there were plenty of parking places closer to the front door. Mama always parked far away whenever she sent Callie into the store by herself. She stayed in the car with two-year-old Brenda, who was napping in the back seat, and smoked a cigarette while nine-year-old Callie did the shopping.

"Now, pay attention, Callie," Mama said. "Get me two pounds of flour—Juanita brand, not that expensive stuff—and a pound of sugar, the one with the picture of the castle on it. That's the small bags, not the big five-pound bags. Don't bring me back big bags. Oh, yes. I need a one-pound bag of harina cornmeal, Juanita brand. The little bag, got it?"

"I know the difference, Mama."

"Well, sometimes you forget. Also—pay special attention—I want you to get me a big handful of chiltepins. You know which ones those are?"

"The little bitty red ones?" said Callie.

"That's right," said Mama. "One big handful in the paper bag. And one of *your* handfuls, not mine. For me, it would be a little handful. But I just need a big handful from one of your hands." She cupped her hand to illustrate the intended quantity.

Callie rolled her eyes. "I know."

Mama opened her old rough-leather purse and fished around. "It should cost two-sixty or a two-eighty at most." She pulled out a five-dollar bill but kept digging. She came up with one scuffed dollar bill and then a couple of dimes, but that was it. She reluctantly handed the five to Callie.

"I want every penny of change. Don't try to fool me and buy candy. I know how much everything costs."

"I won't, Mama," said Callie, lying with an angelic face. She could get away with buying a box of hard candies, which only cost ten cents. The trick was to buy the candy separately. Mama might glance at the receipt when the little girl returned with the groceries, but she wouldn't do the arithmetic.

Callie went into the store and found a cart that rolled straight. Back when Mama first started sending her in to do the shopping, Callie's eyes barely came to the level of the shopping cart handle, and people would smile to see a little girl pushing such an unwieldy contraption. But now that she was taller, she steered the cart like an expert. On the baking aisle, Callie grabbed the bags of flour, sugar, and cornmeal, then rolled on to the produce aisle, where the varieties of dry beans, and red and green chili peppers were heaped loose in bins. Habaneros, pale green gueros, mirabels, jalapeños, and, of course, chiltepins. You couldn't just grab a handful of chiltepins—the little bright red peppers were mixed with stems and dry leaves and broken bits of pepper. She got a little paper bag and picked through the peppers, choosing grape-sized smooth ones with a bright red color. When she estimated she had about one good fistful, she tossed in several more because it was better to have too many than too few.

Her final stop was a rack right at the front of the store by the cash registers, where she discretely grabbed a brightly colored box of jawbreakers. She was tempted by the little packaged cupcakes, but those would be too hard to conceal, and she could make a box of hard candy last for days.

The checker was a nice man with a gaucho mustache who recognized her. He called her Bebita.

He checked and bagged her groceries cheerfully, then handed her the change, two one-dollar bills, two dimes, and four pennies. Only then did she say, "Oh, I'm sorry. I forgot about this," and presented the box of candy.

"You are starting to forget like an old lady, Bebita," he said. "I worry about you." He grinned. "Give me back one dime, please." She handed him the coin, which he tossed back into the register without ringing it up. He winked at her. The little box of candy went into the deep pocket of her skirt.

Back in the car, little Brenda was awake and crying. Mama took the change from Callie and then checked inside the paper bag.

"Oh, Callie, so many!" she said. "I'm not feeding the whole town. You always spend too much. From here on, I will have to do the shopping."

She wouldn't, of course, but it was a nice thought.

On the way home, they stopped by the *carniceria* for pork. Meat was cheaper here than at El Rey, and there was more variety. This time, mama left Callie in the car with the fussy toddler while she bought the meat: scraps of pork from the leaner parts of the pig, jowls and snouts and trotters, and pieces close to the bone, which would be cooked down for hours with spices and chunks of lard until they melted in your mouth and could be rolled into savory tamales and steamed in corn husks.

Mama made tamales once a week, on Saturdays, ten or twelve dozen at a time, and sold them to the families around the neighborhood. Sometimes, she sold them all, in which case Callie wouldn't get any tamales for dinner. This was unfair after she had smelled delicious pork cooking all day in its spicy sauce. But sometimes, there were a few tamales left unsold, and Callie got to eat one or two. On Saturday nights when Mama's husband Mark was home—as a truck driver, he was gone much of the time—she always saved a dozen tamales, and dinner was a feast.

Tonight, Mark Pender was on the road like usual, so there would probably be no extra tamales. But Callie smiled to herself, knowing the secret of the jawbreakers.

ON THE TEN-MILE RIDE BACK to their neighborhood, Callie read one of the books she had gotten from the school library. It was *King of the Wind,* an exotic story about a racehorse. She loved it and adored the beautiful illustrations. She lay in the back seat with her feet up and read while Mama drove. On the other side of the long back seat, Brenda went back to sleep. It was Callie's favorite way to read, riding in the car, soothed by the engine's vibration. She was reaching a particularly exciting part of the story when the car turned onto the potholed gravel road that led to her little dusty neighborhood of San Martín. The ride became too rough and bouncy to read without getting carsick, so she placed a bookmark between the pages and sat up.

Callie savored her Saturdays. When they got home, she carried Brenda carefully into the house and placed her gently into her crib. Luckily, her little sister stayed asleep. Callie hurried through her main chore for the day, cleaning and straightening the room she shared with the toddler, sweeping and dusting quietly because if Brenda woke, it would be Callie's job to care for her. When she was done, Callie was finally able to return to her story of a mute slave boy, an Arabian horse, and their adventures in the olden days. She curled up on her bed, propped by pillows. She hoped for a good half hour to herself.

Mama cooked in the kitchen with Sofía, a small, older woman who helped out with the cooking on tamale days. Sofía often came around on other days, too, because she and Mama got along well and because Sofía had no husband and no kitchen of her own, just a small apartment in a nearby pueblo. She was a *curadora,* a healer, and Mama let her attend to people from around the colonia, either inside the kitchen or sometimes outside in the courtyard.

What exactly Sofía did for people, Callie didn't understand. Somehow, she made them feel better by putting her hands on their bodies or just near them. On days when she was at the Pender house, there were always a few people who came to the back door, knocked, and asked for her. Sometimes Mama would tell them that Sofía was busy and they should come back later, and they always went away quietly and without fuss, but other times, she let them in. They would sit in the heavy wooden chair beside the table while Sofía stood behind them and chanted quietly in Navajo, holding her hands close but usually not touching. Once in a while, she knelt low and hovered over a knee or hip or foot. When they left, they would leave a few coins on the table. Some of the money Sofía gave to Mama, but most went into her little leather coin bag.

Today, Callie noticed there were three people waiting in the courtyard when they got home: an old man in a cowboy hat, squatting on his haunches with his back against the wall, a middle-aged woman, and a chubby young woman. Mama let the two women in first. The young woman, who was fat and round-faced, sat in a chair while the older woman stood behind her, rubbing her upper back in a circular motion. Callie wondered what was wrong with her. It was usually the young people who brought in the old ones to see Sofía.

Callie got to read her book for a deliciously long spell. She was absorbed in her story, savoring the colorful pictures, when she heard a woman sob. She raised her head and listened. It was coming from the kitchen. There were three voices, Sofía's, Mama's, and someone else's, all speaking Navajo. Callie never spoke Navajo, but she had been around the ancient language her whole, short life and understood a lot more than she let on.

The woman's voice, which she didn't recognize, was saying, "Please, she needs the child. The little girl." What was she talking about?

Then there was Sofía's voice, commanding. "Be still! Sit and be quiet!"

Then, there was a young woman's moan. "It hurts! Please! He's not moving! Please let him be alive!"

The older woman's voice again: "La niña pequeña—the little girl could help."

There was more talking she couldn't understand—then Mama's voice, loud, in English: "Callie! Come here, please! I need you!"

Callie sighed and marked her book. At that moment, Brenda let out a little squeak and sat up in her crib. When she saw her big sister, she held out both arms to be picked up.

"Lie down!" said Callie. "It's still naptime."

Brenda let out a howl of disappointment.

Mama appeared at the doorway. "Callie! Come now! I need your help."

"You woke her up!" Callie complained.

"Stop whining and come over here. I'll take care of the baby."

Sofía stood behind the young woman, who sat in the chair backward, straddling the seat. Her face was reddish brown and tears streaked her face.

"I hurt!" she said again, in Navajo.

Sofía saw Callie and beckoned her. "Stand here!"

At Sofía's direction, Callie stood behind the young woman's rotund back. Sofía took Callie's hands by the wrists and guided her.

"Don't touch her, just be very close," said Sofía. "About this far away. Hold your hands close to her back, right here. I'm going to touch you. But you don't touch her."

Callie did as she was told. She didn't know what to expect. Was she supposed to feel something happening? She held still for a few moments. Sofía's hands touched her shoulders, and then she did feel something. Callie held her hands as still as she could, but she began to shake a little bit, and her nose had a tickly feeling that she really wanted to scratch. It seemed as if warm, turbulent water was starting to flow through her fingertips and palms, and she heard a sound like a breeze blowing through aspen trees. She moved her hands from side to side, and the sound changed. The young woman let out a deep sigh. Callie could feel that she was afraid, and wanted to reassure her.

"It's all right," Callie said.

"Be quiet," said Sofía.

They stayed in that position, Callie's hands shaking ever so slightly, which she couldn't help. What was she supposed to be doing? But even without touching her, Callie could feel the fat woman's life pulsing and flowing under her hands. And there was ... something else.

"She has a baby," said Callie.

"Everybody knows that," said Sofía. "Now, stay quiet and let me work."

And so Callie stayed. Her arms ached. Then there was a change—the wind sound grew softer, and the young woman inhaled sharply.

"I felt him move!" she said. "Oh! He moved again."

Sofía took her own hands away from Callie's back.

"Put your hands on her now and say the Hail Mary," said Sofía.

Callie put her hands gently on the woman's upper back, which was warm and sweaty, and did as she was told. She recited the Hail Mary, and Sofía said it with her, and at the end, they said "amen," and they were done.

The young woman sat up straight and moved her head around as if to loosen a stiff neck, then put her hands on the sides of her big belly.

"He's moving!" she said. "He's alive!"

"Of course, dumb girl!" Said the older woman. "I told you. Your baby was just having a quiet day. He sits too long in one place, and it makes your insides hurt. There's nothing wrong."

"It doesn't hurt anymore," the young woman said and turned around to embrace Callie in a damp hug. "Thank you, thank you!" she said in English.

The older woman rooted through her purse and left something on the table, then she and the young woman left the kitchen. Callie wondered if she could return to her book because Mama was caring for Brenda, but Mama said, "Callie, chop the onions and the tomatillos. I have to get Brenda her lunch."

Callie sighed and turned to the cutting board, where a dozen yellow onions and a pile of boiled, peeled, bright-green tomatillos sat. Sofía put her hand gently on Callie's shoulder.

"You are a hand-trembler, Callie," she said. "I always thought there was something about you."

Callie looked up at her, not understanding.

"My grandmother was a hand-trembler, a *hataali*," she said. "She passed the gift to me. I think you have it, too. You should take care of it, practice, and help it grow."

Callie still didn't know what she meant. But everyone seemed happy with her, so she must have done something right.

"My goodness," said Mama. "She left two dollars!"

Callie wondered briefly if any of the money was for her. Probably not. Mama would keep one of the dollars, and Sofía would get the other.

The old man who had been squatting patiently in the courtyard was now standing at the back door.

"Are you ready for me?" he asked in Navajo.

"Sit down. I'll be with you soon," said Sofía.

Callie sliced an onion in half, sliced it again the other way, wiped her nose, and sneezed violently. She blew her nose into her apron, then washed her hands in the sink. She glanced about. Mama was gone from the room, and Sofía's attention was elsewhere, so Callie removed the box of candy from her dress pocket, opened the end flap, and took one bright-green ball, which she popped into her mouth, letting the sweetness spread over her tongue.

A hand-trembler, she thought. *I don't think I want to be that, even if people give me dollars.*

Cooking for Fifty

THE YOUNG MAN WAS JUST ACROSS THE STATE LINE when the clutch failed completely. For the past two hundred miles, every time he stopped, he had to put the old Ford Maverick in neutral, then mash the clutch hard to the floor and ease the car into first gear. When he let the clutch out, it caught just barely above the floor and lurched forward, sometimes killing the engine.

Everything was fine on the highway. As long as he kept going, he could continue on to his destination without interruption. The tiny, underpowered engine got such good gas mileage—for a car made in Detroit—that he could drive for hours on a single tank.

Finally, as the needle dipped perilously low to the E, he exited the highway and rolled into a Sinclair station and convenience store, spent four precious dollars on regular gas, then started the car and tried to pull away. The clutch was dead, worthless. No matter how hard he pushed the clutch pedal to the floor, he couldn't force the transmission into first gear. After many grinding attempts, he shut off the engine. This time, he put it into gear first, then bore down on the clutch and tried to start the car. The engine turned over, the car jumped forward, and the 170-cubic-inch engine died. He put it back in neutral and pushed it twenty feet, so he'd be out of the way of the gas pumps.

He raised the hood in the international sign of car trouble and waited, staring at the engine, wondering what to do. Fortunately, this being the rural west, he soon attracted help. A middle-aged black man with a gold incisor asked him what the trouble was, and when he described his clutch plight, the man taught him a trick.

"Put it in neutral, start the engine, then push the car to get it rolling a little. Hop in, give it a little gas, and start pushing the stick until you find the gear. Once it pops in, keep going until you're going fast enough, then put it in neutral and try to get it into second. Move the gas pedal up and down until you find the right engine speed, and it should go. That's called synchronizing the gears. With a little practice, it's not too hard. You still need to get that clutch fixed, but you can at least get where you're going."

So he tried it, starting the car, pushing it forward, hopping in—and immediately killed the engine. He tried again, and this time, the good Samaritan helped him push the Maverick to get it rolling a little faster. The car found its gear with a pop and lurch and didn't die.

The young man pulled out onto the road, waved to his benefactor, and, with some effort and grinding, found second gear. Third and fourth gears turned out to be easy, and he continued his journey, dreading each time he had to stop but getting better and better at the synchronization trick.

The big city, when he finally arrived, was a harrowing experience, especially since he had only a vague idea of where he was going. His first mission was to locate a bank and, open an account, and become a real person.

The young man was between jobs and between lives. Yesterday, he walked into his old bank in his old town with his last paycheck, which he had cashed, and then asked them to close his checking account and give him that money, too—his life savings in cash: $585.26. A hundred went into his wallet, the rest he stashed in a bank envelope buried deep inside a scratched blue suitcase squeezed into the trunk. After a cheap highway motel, breakfast, lunch, and gas, he was down to seventy-nine dollars in his wallet and coins in his pocket.

On a main street in a busy part of the city, he spotted a bank and pulled into the parking lot, making sure he landed in a spot with no impediments in front so he could do the clutchless starting trick. The other cars in the lot were a lot nicer and cleaner than the old Ford with its cracked windshield and rusting dents on the passenger-side door.

It was early afternoon in late summer, and the parking lot was hot and bright from the reflection of the mirrored windows. The bank was called Capital State, and he figured it was as good as any. He opened the Maverick's trunk, unlatched the suitcase, and retrieved the money envelope. He wondered briefly if he should change into a nicer, or at least cleaner, shirt, but he couldn't think of a dignified way of doing that in a public parking lot.

Inside the air-conditioned lobby, the young man told a well-dressed lady that he wanted to open an account, and she fetched a well-dressed man, who shook his hand and led him to a small office.

The man pulled out several paper forms and a pen and set these in front of him.

"Fill out the first page, down to there," he said and indicated a dotted line at the halfway point.

He picked up the pen and wrote his name and birthdate but then paused when he came to the address line. He didn't have an address yet, of course. He was still between lives. He thought he needed a bank account first so he could pay a deposit on an apartment without using cash. He explained this to the well-dressed man.

The banker leaned back in his bank chair and put an index finger to his cheek.

"I see your dilemma," he said. "Do you have a driver's license?"

He pulled out his wallet and handed over the license. The well-dressed man frowned.

"It's not a picture ID," he said.

"I know. Kansas doesn't put pictures on driver's licenses. At least not yet. I think they're planning to start next year. I have a birth certificate."

"That will help you get a local driver's license, but you'll need a good permanent mailing address to set up an account with us. I could give you temporary checks, but you're going to need a picture ID, or they won't be much use to you."

"What should I do?" asked the young man. "I don't want to run around with all my money in cash."

"I don't blame you," said the well-dressed man sitting back with the index finger pressed to his cheek. He really wanted to help and certainly wanted to be entrusted with the young man's meager savings. "You could get a post office box as a mailing address," he said. "It will cost you about five dollars a month. But here's one more thought. Are you a student?"

"No. Not yet. I might enroll in the spring."

"Hmmm … I was thinking maybe the university might let you have a temporary PO box for free …"

They both sat silently for a few moments. Then the man leaned forward, index fingers on his chin.

"So, what is your plan?" he asked. "What do you want to do here?"

"Well, I just thought I'd get an apartment, then find a job. I don't have any really big goals. I want to go to university when I have enough money saved."

In the banker's mind, gears were turning. He squinted. "Here's a suggestion. Off-campus student housing."

"I'm not a student."

"I know, but I hear co-op houses are lax about that."

"What kind of houses?"

"Co-op housing. Co-ops. There are a bunch of them in the West Campus area, big old houses and buildings with twenty to forty people living in them. Really, that's where you need to live. Forget an apartment. What could you afford? An efficiency on the east side? That would not be good. Cooking on a hot plate, sharing a bathroom." He shook his head in distaste. "No, a co-op is a much better idea. My daughter is a junior at the university, and she lived in a co-op for two years. She really loved the place. Hers was called Prince Street House, and I can give you the address. I don't know what they will ask in deposit, but it won't be much. That's the way you should live when you're young. You get a room in a big house, and you pay one fee a month for room and board. They aren't expensive, but the catch is you have to help with chores. Like mopping the floors or cleaning the kitchen, and that means the house has no housekeeping expenses, and it keeps the cost down. The bonus is you can have a real street address. That's the way to go for young people like you."

HALF AN HOUR LATER, lurching precariously through narrow, one-way streets in an old part of the city, the young man found Prince Street and the house and got lucky when a car was just pulling away from the curb, and he was able to slide the crippled Maverick into the spot. He realized he was stuck there until the car in front of him moved. He'd be on foot for the foreseeable. In a way, that was a relief. Synchronizing gears was stressful.

He knocked on the door of the old, enormous house, but no one answered. After waiting a little bit and knocking again, he just opened the front door and went inside a large vestibule, where off to one side was an office door with a sign:

University Cooperative Council

Main Office

He knocked on that door, and a young man with a bushy mustache opened it.

"Can I help you?"

"I'm ... uh ... I'd like to see about living here."

"Well, that's what we do, but unfortunately, this house is full. We even have a wait list. Sorry."

His heart sank.

"However," said the young man, "There are eight houses in the council, and I'm pretty sure some of them still have openings. But you'll have to check with them. I'll give you the addresses and phone numbers, but it's better just to go in person. The farther you go from campus, the cheaper the rent. Are you a student?"

"Not yet."

"Well, then, being close to campus won't matter for you. I suggest Berkley House. Or Keystone." He handed over a mimeographed sheet with the names of co-ops and their addresses. The names were alphabetical: Avalon, Berkley, Foster, Keystone, Larame, Prince …

"Which one is closest."

"That would be Keystone. It's four blocks west and one street north, on twenty-first."

"Thanks."

He walked. The day was warm and very humid, which he was not used to. By the time he had gone four blocks west and one street north, his T-shirt was soaked, and beads of sweat trickled down his forehead.

It took him a minute to find it. The houses in this area were leftovers from a previous era of prosperity. Tall, cracked columns, deep porches, arched brick windows. He didn't see the Keystone sign until he'd passed it and returned for another look. The small handmade sign was attached to a cement post embedded beside the front gate, which was standing open. He crossed the patio and climbed the stairs to the porch, where there were two mismatched chairs and a threadbare couch. A man with thin hair dripping over the back of his ears and down his shoulders was sitting on the steps, smoking a cigarette, reading a paperback book. He looked up.

"Hey," he said.

"Hey. Ummm … I want to see somebody about living here."

"Okay. You need to talk to Sherry. She's house manager."

"Where is she?"

"I'll go see if I can find her. Wait here." He stood up, put a bookmark in his paperback, and stuffed it into his back pocket, then went inside, still carrying the cigarette.

The young man waited a couple of minutes, then sat down on the couch. The cushion springs creaked. Two girls, both in their early twenties, came through the gate and climbed the steps, chatting, carrying backpacks. One of them smiled at him.

"I wouldn't sit there," she said. "Fleas."

He stood up, wondering if he had been infested. "I was supposed to talk to Sherry," he said.

"She's usually here," said the girl, and breezed inside.

He waited. He had almost made up his mind to just walk in when a cheery young woman, short and pretty, with high cheekbones and flaming red hair, emerged and extended her hand.

"You asked about moving in? I'm Sherry. I'm house manager."

"I'm ... Wally," he said.

"Okay, Wally. We still have a couple of open spots. Do you want the tour?"

"Sure."

She led him through the door at a quick pace, talking fast with a well-practiced spiel.

"This is the main common area. There's only one couch right now, but we're getting another one. Don't sit on that one out on the porch. It has fleas. A guy's supposed to come get it."

She kept going, her guest in pursuit. She led him through a large kitchen that had an ancient professional eight-burner stove, an enormous double oven, and a cutting board that was three feet wide and ten feet long. A giant old stand mixer stood at one end.

"This reefer on the left is for personal food," Sherry said, pointing toward two double refrigerators standing side by side. "Put your name on everything. If it doesn't have a name, somebody will either eat it, or it will be tossed at the end of the week. The other reefer is where the cooks keep the dinner ingredients so that food is off-limits. There's also a deep freeze in the pantry."

They continued to whoosh, entering a large dining room with three long tables. "Dinner is at 6:30 every night except Sundays. Breakfast and lunch food stays in the pantry or in the reefer, and you just use what you need. There's bread and baloney and stuff like that."

She took him down a hall with doors on both sides. "There are two spots left in the house. One is a double room. That's 120 a month. There's also a single room out back, and that's 150 a month."

"I guess I'd rather have the double."

"Okay, your roommate would be Mike. Let me see if he's awake." She knocked gently on one door, listened, then opened it carefully. "It's okay, he's not here," she said. There were two dilapidated desks and a bunk bed with twin mattresses. The bottom bunk had wadded-up sheets and a blanket—the top one was bare. "Mike makes a good roommate. He's a student, but he works as a night watchman. He usually comes in about seven in the morning and leaves for work about ten at night. If you're a regular day person, you'll hardly see him."

The tour swept through another hallway and back to the common room. "That's pretty much it," Sherry said. "Oh, one more thing. The two big bathrooms at each end of the house are marked MEN and WOMEN, but that's just because the health inspector made us do that. Everybody uses all the bathrooms. So don't be surprised if a chick walks in while you're doing your business." She laughed. "So, Wally, any questions?"

"When can I move in?"

"Well, you have to get voted in first."

He looked at her, confused.

"I know," she said, "but it's not a big deal. I'm sure everybody will say you're okay, but it's house rules. You have to come to dinner, and then you have to stand up and introduce yourself and say why you want to live in the house. If we accept you, and we probably will unless you say something really awful, then you can pay the deposit and choose your two chores."

"What are the choices for chores?"

"I'm not sure what's left. But there are enough chores so everybody can have two when the house is full. Except for cooks. That job is so hard it counts as two jobs. Food-buyer is also two jobs. Also house manager, which is my job, that's a double."

"How much deposit?" he asked.

"Half the first month's rent," she said. "Since you want the double, it's sixty dollars. Can you come to dinner tonight? Another guy is coming to look at the house this afternoon, and it's better if we can see both of you at once."

"I can come. Six-thirty? I'll be here."

"Perfect! I'll see you tonight, Wally. Now I have to get back to work."

"Thanks, Sherry!"

She whooshed away, leaving him alone in the common room. A girl came into the room, big-boned and dark-skinned. She gave him a curious look, and he smiled back at her. She plopped on the one couch, opened a notebook, and started writing. He opened the door to leave, then turned back.

"Excuse me. Uh … do you know the zip code of this house?"

She looked up at him like she doubted his intelligence but rattled off the number before returning to her notebook. He recited the zip code a couple of times under his breath so he'd remember it.

Now, to return to his car, retrieve his precious cash from the trunk, and find a bank. It didn't have to be Capital National, just any bank within walking distance, and then he'd have a checking account and an address, and he'd be an official human being with a name and a place to live.

The food at dinner was passable, though bland—pinto beans with thick chunks of tomato, chewy brown rice, a single filet of some variety of white fish, and a dull yellow sauce on top. Wally was nervous but made himself eat it all. If they didn't take him, at least he'd have gotten a free meal. Well, they better take him. This was his official mailing address, as far as University State Bank was concerned.

"Everybody settle down," said Sherry. "Y'all can keep eating, but I want to introduce you to our two candidates. Meet Wally and Jerry."

Wally and Jerry both waved. Jerry was younger than Wally, with a long, thick beard that would have looked at home on a Mennonite.

People were starting to scoot their chairs back and collect their plates, but Sherry gave them all a fierce look. "Guys, we need to give our undivided attention to our guests here, just for a couple of minutes. Then we can vote, and you can get on with your night. Wally, you first. Tell them your name, where you're from if you want, anything else you want to say about yourself, and why you want to live at Keystone."

Wally stood and looked around at the twenty or so people sitting there looking at him. They were about evenly divided between males and females. Among the men, facial hair was the rule, as was general unkemptness. Most of the girls were younger, but a few were older, in various types of Earth-Mother garb. The large, dark girl who had revealed the zip code was eyeing him up and down.

"Hi, I'm Wally. I guess you know that already. I just moved to the city …"

"What's your last name, Wally?" asked one of the older male denizens.

"Uh … Stein."

"Where are you from, Wally Stein?"

"I'm from Lawrence, Kansas, though I was born in Eureka. We moved to Lawrence when I was a little kid. Like I said, I just drove in this morning and am looking for a place …"

"Why do you want to live here?" asked Sherry.

"Well ... because it's a big city with a lot going on ..."

"No, I mean, why do you want to live at Keystone House?"

"I ... uh ... want a place where there is a community," said Wally, hoping that sounded good. "So ... I won't just have to stare at the walls when I come home ..."

"You can stare at Sherry," said a dude, and several people laughed.

"Yeah ... anyway, I'm willing to work to keep the house nice, and I can get along with anybody ..."

"You have to respect the food in the reefer," said another guy. "You can't bring in a bunch of scuzzy friends and let them eat our stuff."

"Robert, shut up and let him talk," said Sherry.

"I ... uh ... don't have any friends yet," said Wally. "Scuzzy or otherwise ..."

A young man with uncharacteristic short hair said, "I hope you don't have insect phobia."

"What?" said Wally.

"There are these roaches that climb the walls and go flying straight at you. Even though we have the place sprayed."

"That's because they come in from outside," said another guy. "Anyway, they only fly when it's mating season."

"I'm not scared of bugs," said Wally.

"Are you allergic to cats?" shouted one of the other girls.

"Cats? No," said Wally.

"Good, because there are fuckin' cats everywhere," said the girl. "Keep your windows shut when you're gone because there's a big yellow cat who will get in your room and shit in your bed sheets. I'm not kidding."

"Oh, come on, Jonie," said Sherry. "That happened exactly *once*. Now everybody shut up and let Wally talk."

"Yeah, Beaver, stop giving Wally the business!" said another tenant. General laughter.

Wally, thoroughly rattled, went on to tell them he would help do chores and not complain, always pay the rent on the first of the month, and be quiet at night.

"That would put you in the minority," said Sherry. "Anybody have any questions for Wally?"

Blank looks. Some people resumed quiet side conversations.

"Okay," said Sherry. "Jerry, you go now."

Jerry had not yet said a word. He was short and thin, with a wash-worn white T-shirt with yellow pit stains. It looked like neither his hair nor his beard had been trimmed or washed in recent memory.

He stood up. "Hi, everybody, I'm Jerry Lewis …"

All three tables erupted in laughter.

"I know, I know," he said, "but that's really my name. I'm Jerry Fox Lewis if you want to call me something else. Otherwise, I'm just Jerry."

"What do you like to do, Jerry Fox Lewis?" asked yet another guy.

"Um …" He was stumped by the question and took a full twenty seconds to respond. "I … like to get high and listen to records."

Chuckling.

"I … I don't know, really … I go to bars and hear bands …"

Several awkward seconds of silence.

"Okay," said Sherry, "Does anybody have any questions for Jerry before we vote?" Heads shook. Quiet, unrelated conversations continued. Sherry turned to the two guests. "If you guys would wait in the living room for a few minutes, we'll discuss you and then vote.

Wally and Jerry went to the living room. Wally sat on the couch while Jerry walked along a shelf along the wall that was stuffed with hundreds of worn record albums. He slid them out one by one and exhibited approval or disdain for each. *Cream? … acceptable … Jerry Jeff Walker? … buncha country shit … Three Dog Night? … are you fucking kidding me? … Bad Company? … All right, I'll take that.*

Wally couldn't hear what they were saying in the next room, but there was a lot of mixed conversation and laughter. What if they rejected him? He'd have to find another place, then go back to the bank and straighten it all out …

"Okay, guys, come back in!" called Sherry from the dining room.

When they returned, everybody was getting up and collecting their dirty dishes. Sherry came over and smiled. "Congratulations, you're both in," she said. "I declare this house officially full. Hurray! Now, come see me in the office and give me a deposit, then pick your chores."

In the tiny office, which in the 1920s had probably been a servant's quarters, Jerry handed Sherry seventy-five dollars in cash for his single room, and Wally gave her sixty. She wrote them each a receipt.

"Your first month's rent is due on September 1st, which is next Friday. You can go ahead and move in whenever you're ready. But, please, seriously, pay the rent on time. The one thing I really hate about this job is going around getting everybody to cough up. Listening to a bunch of excuses pisses me off."

She pulled out a handwritten chart on a long sheet of paper. "There's not much to choose from," she said. "There are only three jobs left. Clean the common bathrooms in the annex on Tuesdays, vacuum the floors in the annex on Fridays, and cooking on Saturdays. Cooking counts as two jobs."

Wally hesitated, but Jerry picked up a pencil and wrote his name beside the two cleaning jobs.

"That makes sense, Jerry, because your room is in the annex anyway," said Sherry. "Wally, I guess you're a cook. If you don't think you can do it, then you have to find somebody with two other jobs and get them to trade."

"I can do it," said Wally. "I worked in a café as a short-order cook for a while, mostly eggs and burgers and stuff. But I've never cooked for this many people at once."

"There's a book in the kitchen that all the cooks swear by," said Sherry. "It's called *Cooking for Fifty*. It's got a lot of great recipes and tells you everything you need to buy. Since twenty-eight people eat dinner, at the very most, you just cut every recipe in half."

"I'll give it a go," said Wally. "I thought you said there were twenty-five people in the house."

"There's two guys who are boarders. They just pay thirty dollars a month, so they can eat dinner here six days a week. They're both from Iran." She pronounced it "I ran." "There's also Beva. She boards, too, but she hangs out at this house so much she might as well be living here. If that's everything, I'll see you guys around. Now, I gotta finish up some double-fucking-entry bookkeeping."

Jerry Fox Lewis turned and walked out the front door without another word. Wally stepped out onto the porch, looking up and down the street. Young people were out in the early evening light, bicycles whirred by, several faraway conversations mixed and merged together. Music from a couple of radios competed with the city sounds. He tried to imagine what this street looked like a long time ago when rich people inhabited these huge old houses.

It was a long walk, but he decided he'd better leave his car parked where it was, retrieve his suitcase, and establish himself in his shared bedroom with his unknown roommate. He wondered if … who was it? … Mike? He wondered if Mike had been at dinner.

He walked the one block over and four blocks back to the Maverick. His homeless, nameless interval was over. He still needed to get a state driver's license to find some kind of a job, but he wasn't between lives anymore. He wasn't some shiftless, homeless schmuck.

Now, he was Wally Stein of Keystone House.

Unauthorized

JIM EDELSTEIN WAS THE ONLY DAD any of the boys knew who had a 'study.' It was a dark room on one end of their house, paneled with maple veneer, with a dark desk and an even darker leather chair that could lean way back, and bookshelves on three sides, filled to about half capacity with books, mostly medical books, since he was a urologist, and twenty silver- and gold-plated trophies taking up the rest of the shelf space. The trophies were of varying sizes depending on whether they represented first, second, or third place or some other notable ranking, but each was of the same gleaming stylized figure: a man aiming a bow, his right arm arched back in the full draw position and the bow extended in front. There was no arrow and no string, however, which would have been impractical at such a small scale. Jim was a competitive archer, and when he was younger, he traveled the state for archery meets and won many awards. He still occasionally strung his old bows and thunked arrows into a backyard target, but he no longer competed.

Dr. Edelstein sat in his study, in his leather chair, pretending to read a medical text. He missed the pipe he used to smoke, which would have made a dignified prop. Two boys sat in leather-trimmed chairs in front of him as he pretended to be waiting for a stopping place in his book before he dealt with them. The boys were fourteen and fifteen years old. The older one was his son, Walter, and the other was Walter's best friend, David Monk, who lived a few houses away. The boys waited without speaking for the doctor to turn his attention their way. They knew he was trying to make them sweat.

Finally, he reached across his desk and retrieved a bookmark, stiff gilded cardboard with a tassel on one end, and placed it between the pages, shutting the thick volume. He looked at the boys over his glasses. This was the moment when most dads would have said something like *Well, what have you got to say for yourselves?* But Jim believed in getting straight to the point.

"Walter, whose idea was it?" he asked.

"It was mine," said Walter. "We weren't even taking the car that far. It's just that Rory said he could give us a ride, and then at the last second, he said he couldn't, so we didn't have a ride ..."

"That was not the question," said Jim. "I asked whose idea it was. Let me ask the same question again. Okay, David, whose idea was it to take my car at eleven o'clock at night without permission?"

The two boys looked at each other. Walter shrugged. David cleared his throat.

"Well, Walter said he thought it would be okay as long as we took care of it, and didn't ..."

"But you didn't take care of it, did you?" said Jim.

"No, sir, but it wasn't Walter's fault. He parked the car really carefully, and there wasn't even another car nearby. But when we came out of Kelly's house ..."

"Kelly? Is that the girl who had the secret party?"

"She was ... yeah, it was her house. When we came outside to go home, there was a police car, and the policeman told us that a lady had hit our car ... I mean your car, while it was parked. It wasn't parked wrong—it was right next to the curb. She just smashed into it. The police arrested her for being drunk."

"I see," said Jim. "So, Walter, you had something in your hand when you came outside to drive home, didn't you?"

"I had a beer," said Walter. "I set it down on the sidewalk. I wasn't going to take it in the car. I just forgot to leave it inside the house."

"And the officer saw you put down the beer?"

"Yeah."

"Please say 'yes' or 'no,'" said Jim, "not 'yeah' or 'nah.'"

"Yes," said Walter.

"Yes, what?"

"Yes, the cop, the officer, saw me put it down, and he asked to see my license, so I gave it to him."

"You mean your learner's permit?"

"Yes, and then the officer asked where I got the beer, and I told him the truth, that it was from inside the house, and I hadn't been drinking and driving, and that's when he called on his radio, and two more police cars came, and they went inside and found the beer."

"That's when they called me?"

"A whole bunch of other people were there, too. They called everybody's parents."

Jim leaned farther back in his leather chair. "So, I'm going to ask you, David. Whose idea was it? And I don't mean the idea of taking my car without authorization. I mean, going to this secret party at this girl's house, where there was apparently zero supervision."

"It wasn't a secret," said David, "everybody knew about it."

"Everybody? I certainly didn't know about it," said Jim. "I don't think your parents knew about it."

"I mean the people at school," said David. "I mean my school."

"But not Walter's school," said Jim.

"I don't think so."

"So, what I want to know, David is how Walter found out about it."

"I guess I told him," said David.

Jim sat upright and rolled his chair forward. "So, what I'm understanding, is that was *your* idea to go to this unsupervised high school party, but Walter's idea to take my car without permission."

"Rory Tisdale was supposed to drive us. He has his license," said Walter. "He just backed out at the last second. I know I should have tried harder to get another ride, but I didn't know who else we could call."

Jim looked up at the top shelf in his study as if he were checking if his trophies were still there. The leather chair squeaked as he shifted his weight.

"All right, guys," he said. "I'll be straight with you. I talked to my insurance company, and they will cover the cost of repairing my car, though I can hardly believe it's not totaled. They will go after the lady who hit it and try to get her insurance to pay, but who knows? Walter, if you had been driving at the time, it would have been much, much worse. For one thing, you would have said goodbye to a driver's license for a long, long time. As things stand, I'm not sure you'll be ready any time in the next year. But we'll have to see."

They were pretty sure he was bluffing. But that was a pretty harsh threat.

"I'll tell you what, then. David, I talked to your mother, and she's disappointed in your judgment, as you might expect. But what your parents do with you is up to them. Walter, you are grounded, pure and simple, for the next month. Go to school, go to your music lesson, come home. That's it. Also, I think it would be best if you guys took a break from each other for a couple of months at least. David, you can go home now."

The boys exchanged looks. The truth was they didn't see much of each other anymore, ever since Walter started going to the gifted high school. A few years ago, they had been inseparable, they and their other friend Randy, but in the last couple of years, Randy had fallen in with some other kids from high school, guys more his bent, who were into shop and tinkering with radios. Nowadays, Walter spent more time with his gifted friends. David had places he had to be most weekends. That rogue party Friday night had been an exception and a lot of fun, and they'd enjoyed each other's company. It was just bad luck the way the night ended.

David walked home. Walter went to his room and shut the door.

Doctor and Mrs. Edelstein had hoped Walter would grow accustomed to the world they were trying to build for him and thrive in it—mingling with other kids like him, the super-smart ones, the prodigies, the exceptional. Shepherd Academy here in this small city had few attendees as smart as Walter, but at least they weren't the public-school kids Jim worried about, the kind who seemed to end up in the newspaper for the wrong reason, who got in fights, joined gangs, took drugs, went to unsupervised parties.

The real hope they had for Walter was the camp in Wisconsin that they sent him to every summer. When he was young, Walter loved it and talked about it all the time. Camp Pursell catered to the best and the smartest kids in the country and required two rounds of testing just to qualify for. And once a boy or girl was accepted, it cost like a semester at a private school. They had never mentioned this to Walter, but the financial burden just made it more distressing that Walter didn't seem to like it anymore, even though, as a senior camper, there were a lot more challenging activities in addition to the usual hiking and canoeing on the Boundary Waters.

They had hoped he would cultivate lifelong friendships among the maximally gifted. However, except for one girl he seemed to particularly like, Walter didn't phone or correspond with the handful of friends he made there.

Wendy came into the study. "Jim, I just saw young David on the way out. He looked depressed. I hope you weren't too hard on those boys. I think Walter learned his lesson, and we can't blame him for the accident."

"I wasn't being too hard. I just grounded Walter for a month, but I also said they shouldn't hang around together anymore."

"I was afraid of that," said Wendy, "it's just that those kids have been friends since Walter was six and David was five."

"It was a serious thing they did," said Jim. "There have to be consequences. I like David, but the last few times Walter got involved in serious mischief, that boy was right in the thick of it."

"I suppose you're talking about that party last winter …"

"Well, yeah. That and other times. I know Walter, and he has better sense than to be at a party where there are drugs. It's David that I worry about."

"Come on, a neighbor called the police because she thought she smelled marijuana. They didn't find any drugs."

"Walter admitted it!" said Jim. "I know he said it was some older boys who weren't even invited to the party, but he should have left as soon as he became aware of it. No, he and David were right in the middle of things. We were just lucky the boys with the drugs left before the police got involved."

Wendy sat down in one of the straight-back chairs. "I'll tell you what worries me, Jim … he just doesn't have that many friends. We always said we wanted him to have as normal a childhood as possible. Patricia may not be a mental whiz like Walter, but you have to admit she's just a happier person. And she has more friends than we can count …"

"I've worried about her, too, believe me," said Jim. "Frankly, Patty may already be beyond our control. I just read an article in *American Psychology*. The friends a kid has when he's in the twelve-to-seventeen age range have the most influence over his development into an adult. At fifteen, Walter needs to be in the company of … well, we might as well be honest … a better class of kids. Whether or not it's déclassé to say it, these are the scientists and doctors and congressmen of twenty years from now. They're going to *run* this country. We were lucky that we discovered how special Walter was when he was young. Otherwise, he might never have gotten the head start he deserves."

Wendy sighed. "Sometimes I wish we hadn't found out for a few years," she said. "I'm not sure we did him any favors."

"You don't mean that," said Jim. "We've given him *nothing but* favors." He picked up a medical journal off his desk and paged through it for something interesting to read.

Everything Is Figured Out

WALTER AND HIS FATHER examined their options. The artist had come with potential candidates for the album cover. The three of them sat in the producer's office at Sunrise Records in Kansas City, where they had just listened to the final mix of Walter's album *The Spirit of the Child*, and now they were trying to wrap up an important bit of housekeeping—choosing a cover.

"I like the one that doesn't have my face on it," said Walter. He had been asked his opinion, but that was not the choice Jim and the cover artist were hoping for.

The artist, whose name was Winston, flipped through the mock-ups one by one as if he were doing a card trick. He kept lingering on the one he liked most. There were three options because he always gave his clients three options—unless they wanted more than that. He'd done as many as six full mock-ups for a certain persnickety violinist. But as a rule, you gave them three. It was generally understood that one was the artist's real choice, one was acceptable, and the third was a throw-away just so there'd be three. The problem was Walter was preferring the throw-away.

Winston knew what to do when the client leaned toward an incorrect choice. He laid all three concepts out on the table side by side in a neat row.

"Okay, we can work with that, but let's talk about the merits of each one objectively before we decide." He pointed to the twelve-by-twelve mock-up to his right. It showed Walter from the side, eyes closed, playing the piano, leaning over the keys, lips held tight as if he were concentrating intently. Only his face, his right hand, and the middle piano keys were in focus. It was a good photo, but it made Walter look about thirteen years old. The pimples on his cheek had been airbrushed out. "What makes this one good is that it's about you. The emphasis is on your face and the creativity that's spilling out of your mind through your fingers and onto the keys. I know it makes you look young, but that fits with the album title. It looks like there is a youth, and the spirit of the youth is flowing through the piano and out to the listener."

To Jim, the choice was obvious—defer to the cover designer. The guy was a professional, had done several dozen albums for serious musicians, and had a good feel for these things. Just go with the one the designer likes and move on. But Jim shifted in his chair and kept his mouth shut.

"Then we have this one," said Winston, tapping another mock-up. The concept was pretty cool—it was a super close-up of Walter's left hand pressing the keys of the Steinway, which gleamed from the studio lights. It could have been anybody's hand, except Winston had him put on a sweatshirt for the photo, and the gray, thick cloth of the sleeve suggested a young man (or, from Jim's point of view, a hoodlum). "I love the graphic excitement of the picture. You can almost hear the music. I understand why you like it. Now let's talk about this one." He tapped the one in the middle. It was Walter from the back, showing his head from a three-quarters view so you could see his right ear and part of one eyebrow. Again, he was in the act of playing—he had actually just noodled études for ten minutes while Winston stalked in a circle with his Leica, snapping as the synchronized lights popped. "This photo is good, but now that I think about it, it's sort of generic. To me, it says, 'Here is a youth playing the piano, but there's no way to tell if he's playing Brahms or Chopsticks.'" He chuckled. No one else did.

"So I keep coming back to this first one. You can actually see the intensity on your face and how young you are, and that's what we want people to think when they are considering buying the album."

"That certainly makes sense," said Jim. He wanted to say, *Please, Walter, this is a clear choice.* But it had to be his son's choice.

Jim and Winston waited for Walter to say something, to make the right decision. Walter tried one more time. "I just don't like looking at my own face. The record is not supposed to be about me. It's about the music."

"I get you," said Winston. "But remember, nobody likes how they look in pictures. Just like nobody wants to hear the sound of their own voice on tape recorders. But to me, this one says it all: *I am a creative young man. Here is my music. Here is my soul.*"

Walter looked at his dad, who was scrutinizing the cover and nodding thoughtfully.

"Okay," said Walter. "Whatever you think."

"It has to be your decision," said Winston.

"Yeah," said Walter. "I guess you're right. I just don't know if I'll be able to look at this in a year and not think I look like a little kid."

Winston laughed and restacked the proofs, his preferred choice on top. "I know, I know," he said. "But believe me, this album is going to be something you'll be proud of the rest of your life, wherever your career takes you."

The correct alternative having been selected, Walter and his dad got back in the car for the hour-long drive home. Walter didn't say much.

Jim couldn't see why his son wasn't excited. This was a real record album. It would be sold in stores, mostly locally, but there was a chance it would break out and be heard in other places, too. Unlike the first record that Walter had recorded last year, a collection of eighteenth-century show-off tunes by classical-era composers like Haydn and Schubert, this one consisted entirely of original compositions by Walter. Last year's recording was done locally on a shoestring, but this time, Jim was spending the money. The record company promised a real promotion campaign. *Spirit of the Child* wasn't a vanity project by a precocious kid from a rich family—it was a genuine work of art. Walter put his heart and soul into the compositions and spent several hours in a big-city studio getting them properly recorded on a Steinway Model M.

He should have been giddy or at least satisfied with the accomplishment, but when the recording sessions were over, Walter showed little further interest in the project. Jim Edelstein had to step up and go the last mile, get the album cover designed, hire a publicity firm. Why had Walter stopped caring about something he did so very well? What was going on in his son's mind?

"Well, that part of it is done," said Jim, breaking the car-silence. "We're in the home stretch. In six weeks, we'll be doing our favorite part—opening the box of records, taking the plastic off the first album, and putting it on the turntable."

Walter nodded but didn't respond. He watched the suburbs give way to farmland in the Kansas River valley.

"After this, I think I need a break," said Walter.

"We *are* taking a break," said Jim. "Nobody expects you to record another record anytime soon. Besides, you have to focus on school and getting ready for the Number Sense competition."

"I mean ... I need a break from the piano," said Walter.

"I understand," said Jim. "You're experiencing a kind of letdown that comes when you finish a really tough project. I know about these things. But you can't let your skills lag. And honestly, an hour and a half a day of piano practice isn't too much to ask."

"I don't know ... I'm just tired of it. I'd rather put my energy into other things."

"Like Number Sense? You do need to work at it. And calculus. You slipped to a B last semester. And you just barely got through European history."

"Dad, I made an A in Euro history."

"An A minus, as I recall, and only because we made you give it a big push right at the end. But you're right, piano can't be everything. Just make sure you don't let your finger skills get rusty. Play an hour or so every day, at least. But I'll start helping you drill for Number Sense. We should be doing that every night."

Walter lowered his voice. "Uh ... I'm not doing the competition this year."

Jim looked at him sideways. "What are you talking about? Of course, you're doing the competition."

"I didn't sign up for it." said Walter, "Really, I need a break."

"You told us you were competing this year. I assumed you would sign up. Did you forget? I'll talk to that teacher, the one who runs the Number Sense club. What's his name?"

"Dr. Butler," said Walter. "But, Dad, please don't talk to him. I already told him I wasn't going to do the UIL competition. He gave my spot to another guy."

Jim shook his head. "I can't believe you, Walter. You came in *third place* in the state last year. You could win it all this time. What about scholarships? First place in a statewide math contest is the kind of thing the good schools look at. You always wanted to get into MIT. We may be well-off, but it would really help if you get a decent scholarship."

"You guys want me to go to MIT," said Walter. "I really don't care where I go."

"Jesus Christ!" said Jim, then felt bad about saying it. He made himself breathe slowly for a few seconds. "I'm sorry, Walter. You're tired, I get it. Let's drop the subject for now. But this is not the time to start letting us down. I mean, start letting *yourself* down. We'll discuss it later when you've had some rest."

Jim stared straight ahead. *He's that age. He thinks he has everything figured out. But, still ...*

They didn't speak the rest of the drive.

As they approached home, Jim turned onto Hackberry Street toward their surprisingly humble house in their average middle-class neighborhood. They could have bought one of those nice houses in Stone Meadows. Jim had even talked to a real estate agent a couple of years ago. But he and Wendy agreed the children should come first, getting them a good start and a proper education. Maybe that had been a mistake. In a better neighborhood, Walter would have had better friends. His sister Patty, at least, had stayed out of trouble, though she had otherwise proved a disappointment. She was on track to graduate in May but probably in the bottom third of her high school class. If she got into any halfway decent college, they'd be lucky. Otherwise, the only option was a junior college. But Walter was different. He had the genetics and the brains. No excuses not to be great.

As they pulled into their driveway, Jim finally played what he thought was his strongest card.

"Your mother will *not* be happy," he said.

Sleep or Play

WALLY FORGOT TO LIGHT the big oven until it was nearly five o'clock. The old commercial double-decker took at least a half hour to come up to temperature, and the fish required a minimum thirty minutes to cook. When he did remember, he was sitting on the porch swing reading a long music review in the college paper when two girls walked past on the sidewalk, and one of them asked, "Hey, what time is it?" and the other girl had replied, "It's almost five," and Wally had thought *Holy, shit! The oven!* and dashed into the kitchen. He dialed the temperature to 425°F so that the top half would be hot enough to get the fish started. Then he'd rotate the full sheets every few minutes so they cooked evenly.

It was Wednesday, one of Wally's two cooking days. In the three months since he'd moved into Keystone, Wally had gone from being an assistant cook on Saturday nights to full cook on two nights a week. Cooking was not nearly as hard as everybody seemed to think it was. You just had to follow the recipes and pay attention to cooking times. His first cooking partner was William Wade, an older guy in his late twenties who had spent some time as a line cook in a café and knew some kitchen tricks to improve efficiency. William had moved out in mid-October, so a new girl named Francy came in as sous-chef, and Wally got a battlefield promotion. Francy wasn't terribly interested in cooking, but at least she did what she was told. She was passably cute and "into film," and Wally liked talking movies and flirting while they chopped vegetables.

The Wednesday head cook slot opened up the following month, but Sherry couldn't persuade anybody at Keystone to step up and take the job. A skinny hippy from France who called himself Poto was willing to be a chef's assistant, but only an assistant. Wally got the idea that maybe they would cut his own rent if he cooked on both nights, and Sherry jumped at the suggestion. Wally took the two double jobs, and his rent was lowered to a hundred dollars a month. Not bad, especially since Wally hadn't managed to find much in the way of employment on the outside.

Armed with a resume filled with odd jobs in another city, zero references, and a Social Security card so wallet-worn it was mostly illegible (he filled in the numbers with a ballpoint pen), the only gig he'd landed so far was part-time grunt labor at a liquor warehouse for $3.75 an hour, twenty hours a week. It was better that the job was part-time because it was so physically demanding—hauling cases of cheap wine and bottom-shelf liquor in and out of boxcars and onto metal shelves, then down from shelves onto trucks. The first few nights after work, he had lain in bed with throbbing shoulders and a sore back, but he got used to the exertion after a couple of weeks.

Wally was chopping stalks of celery when Poto, the Wednesday sous-chef, walked in. He didn't put on an apron but waited dumbly by the cutting board for Wally to ask him why.

"Are you gonna work?" asked Wally. "There's six heads of lettuce in the reefer that need chopping, then carrots."

"Man, I need to tell you something," said Poto. "I switch jobs with Jerry Lewis for today."

Jerry was the champion house stoner, a nonstudent with no employment and no visible means of support, but he still managed to make $150 rent every month if Sherry badgered him. He cultivated a reputation for uselessness as a hedge against effort.

Wally moaned. "You mean you switched with Jerry just for today?"

"No, I mean today every week," said Poto. "I sign up for Monday cook with Peter. Jerry will cook today every week. Peter and me have chemistry together." He meant chemistry, the academic subject. "We can talk about the chemistry while we cook."

"Okay. I guess."

Poto left. Wally continued to chop, periodically checking the thermometer on the creaking, popping oven. He looked at the big wall clock. Quarter past five. Where the fuck was Jerry? Wally took off his apron and went out the back door to the annex, a stand-alone building with eight single rooms. Through Jerry's door came the sound of "Hot 'Lanta" by the Allman Brothers. Wally banged on the door, then opened it. Through a pungent cloud, Jerry could be seen on a beanbag chair against one wall, opposite his stereo, which was much better equipment than most semi-vagrants could afford. On the bed sat a friend of Jerry's with long, unwashed black hair. They both looked up at Wally with red eyes, pleasantly curious.

"Hey, man, Poto said you switched with him for assistant cook," said Wally.

"Yeah," said Jerry. "I said it was cool."

"Well, it's Wednesday. It's right now. I need your help."

Jerry thought it over, then said, "Okay, I'll be there in a flash," by which he meant sometime in the next fifteen minutes.

"Really, man, I need help," said Wally. "You're supposed to be in the kitchen by five."

"I was there ten minutes before five, and you weren't there, so I decided to mellow out until you were ready."

The friend on the bed said, "Hey, the dude needs help, Jerry. Go help him."

"Okay. Okay. I'll be there in three shakes."

Wally went back to the kitchen and chopped. There was exactly one really good chef's knife in the kitchen, a professional workhorse with a fourteen-inch blade. Despite its permanent stains and a wooden handle somebody had decided to paint Day-Glo pink. It was a good-quality knife that could be honed to scalpel sharpness, and Wally made sure it was hand-washed, dried, and left to hang on a wooden knife rack beside the stove. The cooks called it "The Big Pink Knife." On many days, Wally found the knife wet in a dish drainer or, worse, put away damp in a drawer to rust. No respect for good tools. Sheesh!

Wally had begun the sous-chef's job of peeling the carrots when Jerry finally strolled in, along with his nonresident friend, both giggling over some shared point of dope humor. Wally put Jerry to work chopping lettuce, which he did inefficiently while discussing the importance of Jeff Beck with his companion. Wally turned his attention to the evening's entre.

The twenty-eight large catfish filets were sprinkled with "black seasoning," which was a blend of black pepper, cayenne, onion powder, garlic powders, and brown sugar, then brushed with a light coating of oil. A couple of the filets were still frozen in the middle, but they should thaw out before the fish went in the oven. Wally turned his attention to the rice. Unlike its pale, polished cousin, brown rice was cooked uncovered in a rolling boil in an enormous pot. The Keystone kitchen served it every night, a staple that was never particularly liked or appreciated, but the residents loaded up on it, and there were two fifty-pound bags of the stuff in the pantry.

Wally noticed that Jerry had finished chopping the lettuce and was just standing there, gesturing as he talked to his friend. "You're crazy!" he was saying. "The new Beck Group is miles better than the old one. The original band sounds too much like the Yardbirds."

"Hey, I need you to chop the carrots, too," said Wally.

"Okay, man." Jerry picked up a carrot and started slicing.

"Peel them first," said Wally.

"Why?"

"Because the peels taste like dirt. Peel them. Pretty please."

"Whatever."

When the big stock pot was steaming ferociously, Wally poured in the rice, turned down the burner to medium, then set one of the counter timers to thirty minutes. He checked the oven. Almost hot. He opened the reefer and shook the large bowl of Jell-O. It was set. Everybody hated Jell-O, but they had tons of the stuff, so it was made most mornings for dessert that night, and most people ate at least a little of it. This batch was orange, which described its color rather than flavor. Wally considered decorating it with canned orange slices, but that would be a waste of perfectly good canned orange slices.

He looked up at the clock. Time to put the fish in the oven. He carefully lifted one of the awkward aluminum sheet pans of fish and turned to tell Jerry to open the oven. He was gone. Of course. As was his friend.

Jesus!

Nixon, a tall, quiet guy with hair that draped below his shoulder blades, strolled into the kitchen for a beer. Nixon was the oldest guy in the house—he had to be thirty. A nonstudent, he was friendly but not outgoing and always seemed to have plenty of money. Everybody assumed he was a drug dealer.

"Hey, Nixon!" said Wally. "Can you grab the oven door for me?"

"Sure."

Nixon pulled the heavy black metal door down, and Wally slid the awkward sheet into the top rack as a blast of heat wafted through his hair. Wally returned with the other sheet and maneuvered that one below the first. Nixon closed the oven door.

"Thanks."

"Sure."

Nixon put a quarter into the coke machine, extracted an empty beer bottle, inserted a second quarter, and took out a longneck beer, which he popped open and took a long pull. He smiled and nodded at Wally. "Fish, huh? Sounds good." He wandered away.

There were three vertical stacks of bottles in the Coke machine, two of them stocked biweekly by the Coca-Cola distributor, the third left empty so that the house could fill it with beer bottles. Alternating the full beers with empties made the cost of a beer fifty cents. (It violated the distributor's policy to use the machine for that purpose, but the delivery guy was cool about it.)

Now that all dinner components were in process, Wally went in search of Jerry.

Once again, stadium rock pumped through Jerry's closed door. Wally opened the door without knocking, and Jerry looked up inquisitively from his position on the bean chair.

"Where'd you go?" asked Wally. "You're on cook duty."

"I chopped the lettuce and carrots," said Jerry defensively.

"You're supposed to hang around and help with other stuff."

"Like what?"

"Whatever I need," said Wally.

"Well, if you need me, come get me," said Jerry.

It was dawning on Wally just how much he'd been screwed by Peter, the Monday chef.

Dinner was a success, measured by the very occasional compliments but mostly by the fact that it all got eaten. They even ate the turnip greens. Keystone was a member of an organic farming cooperative that provided fresh vegetables to a dozen co-op houses. Tomatoes, peppers, carrots, corn, and potatoes came in by the boxload, depending on the season. The cost of the often-misshapen vegetables was minimal, and they were generally pretty good but required copious washing. However, the greens—collards, mustards, chard, and turnip greens—were so unpopular that the farm gave them away by the bushel without asking. Wally was one of the few cooks who actually bothered to prepare them. With other cooks, the greens ended up as compost.

The first few times he presented his diners with "Greens with Pot Liquor" from the *Cooking For Fifty* book, they had been ignored, except by the boarders from Iran, who gobbled them up. But after a few brave young men and women took the plunge, Wally's greens gradually became accepted, if not beloved.

Wally always served himself last when he was the cook, though he was allowed to cut to the front of the line if he wanted (Jerry, who had done next to nothing to prepare the meal, took quick advantage of this privilege). There were two extra fish filets tonight, as there had been two no-shows. Wally let himself have one of the extras and offered the other to the boarder Beva, who had arrived at dinner late.

Most of the diners were finishing and scraping leftovers into the compost bucket, which would be returned to the farm at the end of the week. Wally had put a large handmade sign above the bucket that read "NO MEAT SCRAPS," but noticed that a lot of people were scraping fish remains into it anyway. Maybe they weren't aware that fish was "meat." He'd have to pick them out later, a job he hated, but you couldn't put meat in compost without attracting rats, according to the farmers.

Beva sat across from Wally as diners pushed back chairs and picked up their plates. Wally liked Beva, though some others found her annoying. She was loud and nosey ... she loved finding out about people and their stories. Lately she'd been talking to Wally, asking so many questions it was more like an interrogation, but he didn't mind. Beva, for her part, was very forthcoming and candid about her own life, which everyone who knew her found out quickly.

She was from Edinburg, in the Rio Grande Valley. She was twenty-four, the oldest of two girls and five boys. At sixteen, she'd had an abortion in Mexico. At nineteen, she'd married a man ten years her senior. At twenty-one, she divorced him after he came home drunk and punched her, breaking a rib. She was hoping to get into law school but was taking a year off from college before her senior year. She rented a one-room apartment with a shared bathroom, which is why she spent so much time at Keystone.

Lately, she'd taken to Wally because she liked a challenge. He didn't divulge personal information easily, which made it more fun.

"So, you're from Kansas?" asked Beva. She knew the answer already.

"Yeah. I was born in Eureka," said Wally, "but we moved away when I was two."

"Do you like Kansas?"

"Not really. It's hot in the summer and cold in the winter. And every spring, we'd have five or six tornadoes. It's really pretty out in the farm country, though, when the crops are all growing."

"Hmmm. Do you have any brothers or sisters?"

"Um ... yeah. I have a sister, but we're not close. I've ... kind of left my family behind."

"Why?" asked Beva. She watched him intently with brown-black eyes.

"I ... I just had to get away from them. They're okay people, but it was really a suffocating place to live."

"Do they know where you are now?"

"Sure they do," said Wally. "I mean, they know I'm in this city. I'm pretty sure, anyway. I'm just not ... but, anyway. How about you? Do you get along with your family?"

"Sure, as long a certain subject doesn't come up. My mom got really mad when I got married and moved away. She just thought I was doing it to get out of the house, which was true. Then she got mad all over again when I got divorced but refused to move back home. In our culture, it's kind of understood that the oldest girl stays home and takes care of the parents until they croak."

"What a fate," said Wally. He finished the bonus filet and scraped up a few remaining bits of turnip greens. "Okay, I'm done." He picked up his plate and headed for the kitchen, and Beva followed. The evening cleaning crew was picking up the saltshakers and stray silverware and wiping down the tables. They wanted to get their co-op jobs done so they could get back to studying or whatever else they did in the evenings.

"Hey, come sit with me in the living room," said Beva. She walked into the large common room and flopped onto the couch, spreading her large thighs wide like a man so she took up at least a third of the available area. Wally sat beside her.

Two Iranians were attending to the house stereo, an old GE Deluxe Wildcat that had been abandoned to common ownership. They had put on a new record (which would have horrified an audiophile) and pulled up two chairs to listen. It was a new recording of old-school jazz, and the two well-dressed foreigners in their open collars nodded rhythmically, discussing the music in Farsi.

Other people walked through the room, but nobody stayed.

Wally turned to say something to Beva when she suddenly leaned over and planted her large hand on his thigh, high up near his crotch.

"Hey, you wanna go get a beer at the Well?" she asked.

"Okay," he said.

The Well was a small bar two blocks away. In a previous life, it had been a tiny gas station. The night was cool and pleasant, and Beva and Wally walked there slowly. Despite its size, bands sometimes played the Well, taking up to half of the available floor space, but not tonight. There were only five or six other customers in the bar.

When they had settled down at their table with house beers, Beva leaned forward and looked at Wally intently.

"You really are a mystery," said Beva. "Don't get me wrong. I like you a lot. But I know almost nothing about you. You're from Kansas. That's all I know. I don't even know how old you are."

"I'm twenty-four," said Wally. "No ... I'm sorry ... I'm twenty-five."

"See, even *you* don't know who you are."

"I was just ... I had a birthday not too long ago, and I'm not used to saying it. Really, I'm not *that* dumb."

Beva laughed in her too-loud manner. "I'm just messing with you, Wally. You're a funny guy. I like to find out about people. Especially if I'm attracted to them, and I'm attracted to you." He must have looked a little alarmed because she quickly added, "Don't worry, I'm not searching for another husband, and I damn sure don't need a boyfriend."

A young waitress in cut-off jeans and a tank top walked by their table. "You guys doing okay? Let me know if you need anything. The longnecks are fifty cents tonight."

"Thanks, yeah, we're good for now. We plan to keep on drinkin'." The waitress walked away, and Beva leaned close to Wally. "I could get me some of that," she said. "She is *cute*. Yum!"

Wally glanced over at the waitress. She was indeed cute, but ... "Uh, Beva ... are you ... do you like girls?"

"I like everybody," said Beva. "And if you're asking if I'm bisexual, the answer is abso-fuckin'-lutely." She took a big gulp of house brew. "How about you, Wallace? Do you like to roll around with nice, cute boys now and again? No judgment here."

"No ... sorry," said Wally. "Actually, I'm not sorry at all. I like girls." He swigged his own big slug of beer.

They had two more beers apiece and chatted. They talked about the city, which Wally had come to love, but Beva thought was changing for the worse.

"I moved here right after I got divorced. That was just three years ago, but this whole neighborhood was different back then. This is the only cool bar left. There used to be about five great bars. Some of them are still bars, but now they've turned into these frou-frou places decorated with ferns and junk from flea markets. Also, they all raised their prices, trying to attract the 'better' clientele." She put up four fingers in the classic air-quotes gesture.

"I don't know," said Wally. "I just really like living in a big city. I've had enough of small towns. I came here because I was sick of ..." He let it trail off. "I'm sorry, I'll shut up."

"No!" said Beva. "Don't shut up. Say what you were gonna say. You moved here because you're sick of ..."

Wally raised his glass to drain his beer. "You know how they tell you that small towns are great because everybody knows everybody? Well, I think that's a double-edged sword."

"A double-edged sword," said Beva, finishing her beer as well. "I like it. Keep going."

"I spent my whole life with everybody knowing who I was," said Wally, "and I got sick of it. Not only does everybody know you, but they think they know everything about you, and they fucking don't!"

"They fucking don't!" said Beva.

Wally realized he was probably going overboard, but he liked this rare tipsy moment and hadn't talked to anyone nonjudgmental in a long time.

"I want to be a stranger in town," he said. "I have a God-given right to be a stranger. By God."

"By God!" said Beva. She clinked her beer bottle against his as a toast, even though both bottles were empty. "So, here's a personal question, Wally boy. You may answer or not. No worries either way. But my friend ... seriously ... have you had your heart broken?"

Wally started to speak, then tried to smile, but the smile was mixed up with a bad memory, and it ended up being something awkward between smile and pain. It must have looked bad because Beva leaned over and took both his hands.

"It's okay," she said.

He swallowed with difficulty and realized tears were coming out of his eyes. Beva reached her big arm across the table and, pulled the back of his head toward her and rubbed his cheek against her cheek. "It's okay, my friend, my favorite stranger."

Wally took a deep breath. "I'm sorry. Yes," he said. "My heart has been broken, but ..."

"Good enough," said Beva. "You don't have to go into it." Uncharacteristically, she was letting him off the hook.

The cute waitress came over to their table again. "Last call," she said. "We can't serve after 11:45."

"We're good," said Beva. "You wanna go, Wallace?"

"Yeah, let's head back to the house."

They walked back to Keystone holding hands, like they were boyfriend and girlfriend, though they were not and never would be. When they got to the house, she followed him into the common room. At the folding table at the other end of the room, four guys were playing a board game.

"I'm coming after Fortress Africa!" said one guy and rolled the dice. These were the serious players in a game that might go till dawn.

Beva stood very close to Wally, looking up at him with her intense brown eyes, her most striking feature. "You okay now?"

"Yeah, just really tired," said Wally.

She leaned close to his ear. "Are you too tired to play?"

Getting her drift immediately, Wally grinned. "No," he said. "Definitely not that tired."

They headed for Wally's room, empty of a roommate at the moment. They climbed the ladder to the top bunk, which was crowded with the two of them, especially with someone of Beva's girth. Getting undressed was hilariously difficult, but they managed.

A little later in the evening, Wally became alarmed at how much the bed squeaked, but there was nothing he could do about it. She ended up staying the night. They fell asleep spooning on the twin mattress.

At 6:45 a.m., the door opened, and Mike came in, unbuttoning his night watchman's shirt. He was surprised to see her but not annoyed.

"Hi, Beva," he said.

"Hi, Mike," she said. "I'll be out of your hair in a few minutes."

"No hurry," said Mike. He got a toothbrush, toothpaste, and a towel out of a middle drawer and headed for the bathroom.

No Controls

Professor Wendt liked to walk briskly whenever he was on the Kansas University campus. It was his only form of exercise. But today, he was walking with Maxwell, one of the graduate teaching assistants, who had an annoying habit of ambling when he talked. The professor found himself pausing and turning sideways repeatedly so the younger man could catch up.

"I just don't see why you can't make it a proper experiment," said Wendt. "What you're suggesting is interesting, but you need to include more controls if you want meaningful results."

"I understand," said Maxwell. "But we don't see this as a classic experiment. I just want to determine if something real might be happening. If it looks like there could be a genuine effect of some kind, then we can go to the next step and design a series of tests."

"But you do want to use controls, right?" asked Wendt.

"Absolutely. But the whole situation is necessarily subjective. We have five graduate student volunteers, plus our guy Albert. They'll all fill out questionnaires about current pain levels—then we have them all sit in chairs in a circle. Everyone will be instructed to sit perfectly still and stay silent before we even let the kid in the room. We'll do everything we can do to avoid unconscious visual cues."

"Sounds perilously close to a séance," said the professor. "Who else is going to be there?"

"Just me and Kirk Rosen," said Maxwell. "I'll be watching our subject, but Kirk will focus on Albert and the volunteers. He'll watch for anything that looks like a cue, unconscious or otherwise."

"And the cost of the whole experiment is just one hundred dollars to the family, right? You're not paying your grads anything?"

"Not a dime. They do get credit for volunteer hours, which is only fair."

"I suppose," said Wendt. "How old is the kid, by the way?"

"Fourteen. His parents will sign the consent, and they'll be with him, except for the actual experiment. We'll keep it as short and simple as possible."

They had reached Fraser Hall, which housed the psychology department. The professor stopped on the front steps and faced the TA. "Okay, write up a summary plan and give it to me tomorrow. Do you have a room?"

"Just one of the small classrooms up on the fifth floor. They should all be available on Saturday."

"Well, nail that down and double-check with Dr. Rangell."

"Will do. Thanks." The TA turned to leave, but Professor Wendt called him back.

"Max, one more thing. This guy, Albert, where did you find him?"

"He's an old friend. We played Lacrosse together junior year. Before he got hurt."

"What happened? Did he get hurt playing Lacrosse?"

"No, it was a bicycle accident. He swerved to miss a guy stepping off a bus, and he hit a road sign. It crushed one of his vertebrae. He's had two surgeries. They had to insert a rod in his spine, but he's had a lot of pain ever since."

"Poor guy," said Wendt. "But my concern is that any touch at all—even gentle touching—might induce pain. The subject might find it impossible to hide it."

"We were worried about that too, but the way I understand how the boy works is that he doesn't touch. He believes he can locate pain by holding his hands a couple of inches from the person. He never actually touches anybody."

"Well, all right," said Wendt. "Go ahead and reserve a room. I'll look over the proposal and let you know as soon as I can." He turned and mounted the stone steps into the building.

"Son, I will leave the decision to you," said Roger Monk. "I just think this is an opportunity to understand what is really going on. Just calling it a miracle is not enough. Scientists like things they can measure, and nobody has ever tried to measure what you can do."

"I don't mind going once," said David. "I'm just afraid they're gonna say, 'We couldn't find anything, so you have to keep coming back.'"

They were sitting in the Monk living room. Mom was making supper, and Dad had just gotten home from work. David should have been doing his homework but was reading a *Life* magazine with a picture of a space-suited astronaut on the cover. The astronaut was not one of those who had actually flown to space, but the magazine said he was scheduled to go later this year and would stay in space a lot longer than anyone else, even longer than the Russians had. The space suit he was demonstrating was a newer kind that could be worn for hours without the astronauts getting all itchy and sweaty. David put down the article.

He didn't want to go to the college to be tested. At first, he had thought it would be okay. Dad said it would help science, and David thought that might be a good thing. If they understood what was happening, maybe they could invent a machine that did the same thing, and David wouldn't have to do it anymore. Plus, they said they'd pay one hundred dollars no matter what they found out, just for David's participation. That was wildly attractive, especially since Dad told him he could keep the money (although it would go into the bank for David's future benefit—not a shopping spree). But the more he thought it over, the more he feared that if they did find something unusual, they'd insist that he keep coming back again and again until they understood it.

It had been Dad's friend from the office—a man who also went to the First Christian Church—who suggested they should contact the University of Kansas, where his own son was a graduate student. When David agreed, Dad had been really pleased. David hated disappointing anyone, least of all his parents. If he backed out now, it was Dad who'd be embarrassed.

Roger Monk sat back in his favorite armchair and crossed his leg, revealing a long swath of over-the-calf black socks. "I can't promise they won't want you to come back," he said. "I also can't promise they'll keep paying a hundred dollars. On the other hand, if they did keep testing you and paying us for it … son, that is a *lot* of money. It could help pay for your college. I know that's not something you care about right now, but it is coming up in a few years. You can't really make it in the world today without a college degree, and we're trying to save enough to send you."

Guilt—subtle but potent. He had to let the college people watch him work. There was probably no getting out of it. But the truth was, David didn't want to help people anymore. He knew that was selfish, but he had never asked for the gift. He liked the idea of making money, but he truly didn't care if he ever went to college. But since Mom and Dad really wanted him to, he probably had no choice.

His best friend Walter complained a lot about never getting to do what he wanted. Walter's parents weren't content to just let him be a genius and get straight As—they made him take music lessons, too, and enter all kinds of competitions. Walter was just as special as David, in a different way.

David's folks, at least, let him live a more normal life. Walter's parents talked about their son's special talents all the time. David's parents kept knowledge of the gift to themselves and the people at church and among their close circle of friends. But they also let David know, through hints and suggestions, that he owed the world some part of himself. They didn't demand that he use his gift, but every time he showed reluctance, they couldn't hide their disappointment.

However, money had never changed hands before. Dad had always rejected offers of cash in exchange for David's help, even grateful generosity after the fact. If they insisted, he told them to donate to the church. Until now, the subject of money had seldom even come up. But a hundred dollars for a chance to help science … that was not trifling.

"Okay, I guess I'll go," said David. He would have to give up a Saturday. Again.

"Very good," said his dad. Roger Monk picked up the *Life* magazine that David had been scanning and read the cover blurbs. "Wow. They say this guy is going to orbit the Earth over twenty times. That's incredible. One of these days, people will be living in outer space." Dad was changing the subject so that David wouldn't have a chance to change his mind.

THEY WERE KEPT WAITING for forty-five minutes in a small office off of a big, echoey hall. David tried to read a science fiction paperback but couldn't focus. Dad looked around the room and wiggled his foot. Twice, a young man named Kirk came in to assure them it was all going to happen—the test was taking longer than expected to set up, but they would be ready very soon.

Finally, a different young man came in and introduced himself as Maxwell Heston.

"We'll get going in just a few minutes," he said. "First, I'm going to read a statement that will describe the scenario. After that, you'll be able to ask questions before we start." He unfolded a sheet of typing paper and read aloud:

"Inside the room, there will be eight people seated in chairs in a circle, spaced two feet apart from each other, facing outward. I will also be in the room, as will the other researcher. We ask that no one else accompany you. When you go in the room, I will show you where to step inside the circle. After I introduce you, please do not speak to any of the seated participants, either before or during the test. They have been instructed not to speak to you. One or more of the people in the chairs may be experiencing chronic pain. We would like you to try to identify this person or these persons. Please do not point or otherwise indicate a choice. If you have a question, please ask me. We also ask that you not touch any of the participants. We will leave it up to you to decide how long you want to stay inside the circle. You may take as long as one hour. When you are ready to stop, just tell me, and you should then leave the room again without speaking to anyone but me. You will then return to this room, where we'll ask you some follow-up questions about your experience."

He looked up. "Okay, I guess that's about it. Do you have any questions before we start?"

David shook his head, but his dad spoke.

"I know you say you don't want me to influence what he does, but couldn't I just observe from the side if I agree to stay quiet?"

"No sir, I'm sorry," said Maxwell. "We need as few distractions as possible in the room, both for your son and for the participants."

"All right," said Dad. "David, I'll be here when you're done."

THE ROOM WAS BRIGHTLY LIT with fluorescent office lights. There was a clear chalkboard but nothing else to indicate the room's usual purpose. When David came in, the eight volunteers were seated quietly.

"This is David," said Maxwell. "I want to remind everyone in this room that if they must speak, they should speak only to me."

He pointed to the space between two of the chairs, and David walked between them into the inner part of the circle. The participants sat perfectly still, eyes open, expressionless. Each chair had a piece of notebook paper taped to the back, with the numbers 1 through 8 written in black marker.

It was strange to have no input from people he helped. When he was called to a healing, often there were relatives, ministers, sometimes a nurse, or other caregivers. The infirm usually engaged with him, if they could, telling him about their suffering, making small talk, often apologizing for the trouble they were causing.

There were six men and two women seated in the chairs. Most looked to be in their twenties. A couple of the men may have been a little older. One of the younger men had a short, neat beard, which reminded David of a jazz musician. The young man who had greeted them when they first arrived stood off to one side, holding a spiral notebook and pencil. Maxwell moved to the other side of the room and stood with his arms crossed.

David had expected someone to say, "Okay, start," or something like that, but everyone just waited. For him.

He walked slowly once around the circle. They were sitting too close together—their energy fields, which David thought of as large glowing eggs, were almost overlapping—but he knew immediately which person was ill. Number 4. The pain, which looked and felt like a thick green electric fog, was strong in the room, and David could detect it through his forehead without even raising his hand. After one pass around the circle, he reversed direction. Standing outside the circle, the man with the notebook slowly shifted positions one way or the other as he observed and took notes.

David raised his right hand and placed it a short distance from the back of one woman's head. What he was doing was for show. Today, he had a chance to fix things in his own life, and he wanted the college people to take him seriously. So, he moved slowly from one person to the other.

Number 4 was wearing a white long-sleeved shirt, like the kind people wore to church, but no tie. His short hair touched the top of his ears and spilled over slightly as if he had missed his usual haircut last week. Like everyone else, he sat perfectly still. David made a point of taking no more time with him than with the others, but the pain was sharp and resonant, centered in the middle of the man's back just below the level of his ribs. David moved on to the next person, taking his time. He had to make this look right. He decided to walk three full times around the circle.

He found no one else with identifiable suffering. One of the older volunteers, Number 2, seemed to have a headache, which David could just catch a glimpse of when his hand was close to the back of the man's head, where the vision part of the brain lives. One of the other men, Number 8, sneezed, wiped his nose on his sleeve, and muttered, "I'm sorry." The notetaker looked at his watch and jotted a note. David accidentally brushed the back of Number 3's neck, which caused her to flinch. The notetaker wrote something, again looking at his watch. Whenever David passed behind Number 4, the man in the white shirt, David felt worse about himself.

After the third pass around the circle, he looked up at the head researcher.

"I … I think I'm done now. Can I stop?" he asked.

"It's up to you," said Maxwell.

"I'd like to stop."

"Okay, that's fine. Now go on back to that room you waited in, and I'll be down to speak with you in a few minutes. Then we should be done for today."

David left the circle and went out the classroom door. When he got back in the room where they had begun, Dad was sitting with a copy of *National Geographic*— legs crossed like usual.

"How'd it go?" Dad asked.

"I couldn't help him," said David.

"You mean you couldn't help his pain?"

"I couldn't see it."

"Oh," said Dad. But he didn't understand.

David tried to clarify. "Somebody may have been hurting, but I couldn't tell which one," he said. Then he added, "I can't see people like I could when I was little. I guess it's going away."

"Do you want to go back and try again? It was probably just too strange of a situation. You can give yourself time to relax. I'll talk to them."

"No," said David. "I just couldn't see it."

The door opened, and Maxwell and the other graduate student came in.

"You did very good, David," said Maxwell. "Now, let's talk about what you experienced."

"Okay," said David.

Both graduate students sat down in wooden chairs, Kirk still with his notebook and Maxwell holding a clipboard and a pencil. "Let's go through the questions one at a time," he said. "Some of them are yes-no questions, but for some, I will ask you to give me a number: one through five. In each case, one means very weak or no effect, and five means very strong effect."

"Okay."

"First question, yes or no: Did you feel you could detect anyone in the room who might be experiencing pain?"

David swallowed. "No," he said quietly.

Maxwell looked up. "None? Nothing at all? Are you absolutely sure? You could not detect any discomfort in any of the subjects."

"No. I really couldn't."

The two graduate students looked at each other.

"Well, what do you want to do?" asked Maxwell, addressing Kirk Rosen.

"That's it," Kirk said. "If he answers 'no' to the first question, then the others are all moot."

"I … I suppose you're right," said Maxwell. His face betrayed his disappointment.

"Maybe he could try again," Roger Monk suggested. "I think he was probably pretty nervous."

"No, really, Dad," said David. "There was nothing. I wasn't nervous. I just didn't feel anything. Doing it again won't make any difference."

"Then I guess we're done," said Maxwell. The two graduate students stood up. "Thanks for helping us. Mr. Rosen can show you out. The bursar's office should send you a check in a few days. If it hasn't arrived in a week, call them. But I think it will be no problem."

Kirk Rosen and the two Monks went out into the hallway while Maxwell stayed behind to write up what would be a disappointingly short summary of his experiment. Some of the student volunteers were still mingling in the hall, and several of them thanked David warmly as if he'd accomplished something.

Maxwell sat in the office scribbling in his own personal shorthand, which no one else could read. He'd type it up this afternoon. *What went wrong?* he thought. Was it like the father said? Was the kid just nervous? Or maybe young David's reputation was based entirely on placebo effect and wishful thinking, which Maxwell and Kirk had successfully neutralized. If that were true, then the experiment was a success and provided real data.

Kirk Rosen came back into the room.

"I think he was holding back on us," he said.

"Really? Why?"

"Let me tell you what I just saw out in the hallway. As the kid passed everybody, they told him thanks, and he just nodded. He obviously just wants to get out of here. But when Albert shook his hand, the kid said, 'I'm really sorry.' He said it very clearly."

"He's just sorry the experiment didn't go like we'd hoped," said Maxwell.

"No … it looked like he was apologizing to Albert, specifically. He didn't say 'I'm sorry' to anybody else. I'll bet he knew Albert was the one with the back pain."

"Maybe Albert gave him some unconscious cues, like wincing when he walked."

"Maybe," said Kirk. "I don't think so. I was watching him like a hawk, and I didn't see anything. No, that kid identified our subject. I'm about 99 percent sure." He consulted his notes. "I watched how he interacted with everybody else. In every case but one, he held his hand very, very close. About an inch or less. With Albert, he kept the hand back at least six inches, like he was afraid to get too close. He also spent less time with Albert than anyone else, significantly. I timed him."

"Maybe he just didn't want to do it after all. I thought he was fine with it. At least, his dad said he was. But I guess he was apologizing for letting everybody down."

"I think he apologized because he could have helped Albert but chose not to," said Kirk Rosen.

Wally's Late-Night Library

S HERRY TRIPP HAD LIVED IN KEYSTONE for two years, serving as its manager the second year, and had her pick of bedrooms. She could have chosen one of the bigger, brighter, airier upstairs rooms, but instead, she lived downstairs in a small windowless room at the end of the hall. It had not been intended as a bedroom when the house was built in the 1930s. Most likely, it was a large storage closet. There was just enough room for a twin bed and a desk with a lamp, a low two-tier bookshelf with a small portable record player on top, and a chest of drawers. A tiny tensor light was attached by a clamp to the bed's wooden headboard, and a floor lamp pointed straight up at the ceiling to provide general illumination. When both lights were off, it was dark as a cave.

Beva said that Sherry was prone to bad headaches and preferred the darkness when she had an episode. Most people supposed the real reason had to do with her boyfriend, Nicholas Symansky.

Nicholas didn't pay rent, but then he didn't eat much, either. He liked to sit cross-legged on Sherry's bed with only the sharp yellow glare of the tensor light or sometimes on the front porch while he read poetry, philosophy, and speculative fiction paperbacks. More annoyingly, he would sometimes sit for extended periods of time in the common room, plucking notes on the house guitar. It was an old Kaye dreadnought with ancient strings, abandoned by a previous tenant, which typically stayed propped against the wall in the common room. It was impossible to keep in tune, but Nicholas would pick it up and play, not songs or chords, but endless major scales, up and down the fretboard. After playing an exasperatingly slow C-major scale, he would start again with D-major, up and down, over and over.

Nobody complained openly to Sherry about him, but there was a lot of gossip, especially lately. The man was obviously crazy. Maybe not dangerous-crazy, hopefully not, but it was clear to anyone who spoke to him that some gears were missing. Residents who had known him the longest had seen his decline.

Nicholas had been a paying member of Keystone House a year ago when he and Sherry first became a couple. He was a deeply thoughtful man in his late twenties who spoke infrequently but was generally pleasant. His only distinct eccentricity was his habit of sitting on his bed naked, partially covered, in lotus position, with the door wide open to the common area. Sometimes, he read in this state, and other times, he sat silently with his eyes closed, presumably in meditation. In that first year, he lived in one of the nicer single rooms. He was said to be working vaguely at a doctorate of some kind.

He and Sherry had become lovers over Christmas break. When students and nonstudent residents returned in January, Sherry and Nicholas were inseparable. Wherever Sherry went, Nicholas usually tagged along, except when she went to her part-time receptionist's job at a doctor's office. When she went to her classes, he sometimes audited them just to be near her. The two of them were often found sitting on the porch swing, absorbed in low conversation. When Sherry went out to clubs or events with other friends, Nicholas went as well but contributed little to the conversation.

Early in the summer, the two had a falling-out, and Nicholas disappeared. When asked, Sherry said, "He's not trying to make himself better. I couldn't put up with that." No one saw him for the next six months.

Late in the fall, he returned. To those who knew him, the difference was alarming. He had let his thick brown hair and dark beard go completely unruly, deep eyes peering out from under thick, untrimmed eyebrows. He had been in Los Angeles, Sherry said, squatting in a vacant house with other homeless people and had dropped a lot of acid. He had spent time in jail for vagrancy and unlawful entry.

Why she took him back baffled everyone. Beva said that Sherry was a "compulsive nurturer." Since Nicholas had no money, he stayed with her in the dark room at the end of the hall, sitting on the bed in silence, sometimes reading dog-eared paperbacks but saying little. Sherry provided him with money for food and brought him leftovers from dinner. He was suspected of pilfering food and drink—clearly labeled with other people's names—from the reefer, but no one ever caught him.

For Wally, there was another problem. He had moved to Keystone with two large cardboard boxes of books, some of them paperbacks, their covers worn and their pages yellowing, and some more sturdy hardbacks. About half the books were his own, collected since he was a teenager, and the rest had been bequeathed by a friend. When Wally moved into the double room with his nocturnal roommate, there was no bookshelf, so he improvised. He found a stack of unused cinder blocks behind the annex, which he brushed off and hosed out the spiderwebs. He then placed six of the large bricks along one wall in his room in two stacks, with salvaged boards in between to serve as shelves.

His books were placed in a vague but logical order: small science fiction and adventure novels on the top shelf—Clarke, Heinlein, Le Guin, Hubbard, Farmer, Asimov, all the greats of the fifties and sixties. The second shelf was devoted to philosophy, poetry, and history—especially history of the West—along with classic novels by Steinbeck, Hemingway, Faulkner, Joyce. On the lower shelf were books about film and filmmaking, books by famous directors, and some biographies of musicians, both jazz and classical. The film books were Wally's, but the music-related titles had come in one swoop from a friend—He hadn't read many of them. Finally, on the floor were large art and photography books and hardbacks of all types.

It was a satisfying collection, and there was plenty of room for additions from the numerous small local bookstores that dotted the university area. Occasionally, he would let a friend borrow a book, but Wally was possessive of them, and everybody at Keystone knew it and respected his library.

He first noticed that a few books were going missing when he was discussing 1930s poetry with one of the student residents, and to make a point he went back to his room to retrieve a book by the radical poet Kenneth Patchen. There was an empty space where the book had sat just a couple of days ago. Lending out books was stressful enough, but somebody just taking them out of his room without asking was not acceptable. At dinner that night, he asked pointedly about the Patchen volume, but nobody confessed.

After dinner, Wally returned to his room and checked the four rows of books carefully. He didn't have any sort of regular inventory list, but he knew his books pretty well. Three or four of them were definitely gone. Another poetry book by William Blake, a novel by Howard Fast, a biography of the filmmaker Truffaut. Most of the bedroom doors in the house had locks, but they were only thumb locks you had to turn from the inside—most of the keys had been mislaid in an earlier age. There was little he could do.

He spotted one of the purloined volumes two days later. Nicholas the Mad was reading one of Wally's science fiction novels while seated on the steps in front of the house. Nearby, Sherry rocked back and forth on the porch swing with a textbook, studying. Nicholas was so focused on the book that he might have been biting his lip, though it was hard to tell under the old-testament beard. Wally hated to interrupt, but there was a principal at stake.

"Hey, Nicholas," he said. That was the only salutation he could think of. Nicholas did not look up, but Sherry did. Wally waited. No response.

"Earth to Nicholas!" said Sherry. "Hey! Somebody is talking to you!"

He looked up at her, expressionless. She pointed at Wally, and Nicholas's dark, scary eyes turned to him. Not confrontational, not even curious.

"Hey, man, is that my book?" he asked. Of course, it was. For one thing, he recognized it from the initials "WE" written along the face of the pages in Magic Marker, unmistakable, personalized from a previous life. Nicholas looked at the book, then back to Wally.

"It's a good book," he said. Not defensive, just stating a fact.

"Uh … well, man, just … you need to make sure I get my books back. People have been borrowing them without asking and … I want to keep my books …"

Expressionless eyes. Did he even understand what Wally was saying? Wally tried again. "It's just that … you know …"

Sherry cut in. "Nicholas, did you take his book without asking? That is *not cool*!"

A hint of sadness came over the bearded one's face. "I'm sorry," he said quietly, not to Wally, to Sherry.

"I mean, it's really okay," said Wally. "I don't mind. I just need you to ask."

"Okay," muttered Nicholas, again to Sherry. He returned his attention to the small, ragged book—*More Than Human* by Theodore Sturgeon.

What more could Wally do? He had to go to work.

It was Wally's last week at the liquor warehouse, but it would be a tough one. Two boxcars of wine had come in the night before as the company stocked up on swill for the holidays. Wally and the other two guys on the shift would be moving and stacking boxes most of the day, eight boxes per level, four levels high, stacked alternately so they locked together and wouldn't shift when the forklift picked them up. Box after box, palette after palette. It was backbreaking work.

Last week, he'd heard about a job at the official campus bookstore, sorting and inventorying textbooks and loading them onto the shelves. It still involved a lot of lifting and carrying, but boxes with twenty copies of *An Introduction to Asian History* were a lot lighter than cases of High-Steppin' wine in the quart size. Next week, he'd start at $4.75 an hour, work more hours in the week, and it wouldn't leave him wiped out at the end of the day. Plus, the bookstore was walking distance, and he wouldn't have to drive the Maverick. He wanted to find a nice legal place on the street for his car and then leave it there. Just fixing the clutch had cost him his first two paychecks, and now the muffler was rattling.

That night, despite Wally's exhaustion, he had trouble falling asleep. He'd taken three aspirins before bed, but his shoulders throbbed. Eventually, he drifted off.

The sound of the door opening didn't wake him, but a shaft of light from the hallway struck his face, and he opened his eyes. Somebody was standing in the doorway—backlit. Wally raised himself upon one elbow. *Mike?* No, it was Nicholas. Wally could identify him from the outline of the head. He appeared to be stark naked.

Nicholas floated into the room, went straight to Wally's bookshelf, and crouched—the light from the hall light washed across the book titles. Nicholas must have seen Wally looking at him but ignored him. He took out a book from the second shelf, put it back, selected another one, put that one back, then picked a third one and spent a full minute reading the description on the back. Then he sniffed it and read some more.

Wally had to get control of his own situation. "Hi, Nicholas," he said.

The silent intruder glanced at him but returned his attention to the book.

"You know, you really have to ask me," said Wally. "I don't mind if you borrow them, but you gotta ask. And make sure you bring them back."

Nicholas stood up and walked toward Wally on the top bunk. Was this a confrontation? Wally wondered if he should jump down off the bunk to put himself in a little better defensive position. But Nicholas stopped a few feet away.

"I *know* who you are," he said.

Wally hesitated. "Um … well, this *is* my room, man, and …"

Nicholas turned and walked away, holding the book close to his chest. When he reached the doorway, he turned sideways and looked back. His body hair and genitals made a strange profile.

"Don't store chemicals in here," Nicholas said. "It's not safe." He turned and disappeared down the hall with Wally's book.

Wally, unnerved, climbed down the ladder and went to the books along the wall. He wasn't sure which title Nicholas had purloined, but he thought it was a book by C. L. Moore, one of the few women working in the science fiction genre. Also, it was a book Wally had not yet read. What could he do? He'd ask Sherry to retrieve it for him tomorrow.

He shut the door, climbed back up on the bunk, and lay there, aching over much of his frame, wide awake.

Walter Phones Late

DENISE MAYBERRY WORKED HARD to finish her paper for tenth-grade world history. It was an economic analysis of the British Protectorate of Hong Kong, with estimates of the city's current and future population, per capita income and financial growth, and alternative scenarios should it remain autonomous or be taken over by Mao's Communist regime. Worth a quarter of her semester grade, the paper was due in the morning, and Denise had put off working on it as long as possible despite her well-earned reputation as a self-starter. The truth was she didn't give a shit about Hong Kong.

It was the world history teacher, Dr. Slocum, who had given Denise the assignment. He knew her family had lived in Hong Kong for a couple of years when she was in elementary school, so maybe he thought the subject would be right up her alley. In fact, she had very few memories of the Far East, and most of those involved stifling restrictions on where she could go and when she could see her friends, the children of other expats.

The only positive thing about having to research this particular subject was that her father had several books about the city and its culture, acquired when he was assigned to the province by his company, an international insurance conglomerate. The books were a bit out of date, but there was no way her teacher could know that, so she dove into them and shoveled out information willy-nilly until she thought she had enough for a paper and then tried to hammer it into something coherent. At least it looked impressive that she could cite five diverse sources. It would have been a hard job even if she *had* cared about Hong Kong. She had difficulty focusing and kept looking up at the clock.

Walter was supposed to call a few minutes after 1 a.m. That would be midnight in his time zone when the long-distance calling rates came down.

She was pretty sure she loved Walter Edelstein. It was not a heart-pounding, breath-panting, obsessive attraction the way love was portrayed in young romance novels, but she thought about him a lot. He must have liked her as much as she liked him, or more because he wrote her many letters. It was also his idea to call her on the phone about once a month. Apparently, his parents didn't mind as long as he called after midnight and kept the calls to a strict fifteen minutes. Denise didn't know how much it was costing the Edelstein family, but she had picked up on the fact that his dad was a doctor, wealthy by small-town standards.

They had met at Camp Pursell in Wisconsin, a sleepaway camp for "intellectually gifted youth." She had learned about it from some brochures at her school and somehow talked her parents into sending her. The Mayberrys were pretty well-off, but Pursell was priced like such elite places always were, and they were already paying for private school. They weren't eager to start a summer tradition that would cost them thousands more dollars before their daughter was even out of puberty. However, the brochure said there were "camperships" available to the sufficiently brilliant and motivated. Denise took the camp application test at her school, aced it easily, then applied for a reduced rate and got that, too. All while she was eleven years old.

After going to such trouble, it turned out she didn't particularly like Pursell. Many of the kids were "gifted" only in the sense of being rich. One girl's father was a US senator, and another was Ambassador to Mexico. There were also some kids from Europe, the sons and daughters of international businessmen. She did make friends but often felt overwhelmed and out of place. Camp activities were fun, and Denise liked canoeing in particular. The camp also offered computing classes. Hiking, swimming, and campfire songs were interspersed with the compiling of punch card stacks, designing programs that could run on the camp's computer.

She noticed Walter that first year but didn't have the nerve to speak to him until the last week of camp. He was going through an awkward puberty, and his voice was changing, which gave it a rusty-hinge timbre. But he was nice to her and stood out as more intelligent than the supposed geniuses at Pursell. On the next-to-last night of camp that term, there was a dance with a hired band, and the two of them had slow-danced together several times under the fierce gaze of the counselors. Before the night was over, they had even kissed surreptitiously and exchanged addresses and phone numbers.

To her surprise, Walter had written, and Denise wrote back. His letters were heartfelt and detailed, though often sad. He was not happy at home and lived under constant pressure to be the best and smartest at everything, something Denise could relate to. His dad, especially, leaned on him to excel at both academics and sports and browbeat him into taking intensive music lessons when it turned out he had a natural talent for that as well.

For her part, Denise tried to keep his spirits up by telling him about the more interesting aspects of her own life and recommending books they could both read and discuss. He was generally game for that. Once, she had even suggested a classical book she was being forced to read at school, *In Praise of Folly*, by the Dutch theologian Erasmus. She was half joking, but then she was delighted a month later when he mailed her a short book review—in Latin. She located a Latin dictionary in her father's library and did her best to translate. The Latin was simple and full of errors, but the whole exercise was hilarious and made her like him even more.

The second summer after they met, her parents let her know she wouldn't be able to attend the same term at Pursell due to a conflict with a family trip to Italy. They would let her register for first term if she wanted. The camp had two full terms per year, June into mid-July and July into August, meaning she wouldn't see Walter if he went to second term as usual. She told this to Walter in a letter and let him know how much distress this was causing her—she pretended she was worried about missing *all* her second-term friends, but really it was just Walter. That was the first time he called. A postscript at the end of his letter said he would call her on a particular Saturday at 11:05 p.m. eastern time.

She mentioned to her parents that a friend from camp might be calling late at night. They probably didn't believe her. She wondered if it would actually happen, but nonetheless, on the appointed Saturday night, she sat beside the living room phone, ready to pick up at the first ding. Her dad had gone to bed, and her mom was watching a late movie in the den. Denise sat on the couch with the phone in her lap and her hand on the receiver. When the phone did ring, at precisely 11:05, she jumped and picked up immediately. It was Walter. His voice had settled down and deepened in the intervening months, but he sounded just like she remembered.

Her mother had heard the interrupted ring and came into the living room and made a little "Who is it?" gesture, so Denise covered the mouthpiece with her hand and stage-whispered, "It's a friend from camp. I told you."

"I hope her parents know she's calling," said Mom. "It can't be cheap," but she let Denise have her privacy. She and Walter talked for half an hour about everything and nothing in particular, and at the end, Walter promised he would make it work so he could see her that summer. In the end, he just told his parents he wanted to switch to first term at Pursell. He didn't bother saying why, and they didn't ask. They were just happy he was still willing to go after they'd heard nothing but complaints about the genius camp for two years.

When they got the phone bill a month later and saw the late-night call to New Hampshire, Dr. Edelstein put two and two together and confronted Walter. He confessed that he had called a girl from Pursell that he really liked. His father made him promise to keep such calls to once a month, after midnight, and hold them to fifteen minutes. Walter agreed.

That second summer, the camp counselors became aware that these two adolescents were inseparable. This was a common situation at every co-ed camp, so the staff kept a close watch to avert hanky-panky. They were not entirely successful. One day during afternoon free time, Denise and Walter met privately behind the row of hay bales at the archery range. That time, they just talked, but Walter came up with a plan for them to sneak out of their cabins after lights out.

That night at 11:30, Denise slipped out of her bunk, bunching the pillows under the blanket to simulate a human shape, as if that would fool anyone, and crept to the door of her own cabin. A girl she didn't know well sat up and looked at her inquisitively. Denise just grinned and put a finger to her lips, and the other girl just returned the grin, winked, and lay back down. Among campers, there was a code of silence about harmless shenanigans. The other girls would all soon know about Denise's late-night escape, of course, but not the staff.

Denise found Walter waiting for her behind the stables. They could have stayed there without being discovered, but it reeked so badly of manure that they abandoned their original rendezvous point in favor of the far side of a grassy hill near the parking lot, where Walter spread out a blanket. The encounter was tame even by teenage standards. There was a lot of kissing. He kissed her lips and licked her neck, and tentatively placed his hand on her small breast over the XXL T-shirt she used as a nightgown. It was a timid meeting, but to thirteen-year-old Denise, it was erotic heaven. They stayed there for half an hour until fear of discovery sent them back to their cabins.

Three days later, they pulled the same stunt again, with similar intoxicating results. That night, they spent much longer together, and after kissing for a while, they lay together holding hands and looking at the stars and talking about their lives with parents who expected only excellence from them.

Walter's childhood had started out conventionally. He was a post-war American kid with a bike and friends and loved to range far and wide up and down the streets and alleys of his middle-class neighborhood. In his earliest memories, the block was so new there were very few trees—just saplings a few feet high supported by guy wires staked to the ground—so the summer sun was brilliant. On hot summer days, Walter's family would drive out to a state park called Clinton Lake with a gleaming fiberglass canoe strapped to the top of the car, where Walter played in the water and his sister Patty sat on the shore in her two-piece bathing suit listening to a battery-powered record player stacked with 45-rpm records, reading movie magazines.

When it snowed in the winter, Walter and his friends formed a gang that roamed the neighborhoods, seeking out snowball combat with other gangs of kids. Spring, summer, and fall, they played an endless game of backyard football at his friend David's house and kickball when they tired of that.

Nothing about school was difficult for Walter. He made A's without trying and was the fastest kid on the track team. His dad was a urologist, so Walter saw him mostly in the evenings and on weekends while his mom worked part time at the University of Kansas. He was aware early on that they had more money than the other families, but he never knew anyone who was poor.

One Saturday, when he was nine years old, his dad and mom drove him to the college campus, where they met with a lady professor. She sat him down in an empty classroom and gave him a written test while his parents went to lunch at a campus cafeteria. It was a strange test, not like the normal school kind. It had questions like:

Which of these shapes would fit inside this shape? or

$6 + 6 \div 6 + 6 \times 6 - 6 = ?$

Walter didn't see the point of it all, but he liked getting the right answer, so he did his best.

When it was all over, and his parents returned, the professor made them all sit and wait for half an hour while she scribbled over the pages with a red pencil. Finally, she spoke. "Mr. and Mrs. Edelstein, would you like Walter to leave the room while I give you the results?"

Mom and Dad looked at each other, and Dad shrugged. "No, I think it's okay if he hears it," he said.

"Very well," she said. "Your son scored a 155."

"Oh, my," said Mom.

Walter had no idea what they were talking about, but he figured out very quickly that 155 was a good score.

The professor elaborated: "Anything over 120 is considered 'superior.' The range of 145 to 160 is the highest the test can accurately measure: 'very gifted or highly advanced.' Your son shows remarkable intelligence."

Very gifted. Highly advanced. These words would come to define Walter's life.

He told Denise the music part was his own fault. He had wanted to play piano ever since he saw Victor Borge perform on the Ed Sullivan show. He loved how Borge clowned around and cracked jokes in a funny accent while playing effortlessly. Piano looked fun. After a couple of weeks of pestering, Mom took him to a music teacher she knew through her job at the college. She gave him a few lessons, then declared that Walter was "naturally gifted" at music.

There it was, that word again. His parents paid for lessons with that woman for a year then, at the first teacher's suggestion, found him more advanced instruction in a nearby city, a fifty-minute drive each way every Saturday to see a male music professor. Lessons became more demanding. Walter's parents alternately cajoled and flattered him into practicing, but it was fear of not being the best that drove him. He devoted up to two hours a day to the piano, on top of private tutoring in math. Normal childhood slipped quietly away.

Walter didn't love playing the piano, almost never played for relaxation or pleasure, though he taught himself a few jazz tunes, and those were fun. Mostly, piano was just another thing he had to be good at and wished he could be rid of.

Denise had it easier at her house. She had two little brothers four years younger—twins, who required much of their mother's attention. Anything Denise achieved at school was her own doing. She was good at math, took advanced classes ("high honors" classes, they were called), and then asked and received permission to take subjects ahead of her own grade level. She ended up in classes with a couple of brainy girls like herself and two dozen unruly smart boys, who both looked down on her and were intimidated by her.

At first, her parents were just pleasantly surprised at her genius, then thrilled. They never pushed her. They didn't have to. Denise succeeded at everything she tried. Still, the longing to be a regular teenage girl was strong and growing. Walter understood. She could talk to him, and he to her, without trying to pretend she was anything other than a super-smart, slightly gawky girl a little tall for her age.

They met surreptitiously twice more that summer session, but a couple of days before the end of term, the planned rendezvous was thwarted when Walter was caught sneaking out of the boys' dorm area. Denise listened from her hiding place as the counselors chewed him out, and he improvised a story about wanting to play a prank on a boy in another cabin. They let him go, but it was a serious infraction that would elicit an official warning and a letter to his parents.

Denise waited in the shadows, then snuck back to her cabin feeling guilty.

On the last day, they hugged and vowed to remain friends for life. Walter would write her regularly and call monthly. Unfortunately, circumstances prevented them from seeing each other in the flesh for three more years. The next summer, Walter's schedule had not allowed him to attend Pursell at all. The summer after that, it was Denise's turn when her family spent most of the summer in Spain.

Her parents weren't aware of Walter's 1 a.m. phone calls. After Walter told her the calls would have to be very, very late at night, Denise invented the trick of secretly unplugging the downstairs phone on the appointed evenings after her parents went to bed. The phone in the upstairs hallway had an extra-long cord that would reach her room where it sat on the floor, ringer volume turned as low as it would go. (Only once had she forgotten to plug the downstairs phone back in afterward, but her mother had blamed the housekeeper.)

The phone rang, and Denise answered instantly.

"Hey, girl," said Walter.

"Hey," said Denise.

They made some reorientation small talk for a few minutes. It took only a short time before Denise felt like she was picking up a conversation from yesterday rather than last month.

"You remember that idea I told you about?" asked Walter. "The mountain road trip?"

"Yeah," said Denise. "Are you going to do it?" He had been mentioning the plan to take a clandestine vacation for a couple of months now.

"It's going to happen. In two weeks. We get a four-day weekend for Memorial Day, so me and my friend David are going camping. He already talked his parents into letting us take his mom's car."

"I thought you said David didn't have a license yet."

"He doesn't," said Walter. "That's what's crazy. But somehow, David talked them into it. I've had my license for nine months now, so I'm gonna drive their car."

"Why would they let you take their car?" asked Denise. "Do they trust you that much?"

"I guess they do. I don't know what David said to them, but his folks are cool with it. Not like mine. My dad doesn't trust me to drive his car to the drugstore. But I was over at David's house last weekend, and all they said was, 'Okay. Just obey all the traffic rules and be careful.' Of course, part of the deal is that we're supposed to be just going to Perry State Park, which is just barely outside the city limits."

"But you're not going there, I take it."

"Nope," said Walter. "We'll load up the backpacks and the tent and say, 'See ya in four days,' but then … we just keep going west. They have no way of checking on us. It'll be sweet. We'll just hit old Highway 70 and keep driving till we get to the Colorado mountains. I heard it will take about eight hours, but screw it. We can hike all over the mountains, then head back Sunday morning. Then it's just 'Hi, folks! Had a great time by the lake!'"

"You're sneaky. What do your parents think about it?" asked Denise.

"I haven't sprung it on them yet. I'll wait till about two days before we go, then just casually mention it at dinner. What can they say?"

"Your dad won't be happy, I bet."

"He's never happy. But what's he gonna do about it? I'm seventeen."

"I worry about you, Walter," said Denise. "One of these days, you'll get in real trouble."

"Me? One step ahead of everybody. I'm a genius, you know."

Denise laughed, then suddenly worried she was being too loud. They were silent for a few moments."

"Hey, girl," said Walter.

"Hey, boy."

"You wanna talk about what we talked about last time?"

"About you kissing me? I could go for that."

"Kissing and … other stuff, you know." Walter lowered his voice. She liked it when he did that. She imagined him as a sexy singer on stage with a microphone.

"Okay," said Denise, "but we only have a few minutes left."

"I can push it a few more minutes if I want. They won't kill me."

"Okay." Denise lay back on the pillow on the floor. She was lying on the soft carpet of her bedroom in the dark. "You start."

"First, some important information. Do you love me?"

"I believe I do," said Denise.

"Very well," said Walter. She heard him take a deep breath and exhale slowly. "We're on the shore of a lake, and nobody is within miles. Now I put my arms around you and lie you back on the grass."

"*Lay* you back," said Denise.

Walter chuckled. "You know that's what I really like about you," he said. "It's your perfect grammar."

"I just need things to be perfect," said Denise. "Now, keep going." She shut her eyes.

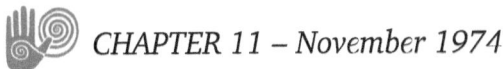

A Flying Leap

WHERE IS SHERRY?

Nicholas Symansky asked himself that question often. Sherry was his touchstone, and he counted on her to guide him here in the sun world.

Sherry couldn't follow him into the spirit world, where he preferred to live, where his true self lived. But every day and every night, he had to spend part of his time in the sun world, where his ego lived, and there Sherry was his indispensable muse and mother.

I cannot live with myself anymore.

But then, who is living with whom? Who is speaking when I say, "I cannot live with myself"? Philosophers had, for thousands of years, pointed out the absurdity of the self. If "I" cannot accept "me," then who is false and who is true? What is the self, and what is the ego? And must these concepts always live with each other, or was it possible they could depart as friends and never meet again?

Where is Sherry?

He rose from the mattress and stood in the dark. A bright light shown under the bottom of the closed door, a bluish light that meant out there the sun world was thriving, filled with people who imagined they were independent souls but were really just ants swarming in devious patterns around the hive, which was the real soul.

Where is Sherry?

He opened the door to the hallway, and the brightness of the daylight coming from the window at the end of the hall made him reflexively cover his face with both hands. But he had to face the light because the sun world could not be ignored for long. It was attached by an umbilical to the spirit world, through which the two worlds fed and sustained each other.

Nicholas walked down the hallway and looked out the window. It faced the courtyard, and in the middle courtyard was a small, cluttered garden where some plants grew in an orderly and planned manner while other plants invited themselves to live among them, and that was a system that reflected the truth of the sun world—the parts that imagined themselves to be the true and orderly ignored or reluctantly accommodated those that knew themselves to be just as true but disorderly. Whose world was the garden?

Nicholas took his body to the restroom. There were times when he could not ignore the sun world, such as a time like this when he needed to piss. Once, he had pissed outdoors in a park where he had been sleeping, and a uniformed servant of the sun world had seized him and put him in handcuffs for following this utterly sensible and ancient reflex. Since then, he had tried to obey the rules of the sun world and only piss where it was allowed.

At the sink, he ran water over his hands and splashed his face, and looked at the mirror. The glass had been recently cleaned, and the face was so clear and yet so alien that he had to look away.

The door opened, and a young woman came in. Her eyes popped wide when she saw him, and she muttered, "Excuse me," and went back out the door again. Nicholas made himself look at the face in the mirror again. The eyes were two slightly different colors. Had this always been true?

Where is Sherry?

The door opened again, and a guy came in. It was Steven, a graduate student. He knew Nicholas and had been kind to him in the past.

"Hey, Nick," he said. "You have to put on some pants, man. You're freaking out some of the ladies. Show some respect, okay?"

Nicholas looked down at the hairy, skinny body that sometimes contained his spirit self. Such a sad, sad thing. There were pink scars in ridges on his right thigh where he'd had a compound fracture that required surgery, a motorcycle accident lifetimes ago. Thick black hair grew over his abdomen and extended downward in a tangled riot before diverting around his dick and balls and onto his upper thighs. But no hair grew on the pink scars.

"Okay," he said. "I'm sorry."

He left the restroom and went back to the small dark room at the other end of the hall to find pants, shoes, and a shirt and earn the approval of the sun world.

Before he went into the room, he turned and spoke to Steven, who was still standing by the restroom door, making sure Nicholas complied with proper behavior.

"Hey, man, where is Sherry?"

"I don't know," said Steven. "Isn't this when she usually goes to her job? She's probably at work."

"Oh, yeah, okay."

The sun in the sun world sometimes felt warm, and sometimes that feeling was mute or missing. Today, it was warm. Nicholas walked on the sidewalk unless someone came the other way, and then he would step aside and watch them pass. Some people looked warily at Nicholas when they passed him as if he were an animal that might pounce and rip flesh. He wasn't sure why some people were afraid of him. Maybe he wasn't invisible, but he felt translucent like a jellyfish or a mist. Maybe they didn't understand that he was a spirit and didn't share their world.

A dozen people waited at a bus stop. Nicholas sometimes took the orange campus bus, which he was allowed to do. He couldn't take the blue bus, which was larger and louder and went longer distances, because on that one, you had to put coins into a slot; two quarters, *ka-chunk ka-chunk,* and then the driver would let you on. But Nicholas seldom had quarters. Back in Los Angeles, he had sometimes stood on the sidewalk or squatted with his back against a building, asking, "Spare change?" to each person who walked by. Most of them didn't see him because he was invisible, but once in a while, someone would drop a coin or two into his leather cap, though they seldom looked at him.

He was not invisible to the men who ran the stores and offices. They would often come outside and tell him to go away. Those men would look him in the eye, so Nicholas knew they could see him. They were usually polite unless he didn't feel like moving and stood his ground. Then, sometimes, they would yell or go away and return later with a servant of the sun world, and then he would have to leave or be taken prisoner. Sometimes, when his sun world body was hungry, he allowed this to happen because, in jail, there was food and a place to sleep.

He did not ask for spare change after he returned to Texas. Some people on the street did, mostly bearded spirits like himself, but Nicholas didn't feel the need for coins, especially since he could ride the orange bus and no one would bother him. He stood apart from the people at the bus stop, male and female, most of them carrying backpacks or briefcases. They could be innocent, but … some of them might be carrying munitions. It was important to keep distance between his body and theirs in case there was an explosion.

The bus roared around the corner and squealed to a stop in front of the people, exhaled in an angry *whoosh*, and the door flew open. A couple of people got off the bus, and then the crowd surged on. It was too crowded for his liking, so he didn't get on. He wanted distance around himself today. The door shut, the bus inhaled, rumbled, and roared, and took off, leaving behind a metallic cloud of soot.

Nicholas resumed walking up the same street. It was many blocks to campus, but he had the time. Today, he wanted to see and listen to the great clock, which was in the center of the large square surrounded by gray buildings. Down, deep under those buildings, hazardous chemicals were stored, probably unsafely.

The clock was really four clocks that sat at the top of a tall, gray tower. The tower was safe, Nicholas was fairly sure. No volatile chemicals or explosives, just books and, papers, and clockworks. Each clock face pointed in one direction of the compass, and a person from either world could see it for blocks around and hear it for miles. Three times every hour, the clock gonged a phrase from a song, every fifteen minutes adding another phrase, until on the hour, the clock would gong out the whole song, followed by a solemn toll for the hour.

After walking the many blocks, Nicholas arrived at the square and at the clock, and waited. The sun was very warm, and his body perspired, so he found a place to sit in the shade on a low wall along the street and waited for the gong. The hands of the clock, which he could see if he craned his neck, were nearing straight up noon when the entire song would play, and then the bells would ring twelve times.

Nicholas had come to understand that the clock was speaking, not in regular language, but in some sort of code. The message wasn't in the bells but in the pauses between. It was a simple code, he thought. He wasn't even sure the message was for him, but he needed to understand it or try. Yesterday, he thought he was beginning to understand what the clock was saying. It was suggesting or urging some action on someone's part.

If he could only go all the way up to the observation deck, feel as well as hear the clock's voice, perhaps then he could fathom its intention. He had tried once, a few weeks back, but the officious lady at the desk next to the elevator had told him the deck was closed to visitors, and the stony glare from a uniformed guard dissuaded him from trying to slip past her and climb the hundreds of steps.

Several years ago, a man who thought he understood the clock had taken the elevator to the top, to the platform right beneath the giant clock faces, and fired a rifle over and over into the scatter of people below to murder and create panic. That was before Nicholas came to the city, but when he heard about it, he knew the man must have misunderstood the clock because it was not saying anything about murder. But … what?

The square was filling with people. Some walked, some stood and chatted, others sat on the patches of grass. Nicholas caught a whiff of fried food, and it made him hungry. Perhaps he would cross the street in a little while and ask for change, something he had never done in this city, but his only other choice was to wait for Sherry to come home, and perhaps she would give him some money. But he couldn't go until the bells spoke and the song played.

Few people knew it, but the song had a name, "Westminster Quarters." It consisted of four notes—G sharp, E, F sharp, and B; then B, F sharp, G sharp, and E—repeated twice through. Sometimes, to focus his thoughts, Nicholas would pluck those notes over and over on the old guitar in the common room at Keystone.

The hour approached, and Nicholas held his breath. Then it came—the loud, loud song, which could be heard in both worlds. He breathed steadily and prepared himself to listen to the toll. The great bell gonged, and he strained to hear the message between strikes. It was a moan or a mutter, and it was hard to make out. It was so low-pitched. Twelve times, the bell tolled, then the low voice trailed away. Perhaps he was too close to …

A woman's high-pitched voice startled him.

"What is he DOING?"

Then a man's voice: "Oh god, no!"

Then other voices, "What?" and "Holy shit!" and "He's not gonna …"

Nicholas looked around. The faces were all peering upward, eyes shielded by cupped hands. Nicholas looked up himself. High above, just below the great clock face, a tiny dark figure stood, arms raised. Then, it leaned forward and dove.

A woman screamed. The dark figure, still in a diving pose, fell for a count of four, then hit the concrete—*whoomp!*— just fifty feet away. He bounced, flipping over, arms and legs flying, then came to rest face down and was still. It was a man in blue jeans and a dark blue shirt.

Suddenly, everybody was talking at once, and nobody was listening. A few feet from Nicholas, a girl covered her face with her hands and said, "Oh, Jesus, oh

Jesus," over and over. Nicholas looked back at the figure on the square, resting with arms extended, peaceful.

He heard a whistle blow, like a coach's training whistle, and a man with a deep voice shouting, "Step back! Step back!" which was not necessary because people were moving away quickly, the square clearing out all at once.

A young man standing close to Nicholas turned to him, eyes wide.

"Did you *see* that?"

Nicholas, not invisible, nodded. Somewhere, a siren wailed, getting closer. He looked up at the clock, now silent.

"What did you say to him?" Nicholas asked the clock.

Changing Circumstances Require Innovation

OGER MONK'S BUICK was no longer parked in front of the house because his company stopped providing cars to its salesmen. David heard his parents talking one night in their bedroom, and he knew something unpleasant was happening. They talked in forced, quiet voices at first, but after a while, they forgot to use their quiet voices.

"How can they cut your commissions?" Mom was saying. "You already practically work for free."

David knew almost nothing about what his father did for a living, except that he sold equipment used by dairies, and commissions were what he got instead of paychecks like everybody else's dad. Whenever the word came out of his mouth, it was always Dad complaining about them. "Seems like they could give better commissions for the really high-dollar equipment," he'd say, or, "I can't believe they call that a livable commission."

One day, Dad drove the company car to work, but that evening, one of his work friends gave him a ride home, and they never saw the Buick again. Mom asked hopefully, "Is your company car in the shop?" and Dad replied, "No more company car. It's not just me. It's all the salesmen. We either use our own cars or go hungry. They haven't been giving cars to the young salesmen in two years. I really don't want to talk about it."

Supper was grim and quiet. Dad watched his favorite TV show, *The Bold Ones*, but with little interest, then went into the bedroom and shut the door. Mom stayed for a while, watching some show she liked, but then followed Dad. There was more quiet conversation.

"I just have to make it work," Dad was saying. "I'm the provider for this family."

"I could just make some calls," Mom said. "It can't hurt."

"I don't want you working, and that's all there is to it," said Dad. "Cathy, you take care of this family and this house. It's your full-time job."

"David is fifteen," Mom said. "All I do all day ..." Then her voice dropped, and David couldn't make out what was said.

Dad had never wanted Mom to work outside the home. David knew that because it got said often. Dad must have had a change of heart, though, because the next Saturday, both his parents left in the big Chrysler station wagon and returned three hours later. Mom was driving the station wagon, and Dad was behind the wheel of a sky-blue Ford Mustang Fastback. It was a used car. David could tell because, despite a shiny coat of wax, there were numerous painted-over dings on the left side back toward the taillight. Still, it was flashier than their other car. Several neighborhood men came over to discuss and admire it, and Dad seemed happy. From then on, Dad drove the Mustang and left the old station wagon for Mom. Two weeks later, Mom got a job downtown at a travel agency.

The whole dairy industry was in a slump, Dad said, and the big milk companies weren't replacing equipment anymore. They were just repairing what they had. One evening, he came home to announce he was changing jobs. His schedule changed as well. Instead of leaving the house at seven-thirty and returning at six-thirty, he was home until well past 9:00 a.m. but then didn't come home until after eight in the evening. Sometimes, he ate supper with David and Mom, but usually, he didn't. Also, he worked every other Saturday. Instead of a suit, he wore a knit shirt with a logo that read "Harold's Sporting Goods." He also had a sweater with the same logo, which he wore on cold days.

Things were still tight financially. Sometimes, David overheard Mom say, "Roger, we don't need all this space." Dad would mutter, "I don't want to discuss it. This is our home." David wondered if they'd have to move.

Early that spring, his best friend Walter did move. The family got a nicer house than the one they had lived in for ten years, two doors down from the Monks on Hackberry Street. A huge moving van pulled up in front of the Edelstein house, and four men spent much of the morning hauling out chairs, tables, mattresses, and boxes. When Dad was leaving for work, he watched the process for a few minutes and then said, "I guess the Edelsteins are finally saying goodbye to the middle class."

David got to see Walter's new house a few weeks later. It was on a wider, fancier street where the houses had large circular driveways instead of garage doors in front. Walter liked the house, especially since his bedroom was in the front corner, far away from his sister Patty's and even farther from his parent's bedroom in the back of the house. The Edelsteins bought a second piano, a beautiful white baby grand, which they put in the immense living room next to a sunken area they called the "conversation pit." The old upright piano, the one that actually got played, was placed in a "family room" on the other side of the garage so Walter wouldn't disturb anyone when he practiced. Patty, who attended junior college in a nearby town and had battalions of friends, was delighted with the new house and took over the living room and its conversation pit for the loose social gatherings she hosted every week. Dr. Edelstein had a larger study for his books and archery trophies and seldom came out. His mother, Wendy, started painting again, an avocation she had enjoyed pre-children and occupied a studio that jutted into the large garden, in which Wendy puttered when she wasn't painting colorful pictures of nineteenth-century French clowns. The physical separation of the Edelsteins was complete.

A new family with two very small children moved into their old house. Battered toys accumulated in the front yard, which was almost never mowed. Wendy's carefully tended flowerbed was filled with gray gravel, but weeds poked through anyway. With the loss of its one modestly wealthy family, David's block slipped a couple of notches.

Still, everybody assumed that the Monks, with their shiny Mustang and perfectly groomed yard, must be doing well.

On Sundays, Roger and Cathy Monk came home from church a few minutes after noon. David had stopped attending, and his parents quit trying to make him. Cathy thought that if they just left him alone, he'd return willingly of his own accord.

David told his parents that he was not feeling the healing power much anymore. He was lying. The truth was he could feel the presence of pain in others more keenly than ever, even without trying, unless he made a conscious effort to block it out. Just the act of walking past or standing close to the infirm made him aware of their suffering. He had a right to ignore them. It was his life.

He was still asked—very occasionally—to perform a healing for someone, usually a church member. This generally happened on Sundays, if it happened at all.

Pain appeared in his mind in various colors and hues. Generalized throbbing or aching pain was red or pink. That was the easiest to find and discharge. Sharp, stabbing pain was yellow and had a lower success rate. As David tried to find the locus of discomfort, to give it a path to leave the person, it would sometimes jump around as if it were avoiding his grasp. Mental pain, that is, anguish, fear, anxiety, grief, was the most difficult of all, but he could sometimes gather and sweep it away with several minutes of effort. That sort of pain appeared green or brown in his mind, depending on the severity. Diseased or dying parts of the body were shades of gray. Cancer was always black.

Whenever Mom and Dad came home from church with doughnuts, David knew he would be asked to help someone. Dad was trying to butter him up. The number and variety of doughnuts correlated with what they planned to ask of him. Once, long ago, David had expressed a preference for caramel-glazed, and so from then on, a choice of four to six caramel-glazed doughnuts meant a Sunday commitment he couldn't get out of.

One Sunday, Dad came in carrying a box of a dozen Dairy Maid doughnuts and plopped it on the kitchen table before hanging up his coat. Mom went into the kitchen to assemble lunch, usually just sandwiches on Sundays. David was in the living room reading a paperback, and his heart sank.

Please let it be easy, he thought. After lunch, he feigned delight at the caramel-glazed treats, but in truth, his taste buds were changing with adolescence, and now he found them too sweet.

"David, I need a big favor today," said Dad.

"Do I have to help somebody?" asked David.

"You never have to," said Dad, but this was untrue. If David balked, then Dad would start speaking to him about his "gift" and the importance of helping the unfortunate, probing at his guilt.

"Where is it? Is it far away?"

"Not too far," said Dad. "It is out of town but not too far. It's just this side of Kansas City."

David sighed. He would have to give up his whole day.

The place they drove was not terribly distant as the crow flies, it was true, but it took over an hour to get there because it was far off the main highways. Long before they reached the city, Dad exited right and headed miles down a two-lane road through a mix of pastureland and manicured estates with enormous, obsessively symmetrical houses. Some of them had small herds of beautiful cows that looked more like props than commerce. This used to be farm country, but now much of it was just show-off acreage for the very wealthy.

"That style of architecture is called Georgian," said Dad, pointing at one enormous white house far off the road. "They're based on classical Greek and Roman buildings. There are a bunch of them out here."

"Who are we going to see?" asked David.

"Their last name is Charabi," said Dad. "It's spelled with a 'ch' but pronounced like 'k.' They seem to be very nice people."

"Do you know them from church?"

Dad chuckled. "No, not the Charabis. In fact, I'm pretty sure they're Jewish."

"Are they rich?"

"I would suspect they are," said Dad. "Look around. I don't know what the father does for a living, if anything. He might just be really rich." He smiled wistfully. "Some people are born into comfortable circumstances."

"Then how do you know them?" asked David.

"I don't, really," said Dad. "Maybe they found out about the experiment last year."

"The one I failed," said David.

"You didn't fail. They just didn't get the results they were looking for. Anyway, the father—his name is Nathan Charabi—called me a couple of weeks ago, and he really, really wants to meet you. He sounds very nice. I think you'll like him."

David's heart sank. Unless the sick person was beyond hope, and might die soon, there was little hope this was going to be a one-off.

They drove onward down the smooth country road. Dad consulted directions he had written on a piece of stationary in his indecipherable handwriting. He kept looking off to the right and driving slower.

"It's supposed to be eleven miles once we turn off Highway 10," he said. "I should have checked the odometer."

They passed through a rural intersection.

"Davie, did you get the name of that road? Was it 'Moss Creek'? It went by too fast."

"I think it was 'Pine'-something."

"I wonder if I missed it," said Dad, checking the rearview mirror.

They came to another intersection, somewhat larger, and slowed way down.

"That's it," said Dad. "Moss Creek." They turned right. "It should be two more miles. He said it's the second gate on the left."

The road was narrow but well-maintained. Dad drove slowly.

They passed one gate with a high stone arch capped with a wrought-iron horse statue and kept going. In another mile, the road began to parallel an eight-foot-high iron fence. Decorative livestock grazed just across the fence and higher up on a hill behind. They came to a second entrance, which was also arched and had two wide iron gates. Roger Monk turned in and stopped.

On the other side of the gates, a paved driveway climbed up and disappeared over a broad hill, concealing whatever buildings were on the other side.

"He said use the phone when we get here," said Dad. He looked up at the gate. "Do you see a phone?"

"It's probably inside that metal box," said David.

"Oh. Of course. What was I thinking?" Dad got out of the car and studied the gray box attached to one of the stone arches, with electrical conduit coming out the top. He fooled with it for a moment, then swung open the metal cover. He squinted, reading the printed sign above a black push-button telephone. David got out of the passenger side and came over to stand beside him.

"It says 'Security dial 9-2-6-6.' Then there's 'Main House dial 4-8-0-4.' I guess that's the one." He started to punch in the numbers.

"Hey!" A shout came from nearby, the voice of a young girl.

David looked through the gate bars and saw a girl on a horse coming down the road on the other side of the gate. She looked to be about twelve or thirteen, with long, curly black hair that bounced as she rode. She wore jeans splattered with mud spots and a T-shirt that said "San Francisco" in florid script. The T-shirt also had mud on it. The girl was cute, but the horse was positively beautiful, with a long, flowing mane and an iridescent reddish coat, perfectly groomed except for its own mud spots. The girl trotted up to the other side of the gate, grinning brightly.

"Are you Mister Monk?" she asked.

"Uh, yeah," said Dad.

"Just punch zero-six-zero-six," she said. This combination wasn't anywhere on the sign, but he tried it. An electrical whir and metallic snap, and the gate slowly screeched open.

"Thanks," said Dad.

"Drive on up to the house," said the girl. "I'll go tell 'em you're coming." She pivoted the horse quickly and cantered away up the drive and over the hill.

Dad drove slowly through the iron gate and up the driveway. David looked back, and the gate was closing automatically behind them.

At the top of the rise, the house came into view, imposing but not enormous. The walls were faced with red brick. Three rows of perfectly arranged windows sat on either side of two white columns, which flanked a surprisingly modest front door situated dead center. There was an expansive open area in front of the house with some tire tracks here and there but no obvious place to park. The driveway curved around to the right, ending in a wide garage with four doors.

The mounted girl was waiting for them and pointed to an area of beaten-down grass between the house and garage. Roger Monk parked the Mustang where she had indicated, and he and his son got out.

"Wait here, I'll go get him," called the girl, and once more, she rode away, disappearing around the side of the house.

David gazed around at the well-groomed acres, with a neatly arranged orchard of short trees on one side, a dozen matching black-and-white mottled cows grazing on the other, and the house, with its perfect Georgian balance, each side a mirror image of the other. He imagined that somewhere behind the house, there must be a creek that glittered with gold nuggets.

"What an amazing place!" said Dad.

This is a trap, thought David. *I am going to fail. I have to.*

Fruit Basket Turnover

K EYSTONE HOUSE—just like all the other co-ops—always had some turn-over at the end of every semester. During a typical mid-winter break, five or six residents moved out and an equal number replaced them in January. As Christmas approached this year, however, things were different. There was unrest at Keystone and throughout the other UCC houses. Rents were going up big time.

At the usual first Monday night house meeting in November, a man and a woman—very serious people in their thirties—arrived from the UCC head office carrying large handmade pie charts and graphs skillfully drawn in primary col-ors with Magic Marker. These were annotated with serious legends: "food costs," "electricity and gas," and "structural maintenance," among other categories. The very serious people took turns explaining the charts to the Keystone residents in I'm-the-smart-one jargon. One of the UCC houses—Berkley—had lost money for years and was closing permanently. Lease costs for the other properties had gone up, and gas and electricity were getting more expensive every month. The organic farm had raised membership dues by 50 percent. It's not us, folks, it's the real world. Rents are rising. Get used to it.

Wally knew he had a pretty good deal at Keystone anyway, so he didn't get upset. Sherry had warned him that the council wasn't going to keep letting him get cheap rent for cooking twice a week. So, when they told him rents were going up to 175 bucks for a double room and 200 for a single, Wally shrugged and rolled with it. He was getting a regular paycheck now.

But most residents, especially the nonstudents, had grown accustomed to years of bargain rates. Some of them got mad, yelled, and talked over each other as the UCC people patiently tried to explain fiscal reality. A major exodus was soon underway. Two large groups moved out in December—those who just couldn't afford it anymore and those who didn't need any extra drama in their lives because going to college was drama enough. In the end, only eight of the twenty-five members stayed. Wally saw no reason to leave. Sherry was still getting a great deal as manager. Nixon had lived at Keystone for years and wasn't going anywhere. Two brainy female grad students who shared an upstairs room and kept to themselves said they would stick around. Poto, the French guy, was happy in his annex room, and so was Jerry Fox Lewis, the champion shirker.

Over Christmas break, after the chaotic move-outs were finished and the dust settled, no one was sleeping at Keystone except Sherry, Nicholas, Nixon, and Wally—people with no families they cared to return to. Chores and cooking were suspended. A guy from the cooperative council came around and told them to shut off the central heat to save money. This didn't bother anybody until a major cold snap blew in after the new year, dropping temperatures into the twenties and bringing a light dusting of snow, almost unheard-of in this southern city. Wally retrieved his old, musty sleeping bag from the trunk of his car, spread it out on his bunk, covered it in blankets, and managed to sleep bearably well in sweatpants, sweatshirts, and woolly socks. Everybody bundled up except Nicholas, who forewent the usual nudity for a long, colorful dashiki over his hairy, unwashed body. Madness inured him to the cold, apparently.

Sherry's job required that she stick around the house and sign up new tenants for the coming semester (assuring them over and over that, yes, there is central heat—It's just not turned on at the moment). She and Nicholas had a big argument that ended when she called him a fuck-up. While this was indisputably true, it hurt his feelings, so he left the house and wasn't seen again for a few days. He returned even dirtier than before from sleeping in alleys.

Wally could see that the Nicholas soap opera was killing Sherry. The eccentric but brilliant boyfriend had devolved into a large, hairy, unpredictable child. Her blinding migraines, which had abated when Nicholas left for California, returned.

Wally came home from his bookstore job one evening to find a handwritten note on his pillow.

Please come see me when you get a chance – Sherry

He knocked on her door and heard Sherry's faint voice say, "Come in."

It was dark in the room except for the floor lamp, over which a scarf had been placed as a makeshift dimmer. Nicholas sat in the room's only chair, against the wall, almost completely hidden. Wally could see his feet, bare despite the chill, sticking out from under his dashiki. His dark pupils reflected at Wally like a jungle cat in dense undergrowth.

That dude is getting creepier, thought Wally.

Sherry lay on the bed under a thick blanket, a kitchen towel draped across her face. She pulled it off, squinting and blinking, and sat up.

"I have a headache," said Sherry, an explanation that wasn't necessary.

"I'm sorry to hear that," said Wally. "Is it a bad one?"

"I feel like somebody is sticking an icepick in my left eye. Yeah, it's bad. It just fucking blows."

"Aww, man. Is there anything I can do for you?"

"Yeah," said Sherry. "Yeah, you can. Do you know how to do double-entry bookkeeping?"

"Uh … no."

"Can I teach you? It's not very hard." Sherry turned and put her feet down on the floor.

"Sure. What's going on?"

"I need help, Wally. I picked the worst possible time to get sick, and I have to finish the end-of-year report for the council. I should have done it already, but I feel like warmed-over shit."

"You need help with the report?"

"I wish you *could* help with the damn report. But what I need you to do is the other stuff, show the house, sign people up, take their money, give them receipts, explain how the house works. I can handle the report if I can just work on it quietly by myself, but dealing with people is just too much right now. It's okay if you can't do it. I can ask Nixon."

"No, it's fine. I can help you," said Wally.

"Oh, man, I love you," said Sherry. "Basically, you'll be assistant manager. I can sign the checks, but I need you to take the deposits to the bank, pay bills, stuff like that. I think I would have a stroke if I had to face bright sunlight." Sherry stood up, wobbling, shielding her eyes from the glare of the doorway. "Meet me out in the common room in a few minutes, and I'll show you everything you need. I have to go to the bathroom."

"Okay," said Wally and turned to leave.

"Stay away from us!" shouted Nicholas. Wally looked back, startled.

"Oh, shut the fuck up, Nicholas," said Sherry. "Wally is helping me."

"He has a black aura," said Nicholas. "He's probably got munitions in his closet."

Over the next four days, Wally showed the house to a couple of dozen people, all students, and signed up ten of them for the spring semester. No introductory dinners or member votes. With this new crop, Keystone was changing. The new residents were mostly straight arrows, upper-division or grad students who just wanted food and a quiet place to study. A hippy pad no longer.

The two Iranian boarders, who had been sharing an apartment on the east side of campus, signed up to be full-time tenants and brought along another friend, also Iranian. Beva, Wally's best friend in the city, also moved in and replaced Mike as Wally's roommate. Just to make things truly weird, Beva now had a more-or-less boyfriend, a quiet guy named Spencer, with incredibly muscular forearms. He was fresh out of the Army and wore a headband over a military haircut that he was gradually growing out. He didn't mind that Beva had a male roommate, but of course casual friend sex was not in the cards for Wally anymore. A handful of residents from the now-shuttered Berkley House relocated the two blocks to Keystone. Two days later, Wally signed up three freshman female students, who occupied the house's only triple room, and Keystone was full again.

The second week of January, they were allowed to relight the house furnace, and the house became habitable. Move-in week was the usual chaotic scrum of people with suitcases and boxes passing each other on cramped stairs, but they got through it. The first big tenant meeting went smoothly, and chores were divvied up without complaint. Between Nicholas and the migraines, Sherry was having a rough time, so Wally ran the meeting. To his own surprise, he discovered he had a knack for organization. Most of the new people assumed he was co-manager and deferred to his judgment, though he had no official title.

Wally resumed his cooking job just once a week on Mondays. This time, he had a decent sous-chef, a short little Israeli girl named Shoshana, a Berkeley House refugee, who had a good attitude and followed instructions. This improved the job immeasurably.

One night, Wally drifted into the depths of REM sleep when a soft knock came at the door. Wally sat up, disoriented. What the hell? The knock came again, and then the door opened, hallway light stabbing into the room. It was Nixon, wearing ragged cut-offs and a long-sleeved T-shirt.

"Hey, Wally," he said. "Sorry to wake you up, man. Sherry needs help."

"Okay." Wally rubbed his eyes, climbed down from the bunk, and pulled on a pair of jeans. Beva was out of town, so he sat on her bed to put on his shoes, yawning, trying to shake off the sleep.

Out in the common room, Sherry was on the house phone. Nixon stood off to the side, smoking a cigarette, against house rules, but then, he was Nixon.

"So, if there's no bail, how do we get him out?" she was asking.

She saw Wally standing there and turned to him, covering the mouthpiece with her hand.

"Nicholas got picked up downtown," she stage-whispered. "Naked, of course." She uncovered the phone. "Okay," she said. "I think I can be there in about twenty minutes. Thank you." She hung up. "Why am I thanking them?" she muttered.

Nixon said, "You need me anymore?"

"No, that's all right. Thanks," said Sherry.

"No problem." Nixon quickly evaporated.

Sherry's face was blotchy, and her hair was a sleep riot. She wore a large man's T-shirt. It read "Willie's 4th of July Picnic, Liberty Hill."

"Wally, I'm so sorry," she said. "I have to get to the police station on Eighth Street. Is your car close by?"

"Yeah, just across the street."

"Can I borrow it? My car is parked way down on San Jac Street."

"I'll drive you," said Wally. "The transmission takes practice."

"Okay, if you really don't mind," said Sherry. "Let me finish getting dressed, and we can go in a few minutes."

Wally returned to his room to retrieve his wristwatch, which he had taken off when he went to bed. *4:45 a.m. Man!* He did a quick back-calculation. *Five hours of sleep! Well, better than none.* He went back into the common room to wait for Sherry.

She came out of her room, dressed, hair hastily brushed, carrying her purse.

"I don't deserve it, Wally," she said. "This is killing me."

"He's not family," said Wally. "I don't know why you put up with him."

"Because … the cop told me if somebody doesn't come get him, they'd arrest him and put him in a holding cell. I can't stand to think about that. He couldn't handle it. He'd go insane."

"He *is* insane," said Wally.

"Yes, but there's different kinds of crazy. I don't think he'd ever hurt anybody, but he really might kill himself. If that happened, I could never forgive myself."

They walked out to Wally's Maverick, which had sat across the street undriven for the past four days. It took two tries and ten seconds of continuous cranking to finally catch. He fed the engine a little gas to keep it going until it was able to idle on its own.

"I should start this thing every day," he said. He put the transmission in gear and eased out the clutch. He hoped the parking spot would still be there when he returned.

As they drove to the downtown police station, Sherry stared at her hands folded in her lap. There was no traffic at all, and the stoplights blinked in unison.

"I started to love him," she said at last. "I told myself I'd never do that again. And especially not somebody who was that broken. Of course, he was different when I first met him. He was so fucking smart. And kind. He didn't say much, but I considered that a plus. Also, he could play the guitar really well—like, professionally trained—and sing. His voice was beautiful. Now he just sits there with that crappy old guitar plucking notes till I want to scream at him."

"It's not your fault," said Wally. "Anyway, we can't give up on people in general just because we have a couple of bad experiences."

"A couple of bad experiences? Wally, I've been married three times. All before I was twenty-one."

"Wow."

"I know, right? But I'm not quite as stupid as I sound. The first marriage happened when I was seventeen, back in Monterey. I wanted to get out of town so bad I just jumped on the first dude who came along. His name was Carlo. He wasn't a bad guy—just totally not ready for commitment. After six months, we both agreed it wasn't working and called it quits. But at least I had gotten my ass out of California."

"All right," said Wally. "So, what about the other two marriages? None of my business, of course."

"It's okay. It's all ancient history. A year after Carlo, I met Robert. I have no excuse for marrying that guy. He never kept a job longer than three months in his life. The crazy part was that getting married was my idea. He was fine with just shacking up. But I was pregnant and made the mistake of telling my sister Ronnie, who told my mother. She said, 'Young lady, you're doing this right,' and she set it up with church, and flowers and this woman minister that she knew. I was fine with all of it. The wedding was the best part of the marriage. It's the last time I was in Monterrey and the last time I saw my whole family together."

"It didn't last, huh?" said Wally.

"Only about four months. For one thing, I lost the baby."

"I'm sorry."

"It was pretty fucking bad, to tell the truth. She was born way too early and only lived a couple of days. Which was probably for the best, but it was awful. After that, I told Robert I still loved him, but I wanted out. He let me, which was really, really nice of him, and I should have given him more credit. He was less selfish than me. Still, it was the last uncontested divorce I ever had. I swore I would never get married again."

"But you did," said Wally.

"Not really. The third one was not my fault."

"What? How does *that* work?"

"The law is weird in Texas," said Sherry. "I lived with this guy in San Antonio—a hellish man whose name I will never say again—and we rented a house together. The owner said he didn't rent to unmarried couples, so we signed the lease as 'Mr. and Mrs. Eric Stedman.' Shit, I just said his name. Anyway, he was not a good guy and screwed around town like he was seventeen. I finally left him. But then he got a lawyer and made me go through the whole fucking divorce process. All because we had signed that stupid rental agreement, and the state called it 'common law marriage.' Turns out it's just as hard to get out of one of those if one party decides to be a jerk."

Sherry looked up and pointed. "That's the police station. Turn right here."

Wally looked around. "Where should I park? Right in front?"

"Visitor parking is behind the building," said Sherry. "I should know. I've been here more than once."

It was surprisingly easy to spring Nicholas. The cops were happy to be rid of him. They had provided him with a thick cotton shirt and faded work pants. He was still in his black basketball shoes, the only garments he had been wearing when he was picked up on Sabine Street.

Wally waited while Sherry signed some papers in triplicate, and Nicholas sat on a polished wooden bench attached to the wall. He looked more perplexed than crazy. A young officer with closely cropped blond hair stood by, and when the paperwork was complete, he followed them to the front door.

He spoke directly to Nicholas. "Pal, keep your clothes on. You can pretty much do whatever you want if you don't hurt anybody, don't steal anything, and don't go walking around naked as a jaybird. Next time—If there's a next time—we can't just let you go. We'd have to charge you with indecency. You will go to jail, my friend."

Nicholas nodded, then opened the big glass door, stepping outside into the cold predawn air. Wally followed.

The officer stopped Sherry as she was leaving.

"Ma'am, that man needs help," he said. "You can get him into the state hospital if he agrees to sign himself in. If he doesn't, then a judge would have to order it. I just hate to see obviously disturbed people land in jail. We have enough of them already."

"Yes, sir. I know," said Sherry. "He's really a decent guy. And really smart, except when he's doing crazy things like this."

"I'm sure he is," said the officer. "But the law cares what a person does, not how his brain works. Now, have a good day. I hope not to see you for a while."

The three of them walked around the building to Wally's Maverick, sitting lonely in the mostly empty parking lot. Wally opened the driver's side door, but Nicholas stopped and stood beside the passenger door, not moving.

"I'll sit in the back," said Sherry. "You can have the front seat."

"I want to walk," said Nicholas.

"No. No way, Nicholas," said Sherry. "You'd just get picked up again, and the cops said they wouldn't let you go twice. Please, just open the door."

Nicholas still didn't budge, so Sherry reached around him and opened the door for him, popped up the release lever to tilt the seat forward, and climbed into the back seat. Still, Nicholas wouldn't move.

"Get in!" said Sherry. "Now, Nicholas!"

He turned around very slowly, doing a complete rotation of his body while gazing into the distance as if he were a periscope scanning the horizon. When he was again facing the open door, he simply said, "Okay," and slipped into the passenger seat.

Wally shut his door and started the engine. Should he try to persuade Nicholas to put on a seat belt? Probably not worth the effort. He drove out onto the main street, where early-morning traffic was just starting to pick up. In the east, over toward the elevated highway, the sky glowed faintly red. The stop lights had resumed their daytime cycles. The lights weren't timed, so Wally had to wait at empty intersections several times.

"If you go left and find River Avenue, it's one way and has a lot fewer lights," said Sherry.

Wally turned on his left blinker for no one, and when the light changed, he turned left down Ninth Street. It was a college-friendly street with several little bars and cafés, plus gift shops, small bookstores, and a few other businesses like a travel agency and a low-shelf law office. After two blocks, they reached River Street. Wally hit the turn signal and looked left, but no one was coming. As he started to turn right, there was a click and a squeak, and Nicholas opened the car door and bolted, running back up the street in the direction they had just come.

"NICHOLAS!" screamed Sherry, but he was gone. In the rearview mirror, Wally saw him dart between two buildings.

"Shit!" said Sherry. "Shit, shit! That asshole! Why is he doing this to me?" She pounded on the back of the front seat with both fists.

There was no point in turning the car around. "You wanna get in the front seat?" asked Wally.

"I guess."

Sherry tilted the front seat forward and climbed out. For a few moments, she looked back up the street, but of course, Nicholas was nowhere to be seen. Then she climbed in and shut the door.

"I'm really sorry," said Wally.

Sherry started crying and covered her face with her hands.

"I can't do this anymore," she sobbed.

Wally drove back to Keystone. His old parking place across the street was still open, so he slipped the Maverick into it. He followed Sherry into the house. She went into the kitchen and found a dish towel, soaked it in water from the faucet, then wrung it out.

"Wally, I need to be in the dark for a while. I have a bad one coming on."

"I'll let people know they should leave you alone," said Wally.

"Thanks," she said and hugged him. He kissed the top of her head.

"It will be all right," he said, though he had no way of knowing if this would ever be true.

Sherry went into her tiny room at the end of the hall, lay down, and covered her eyes with the wet cloth. Wally turned off the floor lamp and left, closing the door behind him.

In the kitchen, a couple of students with early classes were up, getting cereal and toast. Wally took two eggs from the six dozen in the refrigerator and fried them quickly, flipping them with practiced skill, and slid them onto a plate. They looked perfectly presented, like in a diner, but after all of that, he didn't feel very hungry. He ate them anyway, with Tabasco and salt.

Half an hour later, Nicholas came home. Wally was reading the daily campus newspaper on the couch and looked up as Nicholas came in. He was shirtless, probably having dropped it in the street somewhere.

"Hey, Nicholas, Sherry has a bad headache," Wally said. "Why don't you just stay out here and ..."

Nicholas passed him without a glance and headed back to Sherry's room. Wally jumped up and followed.

"Seriously, man, she feels like crap," he said.

Nicholas opened the door to the dark room, went inside, sat down on the one chair and, took off his shoes, then sat with his back straight, head up, eyes closed. Sherry lay still on the bed, on her back, washcloth covering her eyes. There was nothing for Wally to do, so he shut the door and returned to the common area.

A girl named Franny came into the room. She was one of the three students who shared the triple room.

"Wally, is Sherry in?" she asked.

"Yeah, but she's pretty sick. It was a bad night. Can I help you with something?" Wally was the de facto manager again today.

"Uh, yeah. I hope so. I just need to talk about ... It's just ... Okay, here's the deal. We have to move out. Me and Deb and Lynne."

"Move out?" said Wally. "You just got here ..."

"I was just gonna say ... it's that guy. That guy Nicholas who walks around butt naked. We talked about it. He needs to go. I like this house, and I like you guys, but he is just too damn creepy. He walked into our room yesterday, just like that, while I was taking a nap and Lynne was studying. Just came right in with his big hairy stuff just hanging out. He was saying crazy shit about how there might be something 'dangerous' hidden in the room. We yelled at him to get out, and he did, but still ..."

"I get you," said Wally. "He's pretty messed up. But Sherry is trying to figure out how to get him psychiatric help. He's got some weird issues going on ..."

"I'm sorry," said Franny, "but the three of us talked it over, and we have to move out unless he's gone. I mean, like, *today*. Deb talked to her dad, and he's ready to call the cops. I'm not kidding."

"Okay, please don't call the cops," said Wally. "I'll take care of it. I'll talk to Sherry when she wakes up …"

"Today," said Franny.

The Fourteener

AVID FUSSED with the little smoldering pile of leaves and sticks while Walter lay in their little two-man tent. The flap was open, and Walter's boots stuck out comically.

David was so lightheaded he was afraid he might faint as he tried to coax a smoky, struggling campfire to life. He blew gently at the base of the little pile of dry leaves and twigs in a steady stream, took a deep breath, blew again, then took several breaths to recover. His head swam. The embers glowed, and the amount of smoke was promising, but he didn't want to stop until he had yellow flames going and could build a decent fire.

He had already wasted a handful of wooden matches getting to this point. The twigs were damp, and gusts of wind kept snuffing out every struck match. Finally, when the breeze was momentarily calm, a tiny flame caught and held. He drew another deep breath and blew a steady stream of air, careful not to scatter the little smoldering pile. He felt light-headed , but he kept at it. Then, with a little puff, real flames flickered up, catching the thicker twigs above them. As dizzy as he was, he tended the fledgling fire carefully, adding more and more substantial pieces of wood, and within ten minutes, his head was clear, and a real campfire crackled satisfyingly.

"Got it," he said. "I thought I was gonna pass out."

"Tell me when the fire is hot," said Walter from the tent.

"It's pretty good. You should come on out," said David.

Walter dragged himself out of the tent and sat close to the ring of stones that surrounded the fire. They both stared at the flames without talking.

An hour earlier, they had passed up a perfectly good campsite at what had been their goal for the day, Barr Camp, the halfway point on the trail up to Pike's Peak. But when they got there, already wiped out by effort and elevation, there were so many other campers settling in, including a group of six men in their forties, that after a fifteen-minute rest, Walter and David pushed up the trail to leave the crowd behind. The place felt too civilized anyway, with log cabins, carefully delineated camping areas, and a rustic outhouse. They didn't know that the next place they were allowed to camp was a brutal mile and a half away and five hundred feet higher.

Oddly, David was having an easier time with the altitude than Walter, who was bigger and in better shape. Long before they reached the designated area, Walter was sucking hard at the thin air and pausing to rest every fifty feet. David kept finding himself a couple hundred feet ahead of the older boy, and he'd have to stop and wait. The sun was low on the horizon. They had decided that if they didn't find the official campsite in the next fifteen minutes, they'd give up and camp wherever they were, risking a fine if they were caught. But at the top of a series of hellish switchbacks, they finally arrived at the permitted camping area. A metal cutout sign read: *12,098 FT.*

It had been a long, exhausting day. Walter and David had slept the night before on a lumpy foam pad in the Monk family station wagon parked in a lot just outside Manitou Springs, Colorado. Before dawn, they each ate a handful of trail mix, strapped on their backpacks, and took off up the trail. They were determined to make the peak by midafternoon, then hiked partway back down to camp.

The going was pretty rough at first, and as they ascended higher and higher along relentless switchbacks, the snow-crowned mountains looked stunning in the angled morning sun, a beauty that was hard to appreciate when suffering from hypoxia. Two hours into their climb, the trail evened out and was less steep. They'd met some college students who were coming back down and stopped to talk. One of them, a bearded man in his early twenties, cheerfully described the difficult ascent of the peak the day before, including a hellish last quarter mile over packed snow. He wasn't trying to discourage the young climbers, but that was the effect. They hefted up their backpacks, which seemed to grow heavier each time, and trudged up the trail.

Reality had set in for Walter and David by 5:00 p.m.—they wouldn't make it to the top after all. Of course, they could have driven it—for a small fee, and assuming Cathy Monk's old station wagon was up to the ascent. There was a paved highway all the way to the top. But what would be the point of that? They told themselves there'd be other years, other chances, but it was still a deep disappointment. Pike's Peak was another two thousand feet higher, and to reach it would take at least two or three more hours, which they didn't have. Early tomorrow morning, they'd pack up the tent and hike back down, get the car, and drive eight hours back home before their parents flipped out or called the state police to report them missing. They had promised a midafternoon arrival, which they now regretted.

David fired up his little white-gas backpacker stove to boil water in a small aluminum pot and dropped in a double pack of freeze-dried noodles with ersatz chicken broth. It looked repulsive, but they were famished, and David wolfed his portion down. Walter picked at his share of the gelatinous mess, forcing himself to eat it all despite lingering nausea. When he had finished, he looked better and huddled over the fire, rubbing his hands together. Now that the sun was gone, bitterly cold air was sliding down the mountains, chilling them to the bone. It was the last week of May.

David pulled his woolen watch cap over his ears and tucked his hands into his jacket. Gradually, the evening wind died down as night settled.

Walter propped his backpack against a rock to make a backrest and leaned against it, stretching out his legs beside the campfire.

"You want to drink that beer now?" asked David.

They had intended to celebrate the day's achievement with a toast at the top of Pike's Peak, and so they had brought a single can of Schlitz, obtained surreptitiously from the Tisdale home, stowed in David's backpack. It made no sense to drink it now, dizzy from altitude, shivering from cold, short of their goal.

"Sure, I guess," said Walter. "Looks like we're not going to summit tomorrow."

"I thought the summit was the place we were trying to get to," said David.

"Summit is a noun and a verb. You summit a summit."

"Whatever," said David, and opened the beer can. It fizzed dramatically but didn't overflow. He poured approximately half the beer into his tin coffee mug and handed the half-empty can to Walter. They thumped their half beers together.

"To the summit," said David.

"Which we will never summit," added Walter.

They each took a big swig.

Walter shivered and forced down another gulp.

"I have an idea," he said. "What you and I should do is leave the country for a while. Go on a real trip."

The comment was so unexpected David laughed. "Leave ... the country? What are you talking about? It was hard enough just getting out of Kansas for three days."

"I'm serious," said Walter. "Next summer. It's something we definitely should do."

"Where do you want to go?"

"I don't know. I've heard Spain is pretty cool and cheap. But that's not what's important. We could go to Finland or Lichtenstein. I don't care. I just think we need to get out while we still can. Before I go to college."

"You mean just you and me?" asked David. "I don't think the Gestapo will approve."

Walter sat up. "No, man. We can do this. I want you to think about it. Next year, I'll be eighteen, and you'll be almost seventeen. I checked into it. I can get a passport without even telling my parents."

"Yeah, but what about me?"

"You just have to get one of your folks to sign the application. Start working on them now. You've got a whole year. They'd cave. They're not like my parents."

"It's possible, I suppose," said David, using a stick to push an unburned chunk of wood into the flames. "But what's in Europe?"

"Europeans," said Walter. "People who are not like the goobers around here. It doesn't really matter. I just say, if you get away, make it as far as you can."

"How would we get around?" asked David. "Hitchhike?"

"No, man, in Europe, the trains go *everywhere*. And they're cheap. A girl I know went to Spain last summer, just her and her cousin. They visited about six countries, and stayed in these little hotels that are just for young people, that only cost a few bucks a night."

David mused. "It really does sound great. How long would you want to go for? A month?"

"Shit," said Walter. "Two months at least."

"So, are you giving up going to camp?"

"I gave up on that a long time ago. It's really a bunch of pseudo crap to make special people feel more important than everybody else. I've only gone the last two years because of a friend."

"That girl you talked about?"

"Denise. Yeah. She's the only reason I signed up to go this summer. She thinks it's pseudo, too. We'd both rather ditch it and go someplace together if we can."

"Man, you're getting serious about this chick," said David.

"It's not like that," said Walter. "She's just a friend."

"Yeah … right."

"Okay, she's more than a friend, but it's not like she's my girlfriend. She just has to go through some of the same crap I do. We like to talk. She gets it."

"But she's cute, right?"

"Yeah. But mostly, she's cool. And smart without being a jerk about it." Walter picked up a lopsided chunk of wood, charred from a previous campfire, and balanced it on top of the flaming pile. Thick smoke poured out of it for a few seconds, and then it caught. The fire was getting hotter. "Man, you don't know how lucky you are having a regular family and not having to put up with the shit I have to put up with."

"Oh yeah?" said David. "You don't even know what I have to do."

"You mean that healing racket?"

"Yeah, the healing."

"I thought all that bullshit was over."

"It mostly is," said David. "I just don't talk about it anymore. But there's some really weird shit coming down now … just like—hell, I still don't want to talk about it. I'm not supposed to say anything anyway."

Walter adjusted his position to move a little farther from the fire to keep his jeans from scorching. He waited patiently. Of *course,* David wanted to talk about it.

"I don't know why you let people exploit you like that," said Walter. "You're not a little kid. Just say, 'This is pseudo, and I'm not playing your games anymore.'"

"Man, it's not that simple. I can't just walk away."

"Why? Is your old man giving you shit? I'm telling you, you can't let them exploit you, even if you're legally still a kid. If you're gonna do something pseudo, at least make them pay you through the nose for it."

"I *will* get paid."

Walter studied his friend's face in the yellow firelight, searching for clues that he was kidding. "Really?"

"Yes, really," said David. He pulled his fuzzy cap down, trying to cover the back of his neck.

"How much?"

"The guy paid my dad three hundred dollars."

Walter sat straight up. "What? … You're shitting me!"

"Nope."

"Who pays that kind of money?"

"This rich guy. He lives out at a fancy place on the west side of KC. Way out in the country. He's got about a thousand acres, with horses and cows and stuff."

"Wow!" said Walter. "What does he want you to do? Give him a miracle cure?"

"Something like that," said David. "It's not him. It's his wife."

"What's wrong with her? Some kind of psych thing?"

"No, she's really sick. It's this disease that makes her hurt all over. It's called …" David thought for a moment. " … fibro-something … fibromyalgia."

"Never heard of it," said Walter. "Sounds bad."

"It's awful. She hurts every day. Especially her legs. And she can't sleep."

"Don't they believe in doctors? Are they Christian Scientists or something?"

"She goes to all kinds of doctors," said David. "They give her pills that don't really help, and some of them make her worse. The poor lady is really miserable."

"Why does she think you can help her?" asked Walter. "Whatever's wrong, it's gotta be psychological."

"It's not in her head, man. That's stupid. And I can help. The one time I saw her, I *did* help. I just don't want to."

"So don't do it," said Walter. "You know it's pseudo bullshit anyway."

David didn't respond. The wind had died to silence, and the fire snapped. A small burning chunk of a branch rolled off and landed near the edge of the fire ring. Walter herded it back into the burning pile.

"I gotta piss," said David. He stood up, drained the rest of the beer from his cup, stretched, then walked away from the campsite, farther up the trail. Off in the dark, Walter heard the sound of a belt buckle, followed by a stream of piss hitting the carpet of pine needles.

After a couple of minutes, David came back into the firelight and squatted.

"Listen," he said. "It's not pseudo and it's not bullshit. Don't say that anymore. Okay?"

"Come on, man," said Walter. "It's me. Everybody knows about that weird stuff they made you do in church. I thought you stopped that years ago. I didn't know you took faith healing seriously."

"It's not faith healing," said David. "Church has nothing to do with it. It's just something I was born with. I can see pain, and sometimes I can make people better. Usually. Not always. My parents always said it was a gift. But I didn't ask for it, and I don't fucking want it. I hate it. I thought I was done, and now this guy wants me to come to his house and help his wife. Since I did it once, and it worked, I know he'll want me to keep coming back."

"Man ... you never said anything about it," said Walter. "I really didn't know you took it seriously. But you do have a choice. You can just say no way."

"I can't," said David. "This lady's very nice, and she's sick. And besides ... we need the money."

The Unraveling

It WAS LATE SUNDAY AFTERNOON, and Dr. Jim Edelstein was standing in the small office at the entrance to the Perry State Park, twenty-five miles northwest of Lawrence. It wasn't much, just a desk, typewriter, and shortwave radio on one side, a couple of filing cabinets at the back, and a sliding glass window on the side that faced the road.

"Can't I just look at your guest list?" he asked. "Maybe they were here for a couple of days and then left."

The man in the gray-green uniform and the Smoky hat smiled patiently.

"Sir, this is not a hotel," he said. "We don't keep a list of our visitors' names. We write down the make and model of the cars as they come in, plus the license plate numbers, just to keep track of who comes and goes. Do you have the tag number on the car?"

Jim sighed. "I told you, it's a 1962 Chrysler Town & Country. It's not my car, so I don't know the plate number. I can call somebody if I have to, but you should remember the car. There were two teenage boys, unaccompanied. They would have come sometime Friday morning."

The ranger opened his logbook and took his time flipping the pages.

"We've had several station wagons the past couple of days," he said. "It was a busy weekend. Let's see …" He turned back a few pages and traced down the lists with an index finger. "Ford … Ford … Chevy … Dodge … Ford … Wait, here's a Chrysler wagon that came in Friday at 4:45 … Chrysler Newport, brown …"

"It's a *Town & Country*," said Jim. "Not a Newport."

The ranger turned the page and scanned some more, top to bottom. He looked up.

"Nope," he said. "No such vehicle in the past three days."

"I don't understand it," said Jim. "This is definitely where my son said they would be camping: two teenage boys, fifteen and seventeen. No adults. You must have noticed them."

"Well, sir, with as many people as we get on a holiday weekend, I might or might not have noticed. But I don't recall any teenagers coming in by themselves."

"Okay ... okay, I just need to make some calls. Have you got a phone I can use?"

At that moment, a small bell dinged in the office, and Jim heard a vehicle pull up outside the sliding window. "You'll have to excuse me, sir. I have to attend to state business."

The ranger slid the window open.

"Good evening," he said. "You just barely made it. We're closing the gate in ten minutes."

Jim heard a familiar voice.

"Hi, sir. We don't want to camp tonight. I was just hoping to get some literature."

"Literature?"

"Yes sir, like a map and a description of the ... activities ... things like that. We'll probably come here in the future and just want to find out about the park. You know. For the future."

"I have a park map and a couple of brochures I can give you," said the ranger. "But ... you know what? I think there's somebody here who wants to talk to you." He turned back to Jim. "We may have found your boys," he said, gesturing with his thumb.

After Walter had just driven 375 miles without anybody dying, it seemed like his dad would let him continue the last twenty-five miles home, but Jim Edelstein wasn't about to let him the satisfaction. He phoned the Monks, and they drove out in Roger Monk's Mustang, both parents in the car so that David's mother could drive her station wagon home. David wondered if she would even have noticed the extra 800 miles on the odometer. She wasn't a detail person.

Dr. Edelstein waited with Walter in the front seat of their car outside the gates of the state park, which was now closed. David sat in the passenger seat of his mom's car. He had no idea what kind of tongue-lashing Walter was getting, but he was relieved to miss it. He got the impression that Walter's dad blamed David and David's parents, more than he blamed his own son. It was true that the malfeasance had occurred on the Monk's watch and in their station wagon. But the Colorado trip had been Walter's idea to begin with. David watched the sunset and felt his overworked legs throb.

It was just getting dark when David's parents pulled up. Jim Edelstein didn't even bother to get out of his own car. He just rolled down the window and said, "He's all yours now," and sped away, taking Walter. David wondered if he'd ever see his best friend again.

David's mom got into the driver's seat. She looked so sad it broke his heart, and he felt bad about the scheme they had pulled.

"Oh, Davie," she sighed.

"Mom, I'm sorry we didn't go where we said," said David, "but we did go camping. Once we got out of town, we just changed our minds. I know I should have called you."

"Where *did* you go?" she asked.

"Um ... Pikes Peak," he said, suddenly regretting that they hadn't concocted a backup lie in case the first one fell apart. It had been Walter's inspiration to drive by Perry State Park on the way home and pick up some free maps and literature they could wave around as proof.

"You went to ... *Colorado?*"

"Yeah. It was a lot farther than we thought, but really, really great. We hiked almost all the way up the ..."

"Oh, lord, Davie!" said his mom. "You actually drove across the state without telling anybody. I just can't believe it. In my car."

"I'm really sorry."

"I've always wanted to trust you, Davie. We've been honest with each other. I just don't know what to think. Anyway, your dad wants you to ride with him. I'll see you when we get home. Supper's going to be late."

So, David rode home with Dad. Strangely, his father wasn't all that upset about the secret interstate road trip. He almost seemed ... impressed.

"Pikes Peak," he said. "Wow. I've always intended to get out there someday. Is it nice at the top?"

"We didn't make the top," said David. "What we did see was great. If we'd had one more day ... It's really a tough climb. But we had to get back, so we hiked down this morning. Boy, was it cold last night!"

"I'll bet."

There was still a trace of red in the sky visible through the rear window. They rode in silence. The Mustang's passenger door rattled slightly every few seconds. David could tell that Dad had something on his mind. He finally got around to it when they were almost home, turning onto Hackberry Street.

"I talked to Mr. Charabi today," Dad said. "He told me that Judith was asking about you, if you could come back out and see her."

"I have school tomorrow," said David.

"Yes, of course. But if I picked you up right after school, we could go straight out there. Would that be okay with you?"

"Don't you have work?"

"Actually, I'm off tomorrow. I filled in for one of the floor men yesterday. Mondays are light days anyway."

They pulled into the driveway behind the station wagon. David noticed that streaks of red dirt had accumulated on the rear window. He should hose it off, at least. Maybe wash the whole car.

Dad shut off the mustang's engine but didn't get out. This was going to be a driveway conversation. Man to man, Mom not included.

"There's something I need to talk about, Davie," he said. "It's about Mrs. Charabi. You know, she's very sick."

"I know," said David. "But she said she felt better after I saw her."

"She did. And it was really nice of you to help her. But what she has is pretty serious. They say it's incurable and that she'll have a lot of pain the rest of her life."

"I know," said David. "I don't think I can cure her."

Dad nodded, looking straight ahead. He was silent for a moment. Something was coming.

"Davie, do you know what a retainer is?"

"Uh ... I think so. Walter's sister wears a retainer." The question confused him.

Dad chuckled. "Yeah. But that's not the kind I mean. A retainer is money somebody pays regularly to somebody else to provide a service."

"So ... it's like a paycheck?"

"Well ... yeah ... sort of. The difference is the money gets paid whether work gets done or not. Like some rich people pay a lawyer every month just in case they need him for something. To *retain* him. Keep him handy."

"Okay," said David. "Are you going to get a lawyer?"

"No," Dad said. He laughed and shook his head. "I'm saying that Mr. Charabi asked if he could pay you … us … a retainer. That is, some regular money every week so that you'd be available to come out to his house sometimes … Not all the time, just when Mrs. Charabi needs you."

"But what about school?"

"They wouldn't want you to miss school, of course," said Dad. "Anyway, school's almost out."

David's summer, which he had looked forward to mostly from habit, appeared bleaker.

"I … don't think I want to do that," he said. "Anyway, I'm supposed to start at the Blue Cow on June 8." That was the "Home of Twenty Flavors" ice cream shop he had worked at for a couple of months last summer. It was one of the few places he could work legally before he turned sixteen.

Dad knew his weak spot and pounced.

"What will they be paying you at the Blue Cow?" Dad knew as well as David the ice cream shop didn't pay shit.

"Two-twenty-five an hour. I'm pretty sure. I think that's what Mr. Dove said. He'll give me a raise because I worked there last year, and they don't have to train me."

"Well, that's good," said Dad. "But let's do some calculation. How many hours will you be working? Twenty a week?"

"Twenty or thirty."

"Okay, let's say it's thirty hours. That comes out to …" His eyes rolled upward as he multiplied in his head "… sixty-seven dollars and fifty cents a week. That's before all the taxes and deductions get taken out. Let's just call it sixty dollars. Assuming you get all your hours."

"Okay," said David.

Dad leaned close as if he were confiding.

"Davie, Mr. Charabi would be paying you … our family … three hundred dollars a week. Every week. And you wouldn't even have to go every day. Just sometimes when Judith feels extra bad."

David's shoulders sagged. It was happening. The thing he'd feared since he was a kid was coming true. Healing for a living. As a job. How could he get out of it?

"I don't know, Dad," he said. "It's just …"

Dad waited. He didn't have to argue. David didn't have a good reply, and Dad knew it.

"I do see one difficulty, which is transportation," said Dad. "I can't take you out to the Charabi place if I'm working, and neither can your mom. It's too far for a cab. So we've been talking it over. What if we were to get you a car?"

David couldn't believe what he was hearing.

"I'm just fifteen," he said. "All I have is a learner's permit." David had taken driver's ed at the high school on Saturdays last fall, but his birthday wasn't until the end of September.

"Well, I thought of that," said Dad. "I called the Department of Motor Vehicles, and your case would fit the definition of 'hardship.' They'd give you a license that would allow you to drive yourself to work. In this case, to the Charabi's farm."

David checked Dad's face, lit through the windshield by the yellow porch light, for signs that he might be pulling David's leg.

"You'd get me a car?"

"Yeah. Nothing fancy, of course. Just something nice and reliable from a used car dealer. We can start looking this weekend." Dad was talking as if the issue were settled. David's head swam. "What you'd have to understand, though, is that the car would be for work and nothing else. Work and school, when that starts back up. But the hardship license doesn't allow you to ride around with your friends. In fact, it would have to be just you alone or you and an adult. No going places with Randy or Walter or Rory. Just out to the Charabi's place and back."

"Wow ..."

"Anyway, let's go inside. Your mother is burning supper." Dad opened the car door and put one foot out. "Oh ... and don't tell anybody outside the family about what you're doing, okay? It's important. It's a matter of privacy ... for Mrs. Charabi especially." He climbed out and shut the door. "Also ... let me tell Mom."

David stepped out of the Mustang and pushed the door shut extra hard because the latch had been sticking lately. Thirty minutes earlier, he had assumed he'd be grounded for the summer.

But no. They were going to *buy him a car.*

It Takes Commitment

A<small>T THE FIRST</small> M<small>ONDAY MEETING</small> in February, the members of Keystone House elected Wally Stein as the new house manager. Sherry had been worn flat by the preceding month and could no longer handle the responsibility. Wally offered to take the job himself, and because no one else wanted it, he was chosen. By acclamation.

The UCC board had to approve, but that was mostly a formality. After one interview with the organization's director and secretary—the only two salaried positions on the council—Wally was in. His rent was lowered by fifty bucks, and he no longer had to cook or do chores.

Sherry stayed on as assistant manager, a new position the council agreed to create because she had experience with accounting and bookkeeping. Wally had none, but he learned. He paid the bills, balanced the house checkbook, filed monthly reports with the council, explained to a cook why he should substitute ten pounds of locally sourced cottage cheese for the Galbani Premium Ricotta he had requested, and listened to complaints that were more appropriate for the Monday night meetings. ("Some guy is leaving little black hairs all over the sink when he shaves!")

Wally's first management crisis involved Sherry and, of course, Nicholas. The man needed in-patient psychiatric care, and that had to come from the state since he was a penniless vagabond with no immediate family. The institutionalization of Nicholas Symansky became Sherry's full-time job, and Wally helped when he could. Of the three girls who had threatened to move out, only one did. Sherry got through to Nicholas, somehow, that his nude house patrols were out of bounds.

On a Friday morning, two weeks after his latest encounter with the cops, Sherry drove Nicholas to the state hospital, a drab two-story structure from the 1930s surrounded by a twelve-foot-high wrought-iron fence. Wally went along to keep an eye on Nicholas and distract him if necessary.

The admissions process went smoothly at first. A doctor interviewed both Sherry and Nicholas, who, though he spoke only in terse little sentences, accurately explained his symptoms and history. He told them he'd served in the air force stationed in Korea but had received a medical discharge after showing signs of schizophrenia. This was all news to Sherry.

It was all going as planned. The doctor explained that Nicholas would be committing himself for eight weeks, after which he'd be reevaluated. Then, the papers were placed on the desk in front of him, along with a pen. Sherry bit her lip, and Wally held his breath. Nicholas stared at the papers, then looked over at Sherry, then back to the papers. He didn't touch the pen.

"We need your signature at the bottom of the first page," said the doctor. "That will admit you to the hospital. Then, on page three. That's your consent to let us treat you."

Nicholas didn't move.

"Please, Nicholas," said Sherry.

"It's okay," said the doctor. "He can take his time. Nicholas, you can read the whole thing if you want. But we can't admit you unless you agree and sign."

He stared at the doctor, looked over at Sherry one more time, then closed his eyes and folded his arms. That was it. He was shutting down.

They gave him ten minutes, but he never moved, never responded. At first, Sherry gave him space, and then she begged. "Oh, Nicholas," she said. "Do this for yourself. You deserve to get better. Do it for me."

Nope. Not happening. Closed for business.

The doctor explained that their only other option was to get a judge to sign the order. He gave her a list of the names of cooperative judges and their courthouse phone numbers.

"Here, I'll leave you alone," said the doctor. "You can use this phone." The doctor left. He had many other responsibilities, and persuading Nicholas was not high on his list.

While Wally sat with Nicholas to make sure he didn't wander away or disrobe, Sherry went down the list and called judge after judge until, on the fifth try, she found one in his office who was willing to consider committing Nicholas. He would see them at 11:00 a.m. at the courthouse.

They drove back across town, Wally driving Sherry's car and Sherry sitting in the back seat with Nicholas to make sure he didn't try to bolt at the first stoplight.

"I think you don't care about me," Sherry said. "If you cared, you'd try and help yourself."

Nicholas looked at her with sad, sad eyes but wouldn't speak.

The judge made them wait in the hall twenty minutes, then sent a clerk out to say he would speak to Sherry first, alone. She rose from the bench and went into the judge's office. Nicholas stood up and tried to follow her, but she turned and said, in a commanding voice, "You have to wait, Nicholas." He waited, standing outside the door. Wally stood behind him.

Five minutes later, the clerk came out and got them, and Nicholas walked into the office. The judge was a disheveled middle-aged man with a wrinkled white shirt and loose tie, a shiny bald swath on his head with Bozo puffs on the sides. He probably looked more dignified in a robe.

"Mr. Symansky, do you understand I'm agreeing to mandatory commitment for you in a state psychiatric facility?"

No response. Sad eyes.

He turned to Sherry.

"If you were his wife or an immediate relative, it would be more straightforward," said the judge. "You may understand why I'm hesitant to commit based on the word of a friend. But, the doctor at Travis State Hospital recommends in-patient care, and I take that into strong consideration. If he would just sign his own name, it would make it simple."

Nicholas turned and walked around the expansive mahogany desk. The judge rotated his chair quickly to face him, ready to spring if necessary, but Nicholas stopped a couple of feet short of the judge, raised his arms, palms forward, and shut his eyes. He stood silent as if conjuring some spell in his head.

"Okay, you've got your commitment," said the judge. He signed.

Back across town they went. Sherry had packed a small bag of spare clothes for Nicholas, though he didn't own much, just some faded T-shirts from forgotten concerts and two pairs of jeans. She had run them through the washer twice and sun-dried them on the fence so they smelled fresh. She didn't know if the hospital intended to dress him in some sort of nuthouse garb.

They were kept for fifteen minutes in the waiting room while the papers were filed, and then a nurse came and got them, along with two men in white scrubs. One was black and large, the other Hispanic and thin but taller. Sherry,

Wally, and Nicholas all went into the admissions area, which was as far as they were allowed.

"See you soon, Nicholas," said Sherry with forced cheer. "I'll come visit in a few days." She gave a little wave.

"Take care, man," said Wally.

They both turned to leave.

Of course, Nicholas tried to follow them, and of course, there was a huge violent scene as he yelled and fought the orderlies who wrestled him through the double doors and into the mysterious interior of the mental hospital.

Wally and Sherry made it out to the car without speaking.

"Do you want me to drive?" asked Wally.

Sherry burst into tears. Wally wrapped his arms around her and held her as she sobbed into his chest, standing beside the car in the parking lot.

"I fucking give up!" she cried. "Now I just hate him! Why does he try so hard to make me hate him?"

It was midafternoon when Wally and Sherry returned to Keystone. Wally was due at the University Bookstore at 5:00, so he decided to grab a nap. The house was quiet. Beva was in class. A sense of relief had settled in. Wally shut the door to his room, took off his shoes, and climbed the ladder into his bunk. The room was chilly, so he got under the top blanket.

There was a soft knock, and Sherry came in holding a small stack of paperback books.

"I think these are yours," she said. "I found them under the chair."

There were six books in all: four old sci-fi titles, the Patchen poetry collection, and a mystery by Rex Stout.

"Thanks, just stack them on the shelf, and I'll sort them. But the Stout's not mine," said Wally. "It probably belongs to Mike upstairs."

"Mike Barber?"

"No, the other Mike."

"We have three Mikes."

"The one who lives next to Penny."

"Oh. Mike Young. I'll get it to him."

"Thanks," said Wally, and lay his head back on his pillow. It occurred to him he should say something, so he sat up again.

"Hey, Sherry. I'm sorry for all the bullshit you've been having to put up with. You did a good thing today. I don't think I could have done that."

"Well, it's going to be weird not having him. But maybe I can actually pass some of my classes and not get fired from my job." She placed the stack of paperbacks on their side. "Wally, who is DM?"

"That's a guy I used to know," said Wally. "He wrote his initials on all his books."

"Okay, if I find any more DMs, I'll know it's you." She picked up the Rex Stout novel and turned to leave.

"Oh, Sherry," said Wally. "Remember, I'm here for you. Any time. I'll help you with anything you need, really."

"Thanks, Wally. You're sweet."

She shut the door softly.

Wally lay back down and closed his eyes. It was not the first time he'd made that offer to someone.

Benefits of Therapy

THERE WAS STILL A VACANCY to be filled at Keystone House. This spring semester, they had twenty-four paying residents and one boarder, a Chinese graduate student named He, pronounced "huh." In previous years, they had put up with a short tally, sometimes having as few as eighteen people in a semester. But the economic margins had shrunk, and costs had been restless in an upward direction, especially for natural gas. The pilot lights alone on the ancient Vulcan-Hart eight-burner stove pumped out more gas than some space heaters twenty-four hours a day. And electricity, while stable, was still eating them alive. Wally began taping index cards around the house, reminding people to turn off lights—at least during the day, for God's sake. Still, he often found himself on light switch duty when the students left for class every morning.

If there were no unexpected expenses, and the house was totally full, they would just break even. Wally, who was now in charge of making the ledger balance, had to rent out the last spot in the only triple room to make up for the girl spooked away by Nicholas if there was any hope of avoiding a deficit this month. He asked the other two roommates if they had any friends or sisters who might be interested, but they were happy with the extra space and weren't eager to help. He did manage to find one more boarder, a friend of He named Lao, pronounced "low." That helped the accounting a little. The Chinese ate only at regular evening dinners and did not, like some previous boarders, consider the Keystone pantry a free twenty-four-hour larder to be raided at will.

He posted a notice on the bulletin board at UCC headquarters and another at the Student Union. He considered running an ad in the campus newspaper, but it wouldn't stand out among the dozens of perpetual ads run by rip-off rental agencies and house hustlers.

One Tuesday afternoon, Wally came home from work at 5:30 after a tough day shift unloading boxes of Janson's *History of Art: Second Edition*, a hefty art-school bible that had strained the backs of bookstore clerks for a generation. He was exhausted and shaky, just like some of his hardest days at the liquor warehouse.

As he walked into the common room, he was greeted by a familiar sour smell. Greens were being overcooked again. He should have intervened and instructed, but he wasn't up to it this evening. He did stick his head into the kitchen for a moment.

"Shoshana!" he called. "Your collards are done!"

"Thanks, Daddy!" she replied but made no move toward the pot on the stove.

When he returned to the common room, Wally noticed a girl he didn't know standing by one of the large bookshelves that bracketed the gargantuan fireplace (now blocked and nonfunctional). She was checking out the old books, inherited from decades of previous house incarnations, and politely ignoring Jerry Fox Lewis, who was attempting, as always, to flirt.

"Do you like Badfinger?" Jerry asked.

"Can't say I've heard of him," said the girl, not looking at Jerry.

"It's a group," said Jerry. "Their first album is pretty cool. The second one kinda sucked. They're on the Apple label, you know."

"Hmmm," said the girl, flipping through an old book.

"Yeah. Besides the Beatles and James Taylor, they were almost the only band to record with Apple." Jerry spotted Wally and beckoned him over. "This is the guy you need to talk to," he said. "Wally. He's king of the house."

She turned to face Wally. Her appearance was striking, with a long face and straight, coal-black hair that poured down over her shoulders. She had olive skin and deep brown eyes.

"Hi," said Wally. "Are you interested in living here?"

"Yeah, I think so," she said. "I need a place I can move into in a couple of days."

"Well, we do have one open spot," said Wally.

She smiled, revealing large white teeth and a slight overbite. She held a book she had taken off the shelf and clutched it to her chest.

"My name's Callie," she said. "So you're Wally the king?"

"House manager," he said and swallowed.

"I'm glad you *do* have a room," she said. "That's great. Over at Prince Street house, they told me a girl moved out because some crazy guy scared her."

"Yeah, he made a lot of people uncomfortable," said Wally. "He wasn't dangerous. Anyway, he's gone now."

"Complete schizoid," said Jerry. "Mental case. Walked around the house butt naked." He leaned against the arm of the couch and grinned. Jerry had no intention of going away.

Shoshana called from the kitchen. "Wally! Could you help me move the Hobart?"

"Jerry, could you go help the cooks?" said Wally. "I need to show the house."

Jerry complied reluctantly. Hopefully, he wouldn't hurt himself moving the fifty-pound mixer. Physical strength was not one of Jerry's assets.

"Okay, now," said Wally. "Do you want the three-minute tour? The bed that's available is in a triple room, but it's also the biggest bedroom in the house. You'll have your own desk."

"All right, give me the tour," said Callie. She smiled broadly again, and quarter-moon dimples formed at each corner of her mouth. She turned to put the book back on the shelf, then hesitated. "Have you seen this?" she asked. She showed the title to Wally.

A Toastmaster's Treasury of Humor: Jokes and Stories for Public Speakers

He had not seen the book, of course. Nobody at Keystone House ever looked at any of the old books in the common area.

"I don't know that one," said Wally.

"It's really racist," said Callie. She opened the book to the page she'd been reading and handed it to Wally.

The chapter title: "Negroes." Wally winced and started reading the first paragraph. *Two old colored men are fishing in the rain by the river. One says to the other, "Lawdy, you spoze it ever gwine stop rainin'?"* …

"Yikes," said Wally. "I never saw this." He flipped back to the title page. "1938. No wonder."

"There's also a chapter called 'Polish,'" said Callie. "It's a bunch of 'Polack' jokes. And another one called 'Irish.' At least there's no Navajo jokes. *Then* I'd be pissed off. Just thought you might want to know what kind of books you have out here."

"Thanks," said Wally. "Maybe we shouldn't keep this one." Not sure what else to do, he slipped the book back into its slot on the shelf. "You want to see the house? It's got nice people. No racists."

"Lead on," she said, and the wide smile returned. Extraordinarily white and even teeth.

DINNER WAS CHICKEN CUTLETS and overcooked, mushy collards.

"Guys, if you could listen up a second," said Wally, the way he always addressed the whole house. "We have a guest tonight. She is interested in joining the co-op."

The residents looked up, mildly curious.

"Her name is Callie … uh …"

"Pender," said Callie. "My given name is 'Carol,' but I go by Callie."

"Okay," said Wally. "We're going to let her tell us why she wants to live here, and you guys can ask her any questions you have. Then we'll vote."

"Why?" asked one of the women.

"Because that's how we do it," said Wally. "If somebody wants to move in, we let them talk, and then we vote."

"That's not how you did it with me," said one of the guys. "I just gave you a check and moved in."

"But this is how we're *supposed* to do it. That was different."

"How?"

"Come on, guys, just let the girl introduce herself," said Wally. "It'll just take two minutes."

"She's cool," said Jerry. "She's got my vote."

Callie didn't stand up, but she did talk loud enough to be heard. "Should I tell a joke from the *Toastmaster's Treasury*?"

The residents looked at each other. *What?*

"Just kidding," said Callie. "Hi, everybody. Like Wally said, my name is Callie Pender. I've been living over at the River Grove apartments on South Blanco, but I can't stand the forty-five-minute bus rides anymore, and I'd rather be closer to work and live with people who get along and don't play mind games."

"Oh, there's some mind games going on around here," said Robert, one of the nonstudents. "Nothing heavy. Just the usual girls-and-boys bullshit."

"We have a very normal house with great people," said Wally. "Callie, where are you from?"

"I'm originally from Chinle, Arizona," she said, "which you've probably never heard of. It's on the Navajo Indian Reservation. I also lived in Gallop, New Mexico, for a long time. I came to Texas last year to work and save some money so I can go to school. Unfortunately, I think I'm losing my deposit at the River Grove, so that's gonna set me back a little."

"What do you do?" asked one of the men.

"I'm a massage therapist. A masseuse, if you insist."

That got everyone's attention.

"Really?" said one of the women. "That's … interesting."

"A perfectly legitimate occupation," said Nixon, who seldom said anything.

Callie laughed. "I know it sounds sketchy, but it's not. It's real massage therapy. I studied at Peterson Massage School in Gallop. I'm certified, and it pays pretty well."

"Okay," said Wally. "Anybody have any more questions for Callie so we can vote."

"Yeah," said Shoshana. "Why are you breaking your lease?"

"I had a bad falling-out with my roommate," said Callie. "She's a perfectly nice person if you don't have to live with her. It was a mistake to sign a one-year lease. It's been a rough ride since last September. Last week was the mortal blow. She smashed my hair dryer and called me a whore."

"Holy shit …"

"Oh, man …"

"Wow …"

"That bites …"

Jerry spoke up. "Okay, I say she can move in." He raised his hand. "Who wants to let Callie be part of our house?"

"Wait …" said Wally. "She really needs to leave the room …" Wally looked around and, as far as he could tell, everybody's hand was up.

"Okay," he said.

Bad Judgment by the Boundary Waters

THEY WERE CAUGHT BY BRANDY, who was new on the staff at Camp Pursell. She was barely older than they were. Other counselors might have been cooler about it, pretended not to see, or maybe just chewed them out and sent them back to their cabins. But Brandy was an FNG. That was the unflattering term veteran counselors used for first-years. She felt extra pressure to enforce the Camper Code of Conduct.

She didn't even catch them "in the act," as they say. As Walter and Denise lay together in amazement and exhaustion on the air mattress in the boathouse, they heard footsteps on the gravel, and they both managed to put some of their clothes back on before the lights blazed. Anyone with half a brain could see what they'd been up to. For one thing, a bra was draped over one of the inverted canoes beside the makeshift love nest.

The location should have been perfect. As an unpaid counselor-in-training and canoe instructor, Walter had a key to the boathouse. Neither of them knew that there had been a late-night canoe theft the previous season, so a counselor always checked the boathouse every night after lights out. Brandy had seen the padlock open and the chain hanging loose, so she investigated.

Walter and Denise protested and improvised excuses, but the FNG turned them in.

Expulsion from camp was a given, but first, there was humiliation. For Denise, that was the worst part. Her first bold, genuine sexual encounter ended with the two of them sitting uncomfortably on rustic chairs in the office of the camp director, Ms. Cordrie, with a pair of adults grilling them like they were criminals.

Walter took it better. Only his dilated pupils betrayed his emotions. Denise fidgeted and dabbed her eyes with a bandanna. Perhaps because Walter seemed unfazed, Ms. Cordrie and Mr. Gatzenberg, the assistant director, aimed most of the interrogation at Denise.

Ms. Cordrie took the lead. "What hurts me the most is that you are both campers who have been with us for many summers. You're the kids we don't worry about. You're both sixteen. We count on you to set examples for the younger kids."

"I'm seventeen," said Walter.

Ms. Cordrie leaned back in her heavy gray office chair, which squawked. "Yes, seventeen. I realize that young people your age face a lot of pressure ... to be grown up, to fit in and figure out who you are. And ... if I may be blunt for a moment ... your bodies are changing. You have feelings and urges that are new and exciting. It's like an itch you think you just have to scratch."

Denise had an itch, all right. A mosquito bite on her neck, just behind her right ear, in the twilight zone between itch and sting, and she'd been waiting for the right moment to claw it with a fingernail.

Mr. Gatzenberg cut in. "What Ms. Cordrie is trying to say is that growing up presents all kinds of challenges." (Ms. Cordrie gave him a sharp glance. She knew perfectly well what she was trying to say.) He continued: "But your minds ... your God-given minds ... are growing too, and you're the smartest kids in this country. You have to use common sense no matter what your hormones tell you."

Ms. Cordrie took the floor back. "Denise, let me ask you first. Has this been going on for some time, or was this some sort of ... spontaneous decision ... to go to the boathouse with Walter after lights out?"

In truth, it was neither. She and Walter had been close for three summers and had many heart-racing moments and shared each other's breath on secret occasions in hidden places. However, it was their first true physical coupling. There was no spontaneity. It had been a deliberate, careful plan—mostly on Walter's part, but Denise had been a full, eager participant. It *was* their first time. And it had been taken away, dragged into the open, and ruined in the most awful way possible. She reached up and scratched her neck furiously.

"We never went to the boathouse before," she said. "It wasn't what you think."

It was what you think. It's just not your damn business.

"Denise, we're not stupid," said Mr. Gatzenberg. "What Ms. Cordrie is trying to say is that you were not only being foolish, you were being selfish. If there were to be ... consequences ... outside of anybody's control ... it could be devastating for us."

"What *consequences?*" said Denise. "We were just ..."

"He means that if you were to get *pregnant*," said Ms. Cordrie. "That's one of the few ... outcomes ... that could get this camp closed down."

Scratch, scratch, scratch, scratch.

Denise looked at Walter. He stared straight ahead at the nature calendar hanging on the wall between the two directors. She envied his ability to block it all out, but why, why the *hell* was he letting them do this to her?

Walter, you said everything would work out. Defend me!

She looked back at the two judges, who clearly expected her to answer for her own actions.

"It wasn't like that," Denise said. "We were *careful!*" This was all becoming so awful, awful.

Ms. Cordrie pressed on. "Are you saying you did not actually ... have ... intimacy?"

"No!" said Denise. "I mean ... yes, but he used a ... thing ... protection ..." She couldn't bring herself to say the word *rubber.*

"A Trojan," said Walter.

That was a better word, at least. For a moment, it took the wind out of their sails. Denise looked down at her hands. There was a smear of blood on her index finger.

They were both expelled and sent home. Denise was glad of that, though it made her parents share in her disgrace, and it also meant they had to forfeit the tuition—Denise was on a campership, but the cost was still substantial. They also had to buy her a flight home at short notice. She did not have to endure the ridicule or, worse, the sympathy of her fellow genius campers. She would never attend Camp Pursell again and wouldn't miss it.

There was no big scene with her parents, just a quiet conversation about adulthood and responsibility, and disappointment. She was sixteen, so she wasn't grounded. She had no car to take away. As soon as she got back home to Nashua, she spent a couple of days looking for a job and found one as a typist for a two-person law office. No one in her hometown heard the story of Walter and the boathouse. Her mother insisted she see the family doctor, who gave her a quick checkup and then offered her a prescription for birth control pills. She declined.

What Denise had missed was the opportunity to grow up on her own terms. The actual sex with Walter had been brief and awkward for both of them and a little painful for her, but there should have been more. Two or three more encounters without fear of discovery, to allow them to grow accustomed to each other and to the mechanics of physical love, would have set them both on a healthier path to sexuality in the future, with one another and with others in later years.

She never got a chance to speak with Walter again before they were both whooshed away back to their hometowns and chagrined families. She needed to talk about what had happened. Surely, he could explain things to her, make her see it was all a big, funny story they could tell someday. Had she had fallen out of love with him? After the image she had built of Walter, of the two of them together, it wasn't fair or even possible to discard it all without letting him explain himself.

She wondered whether he would call her on Saturday night. Probably not.

Nevertheless, when Saturday night came, she unplugged the downstairs phone, put the upstairs phone in her bedroom, and quietly shut the door. 1:05 came and went. She lay in the dark, mind full, in no danger of falling asleep. It was nearly 2:00 a.m. when she gave up, put the phone back in its nook, and went to bed. She tried to think about Walter—how grown up he had come to be, his muscular torso, the hair on his chest. She had arrived at camp unsure what she would think of Walter at age seventeen. From their first conversation on the first day of camp, she knew she wanted to sleep with him. They had both taken it so seriously and done everything right. It may not have had the makings of a perfect moment, but it should have been something she could keep and think about for the rest of her life. Instead, she kept seeing adult faces etched with Deep Concern.

Some years had been better than others—1966 definitely sucked.

Things couldn't be left that way, hanging, unsettled. He didn't call her, so she tried to call him. The next afternoon, she told her father she was phoning an old camp friend from another state. He had the decency not to ask, "Is it *that* boy?" He just said, "Please keep it short."

She talked to a woman, presumably his mom, who told her Walter was out playing golf with his father. In all their many conversations, she had never once heard him mention golf. She couldn't picture him doing it, wearing those silly knit shirts and hats and carrying a golf bag.

"Could you tell him I called?" she asked.

"Sure. What's your name?"

"Denise. I'm a friend from camp. I just need to ask him something."

She thought she heard Walter's mom inhale. Or maybe she was just expecting that reaction. Surely, Mrs. Edelstein knew she was *that* girl.

"I'll give him the message," she said. "They should be home about six-thirty."

"Thanks." Denise wouldn't call Walter after 6:30. But she did hope he would call her.

He did—at 1:05 a.m. on the dot. Denise was awake and ready and snatched the phone off its cradle.

"Hey, girl," he said.

She wanted to sound as casual as Walter, but she never could manage it. "Oh!" she said. "I hope I didn't get you in trouble when I called this afternoon."

"No, no," he said. "I would have called you last night, but I had to go see my dad get an award from the Fraternal Order of the Eagles. We were out past midnight. It was a long day."

"That's nice," said Denise. "What was the award for?"

"I don't know—supporting truth and justice and gladness, or something like that. I was passing out the whole time. Then I had to spend all day with him today."

"Your mom told me. I didn't know you played golf."

"I don't," said Walter. "It's just something my dad has been bugging me to do with him. So I finally said I'd try it."

"How did it go?"

"Exactly as bad as you think. I was terrible. Plus, he had these two friends with him, and they kept telling me what a great sport it is and how much fun I'll have when I get good at it—giving me pointers and shit. I'm sure he put them up to it. He just wants something he and I can do together, I suppose."

"That's actually kind of sweet," said Denise.

"I know how he thinks," said Walter. "He wants to keep me close so I'll turn out like him. Or rather, a better version of him. Anyway, golf is not going to be the ticket. I'm bad at it."

"If you practice, you'd get good," said Denise.

"Of course. But I'm sick of getting good at things. I want to let this one go. Maybe if I play with him a few times and wave the club around like a real spaz, hit the ball in the water, he'll give up and leave me alone."

Denise laughed. She waited for him to say something else, but he was silent. Finally, she said it.

"I'm sorry how it turned out," she said.

"Me too," said Walter.

More dead air.

This is your chance, Walter. Tell me why you just sat there and let them put every-thing on me. Weren't you just as scared as I was? Were you afraid they might call the police and tell them you'd assaulted me? Why didn't you just tell them to their faces right then and there what sniveling weasels they both were? Were you glad it was happening to me instead of you?

No. No apology. He just said, "I don't want to live here anymore, Dee. I hate every minute of it. I hate this house and this town. I hate my dad."

"Don't say that," said Denise. "I don't like it when you talk mean about your parents."

"I have nothing against my mom," he said. "She won't stand up to him, but that's not her fault. That's just how she was raised."

"Don't you love her?"

"I guess," said Walter. "At least I know I'm supposed to. She loves me, or at least she says she does. I am her son."

"Then your dad probably loves you, too. He just doesn't think he can let down his father-image."

"He doesn't love me. But he really wants me to be a huge success. I'm not his son—I'm his project."

"Come on," said Denise. "You *are* his son. It's not just the DNA. He really cares about you."

"Dee, my dad and I are not related," said Walter.

"What …?

"He's not my dad. My mom is my real mom, but none of my genes came from ol' Doc Edelstein."

"You mean … he's your stepdad?"

"Sort of," said Walter. "He's legally my father. But we're not related."

"Then who is your biological father?" said Denise. "Did your mom get divorced?"

"Nope. My father, whoever he may be, is a perfect specimen. An excellent number in a catalog. My mom got me by making a withdrawal at the bank."

"You mean the …?"

"Sperm bank, yes."

"So, your folks couldn't have a baby," said Denise. "I guess that's … I don't know. Did they tell you, or did you just find out?"

"Sort of both. When I was twelve, I heard my parents arguing about some-thing, and my dad was doing his usual thing where he thinks he wins arguments if the other person stops talking. My mom was giving him shit about something, and so he yells, 'He's not even related to me!' It worked. She stopped talking."

"That's awful."

"It got worse. They realized I had overheard, and my dad starts saying, 'Oh, Walter, you *know* I didn't mean that. Of *course,* I'm your father, ta-da ta-da ta-da, whatever.' And my mom says, 'We couldn't have another baby after your sister was born, so we found this *great* clinic.'"

"Why couldn't they have any more kids?" asked Denise.

"My dad had this infection that ended up in his ball sack, and they had to cut one of his balls out. And the one that's left can't make enough little swimmers."

"Oh, God," said Denise, sorry she had asked. "That's terrible. But at least your mom could get pregnant again, even if your dad couldn't be your ... actual dad. Did that mess you up?"

"I guess not. I got mad at the time. But I understand now. I wouldn't want to tell a kid that he got born because some guy out in Utah beat off into a test tube." Walter laughed.

Denise didn't think it was appropriate to laugh at that, so she didn't. She adjusted her position on the carpet and leaned back against the bed. There would be no fantasy talk tonight.

"When do you suppose we'll see each other again?" she said. "I guess that's it for Camp Pursell. I don't think they'd let either one of us be counselors."

"I wouldn't take it if they offered me a ten-thousand-dollar signing bonus. I only went because you went."

"Well, I only went because you went. I just wish it had ended better. They were always really nice to me. I didn't make very many friends, but I had a few. It would have been better to go out the front door. You know, everybody hugs and cries."

"Dee, I'm really, really sorry ..."

What are you sorry about, Walter? Please say it. You sound hoarse. Are you crying?

"It wasn't your fault, Walter ..."

Silence. Then he cleared his throat.

"Do you want to just get out of here?"

"Out of ... here?"

"Out of the country. I'm completely serious. You have a passport, right? I'm gonna get one, too. I heard it takes about six weeks if you do everything in person at the passport office."

"I've had one for three years," said Denise. "It's still good. My mother filled out the form."

"I'm going to get mine one way or another," said Walter. "I can forge my dad's signature. It's easy. It looks like somebody held a pen and had a spaz attack. My friend David thinks he can get his mother to sign his application. We can take off anytime we want. Spain ... Portugal ... Hell, if you go with me, I'll let you pick the country."

Was he pulling her leg? "Walter, you're kidding, right?"

"I am absolutely serious. And I don't mean just winter break. I want to get out of here for good."

"But ... we're going into senior year. I'm visiting colleges this fall. What about you? Aren't you applying to MIT? You can't just blow off your senior year ..."

"Fuck senior year," said Walter. "And fuck MIT. Fuck college."

"Wow ..."

She heard him do something with the phone receiver. Maybe he passed it to his other hand. After a few moments, he sighed.

"I'm sorry, Dee," he said. "You're right. I can't just blow it off. But I'm serious about the passport. We can wait till next summer. But the sooner I get one, the better. I need to leave. You can go with me if you want. I hope you do. You don't have to stay a long time. David might go, too. He can come back any time. But I want to be gone. I need to ... resign. Quit. Clean out my desk."

Olympic

ROGER MONK INSISTED ON DRIVING out with him in the Mustang to the Charabi farm, leading the way while David drove his own car.

His own car. It was only his third time to drive it—the first had just been around and around the S&E Food Mart parking lot, with Dad shouting confusing instructions, and the second time was up and down the quiet Sunday morning streets of Lawrence. Now, he was hitting the highway on a workday. This was it. David was driving to work.

It was a '63 Studebaker Daytona, a stubby little baby blue two-door with "youthful" lines and a glove box with the word "Vanity" embossed on the front, for some reason. Dad said the car was made in Canada and got good gas mileage. David was still getting used to it. The gear shift was on the floor, a four-speed. The car lurched as he struggled with the clutch, and he kept forgetting there was a fourth gear. The six-cylinder engine revved like crazy at highway speeds.

Dad was pleased about the Daytona and proud of the deal he'd negotiated at Dotson Used Cars. David, on the other hand, was too busy figuring out how to drive to be excited about his first car.

His own car. With a temporary hardship license in his wallet, David followed Dad down the big highway until they turned onto the small highway. Then Dad slowed down and waved for David to come around and go in front.

He wants to make sure I know the way, thought David. He knew the way. David fuddled with the gears for a moment and shifted into second, checked the rearview mirror for other traffic, then accelerated into the left lane and drove around the Mustang. He took it up to sixty miles per hour and checked the mirror again. Okay, this was starting to feel more natural.

Dad was hanging back six car lengths, one for every ten miles per hour, as they said in safe-driving commercials. David hoped he wouldn't follow him all the way out to the farm. He came to the intersection with Moss Creek and turned right, and Dad followed. Thankfully when they arrived at the gate, Dad didn't try to drive up to the house. He pulled over the side of the road as David turned into the arched entrance.

Dad rolled down his window. "Well, you made it," he called. "Be extra careful driving back this afternoon. There'll be a lot of Kansas City traffic coming outbound." David waved. Dad U-turned the Mustang and headed back home.

David was on his own. He leaned out of the window, opened the gray metal box, and punched in the secret code. With a clang and shriek, the gate opened.

Nathan Charabi was standing in front of the house in casual slacks and a bowling shirt that draped over his thin frame. He had a pipe in his mouth, like Hugh Hefner. David parked, shut off the engine, got out of the car, and locked the door. Immediately, he felt silly. Who was going to steal it?

"Hey, David. Thanks for coming out," Mr. Charabi said. He gestured at the light blue car with his pipe. "Got you a new set of wheels?"

"Well, dad owns it, but it's mine to drive," said David. "I can only drive it out here until I turn sixteen."

"Studebaker makes fine cars," said Charabi. "The little ones like yours are tough as nails. I used to have a V-eight Golden Hawk. Great car. Fast. And you couldn't *kill* that engine." He turned and beckoned David to follow. "Judith's with her physical therapist right now. We'll have to wait a bit. They ought to be done soon. Poor girl had a rough night."

They walked in the front door and through the marble-floored foyer. Mirrors on both side walls made the room look even bigger than it was. A wide carpeted staircase in the center curved up and to the left. Mr. Charabi led David to the right and through a small casual sitting room. This is as far inside the house as David had ever been. But this time, they proceeded through double doors into the cavernous living room. An enormous oil painting hung above the fireplace, a garden portrait of the Charabi family, with Nathan himself standing center, pleased and serious, Judith seated by his side, smiling with her hands folded in her lap, and leaning against her, looking sort of pissed off, a little girl about four years old who must be Lisa. On either side of Mr. Charabi were two young men in sport coats who looked to be in their late teens, also not smiling.

Mr. Charabi noticed David inspecting the painting. "We had that one done seven or eight years ago when we first got this house. Those are my two boys, Robert and Seth. They both live in New York now."

He kept walking through the living room, so David followed. In one corner, standing magnificent on the marble floor was a pedal harp. With a shining white lacquered finish, the tall, ornate instrument occupied the spot where most wealthy families might have had a showpiece piano. (They did have a grand piano, of course. It stayed in the back of the house near the double doors to the patio.) David had never realized how many strings a harp had. Every fourth string was colored, alternating red and black, which must mean something to a harpist.

"Does ... Mrs. Charabi play this?" asked David.

"She used to. She was crackerjack at it, too. A natural. Studied in Italy. She doesn't play anymore because of the problems she has with her hands. When I met her, she was with the Cleveland Symphony. I bought this one for her last year. I was hoping she might give it a try again. Maybe you can help with that."

They went through another set of double doors into a smaller family room. On the other side of a large couch, there was the biggest television David had ever seen. The screen was almost three feet wide, but the polished wood console had to be six feet across. The TV was on. It was playing a game show in color.

A head popped up from one side of the couch. It was Lisa Charabi, grinning.

"Hey!" she said.

"Hey," said David.

Nathan Charabi gestured toward the sitting area. "You can wait here if you want, David. You can look at TV. We get three channels out here, both of the Kansas City stations and Lawrence, too, when the weather is good. If you don't like this show, I'm sure Lisa would be willing to change it for you."

"I like *The Price is Right*," said Lisa.

"That's fine with me," said David.

"Great," said Mr. Charabi. "Can I get you anything to drink? Pepsi?"

"No, thank you."

"Very good. I'm going to be out in the garage for a little while. When the therapist gets done, I told her to come find you, and Judith will be all yours." He started to leave the room, then turned back. "By the way, you didn't bring a swimsuit, did you? I suppose not."

"No, sir."

"I should have told your dad when we talked on the phone. Judith likes to swim in the afternoons when she's feeling okay. Lisa usually does it, too. If you want to join us, I can find you an extra pair of trunks. I think there's some old ones that Seth had. They'd be about your size."

"Thanks," said David. The Charabis had a large swimming pool on the east side of the house. Roger Monk had remarked that it must be Olympic-sized, but Mr. Charabi said it was a "short-course" pool. Still, it was as big as the one in David's high school gym. There were lane lines painted on the bottom.

David sat down on the other end of the long couch opposite Lisa. She curled her legs up under her and leaned against the cushioned arm, facing David. She ignored *The Price is Right* and looked straight at him, grinning.

"Are you for real?" she asked.

This was so unexpected David burst out laughing. "Yes, I'm not in your imagination," he said.

"No, Goofus. I mean, is this thing you do with my mom real? Or is it just psychology?"

"I think it's real," said David. "People tell me that it helps."

"I was just wondering," said Lisa. "My social studies teacher said that faith healers are just after people's money. There's this preacher guy on TV who puts his hands on old ladies' heads and yells at them to be healed, and then they get out of their wheelchairs and do a little dance and stuff. I was always pretty sure it was fake."

"Those guys are definitely fake. They use actors."

"But you're the real thing?"

"I … I can really tell … usually … if somebody is feeling pain. And a lot of the time, I can make it go away. For a while. I can't make somebody walk if they're in a wheelchair."

"Do you make a lot of money?"

"No," said David. "I've never charged anybody. Sometimes people want to pay, and then my dad tells them to give money to our church."

"But my dad is paying you, right?"

"He's paying my dad, yeah. Because we have to drive all the way out here from Lawrence."

"Do you get to keep some of it?"

Lisa's eyes bored into him. Was this a flirt or an interrogation?

"My parents are going to put some of it away. For my college." David pretended to turn his attention to the television.

An enthusiastic announcer was proclaiming, "*The Price is Right* is brought to you by Dove, the beauty bar that creams your skin as it cleans!" Applause.

"Can you heal my foot?" asked Lisa.

David turned back to her. "What?"

"I sprained my ankle playing tennis. It really hurts. Can you make it better?"

"Uh … I don't know," said David. "I might be able to."

Lisa bounced over to the middle of the couch and extended her left foot at David. The pads of her small foot and the bottoms of her toes were blackened.

"Here," she demanded. "This is my bad ankle. I've been hopping around on one foot for two days. It hurts. See what you can do." She wiggled her toes.

What could he do? He reached his right hand toward her ankle, but she quickly pulled back.

"It's okay," said David. "Relax and be still."

"You're not gonna tickle me, are you?"

"No, I don't touch."

The foot came back. David held his hand close to the top of the small, smudgy appendages. There was the soft tingle of living energy. Nothing more. He passed his hand back and forth over the top of the foot and slowly back toward her ankle.

"Should I close my eyes?" asked Lisa.

"No. It doesn't matter," said David. He passed his hand up and down and side to side, then held it very still over the boney bump on the outside of her ankle.

"I don't feel any pain," said David. He took his hand away.

Lisa glared at him for a moment, then burst out laughing.

"You *are* real!" she said. "I didn't sprain my ankle. I was fooling you!"

"Okay," said David and returned his attention to the big Curtis Mathis console. *That was weird.*

On TV, Bill Cullen was saying, "The value of this lovely kitchen set is two thousand one hundred and sixteen dollars, and it can all be yours if you make the best bid on just one of these items!"

A woman's voice came from behind them. "Mr. David?"

He turned around to see a fortyish, blond, stocky woman in some sort of white medical smock. The therapist.

"Yes?"

"Miss Judith can see you now," she said, unsmiling. What was that look she gave him? Suspicion? Hostility? There was a hint of that, David thought.

"He's the real thing, Harriet," said Lisa.

"Very good," said the therapist. "I'll take you back now."

David rose from the couch and followed the woman down a long hall.

They ended up in a room with large windows, floor to ceiling on three sides. Opaque green curtains covered everything but the sliding doors to the outside, which were darkened by amber glass.

Aside from a few outdoor chairs, the only furniture was a long massage table in the center of the room, and on the table was Judith Charabi, face down, with a white sheet covering her back to just below her bare shoulder blades David was alarmed to realize that her back was bare. Maybe she was nude. The sheet covered her legs and buttocks, but her smooth white skin was inviting, and her recent massage had left her glowing and oily. Her black hair was tied into a ponytail and pulled to one side. Her arms were straight down by her side, palms up. She was facing David and opened her eyes, but otherwise, she did not move.

"Hi, Davie," she said. "I'm sorry I'm not decent, but I didn't want to move. If I lie perfectly still after Harriet works on me, I don't hurt as much."

"That's okay," said David.

"I'll just lie here and shut my eyes if that's all right. You can do whatever you want to me."

David swallowed, and his pulse quickened.

He wanted to get started, but the sight of Judith's bare back and curved lumbar, the jut of her shoulder blades … he had to take a moment. The one time he'd worked with her, she had been in the front room fully clothed, and there had been witnesses.

"Where do you want me to do you?" he asked stupidly, then corrected. "Uh … where are you having trouble?"

"I don't hurt very much," she said. "But if I tried to raise my head right now, it would feel like needles sticking into my neck and spine."

"Okay." David walked around to her other side to get a better angle for his right hand.

Deep, slow breath in. Exhale.

He reached out and placed his palm an inch from the back of her neck. His hand trembled, so he withdrew it, opened and closed his fist, then tried again. The trembling resumed, but it was manageable.

He waited until he felt the electric tingling in his sternum like he had completed a circuit. Moving his hand very slowly, he tried to mentally map her body.

The first time he had done this, a few weeks ago, her energy lines had confused him. Nothing seemed in the right place. He had concentrated on specific joints, her knees, and wrists, where he had found pools of discomfort he could collect and discharge. Then he had focused on her headaches, which were harder to locate, but he had tried. He felt he hadn't done a good job. Mr. Charabi and another man, an employee or assistant named Roy, had watched him work, and they made him nervous, especially Roy, a gray-haired muscular man with a wide face. But in the end, Judith said she felt better.

Now that he had all the time and access that he needed, he faced a jumble of contradictory colors and cues. There seemed to be sharp little islands of pain everywhere along her spine and shoulders, but no central source to find and ground. Most of what he saw was dull and out of focus. He started at the top and slowly moved down her body, across each shoulder in turn, and down along each arm to the elbow. Whenever he found a locus of pain, he did his best to make it dissipate. He started again with the top of her head. On the side of her head near the left temple was a confusing location where flashes of light and energy seemed to jump around, and there was nothing to discharge, but the longer he stayed, the more it settled down. After a minute, he continued down again, hand shaking more than usual.

When he reached her lower back, the sheet was a problem. It was bunched up right over her tailbone, so he couldn't get his hand close enough. He didn't want to touch the sheet. It would be better if she pulled the sheet up, but he hesitated to mention it. He skipped the tailbone and continued down the thighs, concealed under white cloth, but he really couldn't identify any special areas. He returned his hand to the base of her spine. That was a significant concentration of wrongness, but he couldn't do anything for it, not with the bunched sheet intervening. He had to move it.

"Um … I can't get close to … the low part of the back," he said. "Because the sheet's in the way. If you could move it … "

"That's fine," she said. To his breathtaking surprise, she reached back with both hands and pulled the sheet down just to the top of her smooth, curved butt and smoothed the cloth with the backs of her hands.

He had meant for her to pull it up, but … this was better. In many respects.

Steady, man, he thought. *It's your summer job.*

He took a long, slow breath and extended his right hand again.

LISA DOVE INTO THE POOL. *Ka-Chunk!*

David treaded water in the shallow end, holding his legs up off the bottom. The red swim trunks were big on him, cinched tight around his waist. The day was sultry, and it felt good to be in the water. He started a slow breaststroke back and forth across the middle part of the pool, where it was about six feet deep.

Lisa, her skinny body in a competitors' one-piece, went off the diving board again and again into the deep end, entering the water with perfect form and very little splash each time. She said she was on the swim team at her school, and he believed her.

Nathan Charabi sat in a plastic chair in the shade of an umbrella beside the pool, reading a tabloid-size newspaper with lots of little headlines and dense type. The masthead said *Carter's Shipping World.* He puffed at his pipe and took sips of iced tea from a tall glass.

David would rather have just driven home, but the Charabis were so nice and went to some trouble finding him a pair of their son's swim trunks, so he felt obliged to swim for at least a little while. He watched Lisa dive while he lazed back and forth across the width of the pool. After a little while, he floated on his back, but that felt oddly decadent. He went back to swimming.

After seven or eight perfect forward dives, Lisa climbed the little ladder and walked to the end of the board, but this time, she turned and faced away. For a moment, she stood perfectly still, then bent her knees and swung her arms for a back flip. She hit the water awkwardly and raised a big splash. When her head emerged, she was scowling.

"Damn it!" she said.

"Language, young lady!" said Nathan, without taking the pipe out of his teeth.

"But I whacked my back!"

"You took off too early. Try it again." He went back to his paper.

Instead of getting out of the pool, Lisa swam over to David.

"Are you going to drive back today?" she asked.

"Sure," he said. "In a little while."

"You should just stay out here. We have about ten extra rooms we don't use."

"I have my own room back home."

Lisa paddled slowly backward, still facing him. "You could stay out here part of the time," she said. "Then you'd be here whenever my mom needs you, and you wouldn't have to travel. Roy has his own room. So does Olivia. She's our cook."

"That's why we got the car," said David. "So I could travel out here whenever she wants me to. Besides, I have my family and friends."

"Do you have a best friend?" she asked.

"Yeah. I guess."

"Is it a girl?"

"No," said David. "He's a guy."

"What's his name?"

"Walter."

"Is he cool?"

"Yeah, he's cool," said David. "He's a genius, and he's perfect at everything. We've been friends since we were little kids, but right now, we're not allowed to hang out."

"Why?" Lisa asked.

"His parents think I'm a bad influence."

Lisa laughed.

From the other side of the pool came a shrill wolf whistle. Nathan Charabi had lowered his paper, raised his sunglasses, and taken the pipe from his mouth. He was smiling broadly.

"My lord, look what we have here!" he called.

David turned around and saw it was Judith, in a bright-yellow bathrobe, open to reveal a two-piece bathing suit. A swim cap was pulled tight over her hair. She was approaching with her own glass of tea, moving slowly but steadily. She walked over to where Nathan was lounging, set her tea on the little table, then let the robe slip from her slim body. She draped it over the back of the chair.

"Have a seat, pretty lady," said Nathan. "I see you're feeling better."

"Yes, I am," said Judith. "But I'm going to do a couple of laps first."

"You need me to help you?" asked Nathan.

"No, I do not," said Judith. She walked slowly and carefully to the side of the pool, turned, and grasped the ladder, then stepped down into the water. Her moves were deliberate but smooth. When she was fully immersed, she did a slow crawl to the end, then turned and dunked under, pushing off, and glided half the length of the pool underwater. When she broke the surface, she swam faster, reached the other end by the diving board, and did a graceful turn. When she had swum the full length, she stopped in the shallow end and stood up to adjust her cap.

"Good job, Mom!" said Lisa.

Judith swam back and forth, slowly and with grace. She was so pretty. He knew she was Mr. Charabi's second wife. What did the first one look like? Why did they get divorced? Was she too old?

A black woman in a pink and white uniform came out to the pool.

"Will you be needing anything, Mr. Charabi?" she asked.

"I'm fine, Olivia," he said. "But these kids might want something to drink."

"I have fresh limeade," said Olivia. "Just made it."

"I want some!" said Lisa. "David, you should try it. She squeezes her own limes."

"Okay, thanks," said David.

"Two limeaids coming up," said Olivia. "I'll bring some canapés, too." She walked away deliberately and efficiently.

"What is she bringing?" asked David.

"Canapés," said Lisa. "She makes them with cucumbers and cream cheese. You'll like them."

It occurred to David this was the first time that he would be served anything by a servant. He watched Judith climb out of the pool, rivulets of water running down the backs of her thighs. She toweled herself off very thoroughly from shoulders to calves, and David watched until he thought maybe he shouldn't.

Twelve to Six

S OME YEARS IN THIS SOUTHERN CITY, there was no true winter—just two or three months where a few spent northers managed to wander in, bringing two or three consecutive days of brisk cold but only the occasional freezing rain or wet sleet. It had even snowed back in January of 1972—eight inches deep in some parts of town—leading to closed schools, traffic gridlock, frustration, and dented fenders. But the kind of winters like they had in Cleveland or Boston or Kansas City—endless gray days with steam rising from the curb grills and piles of gray snow decorated with gum wrappers and dog shit—were unknown in this part of the world. Any given day in any month could be sunny and warm. False springs were taken for granted by the natives and appreciated by the out-of-staters.

Wally appreciated them. During the last week of February, a southern breeze blew across the city, and the sun shone brightly. In the parks, some trees were budding—other trees, like the huge live oaks, began to lose last year's foliage as the new leaves grew in behind them. There might be a few more chilly nights ahead, but no freezes.

Sunshine and warm weather elevated his mood. One day, after his shift at the bookstore ended, he decided it was time to take a chance with Callie Pender.

The woman was not easy to get to know. She worked unpredictable hours, and it was hard to arrange moments when he could casually run into her so they could talk. While one might expect a masseuse to be on duty any time—she said the place where she worked, Sandy O's, was open twenty-four hours. Callie preferred afternoons. She called it the "rush hour shift," which usually wrapped up by 8:00 or 9:00 p.m. On those days, Callie depended on leftovers from the reefer. Wally always tried to make sure there was something available for her. When she showed up at regular 6:30 dinner in the evenings, it usually meant she had a day off.

Callie showed up for dinner one Thursday night. Before the dinner triangle rang—a pathetic little thing with a bad tone and muted volume that everybody hated—Wally quickly checked the campus paper for a movie. There was a Robert Altman picture showing at one of the old theaters downtown. He found her after dinner and asked her if she wanted to go. Sure, she said, but she was working late shift that night and couldn't stay out too long afterward. So, they went.

They had an okay time. Wally wasn't sure it could be called a "date." He wondered if he should put his arm around her in the theater at some point, but he never did. Callie smelled really, really good, a scent he couldn't identify.

The movie was strange—nothing like *MASH* or that great film about the kid who flies in the Astrodome. It had its entertaining moments, but in the end, it left them both baffled. As they walked out of the theater, the downtown streets were mostly empty.

"I guess we're supposed to think that the bar owner murdered her husband?" said Callie.

"I suppose," said Wally. "The other dude was talking about it being an accident."

"So why did Sissy Spacek start calling Shelley Duvall her mom at the end? Aren't they supposed to be the same age?"

"I didn't get that either," said Wally. "I think she switched personalities with the older lady."

"Weird."

"Yep, pretty weird."

He had parked a couple of blocks away to avoid paying for parking.

"You want to get some ice cream, Wally?" asked Callie. "I haven't had any since last fall."

"I don't know," said Wally. "It's almost eleven. We should probably go home."

"I still need to go to work," Callie said. "I'm doing the late-late shift. But we still have time."

"Work? I forgot you told me that."

"I know, I know. I don't normally do the after midnight, but I traded shifts with a girl."

They were on the wide, broken sidewalk on Fourth Street, where it meets the Garrot Creek Bridge. In summer, crickets swarmed the pavement in the yellow halo under the streetlight, and you had to be careful not to step on them, but tonight, there were just a few moths circling in the light. Wally's car was parked on the next block.

"I think Passion Fruit is still open," said Callie. "At least we can walk by. I want a frozen yogurt."

"Okay. I guess. I'm not that hungry." The extra-large root beer he drank at the theater sat heavy in his stomach.

Instead of crossing the bridge, they turned on Duval Street and walked up the hill, Wally's soft drink sloshing around his midsection. He was out of breath. It had been a long time since he'd gotten any decent exercise. Lifting boxes did little for his overall health.

Most of the bars and cafés were closed or closing, but light came through the big window at Passion Fruit. A thirtyish man stood outside, smoking a cigarette. Probably the manager.

"You guys still open?" Wally called.

"Ten more minutes," said the guy. "Come on in."

He opened the door for them, and they entered the brilliantly lit shop with its long white freezer case. The air conditioning inside was bracing. Callie went to the long row and peered down through the glass. A college-age girl with the requisite paper hat and apron waited behind the counter, impatient to close the shop and go home. In the corner, three young women sat at one of the tables, eating ice cream with plastic spoons and chatting.

Wally looked, then looked again. *What? Couldn't be! No way.* One of the women looked very familiar in profile. Black curly hair and an aquiline nose. Could that really be her? She was about the right age. Then she spoke, and there was no doubt.

"He's moving back to Fort Worth," she was saying. "He seriously thinks I'd go with him. Fort. Worth." She laughed. Unmistakable. Wally turned away and pretended to inspect the classic movie posters on the wall.

"Can I get a raspberry?" asked Callie.

Wally kept looking at the posters.

Hmmm. 'Out of the Past'. Now that's a great flick …

The three women rose and scooted their chairs back, still talking.

"Let me grab some napkins," said the black-haired one. She walked right past Wally, and he caught her eye for just a moment. She glanced away, then looked back and lit up in a wide-mouthed smile.

"David?" she said. "Oh my god!"

"Hi!" said Wally.

"I didn't know you even lived here. How have you been?"

"I've been good. Working a lot. How are you?"

She looked at him intently, beaming. "I'm great! I'm going to nursing school. It's fantastic to see you! How long have you been in Texas?"

"About a year now." He glanced over at Callie, who was holding a red dessert cone in one hand and accepting change from the other.

"We need to get together," said the woman. "I never see anybody from the old town anymore. You're looking good. Are you going to the University?"

"Not at the moment. Just working mostly. Not a whole lot going on. Hey, it's great to see you, but I'm afraid we gotta scoot. My friend needs to get to work."

"Well, sorry," she said. "Hey, I'm in the phone book. Look me up sometime, okay?"

"I sure will," said Wally.

This was no time for memory lane. Not tonight.

Callie walked over, licking red yogurt from a waffle cone, grinning. Maybe she expected to be introduced, but Wally just put his arm around her shoulder and guided her to the door, which the manager opened gallantly. Wally turned back for a little toodle-oo wave, then stepped out into the dark night.

"Who was that?" asked Callie.

"Just somebody I knew from back home," said Wally. "Hey, do you remember if we parked on Fifth or Sixth?"

"Fifth, of course," said Callie.

Wally walked briskly down the street, forcing her to walk fast to keep up. He knew the question was coming.

"Wally, why did she call you 'David'?"

He shrugged. "She misremembered. She mistook me for somebody else we both knew a long time ago."

"So why didn't you set her straight?"

"I don't know," said Wally. "I guess I didn't want to embarrass her. Anyway, she wasn't special. Just somebody I used to know."

"Are you sure she wasn't an old girlfriend?" asked Callie, giggling. "Too many bad memories?"

"Oh, god no," said Wally. "Just a casual friend. Really. She's a few years younger than me."

They found the car. A piece of paper was tucked under a wiper blade. Wally feared it was a ticket—technically, he was illegally parked—but it turned out to be a colorful solicitation from the Hare Krishna temple. "Experience Love, Peace and Happiness through Chanting," it said. He tossed it into the street.

"Wally, could you just go ahead and take me to work?" Callie asked.

"Don't you want to go home first?"

"I would, but we'd have to rush," she said. "I keep a work outfit at the studio. If I get there a little early, I'll have time for a shower."

Wally unlocked the car door on the passenger side.

"I never heard of anybody taking a shower at work," he said.

"Well, we do. Sometimes a couple of them. We get oily."

Wally walked around the car and slipped into the driver's seat. He wasn't sure he wanted to know, but his curiosity pushed him to ask the question.

"Okay, why do you get oily?"

Callie sighed. "Wally, we use massage oil. Hey, we're just having a fun night out. Don't make me talk about work."

Wally started the Maverick and pulled onto Fifth Street. "Okay, I won't pry," he said. "Where are we going, anyway?"

"Turn back around and get on the highway," Callie said. "It's south, just on the other side of the river. First exit."

They drove to the access road, then turned up the entrance ramp to the freeway, which fed onto the river bridge. There were few other cars on the bridge. The water below was dark, but lights from the buildings on both sides reflected along the shorelines. Far away, the lights from another suspension bridge glowed.

"Exit there," Callie said. "Turn into the parking lot right behind the sign."

The sign she referred to was enormous and green and read Bail Bonds, with a giant phone number. After they had turned into the brightly lit parking lot, he saw there was a smaller sign on the one side of the building: Sandy O's Massage. Beneath that message, it read: Relax, and, blinking red, Open.

"It's hard to see that sign from the street," said Wally. "If I didn't know better, I'd think this was a place to get somebody bailed out."

Callie laughed. "Yeah, Sandy shares the building. It's funny. We take up ninety percent of the space. The bail bondsman is just a guy with a desk and a phone. But people know where we are."

While they sat with the engine running, Callie turned the rearview mirror to inspect her face. She extracted a lipstick from her purse and gave herself a quick touch-up.

A uniformed security guard walked over to the driver's side window. Wally rolled it down.

"Can I help you?" he asked, then leaned down and saw Callie in the passenger seat. "Oh, hi!" he said. "I didn't see you."

"Hi, Lee," she said. "He's just giving me a ride. I'll be inside in a second."

"No problem." The security guard nodded and walked away.

"We have a full-time guard at night now," said Callie. "I heard that a couple of years ago, some guys with guns came in and forced everybody to get on the floor. They robbed everybody, including the customers."

"What kind of customers do you get in the middle of the night?" asked Wally.

"Well, it's not very busy. Only a few guys come in. Some are night workers getting off their shift. Of course, we have our share of creeps and drunks. But that's what Lee is here for. Mostly, they're guys who just need company. Or maybe they just had a rough day at work and need to unwind."

Wally was sorry he'd asked. Sorry he had taken her here, and sorry he found out where she went every day. Of course, he had always had a pretty good idea.

Callie finished applying the lipstick and pushed the mirror back. Wally readjusted it. She must have picked up on what he was thinking from his silence.

"Wally, you don't think less of me, do you?" she asked. "I know this building looks sketchy, but it's just a job."

"I know," he said. "I don't think less of you … I don't … I really like you," he said. "It's just hard to picture you with disgusting old men. You're so nice."

"They're not disgusting!" she said. "I wish you wouldn't say that. I'm not a hooker. I don't sell my body. I talk to guys, and I listen to them, which is most of the job. I have to hear a lot of sad stories. Some of them just need somebody to touch them, so I do that."

"I'm sorry," said Wally. "I didn't mean to imply …"

"Listen, there's a guy who comes here in a wheelchair, and he asks for me, specifically. He says I really help the pain in his legs."

Wally couldn't really blame her for being defensive. Now he felt like a shithead.

"I'm really sorry, Callie. Don't be mad."

"It's okay, I'm not mad," she said. "If I could make a hundred dollars a day working at a pet store, maybe I'd do that. But here, sometimes, I actually help people. Now, I gotta go." She opened the car door and stepped out, adjusting her dress.

"Do you have a ride home?" he asked.

"I can get a ride," she said. "If I can't, I'll take a cab. It'll be after six o'clock in the morning. Now go home and go to sleep."

"Okay ... I just wanted to make sure ..."

The car door shut. Callie walked away toward the small, dark metal door below the flashing sign. He watched her go. When she reached the door, she hesitated, then turned and came back to the car and opened the passenger door. She leaned inside.

"Hey, Wally, thanks for tonight. I really had a good time," she said. "I liked the movie, even though I didn't understand it."

"I didn't understand it either," said Wally. "But it was fun. I'll see you later, okay?"

"Later."

Wally waited until she had gone inside. He wondered if it was too late to get a beer somewhere.

Fear of Drowning

OVER THE WEEKEND, a spent cold front eased through central Texas, sending temperatures down into the high forties. But within a day, warm, wet winds were blowing from the south, bringing low, heavy clouds and a steady drizzle. Mud accumulated by the front door of Keystone House and on the porch, where people banged their shoes against the railings. By Monday, the rain had picked up, saturating the winter-dry ground and swelling creeks. Muddy water puddled on the broken sidewalks.

Once a week, Wally worked the closing shift at the bookstore. Most days, he walked to his job, but that afternoon, he saved himself the misery by taking his car, even though it meant paying six bucks at a parking garage. During his four-hour evening shift, he would occasionally come out of the storage area where he was sorting textbooks to check the situation outside. Rain was unrelenting.

By the time the store closed at 9:00 p.m., the spring rain was a full-fledged downpour, and water flowed down the wide street in a pair of rivers carrying leaves and trash. Wally eased his car out of the parking garage and onto the main north-south street, where cars glided slowly by with their headlights glaring through the wet. The Maverick's wipers could barely keep up. Rain drummed on the car roof so loud he could hardly hear the radio.

It took him half an hour to drive the ten blocks home, creeping down streets that were flooded curb to curb, hoping the sad little engine wouldn't flood out in an unseen low spot. The brakes were squishy and unreliable. He did get lucky and found a parking place almost right in front of Keystone, even better than the one he'd left that afternoon. He put his wheels as hard against the curb as he could, then climbed over the stick shift to exit the passenger side. The water was only a couple of inches below the level of the floorboards. He stepped up onto the sidewalk and shut the door, then put his head down and splashed for the house.

Safely on the porch, he shook his head like a wet spaniel and looked back at his car, which sat almost up to its doors in the Twenty-First Street river. He hoped the inside of the car would stay dry. There was nothing he could do about it. He shook the water off his windbreaker and went inside.

The usual game of world domination was going on at the smaller table in the common room. The four players had beers from the soft drink machine and a metal bowl of burned popcorn remnants. Wally assumed there was a hopelessly blackened pot in the sink, but he wasn't going to look. One of the guys, Aaron, was between turns and went to look out the porch window.

"Jee-Zus!" Aaron said. "Is this shit *ever* gonna let up?"

(Lawdy, you spoze it ever gwine stop rainin'?)

A girl was sitting on the newer of the two couches with a textbook. She looked up. "The radio said it's flooding in Houston," she said. "Six people drowned."

"That's because it's so flat," said another game player. "There's nowhere for the water to go. Here, at least, we have hills."

Since he had missed dinner, Wally went to the reefer to see what was left over. There was a foil tray with four pork chops in coagulated gravy. He extracted one of them with a spatula and placed it in one of the big skillets with a dollop of the congealed brown sludge. It was too much pan for the task, but it was the only one with a good tight-fitting iron lid. He added a splash of water and set it over a low flame. He found some cold brown rice in a covered bowl, threw that into the pan as well.

Then he noticed that the good chef's knife, the one with the pink Day-Glo handle, the Big Pink Knife, was lying wet at the bottom of the sink.

Man! These people! How many times had he groused about this very subject at the house meetings? He rinsed the knife, dried it carefully, and put it back in the rack.

"Wally?" A quiet voice behind him. It was Sherry. Her face was puffy, and her eyes were half closed.

"Hey, Sherry," he said. "Do you have a headache?"

"Yeah, I do," she said. "Wally, I have the hugest favor to ask. Could you please make me a cup of tea? Hibiscus. There's some in the pantry."

"Of course," he said. "Are you hungry? I could make you a plate."

"Just tea. I don't think I could hold anything else down. I'd make it myself, but I really need to lie down."

"Go on back to bed," he said. "I'll get the hibiscus."

"Thanks, Wally." She slipped out of the kitchen like a ghost.

Wally found the jar of loose herbs, scooped some of the leaves into a coffee mug, then set some water to boil. He checked the pork chop and rice and stirred. They were heating up nicely. He used a fork to take a bite straight from the pan and put the lid back.

When the tea water was simmering, he carefully filled the mug and set a saucer on top. While the tea steeped, he ate the rest of his dinner.

I can't help her.

No, that's not right. He probably still could. He *must not* help her. It was a promise he made to himself before he started his new life. Once, the promise had felt like liberation, like the cell door had been kicked open, and somebody had yelled, "Run, run, you fool! Here's your chance! Go!" Times like this made him frustrated and sad and hate himself.

He quickly washed his plate and toweled it dry before returning it to the shelf. He filled the big skillet with water and left it in the sink to soak. As he had suspected, there was also a large aluminum pot with blackened popcorn kernels stuck to the bottom. He ran water into that one, too. Later, he'd clean them both because he was a good guy.

Really? It's gonna take more than washing the dishes, pal.

He got the cup of tea and poured the contents through a strainer into a small pot and then back into the mug, discarding the used hibiscus leaves into the compost bin. He added a small spoonful of honey to the cup and stirred.

Maybe this is all she needs. A nice cup of herbal tea will make her feel better.

He tapped on Sherry's door, then entered the dim room. The floor lamp was draped in its usual scarf.

"Here's your tea," he said.

She was propped up with two pillows, eyes closed. She opened them halfway. She had been crying.

"Thanks, Wally," she said, her voice small and weak. "Just set it on the desk, okay?"

He did as she asked and turned to leave. But when he got to the door, he paused, shut it, and returned to the bed.

Damn it, damn it.

He sat carefully on the edge of the bed. "Where do you hurt?" he asked.

"It's a migraine. You know."

"But, where specifically? Where in your head?"

"It feels like it's behind my left eye. But it's everywhere, really." There were tears in her eyes. "Wally, this is the worst ever. And I didn't do anything to cause it. I used to blame Nicholas with all his psycho games, but now I don't have that excuse. This one just came out of nowhere, and I think it's going to kill me. I'd rather be dead than live like this."

She closed her eyes. She was trying to keep every muscle in her face still.

"Just lie back," Wally said. "I'm going to try something."

She spoke again, barely above a whisper. "Wally, when I was sixteen, an older boy talked me into shooting up some heroin with him. I swore I'd never do that again. But now, I probably would. I want to die."

"Be still," he said. "I'm not going to touch you." He raised his hand and put the palm close to her forehead.

Her eyes opened. "What are you doing?" she asked.

"I'm going to try and help you. Relax. Shut your eyes."

Could he still do this? He was out of practice.

HE CLOSED THE DOOR SOFTLY BEHIND HIM. Returning to the kitchen, he rinsed out the mug. He felt a familiar exhaustion.

He had wanted to talk to her and explain how important it was to keep this to herself, but she was so tired he had just kissed her between her eyes and smoothed her red hair before slipping away. He spent ten minutes washing and scrubbing out both dirty pans, including the one that was not his doing.

He went back to the common room and looked out the big porch window. Water was dripping off the eaves, but the rain had finally stopped. He remembered the punch line to the racist *Toastmaster's* joke.

"*Lawdy, you spoze it ever gwine stop rainin'?*"

"*Can't say. Always has.*"

He decided to go to bed. He'd sneak in quietly in case Beva and her boyfriend were there. The one time he'd accidentally interrupted them in a physical embrace, Beva had just laughed and said, "It's okay, Wally. It's your room, too. We'll try not to be loud."

As he turned to leave the common room, Aaron called to him.

"Hey, Wally! I forgot to tell you. There was a guy looking for you. Earlier, while you were at work."

"What? Who?"

"I don't know. Older dude. White hair. He asked if anybody named Walter was living here. That's your real name, right?"

"Uh … yeah."

"Yeah, I figured that was probably your name," said Aaron. "Anyway, I didn't tell him you were here. The guy gave me the creeps like he was a cop or something."

"What did he look like?"

"Like I said. Older dude. He was wearing an expensive-looking raincoat, and he had this huge-ass umbrella."

"He didn't say his name?"

"No. He just said he was looking for a guy named Walter … uh … something-Stein."

"Edelstein," said Mike, one of the game players, without looking up.

"Yeah," said Aaron. "I told him I didn't know any Walter, and since I honestly didn't know that was your last name, it was technically true."

"Oh … man," said Wally.

"Creepy dude," said Aaron. "He reminded me of this bill collector who used to come looking for my roommate. I figured he was probably bad news. I hope that was the right thing to do."

"Yeah," said Wally. "Thanks. I'm not sure who that was, but I definitely don't want to talk to him."

Steady. Breathe. Rather than return to his room, Wally stepped out onto the front porch. The air was thick and still, and the street was empty. He looked out at his car. The flood had receded, leaving a streak of mud along the middle of the tires. All around him, everywhere, was the sound of water flowing, running, dripping from the trees and eaves.

Somebody knows my new name.

After months of being Wally Stein, a man with no past, he had let himself believe that no one would ever come looking for him again. He didn't owe anybody money, and nobody owed him. Consequently, he had let himself grow used to feeling like a regular person, with a place to stay, friends, and something to do every day—somebody who was never sought out by anyone.

Well, not so fast, cowboy. How long did you think you could keep this up?

The Fall Tour

"I THINK THIS PROJECT NEEDS ITS OWN ROOM," said Jim Edelstein.

Walter sat at the kitchen table with several stacks of pages and large envelopes, opened and set beside each stack. He was skimming half-heartedly through one enticing letter after another, but his mind was somewhere else. He looked up. "What project?"

"Your college project, of course," said Jim. "How many letters do we have so far? Six?"

"Five," said Walter. Well, they had received six, but one didn't count, as far as Walter was concerned.

Five of the eight colleges he had sent inquiries to last week had already responded. So far, all were "delighted" or "excited" or at least "pleased" that Walter had shown an interest in attending their fine institutions. Of course, he hadn't expressed an interest in any of them. That had been Dad. At mom's insistence, he'd also inquired at KU, but … really?

Stanford, Duke, Princeton, Columbia, and Rice (and, of course, KU) had all responded with various come-on-downs and descriptions of their impeccable programs, glorious traditions, and long histories of producing fine men and women, the leaders and movers of business, government, and science. The grand prize, in Jim's view, was the Massachusetts Institute of Technology, and they had not yet responded. No worries. They would, they all would.

"This is going to get crazy, but we don't want to lose control of it," said Jim, concerned and excited. "We need a central place where everything can be spread out, and we can see the whole pie at once. Every college can get its own spot—brochures, letters from them, and copies of letters we write. This is a complex undertaking, and organization is key."

Walter continued to skim a letter, not responding.

"So … what do you think?" asked Jim. He was annoyed that Walter wasn't infected with the enthusiasm of choosing a college. He should be excited, if not giddy. Typical Walter, but, dammit, this was important. The most crucial decision of his young life. How could Jim make his son see that? Dedicating an entire room of their home to the big decision was a good start. Didn't that convey the gravity of the process?

"Sounds fine to me," said Walter. He opened another letter and read for a moment. He let out a sigh.

"What's wrong?"

"Listen to this," said Walter. "'The men and women of the leadership and faculty of Princeton University are excited that you have expressed an interest in our unparalleled liberal arts programs. Princetonians since colonial days have served humanity and directed the course of world events.'" He looked up. "*Princetonians!* Jesus."

"You know, that's just the way they write, to try to get across the importance of their history. Anyway, Princeton is a great school if you can get in. We have to keep that one on the 'A' list. Anyway, how about the spare bedroom? I think that might be the perfect spot," said Jim.

The room in question wasn't yet a spare bedroom, though that was its designed purpose. Whether the Edelsteins would ever actually have overnight guests was an open question, but so far, the room held only unopened boxes and furniture they weren't sure they wanted to keep. Patty's old twin bed was there, too, because she'd pitched a fit when they moved, demanding an upgrade to a queen size.

Jim walked down the hall to the spare room, surveyed the options, then spent the next twenty minutes stacking boxes out of the way and pushing around the three mismatched tables, forming one long organizational area along the wall. Perfect! There was ample room for the eight candidates, plus a couple more if needed. After they had decided which ones would receive in-person visits, three or maybe four of them, the culls would be pushed aside, and the serious paperwork would be assigned to the largest table. The center position, he had already decided, would be devoted to MIT.

How could he steer Walter in what was obviously the right direction? He was confident Walter would be accepted, and there was a good shot at a decent scholarship if he applied himself and kept his grades up this semester. But Jim knew from years of experience that the worst possible strategy with Walter was to push him, even gently. One of Jim's golf buddies had suggested using mild discouragement to goose Walter's personal pride—not by disparaging the prestigious research university, but by suggesting that perhaps Walter might not be up to the challenge of such a historic institution, which had produced many Nobel laureates (twenty-five, they say—oh my goodness). But reverse psychology wasn't the answer. For the moment, all he could do was help Walter understand what was at stake.

When he was happy with the layout, Jim breezed back up the hallway and through the dining room to the kitchen.

"Okay, I think I have it worked out," he called. "Gather everything up, and we'll …"

Walter was gone. Had he retreated to his room with one of the promotional packages? Nope, they were all there. Jim sighed and set about sorting and carefully stacking the letters and slick brochures himself. KU he placed on the bottom. It might be his wife's alma mater and current employer, but Jim agreed with his son in ruling out that option, even as a "safety." Walter had to aim higher to be true to his upbringing and genetics.

Lately, Dr. Edelstein had been thinking about a certain person, someone he had not given much consideration to in years: the source of the DNA that had produced a brilliant and, until recently, high-achieving son.

He was number D788. There were no recognized standard practices for sperm donation in those days. Some staff at the clinic knew the man's name, certainly, but they weren't saying. That was the man who had come to the rescue of Jim and his young wife. He hadn't donated out of the goodness of his heart—somebody had paid him ten bucks, a nice little bonus for a struggling medical student. But Jim was grateful, nonetheless. Mostly. The situation that necessitated a rescue was his own fault.

As a urologist in the mid-1940s, Jim had treated many young men returning from overseas. A large number of them carried latent or active cases of syphilis or gonorrhea. Even when the diseases were identified and successfully treated—a few rounds of penicillin was all it took—there was often damage to the male reproductive tract. Microscopic scarring in the epididymis or urethra sometimes causes male infertility.

Jim and Wendy were married in 1944 in Salt Lake City, Utah, and conceived a child almost immediately—quite possibly on their wedding night. A few months after Patty was born, in the summer of 1945, Jim noticed swelling in his groin. Since he was a young medical doctor, and it was his specialty, there was no excuse whatever for not letting another doctor look at it. But Jim was also fiercely proud of his own robust health, so he just applied a cold pack in the evenings and took a couple of aspirin, and within a few days, the swelling abated, leaving only a slight soreness in one testicle.

Three weeks later, the pain returned like a fiery demon, and Jim ended up in a Salt Lake City hospital, having emergency surgery at six o'clock in the morning—severe orchitis from a staph infection. It was ridiculous to be laid low by such a pedestrian germ, but there it was. He was lucky that testicles came in pairs. The surgeon told him the remaining one looked undamaged and would compensate for the loss of the other. His recovery was complete, with no lingering discomfort, and he went back to work in a few days.

The next year, Dr. and Mrs. Edelstein and their infant daughter relocated to Kansas, where Jim joined a new clinic as a partner. In what turned out to be an amazingly shrewd move, Jim and three other doctors invested together in a side venture—a Holiday Inn franchise on the east side of Kansas City. Within a few years, the hotel was producing at least half his income.

Wendy finished a degree in economics while raising a toddler. It was quite a challenge, but they could now afford a nanny. They bought a house at a wonderfully low—and locked-in—interest rate. Jim's practice settled into a routine of 10 a.m. to 6 p.m. on weekdays, and Wendy became, for a while, a full-time mom.

When Patricia was potty trained, Wendy and Jim decided it was time for another child, hopefully, a boy who could carry on the family name. At first, they tried to conceive the way many young couples did—by not trying to avoid it. Then, after a few months, Jim began scheduling regular couplings whenever a slight change in body temperature suggested Wendy was ovulating. This went on for over a year, with nothing to show for the effort.

Jim insisted that Wendy be tested first. She saw her family doctor, who referred her to a gynecologist in Kansas City, who poked and looked and felt and then gave the opinion that she was most likely capable of getting pregnant again. Perhaps her husband should have a fertility test.

And so, he did. It was remarkably easy. He just produced a sample, which then went under another doctor's microscope (also out of town because he didn't want to see a doctor he knew).

The first step for the specialist was to estimate the average concentration of viable cells present in a given volume of semen and then assign a number, the "sperm count." After that, other factors would be considered. In Jim's case, it wasn't necessary. There were no sperm cells visible. None. The medical term was azoospermia. He was completely sterile.

When he told Wendy, she was sympathetic, but he knew she was heartbroken. They both wanted another child, but for Wendy, the disappointment was particularly keen because she was an only child herself. It was an emptiness she didn't want for Patty.

They could always adopt. Every day, teenage girls who were "in trouble" were sent away to "visit Aunt Edith" for a few months in another city while attending a "special" school. How important was it, after all, to be biologically related to the child you raised? That was a question Jim couldn't answer, and, anyway, the point was moot. But what about Wendy? She was in the middle of her best procreational years. And she longed to carry another child inside.

When he was first practicing medicine in Utah, Jim had learned about the Teigs Clinic and a doctor who specialized in impregnation with donated sperm.

The procedure was not even legal in every state. While researching his options, Jim read of a Georgia man who had sued his wife for divorce because she had borne the child of a donor. This, despite the fact he had fully supported the insemination. But to the state, the child was "illegitimate," and the divorce was granted.

Jim contacted the Teigs Clinic. They assured him that, although identities were never revealed, the donors were carefully screened for race, genetic disorders, and problematic family histories—cancer, heart disease, diabetes, madness. While he would never know the man's name, they could know *about* him. As far as the law was concerned, the offspring would be 100 percent the Edelsteins's blood child, and no one would ever need to know otherwise.

They talked it over for a few days. Wendy was not just willing—she was excited, thrilled, to have the option open to her again. Jim told his partners he was taking a couple of weeks' vacation, and he drove Wendy back up to Salt Lake City. There, they met D788. Well, they *felt* they had met him after they read so much about him.

Race: Caucasian. Ancestry: German, English, Welsh.

Height: six feet, two inches. Average build.

Eyesight: 20/20.

Hair color: light brown. No signs of androgenic alopecia (inherited baldness).

Additional facts: He was a medical student with exceptional grades. He had played football in college and was an accomplished musician. There was no photograph, but the interviewer had noted his general appearance as "nice looking."

They signed and paid the money. The contract stipulated that they could have up to three months or three attempts to conceive, all for one price. It wasn't necessary. The Teigs Clinic and D788 hit paydirt the first time.

Walter Ryan Edelstein was born in May 1949, on a night when lightning flashed and thunder rumbled across eastern Kansas, and the radio repeatedly warned of funnel clouds.

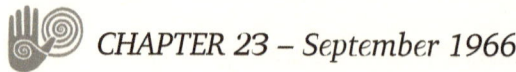

Cities to Live In

DENISE AND HER MOTHER had finished dinner and were clearing the table when the phone rang. Denise was closest to the phone, so she picked up.

"Hey, Girl," he said. It sounded like Walter, but it was so far from his usual calling time that she was disoriented for a moment.

"Uh … hey," she said, hesitating. "Um … Walter?"

"That would be me," he said. "I'm sorry I didn't warn you. Is it okay if we talk?"

"Yeah, sure," she said. Then, holding the phone to her chest, she said, "Mom, can I take this upstairs? I'll help you clean up later."

"Of course, honey," she said.

Denise paused. "It's … just a friend from camp. Could you hang up when I get upstairs?"

Mom smiled slyly as if she and Denise were in on something together. "Sure," she said. "What's his name again?"

"Walter."

Mom took the phone while Denise hurried upstairs. She put the phone to her ear. She could hear soft breathing at the other end.

"Hi, Walter," she said. "I'm Paula Mayberry, Denise's mother. She'll be on the other phone in a second. How are you doing?"

Pause. "Uh … I'm fine," he said.

She wasn't trying to mess with him. She was just curious what he sounded like.

"Well, great," she said. "I hope this call isn't going to break the bank for you."

"I'll keep it pretty short," he said.

Denise picked up the phone upstairs and cut in.

"Okay!" she called loudly, away from the mouthpiece.

Her mom chuckled to herself and hung up.

"Your mom introduced herself," said Walter.

"Oh, god," said Denise. "She didn't have to do that."

"It was okay. I guess she knows all about me, huh?"

"No," said Denise. "She knows you exist. But I didn't tell her any details. Just your name."

"She sounds nice," said Walter. "She doesn't blame me for you getting kicked out of camp?"

"I'm pretty sure she doesn't. I don't think she ever really liked Pursell anyway—a camp for genius kids. She always said I should have a normal childhood, whatever that is. Hey, what's up? Is everything okay?"

"Sure," said Walter. "I just missed talking to you, and I didn't feel like waiting for midnight to roll around. Anyway, since my dad is planning to spend a small fortune sending me to college, a little long-distance bill can't hurt that much. Besides, college is what I want to talk about."

"Okay, good," said Denise.

Really, he didn't want to talk about colleges but rather the cities they were in. Cities he could live in. He started ticking them off one by one. What were the advantages and downsides of each?

Houston? Well, the first thing it had going for it was being far enough away. It was also a big city, but not too big, just enough to get lost in. He'd never been to Texas but heard it was full of roughnecks and cowboys, with a dash of Old South thrown in. Warm winters were a plus, but the summer heat was legendary.

Durham, North Carolina? Probably not. It wasn't out of the question. A small city, but the weather was better, he figured. According to the atlas, it was the heart of tobacco and textile country. It also had a good medical school.

New Jersey? *God*, no. Next.

California? Now, we're talking. Definitely … maybe. Definitely a maybe. Palo Alto is a small town—it's not much more than the university—but it's not too far from San Francisco and San Jose, big population centers with a lot going on. And the brochure made the whole area look like one big, beautiful national park. No winter to speak of, but not too hot either. Put a check mark by that one.

New York? Oh, he could imagine himself in New York. Yes, indeed, he could. It was a place you could get lost in—vanish, even—if you wanted to. If the need ever arose.

Denise and Walter talked for forty-five minutes. Heaven knows what the long-distance bill came to. Prime hours. It was how the phone company made its money.

Denise was applying to a bouquet of colleges with dignified names: Wellesley, Barnard, Bryn Mawr, and Agnes Scott. They sounded more like people, the kind whose name one might drop at a posh party—"I was speaking to Bryn Mawr the other day at the club ..." For sentimental and safety reasons, Denise also applied to the University of New Hampshire. All but the last were top-drawer women's colleges.

"My mom says I'll get in less trouble if I stick with all-female institutions," said Denise. "I don't know why she thinks that. My mom went to Wellesley, and from what she tells me, she got in her share of trouble. Nothing fatal."

"What city do you want to live in?" asked Walter.

"I haven't really thought about it from that point of view," said Denise. "I suppose I should."

"Barnard's in New York."

"I know. It's just a scary thought, living in a city that big, not knowing anybody."

"You'd know me," said Walter.

"So, are you leaning toward Columbia?"

"I might be," he said. "I'm leaning toward New York."

That had never occurred to Denise before, that she and Walter might end up in the same college town, might pick up again what they had barely started, whatever that was. The idea that he might make a crucial life decision based on *her* life decision was contrary to everything she had been taught about crossroads. It seemed ill-advised, at best.

In Denise's family, the story of her older cousin Roxanne was often cited as a life lesson. Roxanne had gone to college in Missouri and found it to be a poor fit. However, despite a miserable, unfulfilling first year, she enrolled for a second— entirely because she had found her first real boyfriend there, and he convinced her that his life would be meaningless without her. Anybody could have told her the punchline—she broke up with him in mid-September, but there she was for another year.

After a month, he started calling and coming around, trying to rekindle their romance, but that ended for good when he was arrested for car theft and booted out of college. The real shocker was that it wasn't youthful impulsiveness or bad choice of company—he stole cars as a weekend job, using his mild demeanor to stay above suspicion as he hot-wired Pontiacs and Chevys in nice parts of town and drove them to a scrap yard to be broken down for parts. He had been doing it the whole time they dated, apparently. It was a harsh lesson. Love is a dangerous thing.

Walter was the boy Denise thought she loved. Most likely. She was fairly sure. And he was suggesting he would follow her, not insisting that she follow him.

Before they hung up, he said a funny thing.

"Have you thought about that thing I said about Europe?"

"You mean taking off and leaving the country? I thought you were just blowing off steam. What's all this talk about going to college been about?"

"It's just an alternate future," said Walter. "It's something I'm keeping open, and you should, too."

"So, you're thinking seriously about it?"

"More than thinking. I'm getting the ball rolling. I'm gonna apply for a passport. And so is my friend David. His life is even more fucked up than mine. He just doesn't realize it yet."

The Good Life

S URE, DAVID HAD RIDDEN A HORSE BEFORE—when he was ten years old at a camp in Missouri. It was run by the Lutheran Church and wasn't really a camp in the usual rustic sense—the "campers" stayed in air-conditioned dorms. During each two-week term, a camper could expect at most an hour and a half of horse-riding instruction, heavily supervised, interspersed with swimming, canoeing, and Bible study. So, the experience of riding on a horse's back wasn't entirely novel. But what an odd feeling—to sit so high with an enormous animal moving and breathing beneath him.

He was on the Charabi property, on a warm, humid day in September, on pastureland next to a small artificial lake shaped like a lazy S, riding a horse called Bumblebee, a mare with a calm temperament suited to an inexperienced rider. Bumblebee was Judith Charabi's favorite mount, but the mistress of the house had not ridden her in close to a year. David didn't have a lot of control over the horse, but Bumblebee was content to follow Lisa's horse, the beautiful rust-red gelding named Osgood. The ride was under control.

Lisa Charabi chattered about her mom and dad and brothers and life on this spacious property, which she explained was named Dulcedo Lake Ranch, while giving David riding tips that he didn't understand.

"My brother Bobby is in New York right now learning to make tons of money— he's with this company that trades stocks and bonds and stuff. He wants his own firm so he can be richer than my dad someday. I can't imagine why. My other brother Seth is the cool one. You'll like him. He's in New York, too, but he's an actor."

She looked back at David, who was passing the reins from one hand to another, gripping the saddle horn with his free hand. "If she balks on you, just give her a little kick in the ribs—not hard—and lean forward. You tell her how fast you want her to go by moving your pelvis forward. That's just a fancy word for butt."

David experimented with several pelvic positions, but they had no discernible effect on Bumblebee. The horse just followed Osgood, sped up when he sped up and slowed when he slowed. No rib kicks were necessary.

Lisa rambled on: "Seth was in an off-Broadway play last year. That means it wasn't one of the famous ones. I wish I could have seen it. He said there were no costumes and no props, just actors, and the script changed every night. Sometimes, they'd even get somebody from the audience up on the stage and make them be in the play, too. It sounds fun but weird. I just wish he'd go out to Hollywood and get into movies. He'd be great. He's really handsome, though not very tall." She watched David ride for a moment. "When you want to turn, turn your head first, then turn your whole body a little bit. That'll let her know to expect a turn."

Clop clop clop clop clop.

Around the east end of the lake they went. Vegetation was thick on the far side, away from the house. Bald cypress trees grew right at the water's edge, with a grove of sycamores claiming the higher ground behind. A narrow clay road turned right, up and away from the lake. Lisa turned Osgood onto the road and up a broad hill, kicking him into a trot. Bumblebee trotted, too, and David clung to the saddle for dear life. They reached the bare top of the hill, and a low stone fence came into view a few hundred feet away. Lisa and Osgood stopped, so Bumblebee stopped.

"Come up and ride beside me," called Lisa.

David pulled the reins left. The horse moved her head left but wouldn't budge. David tried the pelvic turn, but it had no effect. He gave her a slight kick, and she jumped forward, snorting, and David grabbed the horn with both hands. Passing Lisa on the left, he pulled back on the reins and said, "Whoa." Bumblebee stopped and whipped her head around, trying to see what sort of idiot was on her back.

Lisa giggled. "David, you haven't done much riding, have you?"

"It's been a while," he said. "I'm out of practice."

"Do you wanna race up to the gate?" she asked.

"Uh … no … I better not."

She laughed out loud. "I was fooling! I don't want you to break your neck. But let's go to the top of the hill. I'll show you something cool. Stay beside me." She kicked Osgood back to a trot and started up the road toward the distant gate. David's horse fell in behind to her accustomed position, but with some rein tugs and gentle goosing, she moved up beside her stablemate. Lisa extended her left hand out laterally, letting the mare know it was okay.

When they got to the large steel gate, Lisa dismounted and pulled up the latch pin, swinging the fourteen-foot gate open.

"Come on!" she said and beckoned, apparently to the gelding, which walked through the gate. The mare followed, bearing David. Lisa swung the gate shut with a bang, slid back the pin, and remounted.

"What do you want to show me?" asked David.

"It's just up at the top of the hill," said Lisa. "This is our neighbor's property, but they don't mind if we ride on it."

She snicked Osgood into a trot, and David's horse followed. They rode through a stand of conifers, then the road turned steeply uphill, and the horses climbed. The broad, treeless hill was topped with a ridge of pale rock that made a stubby cliff.

Lisa dismounted. "Leave the horses here. I don't want them to hurt themselves. Let's climb up to the top."

David climbed off his horse in what he hoped was a smooth motion, twisting his foot on a clump of grass, and almost fell over. Lisa laughed.

"Do we just leave them here?" David asked. "Shouldn't we tie them to something?"

"Just drop the reins, silly," Lisa said. "Where are they gonna go?"

So David did as instructed, and both horses dropped their heads to graze on the grassy slope. Lisa took off toward the top, and David trudged after her, favoring his sore ankle.

When they reached the short, rocky cliff, Lisa found a break in the limestone outcrop and climbed. She had done this before and was up through the gap in thirty seconds. David caught his breath for a moment, then started to follow, but couldn't find purchase for his left foot. His shoe scraped the rock, kicking loose little avalanches of pebbles.

"Reach up here with your right hand and pull yourself up," said Lisa.

David found a place to grip, then with his shoulder joints stretching painfully and his foot throbbing, managed to pull himself up far enough that he could climb the rest of the way. He sat on the edge of the cliff, out of breath.

Lisa tugged at his shirt. "Come on up here," she said. "You can see the whole thing." She climbed another twenty feet to the highest point of the escarpment, then sat down with her feet dangling over the ledge. David huffed his way up and stood beside her, resting his hands on his knees.

"Now look," she said.

She was right. They could see the whole thing. The double curve of the lake, the pastureland on the other side, the irregular pockets of forest, and, far in the distance, the ranch house, stables, and outbuildings. Beyond that, almost on the horizon, he could see a meander of the Kansas River.

"This place is really big," he said, an obvious comment that didn't match the sight or the moment. As they rested, Lisa's hair whipped in the sharp breeze that was magnified by the cliff face.

Lisa stood up. "We better get back. It's almost time for lunch. We can go swimming later. Maybe tomorrow we can ride down to the river."

"I still have to see your mom," said David.

"Oh, yeah," said Lisa. "That too."

They descended the hill and remounted. David was getting a little better at this—maybe he looked cool on horseback.

So this is what it's like to be rich, he thought.

They rode back across the pasture and through the gate and around the lake to the stables. When he dismounted and handed Bumblebee over to the groom, David hurt in unusual places, especially the bones in his butt right where it met the tops of his thighs, his shoulders, and the ankle he had twisted. He followed Lisa back to the house, walking gingerly.

While the horseback ride had been an unexpected and somewhat fun distraction, David wondered what he was supposed to be doing here at Dulcedo Lake. Nathan Charabi had asked David to come early today, so he'd risen at six, scarfed a bowl of Post Toasties, and driven out through surprisingly heavy Saturday morning traffic to arrive by 9:00. However, nobody seemed in a hurry for his services.

Mr. Charabi was nowhere to be seen. David and Lisa settled on the big couch to wait for Olivia to call them to come to lunch. Lisa turned on the big TV and rotated the channel knob before settling back to watch a program. It was *Bullwinkle*. David had never seen it in color before. Not every show on TV was in color, but all the cartoons were.

Lisa didn't pay much attention to the TV, though. She sat in her accustomed corner on the long couch, facing David.

"Are you coming to Rochester with us next week?" she asked.

"What?" said David. This was new. "Where's Rochester?"

"Minnesota. We're flying there next Sunday. I thought my dad asked you about it when he called you."

"He didn't say anything about it," said David.

"Well, my dad probably said something to your dad. I thought he told you, too. We're going to our house in Minnesota for a few days. It's a pretty place. Not as big as this, but you'd have your own room."

"I don't know," said David. "I have school."

"It would only be for a couple of days while my mom gets her treatment. You wouldn't miss much. I'd miss some school, too, but I hate school anyway."

Olivia walked in. "Youngsters, lunch is ready. It's just sandwiches. Mr. David, I hope you like roast beef."

Lisa hopped up and followed Olivia out. On the television, Rocky the cartoon squirrel was flying through a cartoon sky, the same cartoon cloud going by once per second.

"Young lady, the TV," said Olivia.

Lisa bounded back and switched it off.

Three perfect triangular sandwiches were waiting on three small round dinner plates, with tumblers of iced tea, each one sprouting a sprig of peppermint leaves.

"Is your mom coming to lunch, too?" asked David.

"I don't think so," said Lisa. "She usually just has fruit during the day. But my dad said he's coming."

In addition to the sandwich, each plate had a pickle and a tiny silver dish with some kind of white stuff in it. Maybe mayonnaise, but coarser. Lisa opened her sandwich and slathered the white condiment onto the red meat.

"It's horseradish," said Lisa. "Put a little bit of it on your sandwich. It's hot. The first time I tasted it, I yelled and ran to the sink. But now I like it."

David picked up the little dish and sniffed. It was vinegary and pungent and reminded him of fresh dirt, so he passed on it. The sandwich was perfect—the bread was chewy and the cold meat tender. The plate it had sat upon had the image of a bouquet of flowers turned so that the bouquet was oriented correctly. There was a napkin, so David put it in his lap.

"Hello, daughter and young guest!" It was Nathan Charabi. He breezed in, wearing white cotton slacks and a yellow golf shirt. "I hope you saved me some."

He sat and tucked his own napkin into his shirt and picked up a pickle to take a bite.

"How are you today, David?" he said.

David's mouth was full, so he just tried to smile and nod while chewing.

"I took David out to see the overlook," said Lisa.

"It's pretty up there," said Mr. Charabi. "I hope you didn't lather the horses."

"David rides so slow they didn't even get much exercise," said Lisa.

David swallowed. He wanted to say something, but he couldn't exactly defend his own horsemanship.

Mr. Charabi chewed on his own sandwich. He also ignored the horeseradish. He took a big gulp of iced tea and wiped his mouth.

"David, I asked if you could come out a bit early today because I wanted to discuss something man-to-man."

David swallowed his food and drank some tea to clear his mouth.

"Do I have to leave?" asked Lisa.

Mr. Charabi chuckled. "You can stay, but you're not a man, so you have to keep your mouth shut."

"Daddy!"

"I'm teasing, Lisa! But this does just concern David." He wiped his hands on the napkin and put it on the table. "David, I've never told you about all the doctors and what they're doing for Judith. I'm a real believer in American medicine. I just wanted you to provide an adjunct to her treatment."

"A what?"

"Adjunct. That just means I wanted her to have both—your help with what you can do and the best medical treatment we can give her. And she has been getting better."

"Do you not need me to come out anymore?" asked David, puzzled.

"Oh, heavens no!" said Mr. Charabi. "We still need you. But I wanted to let you know that since school started and you've only been able to come out on Saturdays or Sundays, it seems to me her progress has slowed."

"Sorry," said David.

"It's not your fault, of course. But I did notice that back in August, when you were coming two or three times a week, she was getting out every day and walking around the lake and swimming, too."

"I could try and come after school sometimes," said David. "Unless I have too much homework."

"Well, you are … what … a junior this year?" said Mr. Charabi. "School is very important, and you should be thinking about college. You can't go missing schoolwork. But I've been kicking some ideas around. What if we could somehow … I don't know, *help* you with your studies? It might be a good thing for everybody." He leaned back. "David, have you heard of the DeKalb Academy?"

"Uh … no … I don't think so."

"It's not a school in the usual sense, like your high school. But it does have good teachers, some of the best in the country. They're tutors. They come to you." Mr. Charabi put his fingers together in a peak. "Here's something to think about. I'll be blunt. Why do you suppose that rich kids get the best grades?"

He waited. He expected David to answer.

"I guess … because they have better schools?"

"Some of them do, yes, but the main difference between your run-of-the-mill high school and something like, say, the Perrins school, where Lisa goes, is something else—individualized curricula."

"Indi …?"

Mr. Charabi laughed. "Yeah, I know it's a mouthful. But all it means is that the education is fitted to each student as an individual. Give them the instruction they need where they need it. You see what I'm saying?"

David nodded.

Mr. Charabi continued. "So, each student gets his or her own academic plan. DeKalb does that and goes one better. The teachers work around your schedule. That's how kids who are Hollywood actors get good educations, even if they are shooting a big movie. The teachers work with them one-on-one. DeKalb happens to have a branch in Kansas City."

David wasn't sure what he was supposed to say. Did Mr. Charabi really want him to quit high school?

"Um … I don't think I can just stop going to school …"

"No, no!" said Mr. Charabi. "I wouldn't dream of asking you to leave your high school. But … if you had to miss a day here and there … if you were working with DeKalb tutors … they could help you keep up with your classes. Your grades wouldn't go down at all. If anything, they'd probably go up."

David looked at the China plate, with its perfect watercolor flower. There were crumbs and a smear of grease, which he wanted to wipe off so the plate would be clean again.

"Well … I don't know …"

Mr. Charabi leaned forward again, resting his elbows on the table. "Maybe I'm getting ahead of myself, but I made a couple of phone calls, and there are definitely top-flight tutors at DeKalb who could take you on a couple of days a week. And ... I hope this wasn't too presumptuous of me, but I also talked to a Miss Bishop over at Lawrence High—she's the academic counselor. Do you know her?"

"Uh ... I know who she is."

"She's the person in charge of making sure students are on track to graduate and helps them apply for colleges. Anyway, I spoke to her about your situation, how you might need to be away from school a few days a month. She told me that they could give you a special status so that you don't get counted as absent on those days. Sometimes, they do that for students who have some reason they can't make it to class every day. Usually, they're sick or recovering from surgery or something, but she said your situation would definitely fit the bill. Your teachers would make sure you got all the assignments, and the tutor would know everything about your classes. And they could help you when you needed help, all on your schedule."

David became aware that his mouth was open.

"I guess I'd have to ... think about it ..."

"There's no hurry," said Mr. Charabi. "Talk it over with your parents. Your father says he doesn't see any problems, but it's a big decision, I know."

"Yeah ... I ... I'll talk to them ..."

"No rush, like I said. But there is something I want to toss out to you today. Do you think you could travel with us to Minnesota this weekend? We have a house in Rochester. It's pretty nice. And there's a pool."

"And a hot tub," said Lisa.

"We'd fly out early Sunday and come back Tuesday night," said Mr. Charabi. "Have you ever flown in a private plane before?"

"No." Truthfully, David had never flown in any kind of plane.

"We're not going for pleasure, you know. It's all for Judith. There's a hospital in Rochester where there's a specialist who works with nerve disorders. He wants to try out some new treatments."

"You want me to work with her in the hospital?" asked David.

"She wouldn't be staying in the clinic overnight," said Mr. Charabi. "But she'd be with the doctors all day. You could just relax and swim and see the sights while she's getting her treatment, then you could see her when she comes home in the evening." He was now looking straight at David, eyes boring in. "I'll explain why I would like you to go. The clinic will be running all kinds of tests—some they've done before and some new ones—and this is a chance to see if she's improving.

Anyway, she's had a couple of years' worth of doctors and tests now, and it's all getting a bit old. If you were there, it would help her relax a little bit."

David swallowed. "I'll talk to my mom and dad," he said.

"If you decide you can't come, I'll understand, and so will Judith." He stood up. "Okay, I've talked enough. Think about it and discuss it with your parents. Just let me know as soon as you can."

David thought of one more thing. "Monday is my birthday," he said.

"Were you planning to have a party?" asked Mr. Charabi.

"No," said David. "But I'm turning sixteen. It's a pretty big deal. I can get my real driver's license."

"Then I'll make sure Olivia bakes you her special blueberry cream cake. Now, I have to run, but think about it, David."

"I will."

Mr. Charabi pushed into his chair and left the room. David saw that Olivia had been standing just inside the door silently.

"Are you youngsters finished with lunch?" she asked.

"We sure are," said Lisa.

"It was very good," said David.

"Great," said Olivia. "I'll clear the table. Mr. David, Miss Judith is ready for you."

The Nice Stranger

B Y 9:30 IN THE MORNING, most of Keystone's student residents were already up and out of the house, while the shift workers and shiftless were still asleep. Wally was in the downstairs shower, waking up and thinking about coffee, when he heard a piercing scream. He shut off the water and reached blindly outside the shower stall for his towel. He had not adequately rinsed his hair of shampoo, and soap stung his eyes as he hastily toweled off his head and stuck his head out of the stall to listen. And it came again, a woman's scream, shrill, penetrating, desperate, the cry of someone in mortal distress.

It was coming from upstairs, directly overhead, as far as he could tell. He hopped out of the shower, grabbing his jeans. Skipping his underwear, he pulled on one pant leg, hopped, dripped, water running off his body and onto the bathroom floor. He struggled with the other leg and managed to pull his pants all the way up despite the friction from his wet skin. He sat on the wooden bench where he had placed his sneakers and pulled them on, not bothering with his socks, not tying the laces, and dashed out the door, shirtless.

A sophomore tenant named Robert was coming out of his room.

"What was that?" he asked, wide-eyed.

"I don't know!" said Wally. "Upstairs."

He climbed the stairs quickly, water drops tickling his bare back, with Robert right behind. When he reached the upper hall, all the bedroom doors were closed. He knew the two at the end were rented by students with early classes. The other two were Nixon's room and a single rented by Caryne, a freshman who had moved in mid-semester.

Nixon's bedroom door opened, and there was a girl he didn't know, sleepy-faced with chaotic hair, wearing only a man's size-large T-shirt—Nixon's girlfriend of the moment.

"Is everybody all right?" she said. "I heard a scream!"

That left Caryne's room. Wally banged on the door.

"Hey!" he called. "Are you okay?"

A muffled female voice came from behind the door.

"Yeah ... It's okay."

"Did you scream?"

"Yeah. But it's all right. I'm all right."

"Can you open the door?"

Pause. "Yeah ... Hang on a sec."

He heard rustling from behind the door, then it opened.

Caryne was a small and mousy woman with thick glasses that enlarged her eyes by half. She looked to be fully dressed for class, including a thin yellow sweater and carried a book bag over her shoulder.

"Hi, Wally," she said as if they were casually meeting on the street. "I'm a little late for economics. I gotta try and catch the Temple Street bus."

"What happened?" asked Wally. "Did you scream?"

"Yeah. I'm sorry," she said. "But it's okay now. I thought I lost my wallet, but I found it."

Robert, standing behind Wally, said, "You screamed because you lost your *wallet*? I thought somebody was being fuckin' *killed*."

"No, no," Caryne laughed. "It's okay, really. I couldn't find my wallet, but then I found it. I scream to deal with the stress. It's no big deal. I do that sometimes. Now, I really gotta catch the shuttle bus."

She came out of the room and shut the door behind her, then breezed past Wally and Robert and trotted down the steps.

"Je-SUS!" said Robert. "Wally, you gotta talk to that girl. I thought there was a fuckin' *murder*."

Of course, since Wally was house manager, Robert saw this as Wally's problem. Nobody got the concept of communal living. Wally kept the books, paid the bills, and collected rent. He wasn't their house mother.

"Bring it up at the Monday meeting," Wally started to say, but Robert was already on his way back downstairs. Nixon's girlfriend rolled her eyes and shrugged, then went back in the room. Before she closed the door, Wally got a brief glimpse of Nixon's bare, hairy leg sticking out from under a bedsheet. He had never woken.

Wally went back downstairs. Should he get back in the shower to rinse off the soap and then dry himself properly? Nah. It was too much bother, and he wanted coffee. But he had to get a dry pair of pants, at least, because this one was soaked. He retrieved his underwear and shirt from the bathroom and headed for his room for dry clothes. As he crossed the common room, the door to the courtyard banged open and one of the Mikes—the one who was a law student—came running in.

"I heard a scream!" he said. He had heard it from his bedroom upstairs in the other building.

"It's just Caryne," Wally said. "She misplaced something."

"Huh? ... What?"

Wally waved his hands in a gesture of helplessness and went into his new room to get dressed. Last month, when a resident moved out, Wally had claimed the vacant single room for himself. Beva's boyfriend had decided to be official and pay rent, so he took Wally's space in the double.

It was odd to have his own room again, for the first time in quite a while. It was small, even for a single, larger than Sherry's cave, but not by much. But there were two east-facing windows on the outside wall, and he liked the sunlight in the morning, even after he had worked an evening shift.

He dressed and combed his hair. He was thinning at the crown, and he wondered how his head looked from the back. His maternal grandfather had been bald as a bowling ball, and he worried he might have the ... bad gene. But so far, the hair loss was minor, and he didn't think about it much. What could he do anyway?

There was a tap at the door.

It was Callie. His heart rate picked up a few beats. She managed to look gorgeous even in a man's oversized cotton work shirt. She was holding a piece of toast that was missing one bite.

"Hey, Wally, good morning. Hey, there's a guy out in the front room who says he wants to talk to the house manager."

"Ah, shit," said Wally. "What does he want? We're supposed to get a fire inspection this week."

"No, no," she laughed. "He looks fine. I think he just wants to see the house."

"Okay, thanks," said Wally. "I'll go see him in a couple of minutes. I'm just not ready for the fire inspector."

Callie returned to her room, which was across the hall. She would have it to herself most of the day, as her roommates were both in classes, and she relished the private time.

There was still some coffee left in the large percolator. Wally drew a cup and dabbed in some condensed milk from an open can on the little table. The coffee was a little strong and sour, but that was better than watery. He took a long sip, then headed out to give the usual house tour.

Wally found a man waiting for him in the front room. He looked to be in his mid- to late-twenties, clean-shaven, dressed in well-fitted jeans and a poly-cotton, short-sleeved shirt, with short and neatly parted hair. He carried a small leather bag over his shoulder. Probably a grad student. He smiled broadly when he spotted Wally and extended his hand.

"Hi!" he said.

Wally shook his hand. "I'm Wally Stein, the house manager," he said. "Are you looking for this summer or next fall? We're full up at the moment, but we'll have lots of spots opening in June."

The man laughed softly. "No," he said. "I'm not looking for a room. I just wanted to talk to you for a bit, Wally."

His voice was familiar, but Wally couldn't place it. "Wait. Do I know you?"

The man gave a wide grin. "Yes, you do," he said. "And I know you. In fact, we've had some dealings with each other in the recent past."

Wally peered into his face. The eyes, the slightly bulbous nose, definitely familiar, and the man's voice … wait. No way!

"Nicholas?"

The man laughed out loud. "That's me! And I don't blame you for not recognizing me. I could have told you my name was Fred Friendly, and you'd have believed me."

"Wow … Nicholas. I guess you're out of the hospital."

"Out and about, yes sir," said Nicholas. "Clean, groomed, and medicated. I swear I've talked to three people today that I knew during, well, my bad year, and not one of them knew who I was until I told them."

"I'm afraid Sherry's not here at the moment," said Wally. "She and a work friend went to San Antonio for a couple of days just to get out of town."

"Oh, that's fine," said Nicholas. He looked down. "It's probably for the best, actually. I don't think she's ready to see me, even the new me. I made her life hell, man. I'll never forgive myself for that." He looked around. "Hey, you wanna sit on the porch for a minute? I just want to talk a little bit, and the day is beautiful."

"Sure," said Wally. "You want to get a cup of coffee? There's a little bit left."

"No thanks. I don't do caffeine anymore."

The two men went outside. Wally sat in a plastic chair and Nicholas took the porch swing, washed in a warm swatch of sun.

"So … you doing okay now?" asked Wally. "You all done with the hospital?"

"All done," said Nicholas. "I was the wild man from Borneo for a few days after I got committed—sedated and restrained. But after I settled down and let them help me, I started seeing things differently. And I got the right medicine."

"You're looking good," said Wally.

"Thanks, I feel good. I have been in a psych unit twice before in my life, and this is the first time I actually got something out of it."

"Well, I'm glad they had the meds you needed," said Wally.

"Not just that, the whole program," said Nicholas. "These people take the big view. They help you put your whole life back in balance. Getting enough sleep— and the right kind of sleep—eating good food—I am *done* with meat, by the way. Stuff is just *toxic*. And we learned yoga. Can you believe it? Yoga every morning. Check this out. It's called '*eka pada pranamasana.*' Beautiful name."

Nicholas stood on one foot with the other leg cocked into a triangle, hands together in a prayer pose, and closed his eyes, easily holding the pose without a wobble.

"I'm impressed," said Wally.

"Yep," said Nicholas. "This time, I'm doing it right. I'm getting my body healthy, not just my mind. Sanity is a door you can decide to walk through. And I did. It was my idea to get the shave and haircut. I know it's a cliché, but to be a new person, I want to look like one. But you know what the best part is? Nobody is afraid of me anymore. I can just walk down the street and say 'good morning' to people, and they'll just smile and say it right back."

"That's great," said Wally. "And, really, you should talk to Sherry again. She'd be happy to see you looking so much better."

"I know, and I will see her at some point. I want to do some things first—get my feet under me. I want to approach her as … an equal, you might say. Not somebody who depends on her to keep him in clothes and food." Nicholas looked away thoughtfully, swinging slowly. "Wally, there's two things I need to ask you."

"Okay, shoot," said Wally.

"The first is the easiest, at least for me. I just wanted to say I'm really sorry for all the shit I put you through, and I'm hoping you'll forgive me. And also—thank you for helping Sherry with all the shit I put *her* through."

"You didn't offend me, man," said Wally. "There's nothing to forgive. But if you want, then I do. Consider yourself forgiven."

"Thanks," said Nicholas. "It means more than you think. And … there's one more thing … and I feel really awkward asking this. But … I need a little cash. Just a loan."

"A loan? How much are we talking about?"

"I think forty bucks would do it," said Nicholas. "Here's the story—I actually have some money in a checking account at Riverside S&L. A couple hundred, I think. I just can't get to it because I don't have an ID at the moment. I could get your money back to you in a few days when I get the situation straightened out."

"Why don't you have an ID?" asked Wally.

"The hospital takes all your personal effects when you get committed. The driver's license was in my wallet."

"They didn't give it back when you got out?"

Nicholas bit his lower lip. "Well … Wally, the truth is I was never actually, officially … discharged."

"What? Then …"

"I … checked myself out early. I talked to the administrator, and she made it clear that I had three more weeks of in-house treatment, no matter how well I was doing. I would just have to be patient. That felt like too long to wait. So … I just climbed over the fence after dinner. It was easy. There's an oak tree in the perfect spot on the north lawn, away from the streetlight. Believe me, I'm not the first one to go out that way." He chuckled.

Wally had a hundred twenty dollars cash in a secret spot in his room. It was under the bottom drawer of the old dresser. But …

"I'll totally understand if you can't loan me any money," said Nicholas. "I feel like a dickhead asking."

"I think I can spare you a twenty," said Wally.

"That would really help," said Nicholas. "And it would be just a loan, I promise. I'll get it back to you in a week, tops."

"Okay," said Wally. "Wait here." He got up from his chair.

"One more thing," said Nicholas. "I'm really sorry, but … do you have a belt I can borrow? These pants fit all right, but I feel really stupid walking around without a belt."

"Yeah. I think I have one I never wear. It's a little small, but you're thinner than me."

"Thanks, man."

In a few minutes, Wally returned to the porch with a twenty-dollar bill and an old black belt he had worn as a teenager. Nicholas threaded it through his belt loops, buckled it, then unbuckled and pulled it one notch tighter. He put the folded bill in his back pocket and inhaled deeply, throwing back his shoulders. He started down the steps but turned back around.

"Wait, I almost forgot," he said. "I have something of yours."

Nicholas opened the leather pouch, took out a tiny hardbound book with a blue cover, and handed it to Wally—William Blake's *The Marriage of Heaven and Hell*. "I had it in my pocket when they committed me. They have a rule against hardbacks in the nuthouse, but it was so small they let me keep it. As crazy as Blake is, he helped me find sanity."

Wally took the book, bent and worn from time spent in a back pocket.

"I forgot I owned this one," he said.

"When I was growing up in California, we had a house full of books—books in every room, including the bathroom—and my sisters and I could just grab one anytime. Reading was one of the few privileges we had. When I was going down the hole, it was a habit I kept. I'm sorry."

Wally laughed. "It's okay, really."

"All right, I better go now," said Nicholas. "Thanks for spotting me the loan, and please don't tell Sherry I came by. I'll see her when I get myself better situated. I want to surprise her with how good I'm doing for a change. I'll see you soon, man. I owe you, literally."

He descended the steps and turned down the street, walking at a brisk pace. He bid good morning to an older gentleman walking a small dog. The man returned his greeting warmly.

The Squareback

"How do I look?" asked Callie. She stood straight, shoulders back, chin high. Her long black hair was tied in two braids, and she was wearing a loose-fitting sleeveless dress. She faced Wally for his approval.

"You look fine," he said. "Really fine, actually. Dare I say beautiful?"

"Only if you mean it," she said. "But really, do I look like a woman you would take seriously?"

"You mean if I was a used-car salesman?"

"Any old guy, really," said Callie. "But, yes, a car dealer. Would you want to take advantage of me?"

"I want to take advantage of you right now," said Wally. "But as for car salesmen, they're all scum without exception. But if you wave money at them, they'll take you seriously. You just have to be willing to say, 'I'll keep looking elsewhere, thank you,' and walk out the door."

Wally was about to drive Callie to Tejas Used Cars on the south interstate highway. A few days earlier, she had spotted "the car of her dreams" sitting in the lot, a dark blue Type 3 Squareback, the only Volkswagen on the premises, and decided the time had come to buy her first car.

They were in the room Callie shared with two female students, the only room with a full-length mirror. The look she was trying for was "sexy-serious." She wore a floral sundress that came to her knees but was loose in the chest.

She had tried pairing the dress with cowboy boots, switched to leather sandals, then returned to the boots because they made her taller. She put her hands on her hips, scowled, then put both hands on the top of her head and turned around.

"Can you see my boobs from the side?" she asked.

Indeed, he could when she did that. "Yeah," he said. "What are you trying to do? Sex the guy out so he gives you a better deal?"

"Well, I wouldn't put it that way. But it would be nice if the salesman likes me."

"You offer him money, he'll like you," said Wally. "The trick is to not look like you're in a hurry. Be determined, but let him know you're taking your time making a decision."

"Yes, dear." She opened a drawer and rooted around, then took out a silver star on a leather string and put it around her neck. She inspected the full effect. "Too Earth Mother?"

"More like Indian Maiden," said Wally. "Actually, you do look really nice. Maybe we should go someplace to celebrate afterward."

"I *am* Indian," said Callie. "Half Indian, anyway. The good half. Okay, that will have to do. Let's go. If I get the car, you can buy me lunch because then I'll be poor."

Callie took none of Wally's advice. But she still got her car, and for what she wanted to pay. As she had climbed out of the Maverick, Wally had said, "Take your time. Act like you have all the time in the world. Let the guy show you some other cars, and don't look too eager."

Wally was just repeating sage advice he had been given by others, but she ignored him. When the salesman came out of the office with the usual winning smile, Callie walked with him straight over to the Volkswagen and pointed.

"I like that one," she said. "Can I drive it?"

So, within five minutes of arrival, Callie was buzzing off down the street for a test drive with the corpulent salesman squeezed into the passenger seat. Wally wanted to go along, but the salesman said it was "against insurance regulations," which was horseshit, of course. He was afraid Wally might be the hard-headed husband or boyfriend, and he wanted to work on Callie by himself. As the car pulled away, Wally thought the valves sounded a bit loose. He had no personal experience with air-cooled engines, but he didn't think they were supposed to be *that* loud.

When the little car buzzed back into the lot ten minutes later, the salesman hopped out of the car and hurried into his office, returning a few seconds later with a tape measure. He opened the hatch then measured the cargo space for Callie, who then took the tape from him and measured it herself. He showed her how to lower the rear seats, and they measured the space again.

Wally sat in on the negotiation part of the deal in the salesman's office. This time, the man invited Wally to attend, perhaps hoping he'd provide some masculine reasoning. But Wally just sat in a side chair, sipping a complementary orange soda, and watched Callie smile sweetly, talk softly, and refuse to budge from her offer of five hundred dollars cash—the sticker price on the car was $650. At one point, Callie did employ a tactic Wally had suggested. She looked over at Wally and asked, "Honey, how much was that other little hatchback we looked at yesterday?"

"Uh ... four-fifty," Wally improvised.

"Well ... I suppose I could go for five hundred fifty dollars. Anyway, that's how much I have saved. Otherwise, I'll keep looking."

After some attempts at creating wiggle room, the salesman caved, and the deal was done. Thirty minutes later, Callie was driving a 1968 Volkswagen Type 3 off the lot, with Wally following behind to make sure the little squareback didn't break down on the road. It proved to be a zippy little car, and sometimes Wally had trouble keeping up in his underpowered Ford.

She didn't go straight back to the co-op. She continued south on the highway for a few miles, then exited into an older neighborhood, where she found a specific address: a small house with white gravel instead of a lawn, where a used folding massage table had been advertised for sale in the classifieds. After making sure the measurements of the folded table were what the seller had told her over the phone, thirty more dollars changed hands, and Wally helped her slide the table into the rear compartment of the Volkswagen, above the little air-cooled engine. It fit perfectly, with a few inches to spare. That deal took longer than the car negotiation, not from haggling, but because the fiftyish woman who was selling the table was so affable and chatty. She was a former massage therapist herself and wanted to talk shop with Callie, which they did for half an hour while Wally waited, occasionally looking at his watch. He could have driven himself home, but he had promised her a celebratory lunch.

They found a small café that overlooked the river. The day was warm and beautiful, so they sat at an outside table. They ordered turkey sandwiches and herbal tea.

"So, are you going to quit working at Sandy O's?" asked Wally. "You've got your own wheels *and* a massage table. You can go anywhere."

"I'll stay with Sandy for a little while," said Callie. "She knows I have been thinking of going solo. She even suggested a couple of places where I could rent a small space. But now that I have a car, I don't have to pay for a lease. I'm thinking about running one of those perpetual ads in the campus paper and maybe the city paper, too, if it doesn't cost too much. There's a couple of guys who always ask for me by name at Sandy's."

"Like that crippled guy you told me about?"

"Yeah, like him. He's not completely crippled, but walking is really tough for him, and just getting down to Sandy's is hard. Now I can see him at his house. But Sandy has been so nice to me that I can't quit right away."

Filtered sunlight bathed the café porch. Wally scooted his chair around to get the light out of his eyes and to sit a little closer to Callie. This was the best time of the year in the city, mid-spring. Winter was over, the heat was on its way, but spring days like these were why people lived here.

An older man with short, salt-and-pepper hair came out onto the porch with a drink and a sandwich and selected a table nearby.

"I hope you'll be incredibly careful," said Wally. "If you start driving around the city, you won't have Lee the security guard."

"You could come with me and stand there with a baseball bat," said Callie. "If there's any funny business … WHACK!"

"No, really," said Wally. "I don't want you just driving out to some random guy's house in the suburbs. There are bad people out there. You told me about some of the creeps you get at the massage parlor."

"Please don't say that," said Callie. "A 'massage parlor,' as you call it, is just another word for whorehouse. There are massage parlors in the sleazy parts of town. They stay in business by moving around a lot. A massage therapy studio is licensed and inspected, and the therapists are certified. World of difference."

"I'm sorry," said Wally. "Bad choice of words."

"Wally, I don't mean to sound so defensive, but I've put up with people thinking I'm a glorified prostitute ever since I got my CMP. That after 250 hours of training in anatomy, physiology, kinesiology …"

"I don't know what that is," said Wally.

"It just means knowing how the body moves or is supposed to move. So you don't try moving a body part in some unnatural way."

"Makes sense."

The gray-haired man got up from his table and came over to theirs.

"Excuse me," he said. "Can I borrow that saltshaker? My table doesn't have one."

"Sure," said Wally and handed it to him.

"Gorgeous day, huh?" he said.

"Beautiful," said Callie.

The man returned to his table, opened his sandwich, and sprinkled salt liberally.

Callie finished the last bits of her turkey club and wiped her mouth.

"Back to the sad tale of my career," she said. "Back in Gallop, when I graduated from high school, I interned at a physical therapy clinic for six months, then paid seventy-five dollars for a license. Then I moved to Texas, and the same license cost a hundred bucks. And I have to get recertified every year. The job pays pretty well, but still, it's hard to get ahead. Maybe now I can finally put some money in a real bank. If I can save enough to go to school, I want to get trained in sports medicine."

Wally looked out over the river, where people in rented canoes glided by and families picnicked on the grassy bank. It was a stunning day.

"Do you want to be a doctor?" asked Wally.

"No, not really. I can't imagine how I could ever get into medical school anyway. You have to take a lot of premed courses and then keep perfect grades. No, I just want to try and make a living doing what I'm good at. I never wanted to get rich, just not be hungry."

"Have you ever been hungry, really?"

"Oh yes," said Callie. "We were poor. I remember my grandmother buying cornstarch to eat because it was the cheapest food you could buy."

"Holy shit," said Wally. "I didn't know you could eat cornstarch."

"It's like white sugar—It isn't good for you, but you can stay alive on it. When I was a little kid, I hated the sight of the stuff. It meant we were going through a bad time."

"Back in New Mexico?"

"Arizona," said Callie. "I was born on the Indian reservation. My mom is Navajo. Her given name was Susan Descheeny, and that was the last name on my birth certificate."

"So where did you get 'Pender' from? Is that your dad's name?"

"That was the name of the guy my mom married when I was eight years old, and later we moved to Gallop. I never knew my real dad. He was just some oilman my mom worked for. She got pregnant and had me, and he swore up and down he'd marry her, but he never did. When she got pregnant again, he left before my little sister was born, so we moved back in with my grandmother. That's when we got hungry. Those were the cornstarch days."

"But she finally found a husband, I guess," said Wally.

"Mark Pender was a truck driver. He wasn't home very much, but we had a real house in Gallop. He was not a particularly nice man. He didn't walk out on my mom like the first guy, but he ignored me and my little sister. I hated my Navajo name, so when I went to school, I enrolled as 'Carol Pender' and listed him as my dad. Later, my mom went to the courthouse and made it legal."

Wally checked his watch. "I have to get to work in a little while," he said. "Those physical anthropology books won't unbox themselves." He flexed his shoulder muscles. "Heavy lifting is my life's calling, apparently."

"I'm going to stay here a few minutes," she said. "It's such a pretty day. Though, at some point, I want to open up my new massage table and give it the once-over, clean it, see if anything needs adjusting, and hand wash the head-support pillow. Who knows what nasty faces have drooled on it over the years." She sipped her tea. "Wally, before you leave, tell me something. What *is* your life's calling? Are you going to school at some point? None of my business, but I have a feeling you're not seeking a career in bookstores or co-op management."

"It seems like I'd know what I want to do by now," said Wally. "But I don't." He leaned back and smiled at her. "I know what I *don't* want to do. I don't want to be anybody's personal assistant, be dependent on somebody else's money. I plan to keep my expectations low and my goals simple. I'd like to help people and be useful in the world but never have to do anything I personally think is wrong. I never want to say, 'I'm sorry I did that, but it was my job.'"

"Wow," said Callie. "You and I are more alike than I thought. Have you ever had a job you were ashamed of, like, I don't know, repossessing the cars of poor people or something?"

"No, not really," said Wally. "I did some things I hated doing. But I watched my dad turn himself into a wage slave—kiss the asses of guys who were dumber than he was but had the power. Of course, he did what he had to do because he had a family and people who depended on him. I realize now it's just how the world works. You have to make bad choices sometimes. But at the time, I resented him for it." Wally choked a little, put a napkin over his mouth and coughed. "I'm sorry."

"I'm sorry I brought that up," said Callie.

"It's okay. It was a long time ago. I need to get over it. You can't stay mad forever."

"Sure you can," said Callie. "It's just not good for you. But I've managed to stay mad at a few people in my life."

Wally laughed, then stood up and stretched and pushed his chair in. "Hey, I really do have to go, but I'll see you later on. Are you working tonight?"

"Yeah. I don't look forward to it. I need to let Sandy know I'll be jumping ship in a couple of weeks. She'll be cool with it, but I still feel bad. I'll try and help her find a replacement."

Wally turned, then turned back. "You should get a Volkswagen guy to check your new car. I'm pretty sure your valves are loose."

"Jerry Fox Lewis says he knows Volkswagens. I'll ask him to look at it."

"As long as he's not stoned," said Wally. "A person with brain cells might be a better choice. But it's your car."

He hesitated. *Now? Ah, what the hell.*

He walked around the table and bent to kiss her on the cheek, but she surprised him by turning her head quickly to catch the kiss on her lips. It was quick and chaste, but his heart rate accelerated. He had no follow-up, so he just smiled and patted her on the shoulder. "Bye."

"Wally, sometimes I wish we didn't live in the same house," she said.

"Uh … why?"

"I think you know why," she said. "Now go on. I'll see you tonight."

Wally walked to his car, confused.

Tailing Number Two

H E SEEMS OKAY. *He has a strong voice and a steady gait. Well-developed upper body. A healthy-looking young man in his mid twenties. He's doing fine—has a job and a place to live and a girlfriend. That's all I needed to know, right?*

Dr. Theodore Parsons Hedd had been watching the young man discretely for some time. It was his first chance to observe him close up, evaluate his physical form, listen to his voice. This little café on a beautiful day was the perfect excuse to linger a few feet away, pretending to read a paperback after he had finished his sandwich. There were few people sitting on this outdoor patio, so the restaurant wouldn't shoo him away. But he was done, wasn't he?

Ted didn't want any more of his french fries—he should avoid saturated fats—so he stood up carefully and took his tray to the trash can, tilting the remains of his lunch into the bin. He laid the tray on top, wiped his hands with the last clean napkin, and tossed it in as well.

He wanted to walk away then, check the name off his list, and be done, finally, but he couldn't do that with a clear conscience. For one thing, he was not absolutely certain that the young man having lunch with a pretty Hispanic girl was indeed Walter Edelstein. This was the first good look he'd gotten after three tries.

He'd followed the two from the house on Twenty-First Street miles south to a car dealership, waited half a block away while the girl test-drove, negotiated, and bought a small, boxy used car. He should have spoken to the young man then. There was plenty of opportunity. All it would have taken is a big smile and *Hey, you look familiar. Do you work at University Books?*

But then Ted ended up following both cars to a residential area, where he'd waited an even longer time for them to buy some sort of folding table, and finally to the Mockingbird Riverside Café. What was he waiting for? All his questions but one were answered.

After a few minutes, he decided. *This is ridiculous. Just talk to the guy.* If this man was not, in fact, Walter Edelstein, then Ted had wasted his time. He stood up, making certain he had full balance before taking a step, and walked over to their table. But when he was just a few feet away, the girl had called him Wally, so Ted just asked to borrow the saltshaker. Wally had to be Walter. Almost certainly.

Of course, he could simply have said *Wally. Is that short for Walter? Are you Walter Edelstein, by chance?* Then he would have been a hundred percent sure.

Theodore Hedd, despite his best efforts, he had been known as Ted Hedd his entire life. Throughout childhood, boarding school, the US Navy. For a while during medical school, he tried going by Parsons and signed his name T. Parsons Hedd. But in his first year of residency, his fellow interns found the percussive name cute and irresistible, and that was that.

The young man got up to leave, giving the girl a quick kiss on the lips.

Should I wait a little bit? Then follow? First things first, make absolutely, positively sure this is really the guy. You missed your chance to make it easy.

Ted was in town only a couple more days, and he really wanted to check the young man off his list. To do that, he would have to speak with him, find out about his life, *How's he doing these days? Everything okay?* Nothing in-depth, just the kind of questions you didn't ask a stranger.

The man believed to be Walter Edelstein was gone now, and the dark young woman remained, sipping tea, staring into the distance, smiling softly to herself, lost in her own thoughts. Ted got up, stretched, and twisted. His sciatic nerve tingled, and his quads throbbed, a sign that he should take it slow, avoid any sudden moves.

Aw, what the hell? Just ask the girl.

Ted walked back to the trash and pretended to put something in it, then walked past the girl's table, hesitated, and returned.

"Excuse me," he said.

"Yes?" Her voice was pleasant, not suspicious.

"This is a strange question, but that man you were sitting with, was his name Walter?"

She squinted at him. "Who wants to know?"

"My name's Ted. Just visiting in town for a couple of days. I saw that young man, and it occurred to me that he looks just like the son of an old friend of mine, Jim Edelstein. I haven't seen either one of them in years. But then you called him 'Wally'—I couldn't help overhearing—so it got me wondering if that could be him."

"What's your name again?" Definitely suspicious now.

"Ted ... uh ... Theodore Hedd. Dr. Edelstein was a friend from many years ago, and I knew his son as a teenager. Am I right? Is his last name Edelstein?"

She hesitated with no hint of a smile. "I believe it is. So why didn't you just ask him while he was sitting here?"

"I was going to, but I felt a little embarrassed. He left before I managed to introduce myself. But if his name is Walter Edelstein, that's almost certainly him."

The young woman picked up her teacup and drained the last of the hibiscus.

"Well, when I see Wally, I'll let him know I ran into Theodore ... what was your name again?"

"Hedd, with two 'D's. And yes, some people call me Ted Hedd—the curse my parents gave me, but oh well. Let me give you my card, and maybe he could call me. I'm in town till Thursday. I'd love to see him for a few minutes and catch up, but it's no big deal."

She took the card and examined it. "You're a doctor. From where?"

"St. Louis. I'm in town for a conference over at the university."

She dropped the card into her small purse. "I'll give him the message."

"Thanks. Tell him I'd like to talk to him if he has the time. But it's no big deal. Just a couple of minutes."

Ted smiled and headed for the door. As he headed out through the restaurant interior, he glanced back. She was watching him.

Well, that could have gone better.

When the girl—girlfriend?—told Walter that an old family friend was looking for him, he was not going to recognize the name "Theodore Hedd." That little encounter probably did more harm than good. Walter might avoid him now. All Ted needed was a ten-minute conversation, and he could check this one off his list. Number two, the last of five.

THERE WERE ONLY SUPPOSED TO BE THREE. Maximum. That was not written anywhere, but it had been stated verbally and understood. When Ted finally got ahold of the truth—the actual records—he realized he'd been misled. There were five successful results out of who knows how many attempts. Four of them he had located after years of searching whenever he could find the time. And now that he had probably found the last of them—his second biological offspring out of five—all that remained was to speak to him and confirm it.

Something bothered him, though. When Ted was settled back in his car, he opened his briefcase and removed an envelope with various documents, photos, and a few clippings. He found the yellowed newspaper photograph of a handsome young man with light brown wavy hair and a slightly upturned nose. The caption read, "Walter Edelstein, thirteen-year-old son of Dr. and Mrs. James Edelstein of Lawrence, placed second in the University's Young Artists Competition, held February 6. Walter's rendition of Beethoven's Piano Sonata No. 27 was praised by the judges for its accuracy and spirit."

In the faded photo, young Walter sat at a piano, wearing a suit, head tilted back, and eyes closed as he played. There was very little resemblance to the twenty-five-year-old man that Ted had been discretely watching for the past hour. Longish, jet-black hair, soft black beard, prominent nose. It just didn't fit, even taking into account that a decade had passed. Maybe the guy dyed his hair. Some people change a lot from adolescence to adulthood.

Well, Daniel Chase hadn't looked much like his old photo, either. But then, Daniel, in his twenties was in very different circumstances than the teenager in a bow tie grinning in his school yearbook.

There had been five names in the beginning, and now all of them were associated with real people and faces. Assuming *this* Walter was *that* Walter.

They had all been born between November 1948 and March 1950. Daniel, Walter, Shanda, Belinda, and Joseph. The biological children of Ted Hedd. Donor number D788. It had taken Ted four years to track them all down, using information he was not supposed to have. In doing so, he had potentially exposed the clinic to future lawsuits and put himself in legal jeopardy. He might not have started his quest at all if the first one had not been so easy to find and so unsettling when he did.

Daniel Chase lived in St. Louis, where Dr. Hedd also lived and had his practice, so there was no excuse not to seek him out. Daniel still lived with his parents at the same address they had when they first contracted with the Teigs Clinic for a sperm donor. Ted found him through contacts at Barnes-Jewish Hospital, where the young man was being treated. He accessed Daniel's medical records using a lie. He told the hospital he was collaborating on a paper about heritable neurological conditions. They put him in touch with one of Daniel's doctors, who had been fully cooperative with the supposed research project. Ted was able to verify that Daniel was diagnosed with a rare genetic disorder called Blaine-Fischer disease, and at one point even met the patient.

This was probably a mistake. Since that day, he could never shake the image of the helpless, wasted man in a wheelchair, hollow eyes gazing up because he couldn't raise his head very far. He could still feed himself, but barely. He spoke with great difficulty. With drugs and aggressive physical therapy, said his doctor, Daniel might live ten more years.

Badly shaken, Ted vowed to find the other four whenever they might be.

The second of Ted's progeny, Walter Edelstein of Lawrence, Kansas, was estranged from his family and couldn't be located. He set that one aside and kept searching.

Ted found number three, Shanda Wood, in Provo, Utah. She was happy, independent and showed no symptoms. This made him much more hopeful. Likewise, Belinda Palmer, nee Bell, in Denver, Colorado, was apparently healthy and had three children of her own. He did not ask either of the women to be tested or mention the real reason for his phone calls.

It took Ted almost two more years to find anything on Joseph Coleman. He had lived in Salt Lake City with his parents. There were no medical records for Joseph, no history of hospital stays.

But there was a death certificate. The young man had taken his own life when he was nineteen.

Was he sick? During a very uncomfortable phone call, Joseph's mother told the doctor that she hadn't seen any physical problems in her son, but he had always battled cycles of depression. Whether this was caused by his unfortunate genetic heritage, Ted would never know.

Now, there were more questions than answers. Was this disease exclusive to males? The medical literature was sparse and inconclusive. Ted was more determined than ever to find Walter Edelstein, observe him, persuade him to be tested. On a second call to his parents in Kansas, Walter's mother said she believed her son had moved to Texas, most likely the Austin area. Dr. Hedd was closer than ever to his goal.

Which was … what?

Maybe, when he had enough data, he could write a useful paper, help more doctors spot Blaine-Fischer in its early stages, when it was more treatable. Maybe, through karma, his good-faith journey would help keep his own condition in check.

And maybe, after enough time passed, he'd stop seeing Daniel's eyes in his dreams.

The Milestone

To WENDY EDELSTEIN, David Monk's voice on the phone sounded like Rory Tisdale's. David discovered this fact accidentally when he called the Edelstein's house one afternoon and asked to speak to Walter. Walter's mom called, "Walter, it's your friend Rory," after which Walter answered the phone with "Hey, Rory," and then they both chuckled over the misidentification.

This proved to be useful after Walter was forbidden to have any contact with David. Henceforth, David on the phone would be Rory Tisdale. The real Rory never called anyway, having drifted outside Walter's orbit, but Wendy didn't know that. If she left a message on the little chalkboard that said "W – Rory called," it was immediately understood.

One Saturday morning early in October, David-as-Rory called the Edelstein household. The conversation was short.

"Hey, you wanna go running around?"

"Where to?"

"Doesn't matter," said David. "But I have it now—the holy document, my official License to Kill. It came in the mail yesterday. It says right on it, 'NO RESTRICTIONS.' I can go anywhere with anybody and any number of anybodies. I am free."

"Okay, when?"

"Give me ten minutes. Walk outside to the end of your street, and I'll pick you up."

"Okay," said Walter. "Make it fifteen."

"Cool."

David arrived a few minutes early and made two passes in the baby blue Daytona, circling the block and returning to the same spot three minutes later. On the second drive-by, Walter was waiting and hopped into the front seat.

"Hey," said Walter.

"Hey."

"I have to be back in about an hour," said Walter. "I gotta work on my college essay for Princeton. I told my mom I was going running in the park with Rory. She never even asked why I wasn't wearing running shorts."

"What do you wanna do?"

"I don't know. What do you wanna do?"

"We could go get some beer," said David. "I want to celebrate."

"Who has beer?"

"G and L grocery."

"Oh, you mean go *buy* some beer."

"Unless you have a better idea."

"Okay," said Walter. "You got money? I have two dollars, I think."

"I'll buy," said David.

Strangely, David was the one flush with cash these days. Walter, who was working on Ivy League college applications, was habitually strapped.

G & L Grocery was a small store on the neglected side of town that would sell beer to anyone as long as the store was otherwise empty, which it often was. Nobody could say how long this situation might continue because the store's loose ways had gone from hidden knowledge among a few young hoodlums to one of high school's worst-kept secrets. G & L was now a mandatory first stop for football players headed to parties. Get your beer now before the city fathers get wise.

"Aren't you going out to your private ranch today?" Walter asked. "I thought you went every Saturday."

"Not today. Judith is visiting her mother in Ohio. She'll be back tomorrow, so I'll probably go out for the afternoon. Sunday always takes longer because they usually want me to eat dinner with them. And then they always watch Bonanza, and I usually stay for that."

"Oh, you poor guy," said Walter. "Forced to dine with the rich and then watch a show about rich cowboys. At least there's gunfights."

"I'm pretty tired of it," said David. "It's only a couple of days a week, but it could be any time. That's the worst part. I can't relax. I could get the call any time, and I have to drive out."

"Well, you literally have the easiest job in the world," said Walter. "I don't know what you're complaining about."

"Just want my own life sometimes," said David. The little car bounced over the railroad tracks, and David slowed down, watching for the small, rusty street sign for the forgotten semi-rural street where G & L Grocery hid among mostly empty warehouses.

Underage customers always approached the store from behind. That's what the proprietor, Mr. Leonard, told them to do the first time they were here, testing out whether there was any truth to the rumors. Mr. Leonard explained the protocol: Drive to the street behind, park in front of the now-closed Archer Street Tire Company, walk around the side of the building, come in the front door. If there were any other customers, for instance, a woman buying canned ham and diapers, then you wait and poke around the store and maybe pick up a pack of Slim Jims, and when the coast is clear, you indicate to Mr. Leonard your beverage preference and pay—50 percent pricier than the same beer in a more legitimate establishment. Go out the front door with your Slim Jims, return to your car behind the store, and wait. In a few moments, Mr. Leonard would emerge from the back door with an unmarked paper bag and pass it through the car window. They had pulled this elaborate ruse four times in three months, and it always worked.

It was David who went inside this time. Walter insisted on handing over his two-dollar contribution.

"What do you want?" asked David.

"Schlitz, I guess."

"Schlitz it is."

They were both thinking, but not saying, that if something went wrong, it would be better if David took the heat. Walter was the one applying to MIT, the one who got a 1510 on the SAT, hoping for a merit scholarship and a brilliant future. A tawdry misdemeanor might derail it all. The worst thing that could happen to David is that his parents would be disappointed in him.

Walter waited in the dusty parking lot while his friend disappeared around the corner. David returned in a short time. Too short. He climbed back into the driver's seat and handed Walter's money back to him.

"He says he can't help us right now," said David.

"What? Why?"

"I don't know. He just said he can't sell us any beer right now. He said to come back after dark. There was nobody else in the store. Maybe the cops are watching."

"Ah, man."

No beer today. It wasn't that disappointing because neither one of them had discovered a beer they liked very much anyway. It was just a thing they wanted to do because they could.

They drove back north up Louisiana Street, passing David's high school, where the Lions football team was busy at weekend drills. Early in the season, they were 0 and 2 and had been thoroughly trounced in last night's game, so their punishment was an extra-grueling Saturday practice. David was grateful he had never participated in sports.

"Why do you call that lady Judith?" asked Walter. "Is she, like, a friend of yours?"

"She's really nice," said David. "The whole family is okay, I guess, but the mom treats me like the son she never had. She wants me to call her Judith, so I do."

"I thought they had sons," said Walter.

"Well, the old man does—from his first wife. But they're grown up and gone. Now there's just Lisa. I think Judith wanted to have more kids, but when she got sick, they decided it would be too hard on her body. She might not even survive a pregnancy."

"That sounds really dismal," said Walter. "I guess she must think you actually help her."

"She says I do," said David. "Last week, she got back up on a horse for the first time in over a year. She said it usually hurts too much to sit up straight and get bounced around, but she rode around for half an hour until her husband made her stop. And she's starting to travel again. This weekend, she flew on a plane to Ohio. That's something she couldn't do before. When we flew to Rochester, she had to lie down in this special airplane bed with straps. Sitting in an airplane seat hurt too much."

Walter looked at David and frowned.

"What do you mean 'When we flew to Rochester?' They paid your way to fly with them?"

"Yeah, they took me with them when they flew to Minnesota," said David. "It was not a commercial airliner; it was a private plane. It has room for about ten people and a special bed seat for Judith."

"And you got to go?" said Walter. "Oh my God! You never told me they had their own fucking airplane!"

"I think it belongs to Mr. Charabi's company," said David. "But he's the president and can use it anytime he wants."

"Oh my God," said Walter. "You never mentioned any of this."

"We don't talk much anymore," said David. "Anyway, it wasn't that big of a deal."

"Getting flown on a private jet is a big deal, I think."

"It's not a jet. It has propellers, but it's pretty nice."

"Still … wow. What did they want you to do?"

"Just what I usually do, except I had to hang out all day and watch TV and swim, plus I had a bunch of school shit to do. I worked with Judith in the evening. Just two days, and then we flew back."

"They flew you to another state and put you up in a fancy hotel. Sounds like you're going to the next level. Maybe you'll just work for these people for the rest of your life, be a member of the aristocracy. Sounds like you're set on a path to luxury."

"It wasn't a fancy hotel," said David. "They have a house. And I'm only doing this for another year or so. And if Judith keeps getting better, it will be less and less often."

"Oh, they have a second house," said Walter. "Excuse me. That's very different."

"I really don't want to talk about this stuff," said David. "Come on, I have my fucking driver's license. Let's go *do* something. Find somebody with beer and drink it or somebody with grass and smoke it."

"I really have to head back pretty soon," said Walter. "Listen, I'm not giving you shit. It's just weird to know somebody who's part of the jet set and doesn't want anybody to know."

"It's nobody's business," said David.

Having accomplished nothing but some rare face-to-face and a little conversation, they headed back to Walter's upscale neighborhood. The wind had shifted out of the north, and a hint of chill was in the air. The trees had lost their summer hues as the chlorophyll faded, readying for fall.

"Drop me off in the park," said Walter.

"Okay," said David. "Hey, are you doing anything tonight?"

"We're supposed to have dinner at my dad's club, but I'll be home after eight or eight-thirty. What do you want to do?"

"Henry Friend and his cousin got an apartment, and they're having a housewarming party. We can go back to G & L and score, then go by Henry's and see if there are any girls."

"Who's Henry Friend?"

"He's that guy who … never mind. I guess you never went to school with him. He got kicked out of Lawrence for starting a fire in a bathroom trash can. He's no Einstein, but he has an apartment."

"Where?"

"I don't know exactly. Somewhere south of Nineteenth. If you wanna go, I can give you a ride. Somebody's bound to have some grass."

"I guess," said Walter. "I'll call you when I get home."

David glided the Daytona to a stop at the corner of Parnell Park, near the Edelstein's street.

Walter got out. "See ya."

"See ya."

David looked back over his shoulder to see if any cars were coming. He heard a little thump, and Walter said, "Fuck!" David looked back at the passenger window, but Walter was nowhere to be seen. He heard him again, just outside the car door. "Ah, shit!"

"You okay?" called David.

"Yeah," he heard Walter say, then he stood up into view.

"What happened?"

"I tripped on the curb. Shit! I landed on my fucking hip."

"That was a spazzy thing to do," said David.

"Yep," said Walter. He walked away into the park, rubbing his right hip, limping. David checked his side mirror and pulled away.

SADLY, THERE WERE NEITHER GIRLS NOR GRASS at Henry's apartment. Walter and David did bring a six-pack of beer, which was quickly appropriated and swilled by the dropouts who comprised Henry's pals. After enduring half an hour of cigarette smoke and blasted low-fidelity music, they bailed and headed for the park with their two remaining beers. They parked in the empty lot beside the kids' play area, opened their cans of Schlitz, and sat at the picnic table next to the jungle gym, lit by a single yellow vapor light.

"We have to make plans for next summer," said Walter. "I need to get my passport. And so do you. I heard it takes weeks, so we got to get started."

"I don't see how this is going to work," said David. "We can't get one till we're eighteen without parental consent. Even if I managed it, how do you get your dad or mom to go along?"

"I talked to the guy in the post office. It's not that hard. You don't have to have a parent with you to apply. You just need a birth certificate and a filled-out form with a parental signature. I don't know about you, but I can fake my dad's signature. We can pick up the forms at the post office. He said the most surefire way to do it is to submit the form at a passport office in person, along with ten bucks and an official passport picture. If you're under eighteen, you just show them your birth certificate and social security card. Then you just wait a few weeks, and they mail it to you."

"Won't they at least call your parents and check? A passport is a big deal."

"They won't if you don't act suspicious," said Walter. "Anyway, we can do it at the passport office in KC. I want to get going on this. Let's have our pictures taken this week. There's a place across the street from the university. I think it costs two dollars for two copies. Then, we can get applications and start working on them. Do you know where your birth certificate is?"

"I think I can find it," said David. There was a heavy steel safe in his parents' bedroom closet, which he knew how to open. Just turn the dial to the right and lift the lid. That's where they kept small amounts of household cash, plus various important papers such as their marriage license, car titles, and Dad's honorable discharge from the air force. Nobody ever spun the knob to scramble it, which would seem to blow the point, but Dad had explained the safe was really just there in case of fire. David's birth certificate was almost certainly in there somewhere.

"Mine is in my Dad's office," said Walter. "It's in a file cabinet, but he keeps it locked. They had to take it out when I applied for my driver's license. I just need to pick a time when the file is open so I can grab it and keep it long enough to show the passport people."

"You could just sneak it out and make a Xerox at the drugstore," said David.

"The guy said it has to be the original document. They won't take a copy." Walter sipped his beer and frowned. "I'm going to do this thing and do it right. We need a place to go and a way to get there. I say we set our sights on Spain and pick a month and a day next summer."

"Okay, why Spain?" said David. "Why not someplace that speaks English?"

"Spain is cheap and really cool. That's what Denise says. She's been there twice and went with her cousin last summer. She said there are all these European and American kids who just show up in the off-season when it starts to get hot, and the tourists stay away. There are little hotels and houses to rent by the ocean that cost just a couple of bucks a day. People just hang out and eat cheap food and drink wine and smoke grass right out in the open, and the cops don't mess with you as long as you're being peaceful. And besides, she says everybody does speak English. Anyway, Spanish is easy. I took two years of it, and you took it, right?"

"*No hablo español muy bien*," said David.

"It doesn't matter," said Walter. "Besides, if Denise goes with us, she's fluent, or at least better than we are. Plus, she learned the kind of Spanish they speak in Spain. Castilian."

"Is she thinking seriously about going?" asked David.

"She said she'll go if she can. If it doesn't fuck up getting ready for college—like freshman orientation or something. That's why we need to go as soon as possible after school ends. If Denise goes too, she could get us set up right. She went to a town called Marbella, which she says is amazing. It'll be the coolest thing we've ever done in our lives."

"Okay, let's drink a toast then," said David, raising his beer can. "To Marbella, wherever the fuck that is."

"And to the summit, which we will probably never summit," said Walter.

They thumped their aluminum cans together. Walter drained his beer, turned the can over, and squashed it with a violent slap of his hand.

"OW!" he yelled. He rubbed his hand. "I had a bad angle on that."

David laughed. "That was dumb as fuck. Are you going frat-rat on me?"

"No, I was just trying to squash it so I can throw it away. I should have turned it upside down, maybe ..."

A brilliant light struck them from the side, lighting them up like escapees outside the prison wall.

"What are you boys doing?" It was the commanding voice of authority.

"Nothing," said David, unconvincingly. "Just sitting here talking."

At least it went quickly. The cops had better things to do on a Saturday night than book two juveniles with half a beer and an empty can between them. After some cursory sobriety testing, it was determined that neither boy was intoxicated, and they were made to pour out their remaining beer and follow the police car to the substation by the university, where they had to call their parents. David's parents were disappointed.

Walter's father arrived first. He was just as annoyed with the police as he was with Walter but signed the official warning, agreed to do a better job keeping track of his wayward son, then took Walter home. Dr. Edelstein glared at David as he passed but didn't speak to him.

David's mother came to get him since Dad was working the Saturday closing shift at the sporting goods store. She hugged him in front of everyone, wiped tears from her eyes, signed the release document, and followed him as he drove home. In truth, she was relieved. When the call had come from the police, she had assumed her only son was dead in a mangled heap of smoking metal, his new driver's license in his pocket.

He apologized for worrying her, and nothing more was said about it in the Monk household.

When David got home, there was a note on the pad beside the phone: "Mr. Karabi called. Can you come out Sunday, four o'clock?"

David sighed a little too dramatically.

"I'm sorry you have to do that, Davie," Mom said. She almost never commented about his life as an on-call healer.

"It's okay, Mom. I just wish I could get a Sunday off sometimes."

"I hope you know you really don't have to go all the time," said Mom. "I can speak to your Dad if you want. He should be home in a few minutes. This was always supposed to be on your schedule when you could do it—not all the time. And you certainly shouldn't have to fly across the country on a minute's notice."

"It's really okay."

David tried to find something to watch on TV. He wished they could get the ABC affiliate station like they could on the Charabi's huge color TV. Then he could watch *The Outer Limits*, which wasn't as good as *The Twilight Zone*, but was still pretty good.

Honing the Smarts

DAVID'S FIRST TUTOR, Mr. Catton, came on Mondays, and the second, Miss Blake, came on Fridays. David was surprised the DeKalb people would send two teachers, but that made sense. Mr. Catton tutored Algebra II and science, and Miss Blake taught everything else. Which was mostly English because David was good at history and didn't need help with that or with humanities.

He liked Miss Blake and, at her insistence, called her Ginnie. She was just twenty-six, round and fleshy in a way David found appealing and was pleasant to interact with. Mr. Catton, on the other hand, was a bit of a prig (a word David had picked up from English class). He was just a little older than Ginnie but attempted no congeniality with David. In fact, Mr. Catton always seemed a little bit disappointed in him, like he was being forced to work with a simple boy who needed remedial help with basic life skills. Every question and correction began with an audible sigh.

"[sigh] David, what do you need to do to define the domain of the function?"

"Uh … you mean the domain of 'f'?"

"[sigh] Of *course*."

"Um … figure out what 'x' is?"

"[deep sigh] No. Figure out what 'x' is *not* … *Then* you can find the domain."

David dreaded Mondays. Fortunately, tutoring only lasted two hours at a time. Fridays were no big deal, and he was never in a hurry to get away from Ginnie.

One thing he had not known when he agreed to let the Charabis provide private tutors—all the instruction would be at the ranch house. Though David could go home anytime he wanted, in practice, it meant moving in with the Charabis for the weekend. It was either that or face the highway traffic day and night. David wasn't supposed to be live-in help, but here he was.

They gave him a bedroom upstairs that had belonged to Robert Charabi, the mysterious eldest son. Although he still got on well enough with his family, Robert had severed all ties to Dulcedo Lake and had not, according to Lisa, even visited for the winter holidays in several years. The room David now slept in three nights a week was undecorated and plain, devoid of memories or personality. Seth Charabi's room, on the other hand, had a closet full of clothes, a collection of high school athletic trophies on a shelf, and a bulletin board covered in snapshots, mostly of Seth and his friends camping, skiing, and barhopping,

So now, three months into the school year, David drove out to the ranch house every Friday at 2:30 when school let out. At 4 p.m. on the nose, Ginnie met him in a small downstairs library, and they sat at a dark oaken table and went over his assignments for the week. She was in regular communication with his English teacher, and so David often knew of upcoming assignments even before they had been announced in class.

David had written an essay about an Edgar Allen Poe short story from 1840 called "Man of The Crowd." The story was in a thick book with Bible-thin pages called *The American Renaissance.* David sat across the table and tried to read other Poe short stories while Ginnie whooshed through his essay with a red pencil. She got to the end of the second page, wrote a couple of notes, and looked up.

"David, this is a decent essay. I have a couple of comments, but I am *so impressed* that you typed it."

David had impressed himself with this feat. He had taken Introductory Typing the previous spring semester, drilling to master the "home row" method on a clunky Underwood with a sticky comma key. This was the first time he'd used a typewriter on any kind of official assignment. He did it specifically because he thought it would please Ginnie. He wrote the essay in longhand first, of course. The first page and much of the second had been typed home row style, but toward the end, he had grown tired of erasing and correcting the smudgy typing paper and completed the project using the hunt-and-peck method.

She handed the two sheets back to him.

"I'll give you some free advice that I promise will get you better grades the rest of your academic career—type everything, even little two-paragraph summaries. Even notes requesting extra time to complete a paper. It will be a chore at first, then it will come naturally, and you'll have a leg up for college. College papers have to be typed anyway. I paid my undergrad tuition by typing papers for other students who couldn't type and refused to learn. Oh, and don't use erasable typing paper."

"Why not?"

"Because it smears and gets all over everything," she said. "Teachers hate it, and it's hard to write on."

"But then, how do I fix mistakes?"

"Boldly," she said. "Strike through them with X's and charge forward. Especially when it's your first draft, later you can go back and make a good copy."

Ginnie began critiquing the Poe essay point by point, while David let it sink in that there was no going back from the typewriter. He'd have to type every paper from here on out twice. The idea made him tired. At least he had a new Smith-Corona Coronet Electric portable—a gift from his parents on his sixteenth birthday. Fast and loud with no sticky keys, little physical force required. When you got going, typing could be an act of joyous violence, like firing a light machine gun.

David experienced a wide, insuppressible yawn. He had stayed up late last night for no good reason, trying to bring in distant radio stations on his little AM radio. He did that on too many nights when he should have been resting.

Ginnie paused. "We're almost done."

"I'm sorry," David said. "I haven't been sleeping very well."

"You're a teenager," she said. "You're not supposed to sleep well. Your biological rhythm is changing."

"At least I can sleep in a little bit tomorrow. Unless I drive home tonight. I'm supposed to see Judith at 9 o'clock in the morning. If I start from home, then I have to be up by six."

Ginnie looked at him curiously. "This is none of my business," she said. "But what exactly do you do for the lady of the house?"

David was reluctant to go into it, but Ginnie had asked him so nicely.

"I help her with her fibromyalgia," he said. "It's just something I can do. And if I help her early in the morning, she says it makes her whole day better."

"Is it a kind of massage?"

"Kind of. But I don't touch her. I just hold my hand real close. I know it sounds stupid."

She seemed to be waiting for further explanation, but David looked down at his essay. He saw her comment on the last page.

"What do you mean here when you say, 'What is his motive?'" he asked.

"I meant that you haven't tried to explain why the mysterious man walks all over the city."

"Poe doesn't say."

"Yes, but there are a lot of possible reasons, and he leaves it up to the reader to figure it out. Since it's your essay, you should suggest a couple of reasons."

"It's already 500 words. That was what the teacher wanted."

"Maybe, but add a couple of sentences about why you think the wandering man wanders around—is he looking for something?"

"No," said David. "He just becomes more alive when he's out with humanity. He's like—I don't know—a blood cell flowing through a vein, along with all the other cells."

"Exactly," said Ginnie. "I like it. Say that. Just a couple of sentences in the fourth paragraph."

"Then I'll have to retype it again."

"Yes, you will. You would, anyway. Might as well make it better every time."

They talked a little more—about his upcoming history project on the nineteenth-century labor movement, about whether he and another student should make an eight-millimeter movie for humanities class, about what he wanted from college, where he would certainly end up.

The official time was up, but Ginnie never hurried away. At 6:20, they were still chatting when Olivia tapped on the door and opened it.

"Mr. David, if your lesson is done, supper's ready."

"We're done," said Ginnie. "David, I'll see you … wait … not next week, but two weeks from today, same time."

"Why not next week," asked David.

"Mr. Charabi said you'll be out of town."

"Oh," he said. "They didn't tell me." His heart sank.

"Have a great weekend," she said and walked away, leaving a nice fresh-grass scent in the air. David wondered if it was a subtle perfume, or just the vapors from her skin and breath.

In the small dining room, Lisa was there with a friend from school, a girl named Charlotte, who never raised her voice beyond a whisper if anyone but Lisa was present. Nathan Charabi was there in his usual knit golf shirt.

"What's for dinner, Olivia?" he asked cheerfully, though David suspected he already knew.

"Pizza pie, Mr. Nathan," said Olivia. She was the only person David knew who called it by that old-fashioned term, but she did it very well, with lots of spicy sausage bits and white cheese.

She emerged from the kitchen with the large and perfectly round pizza, already cut into even wedges and a bowl of salad with bright orange carrots.

Mr. Charabi said, "Guests get served first in this house, Charlotte," and held out his hand for her plate. "How many?"

Charlotte mumbled a reply.

"Two slices it is," said Mr. Charabi. He used a spatula to load her plate, then handed it back. He then served Lisa but let David get his own pizza. It seemed he who was no longer a guest, but a member of the household. Maybe that was the point.

The girls talked quietly, with Mr. Charabi politely interjecting a few questions about how Charlotte was enjoying school this year. In a few moments, he turned to David.

"I meant to bring something up," he said. "Judith and I will be going to Minnesota this next Thursday, and she really hopes you can come along."

"I guess I could," said David.

"That would be excellent."

Lisa chimed in. "I'm going to stay at Charlotte's house."

"Hmmm," said Mr. Charabi. "Did you ask her mom if it's okay?"

Charlotte muttered something accompanied by a nod.

"Well, then," said Mr. Charabi. "If it's okay with your mom, too, I guess you can do it. But your homework still has to get done. You girls can't make it a slumber party weekend."

David chewed the pizza, unmatched in crunch and flavor by any pizzeria he'd ever tried.

"David, I truly do appreciate your help," said Mr. Charabi. "Maybe this is speaking out of school, but Miss Judith is going in for some very special testing on Friday. We're not getting our hopes up too much, but the doctors there are very eager to try a new treatment that could make a big difference. She's very nervous, and having you close by will mean a lot to her."

"What are you telling these kids?" It was Judith standing in the entranceway. "We need to keep things in the family." She didn't sound mad. "Did you leave me any pizza?"

"Two slices with your name on 'em," said Mr. Charabi. "And really, dear, we've known Miss Charlotte so long, she's *practically* family."

Charlotte leaned over to Lisa and whispered something inaudible. Lisa burst out laughing.

"I know! I know!" she said.

Extra Pressure on David

THE MAYO CLINIC WAS NOT ONE PLACE but a complex of adjoining and separate buildings spread out over several square blocks in downtown Rochester. David had supposed this trip would be like the last one: He would stay at the Charabi's second home and try to noodle with his schoolwork when Mr. Charabi took Judith in for treatment. But this time, Mr. Charabi asked David to ride along with them to the hospital to "help Judith during the process." He didn't know what that meant.

Mr. Charabi sat up front with the driver while David rode in back with Judith. There was a fold-down table latched into the up position, leaving so much legroom in the backseat he could have done push-ups on the floorboard.

As they rode into town, Judith was silent. David didn't know why. As far as he could tell, she was doing better than at any time since he'd met her. Her mobility was decent. She swam every day and had even ridden her horse, Bumblebee, a couple of times. But today, she just stared out the window while Mr. Charabi chatted with the limo driver about college football.

They passed a building with a long facade that had MAYO CLINIC in giant letters. The car didn't stop there but continued a couple of blocks farther, turned right, then suddenly turned and plunged down a ramp into an underground garage. The limo stopped right in front of a row of brightly lit glass doors, and within seconds, two male attendants came out, one of them pushing a wheelchair. The limo driver opened the car door, and Judith stepped out carefully and sat in the wheelchair, though she could walk perfectly well on her own.

"It's hospital rules," said Mr. Charabi. "Every patient has to ride in a wheelchair going in or out."

The attendants pushed Judith through the door, across a low-ceilinged foyer, and into a waiting elevator. David started to follow, but Mr. Charabi held him back.

"You and I are going a different way, David," he said. "We're going up to the second floor."

Across the hall from the first bank of elevators was another pair of elevators, and David and Mr. Charabi rode one of these up to a larger public room that was teaming with visitors and staff.

"Should I wait here?" asked David.

"No, we've got our own private waiting room. There's a TV there and some tables as well, in case you need to study."

David hadn't brought his schoolbooks, so he lounged on a couch and watched game shows on a TV bolted to the wall. There was a telephone on a small side table next to the couch, and Mr. Charabi made a series of calls that all sounded remarkably similar.

"Hi, Michael," he'd say. "How are things in Detroit? You boys been getting a lot of rain? Tell me some good news." Then he'd mostly listen and make a couple of one- or two-word comments and sometimes write a small note on a leather-covered notebook he carried everywhere. After that call, there was another, and another after that, with only the name, place, and weather condition changing:

"Hey, Boris, how are things in New York? Is it finally cooling off up there? Tell me some good news."

David watched a little TV and, at one point, wandered out the door and down the hall to find the restroom. Many people were in the corridors—patients, visitors, doctors, and hospital staff, but nobody ever came into the little waiting room where David bided his time, and Mr. Charabi made business calls. He found a public bathroom in a far corner of the building. It smelled of solvents and bubble gum.

When he returned to the private waiting room, Mr. Charabi had the phone cradled on his ear, on hold.

"Were you looking for something to eat? There's a decent snack bar on the first floor, right across from the elevator."

"I just had to find the restroom," said David.

"Oh," said Mr. Charabi. "We have our own bathroom right there." He gestured at a closed, unmarked door on an inside wall. "I should have told you." He then popped the receiver close to his mouth. "Paul!" he said. "How are things in San Diego, my friend? Is the weather as perfect as ever? I know, but I think a little cold wind now and again keeps us honest … Yeah, I know. Ok, tell me some good news."

On TV, there was some inane game show called *Supermarket Sweep* where competing teams raced around in shopping carts, accompanied by much whooping and screaming. Since Mr. Charabi had not so much as glanced at the TV since they'd come in, David felt he had the right to change the channel. He didn't know if this was allowed, but there was no one to tell him otherwise. He clicked the dial a couple of notches. On another channel was a rerun of *Candid Camera*. Not classy entertainment, but an improvement. He settled back to watch.

A male nurse or intern came in while Mr. Charabi was in the middle of a call and stood to the side deferentially. Mr. Charabi held up one finger, awaiting an opening in his phone conversation.

"Barry ... hey, I apologize, but could you hold that thought for a second?" He covered up the receiver with one hand, and the attendant leaned over and whispered something to him. Mr. Charabi nodded and said quietly, "We'll be down in two minutes." The man left quickly, and Mr. Charabi came back to his phone call. "Barry, hey. Sorry about that. I'm going to have to let you go. We'll talk this afternoon. Bye."

He rose and stretched. "David, you and I are required below deck."

Inside the elevator, Mr. Charabi pushed a button marked SB2, and they descended. The doors opened to a long, brightly lit hall. There were no patients to be seen down here and no doctors or nurses either. They went through one pair of double doors and, fifty feet farther, another pair. They stopped in front of these, and Mr. Charabi pushed a red button on the wall. In a few moments, the doors opened with a *whoosh*. On the other side, a doctor was waiting for them, an older man with reddish-brown hair and a gray beard. He extended his hand.

"Nathan! Good to see you again." They shook hands.

"Dr. Bland," said Mr. Charabi, "This is my young friend David."

The doctor took David's hand in a firm squeeze. "Good to meet you, David. I'm Hershel Bland. Did Nathan explain what we'd be asking you to do today?"

"I thought I'd leave the details up to you," said Mr. Charabi.

"All right," said the doctor. "David, are you familiar with how hyperbaric treatment works?"

"Uh ... I don't know what that is," said David.

"Basically, it's an oxygen treatment. We have the patient inside a little room where the air pressure is raised, and the percentage of oxygen is higher. That way, their body receives more oxygen than it would normally. Even more than if they were breathing pure oxygen through a mask."

"Is it for Mrs. Charabi?"

"That's right," said Dr. Bland. "As you already know, I'm sure, she has been suffering from a nerve disorder. We've had a lot of good results using hyperbaric therapy on other patients with similar conditions, and today, we're going to try it with her."

Mr. Charabi cut in. "David, have you heard about those chambers they put deep-sea divers in after they've been in really deep water? If they bring them up too fast, they can get a condition called 'the bends,' but the pressurized tank keeps that from happening."

"I've heard of that," said David. "Are you going to put her in a tank?"

"More like a little round room than a tank," said Dr. Bland. "Come on, I'll show you."

He led the way down a short hall. Along one wall, there were a dozen large cylinders and one enormous sign in bright red letters:

NO SMOKING

At the end of the hall was a red door with a sign that said Automatic Lock – Ring Bell. Dr. Bland pushed the button.

"I'll show you the beast," he said. "Mrs. Charabi is already here."

There were two loud clicks, and the door swung open. A man in blue hospital attire, dark-skinned with arrestingly dark eyes, stood aside to let them in.

"David, this is Dr. Patel," said Dr. Bland. "He will be operating the machine."

"Hi," said David.

"Hello."

The hyperbaric chamber was enormous, taking up half the room. It was cylindrical, at least ten feet across, and over twenty feet long. An oval-shaped, heavy door on one side stood open.

David had no idea why he was there. He didn't see Judith. Mr. Charabi went to the open door of the chamber and stuck his head inside.

"Hey babe!" he said. "Are you holding up all right?" His voice resonated.

"I'm fine," Judith's voice echoed weakly from inside.

"David, come have a look," said Mr. Charabi.

Inside the chamber, the floor was raised and leveled. A hospital bed was there, with the back in the upright position, and upon the bed lay Judith. She was holding a *Town & Country* magazine, and the flat fluorescent lights inside the chamber made her look pale. She wore a white hospital gown. Without makeup, colorful clothes, luxurious houses, and furnishings, she just looked sick. She smiled at him softly.

Dr. Patel said, "David, we'll get started soon, but first, I need to explain how this works."

David turned to face the doctors. What were they up to, and what did it have to do with him?

"First, let me just reassure you," said Dr. Patel. "The hyperbaric chamber is absolutely safe. It's been used a million times since it was invented, and no one has ever been harmed."

Why were they telling him this? He tried to swallow dry spit.

"Yes, it's completely safe," said Dr. Bland. "The only thing that could possibly go wrong is for the machine to lose pressure. With the safeguards that are built in, it's nearly impossible and has never happened even once in my career, but if it did, we would just pressure it back up again, and everything would be fine. David, what we want you to do is just treat Mrs. Charabi the way you normally do when you work with her. Pretend you're just back at home. You just happen to be in a strange round room." He chuckled.

David suddenly got it. They wanted him to get into the machine with Judith. He had assumed he'd just be standing by until the process was over. His heart thumped hard, and he felt dizzy.

"The treatment will take two hours. It goes like this: twenty minutes to reach full target atmosphere. While we're raising the atmospheric pressure, you'll notice a sensation in your ears, but all you have to do is yawn and swallow, and your ears will clear. You might have to do this several times. You also might feel a little light-headed at first, but that feeling should go away in a minute or so. There's a chair for you to sit in. We'll keep the chamber at pressure for one hour, then reduce back to normal, which will take forty minutes. The pressure on your ears will happen again, but the cure is the same. Yawn and swallow. Do either of you have any questions?"

David felt a wave of nausea, and his head swam. He's never been particularly claustrophobic, but the big metal submarine frightened him. He didn't want to admit that. He just wanted to back out. Was that even an option? He swallowed again and breathed through his mouth. He couldn't think of a question other than *Do I really have to do this? Is this really my job now?*

Mr. Charabi supplied a question. "Is there some kind of microphone inside so they can communicate with us?" David suspected that Mr. Charabi already knew the answer.

"Of course," said Dr. Patel. "Any questions or comments we can hear, and you can hear us."

The machine swooshed, David yawned, and his ears popped clear. The maneuver helped for a few seconds, and he had to do it again over and over. Inside the chamber, it was quiet except for the continuous sound of airflow.

Propped up in the bed, wires extending from a band around her head, Judith sat with her eyes closed. She didn't yawn but kept moving her jaw, open, shut, open, shut. The only thing she'd said to him, as the door was sealed shut and air started flowing, was, "I'm sorry, David. This wasn't my idea."

He sat in the standard kind of guest chair you find in any hospital room. It was square and straight-backed and was out of place in a room that looked like a spaceship. His head had cleared, but his whole body felt lighter. He was glad they had made him pee before the whole thing started.

Judith pushed a button on a hand controller, and the bed lowered to the flat position. Slowly, in a series of small motions, she rolled herself over onto her stomach. It was more difficult than usual because of the wires that extended from the plastic band attached to her head. The two long wires extended from the band to two of several plugs on a black electrical panel. She removed the pillow and placed it on the floor. After settling herself in with little twists of her body, she lay still.

"I'm ready," she said.

David yawned and popped his ears one last time, then moved in. He couldn't see anyone else, but he knew they were watching. Judith responded best when he started at her head and moved down to her lower spine and buttocks. He stood and raised his right hand, as always, and placed it an inch from the top of her head, trying to clear his thoughts and waiting for the tingling in his solar plexus that meant he had connected with her.

But nothing happened. He removed his hand and walked around to the head of the bed to try again. Maybe the headband and wires were interfering somehow, blocking access to the nerves that descended through the back of her head. He started again, closer to her neck, and this time, he did feel the nerve energy, but it was muted, buried.

He thought maybe he could work from the other side of the table but then realized he'd have to step over the red and blue wires that connected the headset to the panel. It was so much harder than usual that he wanted to stop and call it a day, but they were watching him and expecting him to do his best. Having no choice and wanting it to end, he did his best.

He swept his hand from side to side, closer to her body than usual, locating pain when he could see it, sweeping it up and away. He moved down her body to the upper thighs, then back up again and down again. Sometimes, he thought he could detect her life energy—see its muted colors—but often, it felt as if there were no one there, like ministering to a practice dummy. And she seemed more unbalanced than usual, with all the wrongness and disorder clustered on her left side.

When he worked with Judith, David usually did three full passes along her body, but since nothing was working right today, he performed the whole routine five times. He had no idea if it was doing anything for her.

After some time, he realized she was asleep. He folded his hands and sat back in the chair. Not quite an hour had passed. He needed to pee, but not desperately. He picked up Judith's copy of *Town & Country* and thumbed through it.

David closed his eyes, and his thoughts drifted. *There has to be a plan, a way for this all to end.* He wanted to help Judith, didn't mind helping most of the time, and sometimes felt he was doing some good and it gave his life purpose. His family needed the money. Much of it would go toward his college education and the hope of having his own life. But that seemed so impossibly far away, a future life, future independence. His own place. A girlfriend. A job he didn't hate. Not being a freak of nature anymore.

Maybe Walter is right. Just get on a plane. Go to Spain for a summer. Maybe longer.

He'd heard of people taking a year off before college. Well, this could be his, except it would be a year off from high school. Or just drop out, be one of those kids that the news magazines worried about, a vagabond. Be rid of obligations, live in a cheap place with a beach. A place where there was nobody to tell you it was your duty to give back, that you owed the world your special gift. Maybe he wouldn't come back for a year, two years. Maybe never …

"We are starting the depressurization now." It was Dr. Patel's voice, brittle and sterile through the intercom.

SWHOOOOSH … SWHOOOOSH …

Judith stirred, rolled over carefully onto her back, and then pushed the button to raise the bed into the sitting position. David picked up the pillow and slipped it beneath her head.

"I'm sorry I couldn't help very much," he said.

"No, no, you always help," said Judith. "This is just not the best circumstance. I'm sorry we made you do this."

Nathan Charabi stayed the whole time, though there was nothing for him to do. Dr. Bland had excused himself during the long depressurization to get some work done in his office. Dr. Patel looked over the read-out from the hyperbaric machine, a roll of paper almost twelve feet long with intersecting lines, waves, and squiggles.

"She was having trouble relaxing," he said. "But in the end, she fell asleep."

"I'm sure she'll get more used to it," said Mr. Charabi. "I don't think I could relax inside that big thing."

"I'm sure she will." He returned to the long scroll, making a few notes with a red pencil. Then he looked up again. "Mr. Charabi …"

"Call me Nathan, please."

"Sure, Nathan. Here's the thing. I'm a technician, but I'm also a medical doctor. I care about my patients, even if I don't work with them day-to-day. I have to be honest about what I think is best for them and their treatment."

"Of course," said Mr. Charabi.

Dr. Patel made sure the microphone switch was off. "It's that young man. I really don't think he should be in there during treatments."

"Well, I understand, I think," said Mr. Charabi. "Frankly, it was because my wife finds him comforting. I didn't think it would hurt anything."

"I know. Dr. Bland explained that she was particularly nervous about this treatment." He leaned close. "It's important that she be able to relax. But having the boy in the hyperbaric chamber just isn't appropriate. For one thing, it's a factor we can't control for, and we will have a hard time determining if the treatment is doing any good on its own."

"I suppose you're right," said Mr. Charabi. "I'll explain to her that having David with her is messing with your results. She'll understand. He'll still be waiting for her when she gets out of the chamber."

"That's good. But, Nathan, since I'm being straight with you, it would be wrong not to say what I think. I know this big 'integrative medicine' thing is all the rage these days among the new residents. Call me old school, but from my point of view, having a mystic healer working with a patient is no different from having a witch doctor."

"That's a little too harsh. I wouldn't say he is a mystic. David is reassuring for Judith. And who am I to say that it's just all hooey? Frankly, who are you to say that? I've watched her get better this summer. I've seen hints of her old self ..."

"I'm the first to admit that positive thinking and a belief that something can help is good for patients, no matter what their condition. But in the end, I truly believe that boy and his hand waving is just a placebo—an elaborate, and in your case expensive, sugar pill. What he does may appear to work, but the effect will wear off with time. Invariably. It always does. And probably sooner than later." Dr. Patel unrolled the scroll. "Let me show you something."

Mr. Charabi leaned over to look, but the graph meant nothing to him.

"We had sensors attached in three places—one on her scalp and two more on her chest and stomach. I watched the boy work and kept an eye on the meters. I noted a few times when his hand was close to one of the sensors. Such as right here." He indicated a pencil mark on the chart. "There was no electromagnetic response. Nothing the machine could detect anyway."

"Well, I don't know how much a sensor could pick up ..."

"Nathan, these things measure in nanovolts. These little movements in the line are just random little electrical noise it picks up inside the tank—which is very well shielded. If there was anything else real going on—anything at all—we'd see it. But no. No response whatsoever."

Nathan sighed. "Maybe you're right. I just don't know."

A series of three beeps and then a steady tone came from the chamber's control panel, and a green light came on. Dr. Patel touched the microphone button. "All right, folks. We're done. You're back to normal pressure. I'm going to release the door now."

Ta-SHUNK

 *CHAPTER 31 – May 1975*

New Love and Automotive Convenience

WALLY REGARDED CALLIE'S BARE STOMACH in the morning light.

"You're not all that dark, really," he said.

"Well, not in the places where the sun don't shine," Callie laughed. "What did you expect?"

"Your face is Indian," he said. "I just assumed you'd be Indian all over."

"I'm a half-breed," she laughed. "My dad was German-Irish. I don't remember him, but my mother said he had freckles on the top of his head."

A shaft of sunlight sliced through the crack between the curtains and the window, making a sharp knife of light across Callie's stomach and chest. Wally traced the tips of his fingers down her chin, across her neck, and over her collarbone to the top of her right breast, where the skin color shifted toward the pale in an even gradient over an inch or so, except for her nipples, which were a rich chocolate brown. Her torso was light, the tiny light-brown hairs almost invisible. He kissed her above the navel, then lay on his back beside her.

"Come here," she said, rolling onto her side. He raised his arm, and she pulled herself closer to him, draped one long leg across his, and snuggled close. She put one hand on Wally's chest, which was on the hairy side, but otherwise, his body was pale as clean desert bone. The shaft of sunlight lay across both of them. The room was growing warmer.

"Wait, I'll get the curtain," Callie said. She rolled to the left and reached the curtain, tugging it shut so it stayed in place.

"The sun don't shine here, either," said Wally, as he caressed her right buttock.

Callie laughed and swatted his hand away, then rolled back onto him, put one hand beside his head, and pulled him close. He expected a kiss on the cheek, but instead, she bit him softly.

"Ow!" he said.

"That was for calling me an Indian," she said. "You can call me native American or an Amerindian, if you insist, or Navajo-Apache, but *Indian* I am not. I've never been anywhere near India."

Wally chuckled, then held her gently and shut his eyes. The moment must last.

Never sleep with a housemate. That was an unspoken rule of co-op living. Many a free-love commune had disintegrated into jealous bickering because of the basic human instinct to pair up exclusively. Oh well, too late now. He turned his head and kissed her hair.

"Let's just stick around today and do nothing," he said. "I don't have plans." It was Sunday, and he had no bookstore shift. There were always house manager duties, but nothing that couldn't wait. The house was only half full for the summer.

"Sorry, I have a client at one o'clock," said Callie. "He's all the way up on Fifty-first Street. I have to allow time to get dressed and load the table into the car."

Wally looked at his wrist, realized he wasn't wearing his watch, then fished around blindly on the side table until he found it. *A quarter past noon. Ah, man.* He had hoped for another leisurely coupling. *Ah, well.*

"Do you need help with the table?"

"No, no. I can handle it. But I do need to start getting dressed," said Callie. She rolled out of Wally's bed, pulled on her underwear and jeans, and started rooting around on the floor, looking for something. "Where's my T-shirt?" she said.

"You spilled wine on it last night, remember?" said Wally. "You washed it out in the sink. It's probably still in the bathroom."

"Oh, right," she said. "I forgot." She hopped up and opened the sticky top drawer of Wally's battered old dresser and took out one of his shirts. "I'm gonna borrow this." It was a man's large T-shirt with a faded portrait of three long-haired rockers and the legend "CREAM - Royal Albert Hall." Little holes were forming on the edges of the letters. The old shirt was losing the war with washing machines, but it was a classic, so Wally kept it. Callie pulled the shirt over her head and went out the door and back to her own room. She failed to shut the door all the way, and after she was gone, the door slowly opened itself, obeying the law of gravity in the old, out-of-level house until it hung wide. Wally could get up naked and push it shut again, but she was coming back in a few minutes anyway. He closed his eyes and dozed.

What a night! Callie wasn't working late shifts anymore, so her evenings had freed up. Rather than dine on end-of-week leftovers, Callie and Wally had walked together to a little fried chicken place near campus. The food was cheap, oily, and starchy, and they came away with over-full stomachs and grease burps. Not an auspicious start, but they had walked off the heavy meal for an hour, sometimes holding hands. They ended up in a city park beside a creek that gushed from spring rains, sitting on a wooden bench, watching the dusk settle over the city. There, Wally kissed Callie and told her he loved her. She had kissed him back and said she loved him, too.

Okay, everybody at Keystone House had known these two would get together sooner or later. It was obvious there would be a hookup. It happened all the time in college and its periphery.

But this must not be that—not just a few giddy weeks followed by a couple of unremarkable months, followed by a breakup after a pointless spat, a misunderstanding, a minor betrayal, or just boredom.

Not this time. No, Wally had found Callie, recognized her as a kindred spirit, and now that connection must be nurtured and tilled. It had only been a few weeks and then a breathtaking liftoff of a night. He cared for her, and she for him. He didn't have to be cautious around her, careful about what he told her, guarded and circumspect. He could be genuine and honest, an open book. Honest.

Except …

She didn't really know him. If love starts with truth, then this could not be love. *She doesn't even know my real name.*

Callie returned from her room, dressed in a tasteful loose blouse and knee-length skirt. She breezed into the room, tossed the Cream T-shirt back in the top drawer, then leaned over and planted a wet kiss right on his mouth.

"All right, Wally, I'll be back about three-thirty or four," she said. "Maybe we can go swimming at the springs. It's a hot day."

"Swimming sounds fun," he said. He had a fleeting thought. What if he added *Oh, and by the way, my name isn't actually Wally. Have a great day, and drive carefully!*

Callie left, and this time, she shut the door all the way. Wally lay still for a few moments. His stomach snarled—time to get up and see what was left over and still edible in the reefer.

He dressed and was tying his shoes when the door opened again. It was Callie, lips pursed and head down.

"Wally, I screwed up," she said. "Can you help me? I'm in trouble."

"What is it? Need help with the table?"

"No. Look." She held up her key ring, which had a few keys of unknown purpose, a tiny screwdriver, and a little pewter pendant of St. Christopher. He didn't see anything unusual.

"What am I supposed to be looking at?" he asked.

"This," she said and held the keys closer. "See?" She held a little disk of metal between her fingers. It was the wide end of a car key. "The key broke off in the ignition. What do I do? I have a spare key, but I can't use it with the hole plugged up, and the broken one won't come out."

"I'll take a look," said Wally.

The long end of the Volkswagen key was hopelessly embedded in the ignition switch. Wally sat in the driver's seat and tried to get a grip on the slippery metal with his fingertips, but there wasn't enough exposed key to get purchase. *Maybe Mike has a pair of needle-nosed pliers,* he thought.

"It was sticky and wasn't turning," said Callie. "I got frustrated and turned it real hard, and … *POP.* What do I do, Wally? I have to get out to Hyde Park. This is a regular client who can't come see me."

"I can give you a ride," said Wally. "But let me fool with it a minute." He examined the ignition switch. He wiggled the wings of the lock back and forth, then pushed in and rotated the switch. The starter cranked, and the engine came to life, its loose valves clacking.

"What did you do?" she asked.

"The key is in place," he said. "Just push in and turn the whole switch."

"Well, that's nice to know now," said Callie. "Can I still drive it?"

"Sure. Of course, anybody else can, too."

"Then I better get going." She sat in the front seat, turned off the engine, and then started it again. "It works! Thanks for helping, Wally. You know, I might just leave it like this. If I ever need to lock it, I can use the other key, but I don't think I will because I'm not going to leave the massage table in the car anyway. Actually, it will be pretty convenient."

"Just don't tell anybody," said Wally.

"It'll be our little secret," said Callie. "Thanks." She slipped the car into gear and drove away, the little air-cooled engine humming happily.

Hexosaminidase Subunit Alpha

THE KEYSTONE MAILBOX WAS A WOODEN GRID constructed many years ago by a resident, probably in exchange for a month of free rent, but no one remembered. It was four rows tall by eight slots wide, with thirty small cubbies and one big one—for general/junk mail. That was more than the absolute capacity of the house, but it allowed former residents a place to receive mail for at least a little while after they moved out until somebody else needed the slot. The mailbox was painted blue, with scratch marks that revealed an earlier beige color beneath. Residents' names were written on painter's masking tape above each slot. Sorting the mail was a shared job, which meant it was neglected a lot, and mail often piled up on the table, unsorted until somebody—usually Sherry or Wally—tackled the pile.

Wally got mail in his slot every day because all mail addressed to "House Manager," "House President," or, hilariously, "House Mother" was diverted to him.

Somebody, probably Sherry, had already sorted today's delivery pile. Along with the usual bills and solicitations, there was a folded piece of notebook paper with Walter Edelstein written in pencil. When Wally unfolded it, a business card dropped out. It was identical to the card Callie had shown him a few weeks earlier, the one from the odd man at the restaurant.

The note said: "Please call me at your earliest convenience. I'm staying at the Riverside Hilton. I just need a few minutes of your time. It concerns your family in Kansas." There was a local phone number. The note was signed "Dr. Theodore Hedd."

He went to Callie's room and knocked. Her roommate Lynne answered. She was the only other occupant of the triple room because of the light summer load.

"She's out in the laundry room," Lynne said.

"Okay. Thanks."

Callie was folding clothes on the long table next to the dryer.

"Hey, what's up?"

Wally held up the paper and the business card. "Ted Hedd left a note. He wants to see me."

"That creepy guy from the café? So, he's back. Does he say why?"

Wally handed her the paper. Callie read it and frowned.

"Are you going to call him?" she asked.

"Why should I?" said Wally. "I don't know this guy. I've never heard of him."

"Maybe he knows your parents. You said you were from Kansas. Are your parents still there? You never talk about them."

"They're not in Kansas."

"How about brothers or sisters? Grandparents?"

"I was an only child, and my grandparents died when I was little. I have no family left."

"Well, maybe Ted Hedd is wrong," said Callie. "He might be looking for someone else. It wouldn't hurt to call him, would it?"

Wally took the note back.

"I guess not," he said. "But I don't want to do it right now. I'll probably have time this afternoon. Hey, maybe we can hang out tonight. Maybe go hear some music at The Well."

Callie folded a towel, put it on top of a neat stack of four, then folded another. "I'll have to see how my afternoon goes," she said. "I have two paying clients." She picked up the even stack of towels and placed it carefully inside a cracked plastic laundry basket. Then she started folding socks. Wally turned to leave.

"Hey, wait," said Callie. "You know, it doesn't have to be bad news. Maybe it's your parents or some relative you don't know. They could just be trying to reach you or extend an olive branch, or whatever. Heck, maybe a rich uncle left you money."

Wally chuckled. "I don't think so."

"Call him just to get him off your back, if nothing else. Maybe it's a good thing. You don't know."

"You're right. I don't know what he wants, but it can't be good. No good things come out of Kansas. Not for me."

The note with the phone number and the finely etched business card stayed in Wally's pocket until he forgot about it. But then, in the late afternoon, he wondered if he had ordered too much milk from the food co-op, considering there were just fifteen summer residents compared to the regular full load. He thought, *Maybe I better call them and cut it back to six gallons* when he glanced over at the phone and thought: *Oh shit. That guy I'm supposed to call.*

The telephone in the large common room had a lock on the dial, opened with what looked like a handcuff key. This was to prevent outsiders and street dwellers from walking in the front door and using the phone. One bearded and sunburned young man had been found on the phone long distance to Ohio, twenty minutes into a call with his sister. It took five minutes of continuous cajoling before he finally shouted, "I'm done, okay? Are you happy now?" and hung up. However, everybody hated the phone lock, and some took to leaving the key in the lock or the lock off the phone.

The phone was locked this afternoon, but Wally knew where the little key hung just inside the kitchen door. He retrieved it, hesitated, then took the notebook paper out of his pocket and unfolded it. He briefly hoped the phone number would be illegible, but it was written in pencil and impervious to sweat.

Callie would probably be back from her latest mobile masseuse gig within the next half hour. He didn't want her asking, *Did you call Ted Hedd?*

He unlocked the phone lock, placed it on the table with its leather string dangling, and dialed.

Ted Hedd picked up immediately.

"This is Dr. Hedd."

"Hi, I'm … Wally … You left a note in my mailbox."

"Uh, hi. Yeah. Wally, just to make sure I'm talking to the right guy, your full name is Walter Ryan Edelstein, right?"

" … That's right."

"I'll call you Wally if that's what you prefer."

"That's what people call me."

There was a pause as if Dr. Hedd were consulting notes. Then he came back on.

"Wally, I apologize sincerely for just coming at you out of the blue, but I really needed to get in touch."

"Why?"

"It … it has to do with your family back in Kansas."

Wally paused and swallowed. "I am not in contact with my family," he said.

"I understand," said Dr. Hedd. "Things happen, and it's not my business. I actually … contacted your father … and he told me he had no idea where you are.

I'll tell you right now—it was not a pleasant conversation. He told me in no uncertain terms he wanted nothing to do with me, but he did say you might have moved to Texas. That was it. So, with a little detective work, I found you."

"You hired a *detective*?"

"No, no. It was really very simple. When I was in town a couple of months back, I went to the Department of Motor Vehicles and looked through the records of all the people who received a Texas driver's license in the past two years—it's an open record, but there are thousands and thousands of them. I got lucky and found Walter Ryan Edelstein in just a couple of hours of searching. The name and birthday were right, so I knew it was you."

Walter moved the phone to the other side of the table so he could sit on the end of the old couch.

"Okay, Mr. ... Dr. Hedd. You found me. What do you want?"

"I have to tell you about some medical issues that may ... possibly may ... affect your health ... now or in the future. It's a complicated story, but ..."

"My health?"

"That's right, it concerns your ... heritage. Umm ... Listen, Wally, it's something that would be a hundred times easier to explain in person. Can we meet somewhere, either later today or tomorrow? I could come to your house or swing by and pick you up."

Walter paused because two male residents were walking through the common room. One of them spotted Wally and came over to him.

"Wally, I'm sorry to interrupt, but can I ask you a question real fast?"

"What?" Wally covered up the phone's mouthpiece.

"I'm scheduled for bathroom cleanup downstairs today, but I just got put on the night shift at the library. I can't do it. There's no way."

"Then *trade* with somebody," said Wally. "You know how this works."

"Okay. I was just hoping you could suggest somebody."

"Try Justin. Or Mike Spencer, or maybe Mike Ware. Or Nixon. Or maybe that new girl."

"Okay." He went away, disappointed that Wally hadn't said the bathroom doesn't matter anyway and not to worry about it.

Wally looked at his watch.

"Dr. Hedd, I'm sorry. Do you know where B & A Steakhouse is, on Neches Street? Neches at about Eighteenth. I can be there in about thirty minutes."

"I'll meet you there," said Dr. Hedd. "Thanks, Wally. It's really important."

A few minutes later, Wally was still sitting on the tattered couch in the common room when Callie came through the front door. She was frowning but brightened when she saw him.

"Wally, can you do me a huge favor," she said. "I had to park on Twenty-Second. There are a lot of cars parked on the street today."

"It's orientation week," said Wally.

"Oh," said Callie. "Anyway, can you help me with the table? I can manage it, but it's a long haul for my delicate body."

"Sure," said Wally. "Maybe you could do me a favor if you have time."

"Of course," said Callie. "What do you need?"

"Moral support," he said.

WALLY DIDN'T REMEMBER what Ted Hedd looked like, but Callie did. They ordered iced teas and a plate of french fries to share. The fries had just landed on the table steaming hot when the mysterious doctor came into the restaurant.

He was wearing a jacket and tie despite the sticky summer heat, and his clothes hung loose on his thin frame. He scanned the room, which was dark compared to the brightness of the street, and he didn't see them. He started to take a seat at the counter.

"That's him," said Callie. "Shouldn't we wave?"

So, Wally waved, just a little hey-there gesture. Hedd spotted them and came over.

"Mind if I sit?" he asked.

"Sure," said Wally.

"I'm Dr. Theodor Hedd, as you probably guessed." He offered his hand, which Wally took. It was damp and bony, with long fingers.

"I'm Wally," said Wally. "This is Callie."

"I'm his friend," said Callie.

Hedd shook her hand as well.

The waitress came over and asked him if he wanted anything. He said iced tea. Uncomfortable silence.

"You can have some fries if you want," said Wally.

"Thanks."

He took one and ate it, then opened the folder, which held a couple of sheets of photocopied paper.

"Uh … Wally … I have to let you know this is pretty personal stuff." He nodded in Callie's direction.

"I can leave," said Callie.

"No," said Wally. "She can stay. I don't keep anything from her."

"Very well," said Dr. Hedd. "This could relate to you in the future if you two should ever decide to …" He tugged at his tie and looked around the room.

"Get married?" suggested Callie.

"Yeah, that's what I meant," said Dr. Hedd.

"We're not there yet," said Callie.

"That's fine," said Dr. Hedd. "Walter … I mean Wally … I assume you're aware of the circumstances of your birth."

"You mean that my mother got pregnant with a sperm donor? Yes, I know. It's not a secret."

"That's right. Your parents used the Teigs Clinic in Salt Lake City."

"Okay," said Wally.

"Well, I worked there for a year in the late '40s. I was still in medical school. Anyway, that was back when Dr. Teigs was still alive. I knew him personally. An amazing, dedicated professional. He really believed in his mission—helping couples who couldn't have children on their own. He also believed in the right to privacy, so all records were closely kept. The donors were assigned a number, and they never knew how, or even whether, their … donation was utilized. Everything was anonymous. Overall, we … they … had many great successes."

"So, there's no way anybody could find out who their actual father was," said Wally.

"That's true," said Dr. Hedd. "Almost true."

"So what does this have to do with you?" asked Wally.

"Well, let me tell you a little about me," said Dr. Hedd. He ate another fry. "When I got out of medical school, I went the usual internship route and worked at a couple of different hospitals in Utah and then in Missouri. I wanted to be a general surgeon. But after a few years, I decided to go into internal medicine instead. So that's what I did and what I still do."

"So what does that have to do with me?" asked Wally.

"I'm getting to that. You see, I was in my late twenties when I started my surgical residency, but there was a problem. A surgeon has to have dead-steady hands, and I had a tendency to … shake a little bit under pressure. I thought it was just that I needed more practice, but instead of getting better over time, it got worse. Finally, I had to admit that surgery was just not in the cards, so I changed my specialty. I was successful, but my hands bothered me so much I went to see a neurologist. In fact, I saw a few of them over the years. Nobody could find anything physically wrong with me. They kept referring me to psychiatrists. But finally, somebody hit the right diagnosis—I had something called Blaine-Fischer disease. It's very rare. It's caused by an enzyme—or rather not enough of a particular enzyme—and it was causing the nerves in my hands and other places to slowly degenerate. Fortunately, it's treatable. But it's not curable."

"Wow," said Wally.

"I'm sorry," said Callie. "You seem okay now."

"I take two different drugs every day, morning and night. They don't cure the disease, but they do slow down the nerve degradation. It also helps that I do special exercises every day. I'm forty-eight, and I have a full-time medical practice."

Wally had a bad feeling about where this was going.

"Does … Blaine disease run in families?"

"Yes," said Dr. Hedd. "Blaine-Fischer. If the offspring inherits the gene from both parents, it's always fatal, usually in childhood. But if only one parent has the mutation, it's what we call an autosomal dominant gene, which means symptoms can start showing up in your twenties or thirties or even later. Some carriers never develop the disease at all."

"But you did," said Wally. "Your dad had the bad gene, and now *you* have it."

"It was my mother, I think. She died in a traffic accident when she was thirty-five, but she had complained of weakness in her legs. My father is still alive. He has health issues, but he's not sick."

Wally looked at Callie. He could tell she was thinking the same thing.

"So … are you …?"

"Your biological father, I believe, yes."

"But I don't have any of that stuff," said Wally. "I'm not sick."

"That's great," said Dr. Hedd. "But I still think you should get tested. It's called a HEXA enzyme test. I can tell you where you can go. Any one of the major hospitals here can test for it."

Callie asked the looming question. "So … if the files are secret, how did you find out about Wally?"

"After the diagnosis, I went back to the clinic," said Dr. Hedd. "I was friends with the records clerk when I worked there, and she was still there four years ago. I told her my situation, and she agreed to pull the files for me unofficially. It was all very questionable, ethically, but there was no other way to find out what I needed to know."

"So that's how you got my name?" said Wally. "How did the clinic even know?"

"They always follow up with all their clients," said Dr. Hedd. "If a baby is conceived and born, it's in the record. If a name is known, that goes into the record, too. I found you there, along with your birthdate."

"Were there other babies?" asked Callie.

Dr. Hedd swallowed. "Yes … But I can't talk about that." The waitress brought a glass of iced tea for the doctor. He opened two paper packs of sugar one at a time and stirred them in. "Wally, you weren't the only one. But you are the last one. It's taken me years, but now I've done all I can do."

"How many more were there?" asked Wally.

"I really can't disclose that."

"Are some of them sick?"

"I can't tell you that either. I can just tell you that you should get tested."

Wally looked down, silent. Then he scooted his chair back. "Maybe I'll do that," he said. "But right now, I have things to do and places to be. Thank you for letting me know. Have a good day." He extended his hand.

Dr. Hedd took Wally's hand but gripped it for a moment.

"Wally, this is really important. Please get tested. If you're positive for the disease but don't show any symptoms yet, you can start doing things now to mitigate the effects. You could live out a full life, one that's mostly normal."

Wally looked the doctor straight in the eye. "I appreciate what you're trying to do. But I have my own life, and I need to get on with it." He let go of the doctor's hand and stood up. "Let's get going, Callie. I have some business to attend to."

"Wait," said Dr. Hedd. "Please take this. I brought it for you." He started to remove a sheet of paper from the manila folder, then just handed him the folder.

"What's this?"

"It's a medical order from me requesting a HEXA test. Any fully equipped, reputable hospital will honor it. Please get this done. I don't know what it will cost, but contact me at the number on my card, and I'll reimburse the full amount."

Wally took the folder. "All right. I'll think about it."

"Please," said Dr. Hedd. "It took me a long time to find you. This is my attempt to make up for a mistake. It's the best I can do. I've already told you more than I've ever told anyone. I violated all kinds of confidentiality standards. And ... okay, I also probably broke the law. But I owed you the truth."

Wally gestured to Callie, and she followed him to the cashier, where he paid for three iced teas and a plate of french fries. He glanced back at Dr. Hedd, who remained at the table, crestfallen.

"I'm not your problem," said Wally. "You can stop worrying about me. And I'm not your son."

"Of course, you're not," said Dr. Hedd. "You're the son of the people who raised you. I'm just trying ..."

But Wally and Callie were out the door and down the street.

Hanukkah with the Master

AVID FINISHED THE FALL SEMESTER of 1966 with straight A's, though he just squeaked through with an 89.8 in algebra, and the teacher rounded up to an A-minus. Much as David loathed and feared his tutor, Mr. Catton, the man had succeeded in drilling the mathematical concepts into David's reluctant brain and improved his skills sharply.

He stayed with the Charabis every weekend, grew accustomed to the deep, comfortable queen-size bed and having his own bathroom. Delicious meals served to him on a precise schedule, and a pool he could use whenever time and weather permitted. He had a key to the side door of the house, the servant's entrance, and let himself in and out as he pleased.

Typically, he drove out to the Charabi's place early on Friday to treat Judith during the afternoon—give her a few more treatments over the weekend. He would return home before dinner on Monday afternoons. There were weeks when he only caught glimpses of his father.

The fall semester ended December 9, a Friday, so he attended classes that day because it seemed like the right thing to do. Even though there were several official and impromptu Christmas parties that night at various friends' houses, and he really missed his friends, David had promised Judith he would be there for her on Friday by suppertime. His tutor, Ginnie, would not be at the Charabi house today and would not return until the new semester started in January. He would miss her. He would not miss Mr. Catton.

So, on Friday morning, David put his overnight bag into the back seat of the Daytona before he left for school and headed straight for Dulcedo Lake Ranch as soon as classes let out.

For the previous week, decorators had been at work inside the Charabi house and in the pool area, stringing up lights and menorahs for Hanukkah. On Saturday morning, when David went out to the pool for a swim—the air was quite chilly, but the heated pool steamed invitingly—the large doors from the family room stood propped wide open, and two men were slowly maneuvering the big white grand piano outside onto the patio.

Nathan stood by in a big woolly turtleneck sweater, observing the operation, smoking his morning pipe. He saw David's inquisitive look.

"We're having a party next Friday night," he said. "It's a family tradition that we've had to skip the past two years because of Judith's health. We're determined to do it this year. My only worry is the piano, tuning it up and keeping it covered and out here all week. The weather is supposed to be good until the first of the year, but around here, who can say? It will be covered and under the awning, but heavy rain would be a real problem. Anyway, this is the only time I could get these guys."

"Is this for Hanukkah?" asked David.

Nathan laughed. "Not exactly. Hanukkah ends Thursday. Friday is the six-teenth, which is Beethoven's birthday. Judith and I met on the sixteenth at a concert in Boston. So, we started celebrating Beethoven Day as a sort of anniversary. I know you probably think we're crazy, but it's something we love doing, and it's always fun."

The piano movers were struggling to turn the grand just the right way so its massive body could slip through the gap. Nathan went to speak with them and gestured with his pipe. They pulled the piano partway back into the room, rotated it a few degrees, and then slowly rolled it out again, clearing the door frame by a few inches.

Nathan returned to where David was shivering in his bathrobe, not sure if he should risk an errant splash from the pool.

"By the way, this party is very casual," he said. "We'll have a few of Judith's friends plus her sister's family and some of my old friends from the city. Lisa will have a few of her pals from school here, too. We're hoping you will come, and bring a friend or two if you want. If the weather cooperates, we'll use the pool." Nathan became distracted by the piano movers again, who slowly rotated the beast into position under the porch awning and began drawing a heavy canvas covering over it.

"A really fine pianist is coming out for the party—Bobby Steiner," said Nathan. "He has played on every continent except Antarctica, and Friday night, he'll be here just for us. He'll play some Beethoven, of course, but the man can literally do any-thing—show tunes, barrelhouse, rock and roll—and he takes requests. Incredible musician. It will be a great time." He glanced at the piano movers, frowned, and went to talk to them again.

David walked in his cold bare feet to the edge of the pool, which steamed in the morning sunlight. He wanted to jump in and warm his body immediately, but he carefully draped his robe over a chair and gently slipped into the embracing water. When he was swimming in the warm pool, he didn't feel like an impostor, a fake member of the elite.

David returned home Sunday night. It was so strange to be there. His mom was delighted to have him and spent the week hauling Christmas decorations up from the basement and sorting them out. Uncharacteristically, she had spent money on a luxury item—a new iron hearth insert for the old fireplace to replace the old rusty one. A huge and heavy box was delivered by truck on Monday, and it sat in the living room, taking up space until Wednesday when Dad had a day off.

He enlisted David, and together they unscrewed and removed the old plain iron hearth and grate, then spent much of the afternoon reading confusing instructions and banging together the new decorative hearth and adjusting it to fit the space between the bricks.

When it was finished, it was a sight to behold. The hearth raised the level of the fire by several inches, and iron panels extended a foot beyond the fireplace on each side. They were adorned with cherubim and seraphim, playing trumpets and lutes. Mom had intended that they would drag this ungainly Baroque thing out only at Christmastime, but once it was installed, Dad said there it is, and there it stays.

They lugged the pieces of the old iron fire grate down the basement stairs, where they jammed them against the wall beside the old, belching gas furnace. It was a tight fit, but with both of them shoving hard, they did it. David wondered why Dad didn't just sell the old thing as scrap iron.

As preposterous as the new hearth was, Mom loved it and spent the week decorating the living room. At night, they opened the chimney flue and burned oak logs, even though winter had not really settled in yet. David had not seen her so happy in quite a while. Well, the family's financial situation had improved, and it was partly his doing.

Without much going on, the week dragged by. David watched a lot of TV. He missed the big color Curtis Mathis.

On Friday, David went to the Hanukkah/Beethoven party and invited Walter. He wasn't sure his old friend would even want to go since nobody he knew would be there, but Walter was also feeling trapped at home by the holidays. His sister Patty had the right idea and took off to spend Christmas with college friends in Florida. Walter told his mother he was going to a big party in the suburbs at the home of some rich Jewish people and that David was giving him a ride. She agreed because she worried about Walter's social life, and she didn't share her husband's grudge against David.

The morning of the party began with a discouraging drizzle, but by afternoon, the sky had cleared, the tarp was removed from the grand, and it was rolled into position out on the patio. The "very casual" party had, by David's estimate, eighty-five to a hundred guests. Two valets parked the cars. It was weird to hand the keys to the Studebaker over to a stranger, to be parked alongside Cadillacs, Oldsmobiles, and Lincoln Continentals. Inside the kitchen, caterers assembled enormous platters of what Lisa called "Jew holiday food"—latkes, brisket, elaborately twisted challah bread, and roasted chickens sitting on heaps of savory vegetables.

Nathan was in his good place, strolling about the pool area with a bottle of beer, greeting and mingling with the guests, including the young people he didn't know. Judith stayed off her feet for the most part, lounging in a cushioned outdoor chair, close but not too close to the splash zone of the swimming pool. She smiled sweetly at everyone, gripping each person's hand for a moment and looking them in the eye as she spoke.

David had been sure that Walter would sneer at the ostentatiousness of Dulcedo Lake, but his friend seemed to really enjoy himself.

"This is who you work for?" Walter said. "Damn, man!"

Several girls from Lisa's school clustered around the two older boys and chattered flirtatiously. After a while, almost everyone under twenty, including Walter and David, ended up swimming in the warm pool while the pianist, Bobby Steiner, who had driven down from Cleveland, sat in his coat and tails playing Beethoven sonatas, Rodgers & Hammerstein tunes, and Righteous Brothers torch songs.

When the buffet was announced, the boys climbed out of the pool, dressed quickly in David's adopted bedroom, and got in line. They loaded their plates with heaps of chicken and beef and found an outdoor table, which turned out to be the same one where the pianist was taking a break with his own plate of food. When it came up in conversation that Walter had been a finalist in the Young Artists' Competition a couple of years earlier, Steiner prodded him into performing what Beethoven he still remembered. Walter made a show of trying to beg off, but David suspected he was eager for the attention. After dinner, people they didn't know crowded around the piano while Walter worked his way through the Sonata No. 27.

Lisa whispered to David, "You never said your best friend was *that* good at piano."

Walter, who had always claimed to hate the spotlight, played ecstatically. His messy, towel-dried hair made him look like a mad genius. After he'd worked his way through the sonata, with a few forgivable hesitations and mistakes, he went into something different, a jazzy pop number with a bebop left hand at the low end. At the conclusion, David stood up and bowed from the waist as the Charabis and their friends clapped energetically.

Before sitting back down at the piano, Bobby Steiner put his arm around Walter's shoulders.

"I don't know that song," he said. "What's it called?"

"I call it 'Oskaloosa Blue,'" said Walter.

"And did you ..."

"Yeah. I wrote it. I know it's not that good."

"I thought it was wonderful," said Steiner. "Ladies and gentlemen, a big round of applause for Walter. The future of American music is in good hands."

Walter beamed and blushed.

With the accolades over and the professional entertainer back at his job, David and Walter retreated from the patio. At the bar, they brazenly requested beer, figuring it was worth a try. The bartender, an expressionless man in his early twenties, poured each of them a glass without hesitation or comment. They walked around the side of the pool house, where it was darker and more private, sipping from their glasses of beer, which was delicious, refreshing, and hoppy. At that moment, David decided he liked beer.

"This stuff is good," said Walter.

"Did you see the label?" asked David. "It was in German. It's German beer."

"That would make sense for a Beethoven party. I like it."

"Me too. I wonder if we can get this stuff at G & L."

"Probably not."

"No, probably not."

They didn't want to put their wet swim shorts back on and weren't thrilled by the prospect of being adored by giggly tween girls, so David and Walter walked around beyond the stables, watching and listening from a distance to the gaiety coming from the house.

"Did you get it yet?" asked Walter.

"What?"

"Your passport. It's been almost two months. The guy at the government office said six to eight weeks."

"No," said David. "Did you get yours?"

"Not yet," said Walter. "But it should be any day. Maybe the mail is slow because it's Christmas."

"Of course. There's like a billion Christmas cards going through the system."

"I wish we'd started earlier," said Walter. "It was my fault, I know."

"Don't blame yourself," said David. "You had to sneak your birth certificate. But you got it. The passports will probably come right after Christmas. We're not in a big hurry anyway."

"I don't know, man," said Walter. "I'm not sure I can wait till summer."

David tilted his glass up and drained his last slug of German beer. "Stop talking crazy," he said. "You have to graduate."

"Really?" said Walter. "I don't have to fucking do anything. It's my life." He took a moment to kill his beer. "Let's go get another one," he said.

They started back toward the pool area. As they walked past the corner of the stables, a small shape darted out of the shadows and skittered past them.

"Whoa! What was that?" said Walter.

"Probably a fox. They're all over the place out here," said David. "They're real pests."

"Gee, even millionaires have their problems," said Walter.

They stopped at the edge of the light about thirty feet from the bar. Three people were standing there ordering cocktails and chatting with the bartender.

"Let's go up one at a time," said Walter. "You try first."

"Hold up. Wait till these people are gone."

They waited while the three guests lingered, in no hurry to depart.

"Hey, by the way, you still have my birth certificate. And my Social Security card."

"Yeah, I know," said David. Walter had accidentally left the documents in David's car on the Saturday they went to the passport office in Kansas City, back in October.

"I need them. My dad hasn't noticed anything missing, but if he figures it out, he'll flip."

The three guests, with their martinis, left the bar and strolled back toward the main party. David put on the most casual, genial expression he could manage and headed for the bar. The bartender poured him a beer without blinking.

"Thanks. Nice night," said David.

"I hear it's supposed to get really cold after Christmas," said the bartender. "It's risky having an outdoor party this time of year."

The Last Christmas

CHRISTMAS FELL ON A SUNDAY this year. On the Thursday before, much to David's disappointment, Dad's older brother Phillip Monk and his wife Chloe drove down from Des Moines to spend the holiday with the lesser Monks. Mom spent two days cleaning out and preparing her sewing room to serve as a spare bedroom, even buying new floral curtains and a matching comforter for the bed. The presence of the two guests made the already too-small house unbearably close. Nobody had tipped David off that this was happening.

In the past, when the families had spent holidays together, it was always at Phillip's larger house in Iowa, with its sizable bedrooms and spacious backyard, where David could at least find some space without suffocating. But this year, Chloe and Phillip were on their way to see their only daughter Lynette in Coffeyville, and Lawrence was on the way, so nobody could think of a reason not to visit. This explained the expensive fireplace insert—Mom and her sister-in-law had been competitive since she married Dad, who, in Chloe's estimation, was a disappointment as a breadwinner.

Dad and Uncle Phillip got along well enough and usually found things to talk about, but with Chloe, it was always how much they loved their new car, what a wonderful husband Lynette had found, how beautiful Iowa was in the fall, how proud she was that Phillip had won another golf tournament. Mom just listened and smiled, trying not to look miserable.

When Mom built a fire in the fireplace, neither of her in-laws mentioned the new hearth, but Chloe did point out that a few lights had burned out on the Christmas tree. At breakfast on Saturday, Chloe remarked that the stuffy air in the house had given her a headache, so Mom went around the house and cracked several windows open by an inch or two to flush out the stale air. Then Chloe complained that the house was drafty.

Phillip made a point of including David in the conversation but mostly spent his time explaining to his nephew why he should consider Iowa State as a college option. The school, he noted, was well-regarded for its engineering, which, coincidentally, was Phillip's field. Chloe added that David could drive down and visit his parents on weekends as if this were a selling point.

David escaped from the house as much as he could. He and Walter crashed a party on Saturday at the home of some neighbors on Walter's street. No one minded them being there, and David enjoyed flirting with a couple of prep-school girls, but he couldn't stay very long because he'd promised his parents he'd go to Christmas Eve church services with them.

The church Mom and Dad went to now was larger than their old one, and David hadn't attended often enough that anyone knew him. As the congregation sang old carols, he flashed back to the days when he was Young David, the child healer who had shared his gift with the world. Now, healing was just his hustle and contribution to the family's bottom line.

Christmas Day was interminable, and he couldn't leave the house until afternoon.

Neither of the Monk families were lavish gift-givers. Chloe gave his mom and dad a brightly glazed vase to "help brighten up that dark living room." David's main gift was a nice, large, powder-blue suitcase with heavy keyed locks and chrome trim. The brand name, "Skyway," had a cool logo of a jet plane, as if he were a world traveler. It was not a message—his parents didn't give message gifts. It was just something that might be useful for college one day. David gave Mom a mirrored jewelry box because he had noticed the mirror had fallen out of her old one. To his dad, a new socket wrench set because when they put together the new iron hearth and disassembled the old one, David noted that several of the sockets were worn out or missing—a very practical Christmas.

The Christmas ham was really good, and even Aunt Chloe complimented it.

In the early afternoon, David escaped and drove to the park, where he sat in his car and thought. He had few friends, and Walter was obligated to spend the day with his own family. David considered taking a slow, brooding walk along the trail that ran beside the Kansas River, but the wind had really picked up and gotten colder, and dust and trash blew about in the chilly gusts. Fast winter clouds raced across the sky from northwest to southeast. Winter was finally arriving, it seemed. He sat and listened to the radio for a long time, then drove back home.

It was midafternoon, and the Des Moines Monks were on their way out the door to spend a week with their daughter and ring in the new year 1967.

"If it's going to get cold, I wish we'd have a little snow," said Chloe, who did not have to drive in the weather she wished for. "This wind makes my skin so dry."

The cold wind discouraged excessive goodbyes, and soon, Chloe and Phillip were gone. The house was pleasantly quiet again, and Mom went around the house, shutting most of the windows. Later, Dad turned an Ed Sullivan's *Christmas Day Extravaganza*, and David watched it because there was nothing better. They ate leftover ham sandwiches.

The phone rang at about seven-thirty. Phone calls on Christmas Day were usually from extended family. Mom picked it up and then called, "Davie! It's for you."

Really? Who?

It was Nathan Charabi. "Hi, David. Merry Christmas!"

"Hi."

"Are you having a good holiday with your family?"

"Yeah. It's okay. My aunt and uncle were here, but they left."

David thought Mr. Charabi's pleasantries sounded a bit forced. He suspected there was another reason for the call, and he was right.

"David, listen," said Mr. Charabi. "I'm really sorry to ask you this, but … is it possible you could come out and see Judith tomorrow?"

"Uh … yeah. Sure. Is she doing all right?"

"Well, I gotta be honest. It's been a tough week for her. I thought maybe the party just wore her out, but she's gotten a lot of rest the past few days and she's not bouncing back. She has a lot of pain in her legs and back and didn't get out of bed today."

"I can come out in the morning," said David. "I don't have other plans."

"If you could, that would be great," said Mr. Charabi. "You haven't come to see her in over two weeks, and it shows."

Was this a rebuke? It was Judith who had insisted that David spend the holidays with his family.

"I'll come out," said David. "What time does she want me?"

"There's no hurry," said Mr. Charabi. "She's been sleeping very late. But she does want to see you."

"Okay," said David. "I'll be out sometime in the morning."

That night, he slept poorly. The wind blew gusty and cold all night, and he kept waking to the sound of swishing trees in the side yard and dry leaves skittering across the ground. Late in the night, he awoke with a throbbing headache. He went to the bathroom and took two aspirins, then opened his bedroom window half an inch to let in some fresh air.

He finally drifted off into a deep sleep in the very early morning, and so he slept later than usual. When he finally rose, Mom was still in her robe, but Dad had gone to work. Since Christmas had fallen on a Sunday, most offices were closed today, but the retail stores, including Harold's, were holding after-Christmas sales.

"Good morning, Bug," she said, calling him by his toddler nickname. "I made some waffles for you. They're still warm in the oven."

David piled three waffles on his plate and slathered them in butter and maple syrup. They were good, even at an hour old. He poured a cup of coffee, not something he did every day, but he was extra groggy. Mom puttered around the kitchen. She left some dishes dripping in the sink and sat at the kitchen table with yesterday's paper.

"I'm just going to take it easy today," said Mom. "I think I'm coming down with something. Your dad felt a little achy this morning as well, but he went to work, of course. It's this north wind. It just kills my sinuses."

Just to show his appreciation for the Christmas gift, David packed the usual change of clothes, plus his warm coat and an extra sweater, into his new suitcase. It was way bigger than required for this little overnighter. He also tossed in some of his schoolbooks and papers, though he didn't expect to do any schoolwork unless he was terribly bored.

As he said goodbye, his mom unexpectedly stood up and embraced him.

"Davie, you're a good boy," she said. "One of these days, you won't be having to constantly run off at somebody else's beck and call."

"I don't really mind," he said. "I'll be home in a couple of days."

"We'll always be here for you," she said. "Be extra careful today."

"I will."

On the drive out to Dulcedo Lake, David listened to the radio. Between Top 40—songs by the Young Rascals and the Mamas & the Papas—the DJ gave weather updates. Tonight, the temperature would be dipping close to the freezing mark, he said, but for tomorrow night, the weather service was predicting a hard freeze, with an increasing possibility of sleet or snow. David ran the heater in the Daytona for the first time. It stank of hot dust.

David made it to the Charabi's in the late morning. Judith had deteriorated. When David arrived, a doctor was just leaving. If you were rich enough, doctors still made house calls. David overheard him talking to Nathan Charabi.

"I will be out here again tomorrow morning," said the doctor, "but I want you to consider putting her in St. Luke's. There's a lot more I can do for her there."

"I will," said Mr. Charabi. "I'd like to leave it up to her. She hates hospitals, and I don't blame her a bit. But we'll see how she feels tomorrow."

David found Judith in her bedroom. She was out of bed, sitting up in a chair. Her skin was pallid.

"David, I'm so sorry," she said. "I know you were enjoying time with your family."

"No, it's all right," he said. "I had a good week. But my aunt and uncle have left, and my father is back at work today. It's nice to get out of the house."

Judith closed her eyes, put her hands on the chair arms as if to rise, then dropped them back in her lap.

"I'll be ready in a few minutes," she said. "You can go look at television or read a book. I'm sorry I wasn't already on the table."

"You don't have to be on the table if you don't want," said David. "You can just lie on the bed."

"No, I'd rather be on the table. I'll be just a little bit."

"I'll help you, sweetheart." It was Nathan standing in the doorway. "Do you want the wheelchair?"

"No, I can walk. Just help me to the bathroom first."

David left the bedroom and went back to sit on the large sofa in the family room, where, on most days, Lisa would be watching TV. Today, she was nowhere to be seen. He considered turning on the TV himself but knew it would just be soap operas and game shows. He waited quietly, then sorted through the stack of *Life* magazines until he found one that looked promising, an older issue with a really sexy cover photo of the actress Sophia Loren in a sheer nightgown. But when he flipped to the article on the inside, it turned out the subject was the photographer, not the sultry Italian actress. So, he read an article about what astronauts do on their days off.

"David?" It was Nathan. "She's ready for you."

"Okay." David closed the magazine and stood up. Nathan put a gentle hand on his shoulder.

"I don't expect there's much you can do, but if you can make her feel a little more comfortable, that would be enough. I think the stress of the holidays brought this on. I guess I pushed her too hard. She tried to act normal for everyone at the party, but maybe that was too much."

"I'll do what I can," said David.

The curtains were drawn in the back room, and only one low-wattage lamp shown in the corner. At the foot of the table, a small electric heater glowed red. Judith lay prone on the table with a sheet pulled up to her neck, face turned toward him, eyes shut.

David stood beside the massage table for a moment, hesitant about whether he should draw the sheet down. He placed his right hand a few inches from the side of her face, palm outward. Her eyes opened, and her left arm came out from beneath the sheet. She took his hand in her own and gently pulled it to her lips for a soft kiss. She had never done that before, and he was both touched and confused. She let go of his hand, then, with both hands, drew the sheet down to below her shoulder blades.

"I love both my stepsons," she said very quietly. "But if I had one of my own, I would want him to be like you."

Not knowing how to respond to such an affectionate sentiment, David leaned forward and placed a kiss on her hair right above her ear. She smiled weakly and shut her eyes.

Wait. What? Why did I do that?

Placing his right hand near her temple, he began a routine he had done many, many times. Could he even help her? The colors he sensed were messy, confused, and unbalanced. Her energy field was closer to her body than usual and strangely asymmetrical. There was no specific problem he could focus on. But he had to try.

Judith breathed in slowly, held it briefly, then exhaled a quiet sigh.

SHE DID NOT JOIN THE FAMILY for dinner that night. Olivia was off duty, so Nathan had procured chop suey and fried rice from somewhere, along with little boxes of eggrolls and some variety of cabbage salad. Lisa had returned from wherever she had been, and the three of them ate together at the kitchen table. No one felt like small talk. David was hungry and wolfed down his Chinese food using a fork, but

Lisa made a game effort at the chopsticks for a few minutes before losing patience and resorting to silverware.

"It's s'pose to snow tonight," said Lisa. "There's already bits of ice coming down."

"You're not planning to drive back tonight, are you, David?" asked Nathan. "It could be treacherous on Highway 10."

"I'll stay here tonight," said David. He had already promised Judith he would see her once more before bedtime.

"Good. If the roads aren't too bad in the morning, Olivia will make it out here and give us a civilized breakfast."

When dinner was over, and the boxes were thrown away, David sat in his accustomed place on the couch and watched *I Dream of Jeannie* with Lisa while Nathan checked on Judith. After a few minutes, he stuck his head into the room.

"David, she's sound asleep. I think you can just see her in the morning."

"Okay."

David stayed on the couch, and they watched the *Roger Miller Show* before switching channels to catch *Andy Griffith* and then *Family Affair.* Toward the end of that show, David nodded off and awoke when Nathan switched the television off.

"I don't know why I'm so tired," he said.

"Well, go on to bed anytime you want," said Nathan, "And once again, David, thank you for driving out. I know it's not what you had planned for the day after Christmas."

"I don't mind," said David. He roused himself off the couch and stretched.

Nathan was halfway out of the room when he stopped abruptly and turned around.

"David, wait!" he said. "I completely forgot something. You have a present. I'll be back in two seconds." He hurried out of the room, then returned a moment later with a small, flat, white box tied with a thin red ribbon. "Judith picked this out for you. It's just a little something. We forgot to give it to you before you went home last week." He handed the box to David. "I know we're Hebrews, but consider it a Christmas present. You can open it now if you want."

David untied the ribbon and took the lid off the box. Inside was a silver pendant held by a rawhide leather string. It was about an inch high and looked like a cross but with a loop at the top.

"I know it's weird to give jewelry to guys," said Nathan. "But Judith insisted. I hear that surfers out in California are wearing these."

David took the lump of silver in his hand and felt the weight of it. A small card inside the box had a printed legend:

Ankh, the Ancient Egyptian Symbol of Health and Healing.
Sterling Silver 925.

In small, precise handwriting below: To David with Love and Gratitude, Judith and Nathan Charabi.

"Thanks," said David.

"You're very welcome," said Nathan. "I'm sorry I didn't remember to give it to you before the holidays. Now, I'm off to bed. Good night."

David put the ankh back into its box and went upstairs, where he forced himself to brush his teeth before shutting the door to Robert Charabi's room, turning off the lights, and climbing into bed. He was asleep in minutes.

It did snow in the night—thick, sticky stuff that turned to cold puddles on the patio and walkways. When he was little, a morning like this would have found him and the other neighborhood kids dashing around, throwing snowballs, sliding, and laughing. Now, he just gazed out the picture window, waiting for Olivia to announce breakfast. She had braved the slick roads early that morning to serve the needs of wealthy white people because that was her job. As David watched, a blanket of snow slowly accumulated on the roof of the stables and the pasture beyond.

"Mr. David, there's sausage and biscuits," said Olivia. "And oatmeal with berries. You can dig in first while I rouse the other folks."

"Thanks."

"Are you going to stay here today?" she asked.

"I think so," said David.

"How is Miss Judith doing?"

"She's weak, and she hurts a lot," said David, surprising himself with his candor.

"I worried about her all through Christmas," said Olivia. "I could hardly pay attention to my own family." She hurried away to fetch Nathan and his daughter for a steaming hot, abundant breakfast.

We're both servants, Olivia and me, David thought, *discussing the mistress of the house.*

A little before nine, the doctor showed up again, his heavy dark medical bag reminding David of doctors in old Western movies, arriving at the big ranch house to treat gunshot wounds, set broken legs, and deliver babies.

David waited around for a while, then put on his coat and took a walk along the gravel road behind the house, his shoes squeaking in the fresh, wet snow. The small flakes tickled his face and ears, and he drew his collar up. The wind had died down, so the cold was bearable. The sharp air hurt his sinuses.

He re-entered the house through the side by the kitchen, stomping the snow off his shoes and finding a small kitchen dishrag to towel his wet hair. The doctor was talking to Nathan just inside the front door. He was on his way out, having stayed less than half an hour, so maybe that was a good sign.

"I'll have somebody call you later today when it's arranged," the doctor said, buttoning up his big overcoat. "Midday tomorrow. Hopefully, this doesn't turn into a blizzard." He scooted out the front door, and Nathan pushed it shut firmly behind him. He noticed David.

"David, wait ten minutes, and she'll be ready for you," he said. "Then just go on in. I have to make some calls."

David climbed the stairs and removed his coat, hanging it in the large, empty closet, then returned downstairs.

Judith was in her usual place, face down on the massage table.

"How do you feel," asked David.

"I'm better," said Judith, though she didn't sound better. "I had a good sleep. My legs don't hurt as much. Can you work on my legs again?"

So he did. As always, the pain was general and hard to locate, but there were clear rivers of sciatic pain at the top of both legs, extending up toward the spine. That was something David could work with, so he did his best to find, gather, and discharge them. He made three full passes, taking his time with each one. He stepped back for a moment, resting his arm, preparing to go a fourth time, but she stopped him.

"That's good, David, thank you. You can take a break. Maybe again this afternoon?"

"Sure."

"You probably want to go home tonight, right?"

"I can stay if you want me to," he said truthfully. There wasn't much waiting for him in Lawrence.

"I'm … going to go into the hospital for a little while," she said. "Tomorrow. The doctor wore me down, and my husband insisted. They're going to try some new shots. Always new shots."

"I'm sorry," said David. "The hospital can probably help you."

"Maybe. But if you can see me one more time this afternoon, it will help me get ready for the ordeal." She raised on her elbows, and David averted his eyes. She stretched and rolled her neck. "It's better, it really is," she said. "Just a little booster this afternoon, and I'll be ready for tomorrow. I wish there was something for you to do. If it wasn't for this weather, you could swim or ride my horse."

"I'll be fine. I have school stuff I can work on."

David returned to his big, undecorated bedroom. No, he wasn't going to work on anything school-related. He was tired. Working with Judith always drained him, but he was even more worn down than usual. He lay on top of the bed, wondering what Robert Charabi had done in this room when he was bored at sixteen. Read? Play solitaire? Jack off?

Outside, the snow accumulated, turning from wet and thick to soft and fluffy as the temperature dropped. The walkways glazed over. The house, the stables, and the fields were covered in a clean, white blanket. It was postcard-beautiful. Hours passed, and still, the snow fell.

In the late afternoon, David went to see Judith again. She had never dressed in her day clothes. He tried to find and release pain from her lower torso and back with some success. As always, she was deeply grateful. Olivia made sandwiches, which David and Lisa ate while watching TV. David would not be driving home tonight. He thought he should probably call home to update his parents on the situation, but then they started watching a movie called *Blue Hawaii*, and he never got around to it. It was funny to see Elvis Presley cavorting and singing on a tropical beach while David's world iced over.

The highways had become treacherous. County crews were ordered out with their salt and sand trucks. Hazard warnings went out across the Midwest, and traffic slowed to a crawl. David didn't know it, but the perilous county roads of eastern Kansas had saved his life.

Next of Kin

B Y WEDNESDAY AFTERNOON, the sun was out, and the snow on Hackberry Street had devolved to gray slush. An ambulance idled in front of the house, vapor puffing from its tailpipes. One police car, also idling, was pulled up right behind the Mustang in the driveway.

The front door of the small house stood open despite the freezing temperature. A chair was propped against the screen door to keep it from shutting in a gust. The back door was also open, and most windows in the house had been raised as far as disuse and old paint would allow. A police officer in a dark blue overcoat was speaking to a neighbor in the front of the house next door, writing an occasional note in his notebook. Other people, adults, and some young people stood back a respectful distance, talking quietly. A few kids on bicycles peddled up and down the street, leaving narrow, wet trails in the melting snow.

An older man in a gray trench coat and winter fedora came out of the house and spoke to the ambulance driver, who then got out of the vehicle and followed the older man back inside. After several minutes, there was activity at the front door. A police officer came out and removed the chair that held the screen door, setting it out of the way, then held the door as two other men maneuvered a gurney over the threshold and out onto the front porch. A body on the gurney was wrapped in a sheet. A man said out loud what most people were thinking.

"Oh, no."

Roger Monk, age forty-six, found in his living room recliner, deceased. The television was still on. His hands were folded across his chest, and his reading glasses were in one hand as if he had taken a moment for a catnap.

The three men carefully lifted the covered body from the gurney and placed it into the ambulance. They rolled the empty gurney back into the house. After a long, long thirty minutes, they returned with a second body, also wrapped, and placed it beside the first. Cathy Monk, age forty-two, found in bed under the covers, wearing pajamas, scarf tied neatly around her hair, deceased.

The ambulance pulled away slowly.

Given the temperature and condition of the bodies, the coroner estimated the couple had been dead between twelve and sixteen hours—preliminary cause: carbon monoxide poisoning.

Every year, usually at the first big cold snap, the coroner had to deal with a few cases like this. Old, neglected gas furnaces—houses shut tight with people found dead in those homes.

Whispers and anxious questions among neighbors. Then someone spoke to the man in the trench coat. Was anyone else there? A teenage boy?

No, no one else was in the house. What is the son's name?

David.

Does anyone know where David might be? How can we contact him?

No, no one did. Somebody said he had a close friend who used to live on the block, a boy named Walter Edelstein.

WENDY EDELSTEIN HEARD THE PHONE RING just as she and Jim were heading out the door. They were to meet another couple for dinner at a new steak place near the museum. Wendy considered letting the call go, but since Jim was a medical doctor, the phone always had to be answered.

It was a woman in the police department. As soon as she identified herself, Wendy's heart raced, but then she thought, *It's okay. Walter is here. He's in his room.*

"Is this Mrs. Edelstein?"

"Yes."

"We are looking for a boy named David Monk. Do you know him?"

"Yes, I do," said Wendy. "He's a friend of my son."

"Is he there?"

"No, he's not. I haven't seen him in several days. I could ask my son Walter."

"Please do," said the woman. "I'll wait."

Jim fretted by the side door, fully coated and wearing his hat. "Who is that?" he asked. "We're supposed to be at the restaurant in twenty minutes."

"It's somebody from the police department," said Wendy. "They're looking for David Monk."

"David?" said Jim. "What did he do this time? Walter better not be involved."

Wendy crossed the width of the large house and found Walter in his bedroom. "Do you know where David is?"

"Nope, haven't seen him," said Walter, barely looking up from his paperback. "He's probably out at that house ... you know ... those rich people he works for."

"What are their names?"

"I don't know ... Judith and Nathan something. Starts with a C, I think."

Wendy returned to the phone and conveyed the information. "What's the problem?" she asked.

"I can't disclose details, but there's been a death. We need to notify next of kin."

"Oh, my god. Who's dead?" asked Wendy.

"Who's dead?" demanded Jim.

"Ma'am, could I speak with your son directly?" said the woman on the phone.

Wendy didn't want to yell, so she crossed the house again to retrieve Walter.

He spoke on the phone for about ten minutes, describing the house and the ranch owned by rich Jewish people. He remembered the name of the road, Moss Creek. Then, the name of the ranch came to him: Dulcedo Lake. That was all he could recall. The caller thanked him.

"What did he do?" Jim asked Walter. "Do you know something about this?"

"He didn't do anything," said Walter. "Somebody in his family died, and they want to tell him."

"I hope it wasn't his mother," said Wendy. "She's such a nice lady."

"I bet they're just saying that so Walter will tell them where David is," said Jim. "That kid is up to something. I'd bet money on it."

"Oh, Jim, be quiet. You don't know."

"And can we please go eat now?" said Jim, opening the door. "Or do you want to be even later than we already are?"

It took the police, working with a telephone company operator, only a few minutes to arrive at the name Nathan Charabi and identify a contact number. But by the time somebody called out to the ranch, there were only a couple of servants in the house, and David was on his way back home.

DAVID LIVED IN A SLOW-MOVING NIGHTMARE. From the moment he had pulled onto his street and investigators realized who he was, the minutes and hours and days and nights had blurred into one awful twilight. He was not allowed to enter the house, even though the deadly furnace had been shut off, and the water heater as well. He was driven down to the Douglas County Coroner's office, where he met with a young doctor who worked part-time for the office and was filling in because everyone else was on Christmas break. The doctor asked him if he was up to making an identification. He said yes.

In a cold room lit by fluorescent lights, an enormous morgue drawer was rolled open, and the sheet was drawn back. It bothered David that her hair was all squished over to one side. She would never have gone out in public looking like that. If somebody would just give him a brush, he'd make her look more right. But he just said, yes, that's my mother. Her name is Catherine Smith Monk.

His father looked more like Dad, asleep or maybe just resting with his eyes shut. That's my father. Full name? Roger Sherman Monk. The drawers were rolled shut. David signed his name twice, the doctor signed his name below his, and a county employee signed each form as a witness.

Still, he couldn't go home. The city police let him stay the night in a small room they used when detectives and desk employees working all-nighters needed a catnap. The room held two single beds and a sink, like a jail cell.

He didn't expect to sleep, but eventually he did. Late, late in the night, around 3 a.m., he awoke when someone came into the room quietly and lay down on the other bed. David heard him breathing but never turned to see who it was. Half an hour later, that person left, and David was alone again.

The next morning, a police lieutenant bought David breakfast at the café across the street from the police station. He told David that the fire inspector had found that an internal part of the old gas furnace, called the heat exchanger, had broken in a couple of places. It appeared to have happened when pieces of a large iron fireplace hearth had been banged up against it. People should have their furnaces inspected every year, he said, but few of them do.

David's father had not shown up for work on Tuesday, so the store manager had called the police when no one could reach him. This is lucky, said the lieutenant. Many times, people go missing for days before somebody comes looking for them. He added that he was sorry for David's loss.

HE HAD TO MOVE to Des Moines, Iowa. Because he was a minor and an orphan, the only other option would be to put him into the custody of the Kansas Department for Children and Families, which would place him in a temporary foster home. David's only immediate relatives were Phillip and Chloe Monk, who agreed to take him in, at least for now. Everyone thought that was the best arrangement under the circumstances.

That afternoon, Uncle Phillip and Aunt Chloe drove to Kansas to retrieve their orphaned nephew. Chloe, who never approved of Dad and didn't get along that well with Mom, was inconsolable. She sobbed and gushed tears and squeezed David so relentlessly that Uncle Phillip had to say, "*Please*, dear! Let the boy breathe." She calmed down but kept trying to hold on to David as if he were a toddler who might bolt into the street.

In the afternoon, they all went back to the house, followed by an officer in his squad car. David's car, which had belonged to his father, was still parked where he had left it in front of a neighbor's house. At the officer's suggestion, David moved it to the front of the Monks's house. He would never drive the Studebaker again.

David was allowed to collect clothes and anything else he needed. The house was freezing cold but otherwise ordinary, exactly like it looked every day. The faucet in the kitchen dripped every few seconds. Dad's chair was reclined, and his house shoes sat side by side on the floor. When Aunt Chloe saw them, she burst into sobs again.

David filled his new Skyway suitcase with all the clean clothes he could cram into it. He brought his portable typewriter in its little case and everything school-related that he could find. It all went into the trunk of Uncle Phillip's long Oldsmobile 98 hard-top. The officer locked the house, and the Des Moines Monks drove away, taking David east and then north, over two hundred miles, across the state line. The roads were icy in places, and they had to drive slowly. The normally three-hour trip took Uncle Phillip over five hours, including thirty minutes in an Osceola truck stop for dinner.

David wasn't expected to talk, and mostly he didn't. Over the next few days, Phillip and Chloe left him to himself, not knowing what else they should do. Occasionally, Phillip got him to answer questions about school or the mysterious work he had been doing for the Charabis, but much of the time David spent in the spare bedroom they had hastily arranged for him.

Near midnight on December 31, David awoke to the sound of firecrackers popping in a nearby vacant lot. More explosions and firework whistles followed. He lay in bed listening until the fireworks tapered off.

It was 1967.

Dave Diamond and the Clientele

CALLIE PENDER, LMT, had expanded her massage therapy business to include ten regular customers. Her favorite was a sweet guy with long salt-and-pepper hair who called himself Dave Diamond, which sounded like a stage name, and it was. He fronted a small jazz combo called the Dave Diamond Trio, well-known among local music sophisticates but not world-famous. Dave had come to see Callie many times when she worked at Sandy-Os, but since his legs were partially paralyzed, he couldn't drive himself and had to find a ride from a friend or else call a specialized, very expensive taxi. He was thrilled when his favorite therapist told him she was going solo and would be making house calls. He upped their regular massage sessions to once a week—on Thursdays—and enthusiastically recommended her services to his other musician friends. Since discovering Callie's talents six months earlier, Dave Diamond had decided he was going to rehabilitate himself right out of his wheelchair and back to braces and crutches, a real improvement. He wasn't quite there yet, but with Callie's help, he'd made a lot of progress.

Today, Dave surprised her by opening his front door and greeting her while standing upright using forearm crutches, grinning widely.

"Dave!" said Callie. "I've never seen you at eye level before. You're looking strong."

"I've been practicing every day at least two hours," said Dave. "At my current rate of improvement ..." He squinted and pretended to calculate ... "I'll be ready for the Boston Marathon in 1999."

Callie chuckled. "I like that you're working so hard, but you should really consider doing this in an official rehab clinic. Medicaid would pay for it. Seriously, my friend, what if you fell?"

"Then I'd either pick my sorry carcass back up or wait for Thursday to roll around so you could help me up again. Don't worry about me. And Medicaid can kiss my skinny ass."

Callie rolled the table in through the front door of Dave's apartment over a shallow ramp on the threshold. "Where do you want me to set up?"

"Let's do it in the front by the big window," said Dave. "I like the light. If somebody wants to be a Peeping Tom, they'll be bitterly disappointed."

Dave got himself onto the table and lay face up while Callie washed her hands and arranged her massage oils.

"Oh, before we start," said Dave, "is it okay if I write you a check today? I'm cash-poor."

"Sure. Just be sure and make it out to 'Carol Pender.' That's my legal name."

"Carol. Sure."

Callie started from the upper thighs and worked her way down with the rhythm of a pro. She massaged one leg at a time, covering and uncovering parts of his body discretely with a sheet and moving her hands from thigh to calf. She worked the atrophied areas to improve circulation and stretched the muscles that still functioned.

A neighbor, a woman who lived upstairs, walked past the window and glanced in. Dave smiled and waved. She looked like she might wave back, then thought better of it and walked on.

For a man who liked to talk during sessions—not every client did—Dave didn't say much about himself, but he often asked questions. Most therapists avoided personal discussions, but this client was so open and endearing he had a way of drawing her out.

"How's it working out with the new boyfriend?" he asked.

Callie had already revealed how she had fallen for the manager of her housing co-op. Dave kept up with the leading questions, and soon, she found herself describing the strange meeting with Dr. Ted Hedd about mutated genes and chronic illness and how Wally had taken to bouts of sadness and withdrawal. Many times—most of the time—Wally was his normal, sweet, and loving self, she said, full of enthusiasm and energy in bed. But then, sometimes, she would find him sitting by himself, mind far away, staring blankly. If he was worried about developing a chronic disease, he didn't admit it, and he stubbornly refused to be tested.

"I don't understand why he's being stubborn about that one thing," said Callie. "I get that he doesn't want to hear bad news, but doesn't he owe it to himself to find out whether he's a carrier?"

"Of what?" said Dave. "The bad seed? There are things in this world that are dealer's choice every time. I'd say personal medical history is one of those. It's nobody else's business."

"What if he wants to have kids someday? Wouldn't it be the moral thing to find out if you'd be passing a life of misery to the next generation?"

"You said he has no symptoms, right?" said Dave.

"None at all, according to him, and nothing I can see. But if it were me … I would really want to know. But he's in denial about the whole thing. He just says, 'That guy's not my real father,' and changes the subject."

"I'd let him work it out on his own," said Dave. "As a hostage of the medical-industrial complex myself, I say stay away from it as long as you can. Once they get their hands on you—and I speak from experience—they never let you go. Never." He shifted positions on the table. "Could you work on my right thigh a little more?"

"Sure. Let me know when you're ready to roll over."

Callie kneaded the large rectus femoris muscle, which was overworked from compensating for the atrophying muscles on the back of his leg. Then she helped him roll over and gently massaged his upper back muscles.

"When you're done with my back, do that thing with your hands where you don't touch me, okay? I don't know why that works, but it does."

"Of course," she said. "It's called 'Reiki,' by the way. And nobody really knows how it works, even if they say they do."

"I love mysteries," said Dave Diamond. He inhaled deeply and relaxed. Callie held her hands close to his neck and moved them slowly down along the spine. Her hands trembled slightly.

"Oh … yes," he said quietly. "Medicaid and the hospitals can kiss my skinny ass. I have you."

He fell quiet for several minutes, breathing so softly she thought he might have gone to sleep. But he half opened his eyes. "Before I forget, we're playing all next week at the Downtowner Lounge on Trinity Street. Eight o'clock till we keel over. That's your neighborhood, right? Bring your friends. It may be old-fart music, but it's good, and there's no cover."

"I'll try," she said.

"And bring that boyfriend of yours. I want to meet this lucky guy."

"We'll have to see about that," she said.

Mellow and Real

TWELVE NEW RESIDENTS moved into Keystone house for the fall semester of 1975: Patty, Sondra, Ming, and Lilly, high school friends from the northwestern part of the state, all freshmen; Two more Iranians, Abbas and Mohammed, graduate engineering students; Wendy, a premed student whom nobody ever saw; a senior Chinese major named Mike (maintaining the house's number of Mikes at three, having lost one the previous spring); a nonstudent named Willy, who would contend with Nixon for the title of Most Likely to be a Drug Dealer; a couple named Rebecca and James, transfers from a feeder college in a nearby city, hopelessly, giddily in love (and therefore doomed to miserable breakup in the eyes of most); and, finally, Nicholas Symansky. Yes, that Nicholas.

Callie moved out, because she was in love with Wally, and she wanted the relationship to work. She found a small apartment a couple of blocks away. She kept her boarding contract so she could eat at Keystone six days a week. Beva and her boyfriend had broken up, so he moved out. The house was still two residents short of the number required to break even financially. Wally would have to keep working on that.

Only Nixon and Sherry and Beva, and a couple of other residents, remembered the Nicholas from last year. Now, he was short-haired, clean-shaven, and gainfully employed at a campus-area bakery. He showed few traces of the self-destructive, naked lunatic he had once been. It was Sherry who asked Wally if Nicholas could come back. He would pay rent, do chores, and have his own room. She and Nicholas were no longer a romantic item, she said, just good friends. Wally said okay, but he has to keep up with his psychiatric treatment.

Nicholas himself came by to see Wally, paid him back the twenty dollars he owed him, showed him a bottle of pills marked "Thioridazine 50 mg," and assured him he had "patched things up" with the state hospital after checking himself out early and going on the lam for a few weeks. He didn't give details.

The tradename of the neuroleptic was Mellaril, which Nicholas pronounced mellow-real.

"I take my mellow-reals twice a day, with food," said Nicholas. "They made me a little hazy at first, but now I'm getting used to them. I won't skip meds."

Wally took his deposit, gave him a small single room in the Annex, and assigned him to kitchen and courtyard cleanup (which mostly involved raking up leaves and sticks from two large, unruly live oaks.)

Wally wondered if he was making a mistake, and, if so, how much of a mistake? Everybody should get a chance to start over. Right?

The new Nicholas proved to be a changed man. On his first kitchen-cleaning assignment, he was so fastidious that the cooks were impressed. They mentioned to Wally what a good job the new guy had done. And when Nicholas was done with the courtyard, the concrete had been hosed down and scrubbed, all the weeds pulled from the garden, and sunflowers planted, which quickly began sprouting in neat little rows. He presented such an assured, mature presence in the house that many of the younger residents assumed he must be Wally's assistant manager.

Wally started the new semester with two clear personal goals, both painful and difficult. First, he wanted to find Walter Edelstein. The real Walter Edelstein. Tell him what was going on, and give him Dr. Ted Hedd's medical referral. Second, he had to tell the truth to the woman he had come to love, such as his real name and his real story.

No, he had the order wrong there. He had to start by telling Callie the truth. Then he'd try and find Walter.

He invited her to dinner at The Grub Ranch, an enormous venue on the near north side of town that specialized in chicken-fried steak, beer, cigarettes, and noise. Not an obvious location for a heart-to-heart, but on weeknights, the porch wasn't crowded, so they'd have some space to themselves. Wally told Callie he wanted to discuss something serious.

"You're not planning to propose, are you?" she asked. He was taken aback by her scowl. A mock scowl?

"No, I just wanted to talk about something personal." Of *course*, he hadn't planned to propose. But her flat rejection of the idea stung.

"Good," she said, and then she must have picked up his look of dejection because she added, "The Grub Ranch would be a bad choice for something like that. Romance and beer burps don't go together."

"No proposals," he promised.

On a Wednesday night, Wally and Callie drove in Callie's (more reliable) car north on a road that used to be called the Dallas Highway back before a real highway to Dallas was built. They drove past the northern outlier buildings of the college campus and then block after block of cheaply constructed apartments interspersed with dilapidated strip centers until they arrived at their destination, a sprawling one-story wood-and-corrugated-steel building with an enormous neon sign on top. It was a cartoon cowboy holding a green knife and a red fork. Laughter, shouts, and overloud jukebox music reverberated out the big open doors, where waitresses buzzed out with plates of food and drink and back in again with empties and spent dinners.

Wally picked a table on the raised wooden porch, several tables away from other diners.

What is the best way to deliver odd, unexpected, possibly shocking news? Just blurt it out? Or would a little context help soften the outrage? Would she laugh at his caution, get angry, give him a big hug and kiss as a reward for honesty, or throw a beer in his face and storm out?

Or would she just say, *"Wally, I realize now that you're an untrustworthy fraud, and I can never love you. Goodbye"*?

It was fried shrimp night, so Wally ordered shrimp and a draft beer. Callie got the nacho salad and iced tea. He was planning to wait until the food was delivered, but Callie made him cut to the chase.

"What did you want to tell me?" she asked.

"It's about something ... that I need to do," he said.

"And that would be ...?"

"It's only going to make sense if I also tell you something else."

"Such as ...?"

Wally took a swallow of beer. "Last year, when I moved here ... from out of state ... I changed my name." Another swallow.

Callie waited, eyebrows up. "You already told me that 'Stein' was short for 'Edelstein.'"

"Yes, but that's not my real name either. I changed it because I needed ... a fresh start."

"Don't we all?" said Callie. "Come on, Wally, spill it. What did you do? Are you wanted by the police?"

"No, no," he said. "I just needed everything to be different."

Callie waited. No smile, no encouragement. Silence.

"I just thought … now it's time to tell you the truth."

"I should say so," said Callie. "Okay, let's get right into it. You're saying you're not actually an Edelstein?"

"I'm a Monk."

"What? You're a *Monk?* This is getting weird."

"My *name* is Monk. Or it was. Well, it still is. I guess. Legally."

"So you're actually Wally Monk?"

"David," he said. "I was born David Monk."

Callie leaned forward, looking him straight in the eyes. "So … that girl who called you 'David' in the ice cream place …"

"She was the daughter of somebody I knew back in Lawrence."

"I thought that was pretty strange at the time," said Callie. "Okay, before we go any further here, what am I supposed to call you?"

"Wally. Keep calling me Wally. That's who I want to be."

It was Callie's turn to take a slow sip of draft beer.

"Okay … Wally … why are you telling me this now?"

"I wish I'd told you from the beginning," said Wally. "But after it all settled down, and I got a job and a place to live and everything … and a driver's license with the new name … I thought it didn't matter anymore. I could just go on being Wally Stein the rest of my life. But then that doctor showed up …"

Callie interrupted. "Then you really *aren't* related to Ted Hedd."

"No, not at all."

"Then who is?"

"Walter Edelstein."

"So … where is the real Walter?"

"I don't know," said Wally. "I don't even know if he's alive. I haven't seen him in years. But I should at least try and find him."

Callie took a big swig and drained her beer, then scooted her chair back.

"Please, don't leave," said Wally. "I'm sorry I didn't tell you before."

"I'm not leaving," said Callie. "I'm going to the restroom, which you know— since you've been here before—is not a fun experience for women. While I'm gone, you're gonna order us two more beers. And when I come back, you can tell me all the other stuff you've been lying about."

"I'm not lying," said Wally. "I mean, the name wasn't technically true. But it was just the easiest thing to do at the time."

"Why?" she asked. "Why *that* guy? Why steal *his* name?"

"Because I had his birth certificate. I still do. It's … a long story."

Callie stood up. "Two more beers. And something lighter for me this time. Miller or something." She walked away quickly, dodging a busboy with a tray of empty mugs, and headed into the main building.

Acceptance

I N THE FIRST WEEK OF THE NEW YEAR, Walter received two important pieces of mail on the same day. The first was his long-awaited passport. He'd been watching for it, ready to pounce whenever it arrived.

At the Edelstein residence, the mail came in through a brass slot to the left of the front door and landed in a wicker basket on a small oaken side table. The Edelsteins received quite a bit of mail every day, most of it addressed to the good doctor, but also the usual assortment of junk and bills. And magazines. Lots and lots of magazines, popular, news-oriented, and medical, and heaps of junk mail targeted at girls and young women. If the Edelsteins were out of town for even a few days, the mail pile became a Kilimanjaro, with sloping sides of slick, colorful paper that spilled out onto the floor.

It had been seven weeks since he and David had applied for their passports. The new school semester would begin Monday the 9th, so this week was Walter's last hope of intercepting the delivery ahead of his mother. The postman's typical arrival window was between 2:00 and 2:45 p.m., and Walter hovered close by every weekday. On Wednesday, when the mail clump came through the slot, Walter spotted the passport immediately. Brown and official-looking, with a "Do Not Bend" command on the front, the letter had a US Department of State return address. He snatched it up, took it back to his room, tore the envelope open, and removed the blue cardboard booklet.

It was a work of art, this passport. The American eagle was fierce and noble. Walter's picture was goofy, eyes open too wide, hair badly combed, but it was him, and they had spelled his name right. He fanned through the blank, watermarked pages, each one waiting to be filled with visas. He raised it to his nose and sniffed. It smelled of ink and possibility.

He quickly wadded up the accompanying letter, then the envelope, and wrapped both in a loose sheet of paper before throwing the whole crumpled ball into the trash. He opened the desk drawer, removed a stack of used bluebooks, slipped the passport into the back of the drawer, and placed the bluebooks on top.

He returned to the foyer to go through the rest of the mail pile. That's when he saw the big, fat one addressed to him. It was from MIT.

He put it back on the stack. For a moment, he considered spiriting the ungainly thing out of sight into the same desk drawer on top of the passport or someplace deeper, underneath his socks in the chest of drawers, perhaps. Or out into the metal trash bin behind the house. But he couldn't do that. He left it where it was and went back to the family room, sat at the piano bench, and raised the fallboard. He didn't play. He just stared at the keys.

Finally, he placed his fingers on the keyboard. He began playing a slow, mechanical version of Beethoven's "The Tempest"—aka the Piano Sonata No. 17 in D Minor—watching his fingers strike the keys in the right order, automatically, without his input.

Ten minutes later, he heard his mother's voice calling from the front of the house, excited.

"Walter! … Walter! Where are you?"

"Back here!" he called.

She entered the family room, face beaming, holding the fat white envelope, fanning the air with it.

"It's here!" she said. "It's MIT! Open it!"

Walter took it from her. He didn't need to open it. It couldn't possibly be a rejection. It was too thick and substantial. But his mother was standing there, so he tore it open.

Dear Walter,
On behalf of the Admissions Committee, it is my pleasure to offer you …

His mother leaned down and embraced him from behind.

"Oh, baby, this is so exciting!" she said. "I knew you could do it! It's so wonderful." She let go of him and stood up. "I can't wait for your father to get home! I have an idea … let's call him right now! He usually sees patients in the morning, so he's probably in his office."

"Mom, no," said Walter. "Don't call him."

"But he'll be so happy!" she said.

"It's all right. Don't bother him at work. I'll talk about it when he gets home tonight."

"Okay, I'll wait. But I'm going to cook something special tonight. I can get ribeye steaks at Turner's. I'll go right now."

"Mom, please don't!" said Walter.

"But we should celebrate. We have to! You got into MIT! How many kids in the country can say that?"

"But I also got into Columbia," said Walter.

"Of course, but this is the one that really matters. A lot of people get into Columbia. It's a good college. But ... Walter ... *M-I-T*! Think about it."

"I've been thinking about it. It's just that ... I'm not sure where I want to go."

His mother took the envelope from him and folded the letter, tucking it inside.

"I'm going to put this where your father can see it when he comes home," she said. "I can't believe you're not more excited. This is a great day for the whole family. I know it's your decision, but you can't blame me for being thrilled. This is what you and your father have been working toward for the past year. You can't reject it without a lot of serious thought."

"I'm not rejecting it. I'll talk with Dad when he gets home." Walter pretended to return his attention to the piano.

Mom started out of the room, then turned back for a moment.

"Don't get in a fight with him, okay, Baby? I know he can be ... overbearing."

"I don't want to fight," said Walter.

"It's so important to him," she said. "It will make him so happy. Just promise you'll think before you say anything that might set him off."

"I promise," said Walter. He began playing a desultory rendition of Beethoven's Sonata No. 23 in F Minor, known colloquially as "L'appassionata," the passionate song.

His mother called from the front room.

"I'm going to the grocery! Do you need anything?"

"Don't get steaks!" yelled Walter.

Dr. Jim Edelstein came home at 6:45. He spotted the envelope immediately.

"Walter!" he called.

Wendy came out of the kitchen. "He's taking a walk around the park. He said he'll be back by seven."

"Since when does he take walks at night?" said Jim. "Did you see this? He got accepted."

"We saw it," said Wendy. "He says we can all talk about it tonight."

"What's to talk about?" said Jim. "He got in. He should be doing back flips."

"You know it's not that simple," said Wendy. "I think he's had his heart set on Columbia, and this is something he needs time to think about."

"You know Columbia was always just our safety. Now that Massachusetts has said yes, that makes the decision obvious."

"I'm sure he'll come to that same conclusion," said Wendy, "but we need to give him time and space."

"A little time," said Jim. "But not too much. He needs to respond soon. Very soon. It's common courtesy."

"Promise me you two won't get into a fight," said Wendy.

"It's not up to me, but I'll try," said Jim. "I'm not going to start a fight, but you know how he is."

Jim carried the triumphant envelope into the college room, and set it down in the middle of the center table.

The two Edelstein males did not fight. They discussed, sometimes loudly. Jim won the discussion because he was louder and had more endurance. And he was in the right, of course. Wendy gave up trying to moderate and cleared the table. Walter reduced his responses to one or two syllables.

"Sure."

"Whatever."

"I *know*."

It was settled. Walter would sign and mail his acceptance to MIT no later than Friday. Jim would follow up with a formal letter to the admissions office requesting information on tuition rates, on-campus housing, and payment schedules. Everything would proceed as it should.

Walter did what he said. Actually, he just signed the letter and handed it over to his father. The acceptance was sent by registered mail on Friday morning.

SATURDAY, THERE WAS AN AWFUL THING they had to do as a family—attend the funeral of Roger and Cathy Monk.

At the last moment, Jim Edelstein bowed out because one of his patients was experiencing renal failure and had been admitted to Lawrence Memorial Hospital. It was the only time Jim had ever felt relief after receiving news of a diseased kidney.

The service was held at West Hills Fellowship, a large nondenominational church that Cathy Monk had discovered a couple of years ago after a falling-out with First Christian—she had missed its old, retired pastor and found the new one pedantic and overbearing. The congregants at West Hills barely knew David, but Roger and Cathy were well-liked. Aunt Chloe placed the necessary calls, and arrangements were made. Uncle Phillip wrote checks to the funeral home, the church, and Memorial Park Cemetery. He chose that one because the plots were more affordable, and graves were all marked with small, ground-level monuments rather than ostentatious (expensive) headstones. He said his brother would have wanted that, and he was probably right. Roger and Cathy had left only short, boilerplate, outdated wills, and there was a lot to sort out. They had no life insurance. *Typical Roger,* Phillip thought. He dreaded the months of confusion and probate that lay ahead, but he was determined to be reimbursed.

The service was held in the small adjacent chapel rather than the big arena. A couple dozen people attended, including several from the Monks' previous church. The caskets sat side by side, almost buried in flowers. The minister spent some time extolling Roger and Cathy's love of their church, their savior, and each other, and what good parents they were, and how we just have to accept that sometimes we can't understand God's plan even when it seems completely wacky and upside down. Then, a pianist played a recessional hymn because there was no organ in the chapel, and people lined up to smother David in hugs and shake his hand. They promised to be there for him if he needed anything—anything at all.

Wendy and Walter lined up near the back, and when it was her turn, Wendy got her hug and explained that Dr. Edelstein had sent his deepest condolences but that he had a medical emergency.

Walter didn't shake David's hand, but he leaned over and whispered, "I got my passport this week."

David whispered back, "I got mine just before Christmas."

Walter whispered, "The day school is out—We're gonna blow this shithole."

The remark elicited an inappropriate snort from David, quickly stifled.

Wendy told Aunt Chloe, "Those two have been friends since they were little. They can still make each other laugh."

Temporary Arrangements

T HERE WERE COMPLICATIONS. The first and biggest was that David's closest relatives lived in another state. Except, that is, for Cathy Monk's younger sister Charlotte, last legal residence in Topeka, current whereabouts unknown. She had been married three times by the age of thirty and had spent two weeks in county jail at one point for theft-by-check. She would never be anybody's guardian.

Phillip and Chloe Monk were residents of Iowa, which had somewhat different child custodial laws than Kansas, but both states agreed that the age of majority was eighteen. If David wanted to continue to attend high school in Lawrence, he would have to be assigned to a foster home unless either Phillip or Chloe or both were willing to move to Kansas and rent a house or an apartment for David. They weren't. David would finish out high school in Des Moines.

The late Roger Monk family's financial situation was a mess. Phillip took on the responsibility of sorting everything out, quickly discovering that his brother had been cash-poor and debt-heavy. After the costs of lawyer and probate, the value of the house plus the furniture would barely cover the money still owed. Two of the three cars were paid for, including David's Studebaker Daytona, but the Mustang was still a thousand dollars underwater. Everything would have to be sold, and in the end, Phillip was not likely to recover what he had spent getting his brother and sister-in-law buried.

Why do the people with common sense always have to bail out those without any? thought Phillip Monk. Life was unfair to the competent.

David missed the first two weeks of school in the spring semester. On his last day in Lawrence, Uncle Phillip drove him to his old house to collect anything else he wanted before the whole place was closed up. Most of the furniture was gone, but there were still clothes in the closet. He took a few shirts and pairs of pants and sweaters he had not grown out of, but most of it he left behind.

He filled a cardboard box with the books he wanted to keep, his large photography books, and a few art books his mother had given him. He lugged the box into the living room and left it by the door.

While Phillip was poking around the kitchen, wondering if his wife could use any of Cathy Monk's cooking utensils before they sold everything, David slipped into his parent's bedroom. He found the floor safe in their bedroom closet. The combination lock, unspun, opened with a simple turn to the right.

David lifted the heavy lid and poked through the safe's contents. He already had his driver's license and new passport. His birth certificate was still exactly where he had left it two months ago after he'd returned it to the safe. Apparently, it had not been opened since. David retrieved the birth certificate and found an unsealed envelope on the bottom of the safe under a pile of old mortgage statements. Inside was a stack of twenties, four hundred and sixty dollars in cash. He folded the envelope and tucked it into his front pocket.

He heard Uncle Phillip come into the room.

"What'd you find?" he asked and peered over David's shoulder into the closet.

"It's my dad's old safe," said David. "I got my birth certificate." He showed Phillip the envelope.

"You knew the combination?" said Phillip. "I thought I was going to have to hire a locksmith."

"It wasn't locked," said David.

"I should have tried it," said Phillip. "If you're done there, let me have a look."

David stood up and stretched, and it was Phillip's turn to crouch and root through the contents of the metal box.

Phillip came away with a stack of papers he thought might be relevant and then lowered the lid.

"Gather your stuff and put it in the back seat," said Phillip. "We need to head back."

That was the last time David would ever be in his childhood home. Everything left behind would be consigned to an estate sale. A "For Sale" sign would appear in front of the house in less than a month. David glanced back as they pulled away. He never saw the house again.

About halfway back on the drive to Des Moines, David remembered that he still had Walter's birth certificate and social security card stuck within the pages of a book called *Painting with Light – the Photography of Edward Steichen*. Oh well. He'd have to mail them to him. At least Walter already had his passport.

Late that afternoon, a long, black sedan pulled up in front of the house. A large man in a gray jacket and thick wool hat got out and walked to the front door. He rang the doorbell, then knocked sharply. He shaded his eyes with both hands and tried to peer through the windows.

He walked next door and knocked. A chubby woman with a baby cradled in one arm answered and spoke through the screen. They talked for a couple of minutes. He thanked her, touched his hat, and returned to the car.

Driving a few blocks as the light faded, he found a drugstore with a bank of payphones along the wall beside the entrance. He pulled his jacket collar up, fed a couple of coins into the phone, then dialed.

"Sir, this is Roy. I checked his house, and he's not there. Place looks unoccupied." He paused and listened. "Yes, sir, I talked to a lady in the house next door. She said David went to live with some relatives after his folks died, but she doesn't know their names. She thinks they're from out of state." He paused again. "Yes, sir … I'll come on back. I can pursue this better by phone tomorrow. Thank you, sir."

DAVID WAS IN A bedroom that had belonged to a teenage girl. Posters had been on the walls at one time, but all that remained were ghost rectangles of unfaded paint. Chloe had taken her daughter's unclaimed clothes and boxed them up for Lynette to go through later in the unlikely event there was a blouse or T-shirt she might want to keep.

The bed had a flowery comforter, which had to stay for the time being because winter had struck in earnest, but otherwise, the room was bare and genderless. Though he had been here off and on for three weeks, David still had not unpacked his large Christmas suitcase or put away the stack of loose things. That would be admitting that his life had changed forever. He needed a distraction, however, so he lugged the suitcase onto the bed, unlatched it, and spread the two halves into the open position. One side was mostly underwear, socks, and summer shirts, which he stacked in a bureau drawer.

At the bottom of the suitcase, there was a flat white box. It was his present from Judith Charabi. David took out the pendant and held it up by its rawhide string. The ankh. He looked at it closely and realized it had odd little symbols in relief along its surface: a cat, a bird, something wiggly—a snake, perhaps. Another detail he couldn't make out was some sort of insect. Hieroglyphics, he supposed. He stared at it a long time until his vision blurred, and he couldn't quite catch his breath.

Outside the door, Chloe Monk paused. She had been about to knock and ask David if there was anything he needed and to tell him goodnight, but she heard him gasp and cough and then realized he was sobbing.

She went back to the small den that Phillip used as an office and study. He had the papers he'd retrieved from the Monk safe and was going over them one by one, penciling in notes.

"He's crying in his room!" she said. "What should I do?"

"Leave him alone, Chloe," Phillip said.

"But … somebody should be with him. I want to hold him, tell him it's okay."

"Let him be. He's been holding it in—everything that happened. He's finally accepting that his parents are gone. He needs to cry it out."

"I'll give him a few minutes, then knock."

"No. Please leave him alone."

Strange Fruit

CLARITY WAS EXHAUSTING. Nicholas Symansky had emerged from a fog of certainty into a world where his thoughts and actions had to make sense to others as well as himself. In one of his last group sessions at the state mental hospital with Dr. Potter, the psychiatrist Nicholas most respected, he heard something that really got through to him.

"Remember, being well does not necessarily mean there are no crazy thoughts in your head," said Dr. Potter. "I have crazy thoughts from time to time—everybody does. It's your *actions* that have to be sane. You might think, 'I wish I could jump off this building and fly around the city like a bird,' and that's perfectly normal. Thoughts are where we explore ideas, test them out inside our heads. But jumping off a building flapping your arms—that's insane." He flapped his arms spastically, and the patients in the group laughed.

He stood up and walked to the whiteboard, uncapping his marker. A familiar solvent smell drifted across the room. He wrote:

MENTAL WELLNESS IS:

WHAT YOU THINK
WHAT YOU SAY
WHAT YOU DO

"Starting from the top, how important is it to have sane thoughts in your head? Let's say in percentages. Anybody?"

A woman raised her hand. "Maybe twenty-five percent? You can have insane thoughts as long as you recognize them."

"Excellent," said Dr. Potter. "But I wouldn't even give it that much. Let's say 10 percent important." He wrote "10%" beside the first item. "Now, how important is it to the rest of the world what you think?"

A male patient chimed in. "Shit-fire, man. The world don't care what I think." The patients laughed.

"Right!" said the doctor. "The world cares zero percent what we think." He wrote "0%" next to the first number. "Now, how important is what you *say*? We're talking about the world again."

Nicholas spoke up. "When you say crazy stuff, that's when they start worrying about you. But they usually don't call the cops. I'd say 20 percent."

"I'll take that," said Dr. Potter. He wrote "20%" on the second line. "When they let you start wandering around by yourself again—when your doctor says, 'Okay, you're better now, have a good life,'—we do it with the understanding you won't walk around saying things that make no sense, or threaten the 'normal' people." He made air quotes when he said "normal."

"Now, how important is number three in determining whether you are well enough to live in society? How important is what you do? Anybody?" He looked around the room.

"It's everything," said the first female patient.

"Right!" said Dr. Potter. "It's the whole enchilada, as our former president used to say." He drew a big circle around "WHAT YOU DO."

He's right, thought Nicholas. *It's when I couldn't stand the feeling of my own clothes on my body that they put me away.*

Nicholas had learned his lesson. He spoke little, tried to make sense when he did speak, kept his clothes on, shaved every morning, did his yoga routine, went to work, and tried to do a good job. There was nothing challenging about keeping the bakery ovens up to temperature, monitoring the yeast rolls and cinnamon buns, putting the large trays on the racks to cool. But it was something to do, and he enjoyed the accompanying smells.

He took his thioridazine faithfully, morning and night. The antipsychotic drug quieted the relentless agitation that had plagued him before, slowed down his galloping thoughts. But it also left him tired much of the time. Gradually, he grew more accustomed to it.

On nice days, Nicholas walked to work. His usual route from Keystone house to East End Bakery and back took him past the side of a stately, columned fraternity house, Pi Sigma Rho, at the end of "frat row." The house had a second-floor balcony with iron railings on three sides. On weekend evenings, fraternity brothers often congregated and drank beer, shouting at the passersby below, catcalling the girls, and challenging the manhood of the younger male students. People ignored them, for the most part. Occasionally, objects were hurled down and the police got involved. Warnings had been issued a few times, but serious incidents were rare.

As Nicholas was walking past the house on his way home one night, a frat boy deep in his beer had bellowed, "Hey hippie! Got some SPARE CHANGE?!" Nicholas felt the lava rising in his psyche, and he looked up to confront his harasser … only to realize the boy couldn't possibly be speaking to him—the comment was directed at a sad, dirty, and bearded young man waiting to cross the street. Nicholas, with his short hair and white-bread looks, was no longer a target. He was mostly invisible.

His heart still pounded for a time, but the mellow-real kept his emotions leashed. From then on, he walked on the other side of the street. But something about that house stuck in his mind. There was more going on there than met the eye, he was sure.

For one thing, there was a smell. He couldn't tell its origin—was not even sure it came from the Pi Sigma Rho house, but he often caught a faint whiff of some familiar chemical when he was nearby or just up the street from the fraternity. Some kind of solvent, but he couldn't place it and couldn't say why it bothered him.

ON A FRIDAY EVENING, Callie organized a field trip to hear her friend's jazz band. Two members of the Dave Diamond Trio were now her regular massage clients. Besides Dave himself, there was a tall and rotund man named Gage Hathaway who played double bass and suffered from a perpetually aching back from twisting it into unnatural positions five nights a week. Gage lived farther away than Dave, but he was such an upbeat and engaging conversationalist that she didn't mind the extra half-hour drive. He employed her services once a week whenever he was in town.

Callie had promised Dave Diamond she'd gather some of her musically unsophisticated friends and get them out to the Downtowner Lounge before his one-week engagement was finished, and she did. On Thursday, she organized a posse of Keystoners, including Sherry, Nicholas, the Iranians Abbas and Mohammed (the only actual jazz fans in the group), Mike, the Chinese major, and, surprisingly, Nixon and his current girlfriend. A few people in the house said they'd try to make it later but probably wouldn't. Callie asked Wally as well, but he declined since he was working the closing shift at the bookstore. The music wouldn't even start until nine o'clock, meaning Wally could easily drive out after work and meet them, but he begged off. Callie didn't insist.

Callie wasn't sure where she stood with Wally. She also wasn't sure what she thought of him. A night apart might do them good.

By the time Callie and her assemblage got to the club, parked both cars, and got themselves inside, the Dave Diamond Trio was already playing. Tonight, they were a quartet. Dave sat at the keyboard, crutches leaned up against the side of the piano, eyes closed and mouth open, in the moment. The drummer, a bald, middle-aged black man named Keaton, was singing, his head turned sidewise into the microphone (Now *there's* another candidate for physical therapy, thought Callie.) Gage Hathaway played his bass in counterpoint to the drums, bear-hugging the enormous instrument. Tonight, a guest trombonist in a porkpie hat was sitting in, blowing mournful low notes and facing away from the people at the tables.

The lyrics Keaton sang were odd and sad.

The arrival of the Keystone crew almost doubled the size of the audience. When the band finished the song, there was a smattering of applause. Dave responded as if it were an SRO crowd at Birdland.

"Thank you, thank you, ladies and gentlemen! That was 'Strange Fruit,' a tune made famous by Miss Billie Holiday. Because of the movie that came out a couple of years back, *Lady Sings the Blues*, a lot of people think Billie wrote the song, but it was actually written by a Jewish songwriter named Lewis Allen, who was protesting what was happening to Black folks in the South." Dave leaned over and said something to the drummer, then turned back to the mic. "Well, after that, let's brighten this place up with a little Oscar Peterson: 'You Turned the Tables.' Two ... three ..."

It was fun because it was so different. Callie told everybody they should stay in character and drink old-school cocktails, and they did—except Abbas, who didn't drink, and Nicholas because alcohol didn't mix with his meds. Callie, at Nixon's suggestion, ordered a dry martini. When she took the first sip, she winced, but she loved the look of the glass and the olives on a little plastic sword, which fit with the music.

Between sets, a few people left, but more arrived, and most of the tables were occupied. During the break, Dave Diamond stayed at his seat by the piano, so Callie went up on the little stage to say hi.

"Hey, thanks for coming," said Dave. "Did you bring your boyfriend?"

"No, he had to work," said Callie.

"Damn. Guess you'll just have to come home with me."

Callie laughed and returned to her table. Dave Diamond leaned into his microphone for the whole room to hear: "I'm just teasing, Miss Callie ... Ladies and Gentlemen, this is Callie, the woman with the magic hands and the healing touch. By this time next year, she'll have me doing cartwheels up here on the stage."

Sherry leaned over to Callie. "I think he's sweet on you."

"Yeah, he is. But he's a gentleman. No creepy stuff." Callie sipped her martini and tried not to make a face.

Sherry was working on her second old-fashioned of the night. She picked the bourbon-saturated orange slice off the rim and took a bite of pulp.

"Yum! That part I like," she said. "My dad used to order these at dinner. I don't know if I could ever get used to them." She sipped again. "So ... it's not my business, but ... are you and Wally doing okay?"

"We're fine," said Callie. "He just has some things he needs to work out by himself. I'm giving him room to do it. I guess he's confronting his past."

"I know nothing about his past," said Sherry. "He's always been a mystery man. Anything you can share? Or would that be talking out of school? I don't want to pry."

"No, I shouldn't really get into it. If he wants to tell other people, he can. It has nothing to do with me or you."

"Well, maybe it's just the orange slices talking, but I think you two are a good fit. I hope he figures things out."

"Me too."

"I don't know if he told you this," said Sherry, "but he really helped me a couple of months ago when I hit rock bottom with my migraines. I was so sick I wanted to die. I didn't even ask him to help, but he did this thing with his hand." She held up her right hand to demonstrate. "It was sort of like hypnosis. He didn't touch me—he just put his palm close to my forehead for a few minutes and talked really quietly. My face felt all tingly, and when he took his hand away, my head felt a million times better. Since then, I've had maybe three headaches, but nothing like those really bad ones."

"Really? I didn't hear about that," said Callie. "You said he held his hand near your head. Just one hand? Not both?"

"Just the one. His right hand."

"Interesting," said Callie.

"I don't know if it was the power of suggestion," said Sherry. "Maybe I could finally relax because I knew somebody was trying to help. But if he can do things like that for people, he should be something more than a co-op manager. A therapist or a counselor maybe, more like you."

"He's a private person," said Callie. "But I'm glad you told me about that. It makes what I do know about Wally make more sense."

"Hey, I want another drink," said Sherry. "Would you be offended if I ordered white wine instead?"

Callie laughed. "Make it two," she said, pushing her martini glass aside.

Sherry looked over at Nicholas, who sat silent with his eyes closed.

"You holding up all right?" she asked. "Let me know if you need to go home."

No response.

"Mission Control to Nicholas!" she said.

He opened his eyes. "I'm good," he said.

"You'll be okay if we stay a little while longer?"

"Yes."

"Do you like the music?"

"Yes. It's great."

Up on the stage, the drummer returned, adjusted his vocal mic, and sat down, picking up his drumsticks.

"The drum is a heart," said Nicholas.

Sherry glanced at him, but he said nothing more and closed his eyes again. She got up to order two white wines from the bar.

The Korean Word for Hotel

N ICHOLAS OVERSLEPT ON SATURDAY and didn't get out of bed until almost 7:00 a.m. when he was supposed to be at East End bakery. He had been out with Sherry and the others at the jazz club until 1:30 in the morning and forgot to set his alarm.

He rubbed his face and looked at the clock. *Oh, man!*

No time for coffee, breakfast, a shower, or anything else. No yoga. He had really come to love doing his morning yoga routine. *Well, I can't do it this morning.* He dressed quickly and dashed out the front door just as the first streaks of sunlight were starting to hit the roofs of the houses.

He got lucky and caught a city bus at Twenty-Fourth Street, and in the end, he was only about thirty minutes late.

Albert, the manager, was the only one in the store.

"Man, I'm so sorry," said Nicholas. "No excuses. My friends and I were out hearing music last night. I just screwed up."

"Nick, you are literally the only guy in this shop who's ever on time," said Albert. "I can cut you some slack. Tell you what, I've already got the cinnamon roll dough going in the mixer. If you could take over that project, I'll work on the croissants. Give the mixer about four more minutes, then you can roll them out."

Nicholas put on his apron and looked down into the barrel of the large mixer, where twenty pounds of pale, sweet dough was swirling around and around on the large paddle driven by its heavy motor. He felt an involuntary shiver. He didn't like the look of bread dough, and he couldn't tell anybody why, not without revealing something he wanted to forget.

FOR MUCH OF THE YEAR he had spent in the army, 1969, Pfc. Nicholas Symansky had been deployed to Camp Bonifas in South Korea, a large army base near the

Demilitarized Zone. It was a coveted posting because every man there knew he might be deployed to Vietnam at any time. Nicholas was part of a group of specialists who inspected large stores of ordnance, particularly a compound called RDX, making sure the highly explosive substance was secure, stored properly, and showed no signs of leakage or chemical breakdown.

The RDX was mixed with stabilizers and mineral oil to form soft bricks of a sticky, pale-colored putty called Compound 4, or C-4. It looked harmless, and it was, mostly. You could drop it, kick it across the room, bang it with a hammer, even shoot it with a rifle round, and it wouldn't explode. Light it on fire, and it would just burn—hot and bright with a toxic gas—but it wouldn't blow up. Only a primer charge would detonate it, and in that case, the resulting blast was enormous and efficient.

Once, when Nicholas and another soldier were driving across Puja City close to the army base, a tremendous explosion shook the street. They stopped the jeep and looked over their shoulders to see a thick cloud of smoke rising behind some buildings on the next block over.

Alarm bells, horns, then the wail of sirens. They drove around the corner to find a smoking mountain of rubble in the middle of the block, with small gas fires and water spraying from ruptured pipes.

People poured out of the nearby buildings. A US Military Police vehicle roared up, and a pair of MPs got out, blowing their whistles, trying to keep the crowd from getting too close. Nicholas and the other GI got out to see if they could help. A panicked young boy had pointed at the chaos and shouted at them:

"HOTEL! HOTEL!"

The word was the same in Korean and English. A few minutes earlier, it had been a sleek, clean, modern, mid-sized hotel popular with foreigners and diplomats and had now become a smoldering death trap. Anyone staying or working there was buried in dust, twisted rebar, and broken concrete.

Nicholas spent the next four hours laboring alongside other US soldiers, Korean police, and firefighters, digging through smoking rubble, finding pieces of bodies but no survivors. The smell of chemicals combined with the stench of destroyed human beings penetrated his senses. Even when he was handed a gas mask, the odor remained in his sinuses for hours afterward. For several days, anytime Nicholas sneezed, it brought back a sickening whiff of that noxious, unnameable smell.

Later, the forensic investigators determined that the blast had been caused by about sixty pounds of C-4, placed skillfully around the basement. Where it had come from, who had planted it, and why, nobody ever learned. No inventory was missing from any American supply depot, and no group ever claimed responsibility.

Three weeks later, Nicholas had been on inspection duty when everything unraveled. It was the odor of C-4 binder that set him off. Heart racing, vision blurred, he shouted at the walls, the shelves, the stacks of ordnance, making no sense. He was relieved of duty and shipped out to a hospital in Tokyo, then stateside to Eisenhower Army Medical Center in Georgia. After four months, he was given a Section Eight discharge, *Mentally Unfit for Service.*

SINCE THEN, NOT ALWAYS, but too often, Compound 4 haunted his dreams and sometimes his waking life. It was just unsettling how much the damn stuff looked like bread dough. Or rather, how much bread dough looked like C-4. Particularly when loaves were in the proofing box, rising, they made Nicholas's pulse quicken, and he had to avert his eyes.

Nicholas focused on his breathing and made the cinnamon rolls. To be sane is to act sane—the whole enchilada. Nicholas would behave himself. Maybe if there was a slack time later on, he'd sneak into the storeroom and do some yoga.

Despite his tiredness and the little rough moment with the fresh dough, Nicholas had a pretty good day, and it got better as it went. He was cheerful and talkative, chatted amiably with the customers, and told a hilarious anecdote he heard in the state hospital (though he didn't say that part) about a skunk that had walked into a bank lobby during business hours, causing a panicked teller to accidentally trip a silent alarm. He had the whole staff howling with laughter and gasping for breath. He made batch after batch of rolls and cookies.

"Man, you need to stay out late more often," said Albert. "You're on fire today. Good work."

Nicholas laughed, but Albert was right. Nicholas was bubbling with happy energy. When his shift ended, he stayed an extra half hour at the counter so the manager could run a personal errand. It had been his best day at the bakery, and he looked forward to more.

It's when he had finally clocked out and was walking home that it occurred to Nicholas: He hadn't taken his mellow-real today. He didn't skip meds anymore. That was the old Nicholas. When he got back to Keystone, he immediately popped his evening dose with a tall glass of water, then sat on the couch reading the campus newspaper until he began to feel the familiar drag of lethargy overcoming his body and mind. He wasn't hungry but made himself eat some leftovers from the reefer.

When he crawled into his bed, it was only nine-thirty, but he was wiped out. While he waited for sleep, Nicholas thought, *No more mellow-real in the mornings. Nobody should start the day by taking a downer. The medication has done its job, and now I'm better. I'll just take them at night when I go to bed.*

When Sherry checked on him around ten, she found him sound asleep and snoring, so she left him alone.

Something Worth Doing

DAVID'S HIGH SCHOOL in Des Moines was at least twice the size of the one in his hometown. He went to classes, did the assignments, answered questions when asked, but made no effort to make friends. His English teacher remarked that it was refreshing to get a high school junior who typed his papers, and regularly gave him As without commenting very much on the content.

He didn't miss tutoring, but he did miss Ginnie Blake. The last time he'd seen her, it was just "See you after the holidays," and then he'd never laid eyes on her again. Tutoring wasn't necessary anyway because his classes, even algebra, were easier now.

Every evening, he sat at the dinner table with Uncle Phillip and Aunt Chloe. They tried to include him in the conversation, but he had little to say. One night, he overheard them talking. Aunt Chloe said, "We could think about finding a psychiatrist for him," and Uncle Phillip replied, "But, dear, those guys charge like heart surgeons. Just give him time. He'll come around."

After that, David offered some conversational tidbits at dinner about what was happening in school so they would stop worrying about him so much, and it worked. Immediately after dinner he'd say he was going to do his homework and then disappeared into his room. There wasn't enough homework to keep him busy, so sometimes he watched TV with them in the living room.

A couple of weeks after he had moved in with the Des Moines Monks, David got a call from Nathan Charabi. Chloe picked up the phone, and David knew who it was from her responses.

"Now *who* are you?" Chloe asked … "How do you spell that? … With a C? … Oh, you're the people he was working for … Sure, just a second. I'll get him."

Even though the bedroom door was slightly ajar, Chloe tapped lightly on the doorframe with her fingernail.

"David? There's a call for you. A Mr. Charabi?"

David briefly wondered: *Are they sending Roy to pick me up? Are we flying to Rochester? Maybe just down to the ranch for a few days?* He could hope. But no, Nathan Charabi was calling him to make it official that David's services were no longer needed. He was being let go.

"David, we're so glad to hear you've found a place to settle and relatives who could take you in. After what happened—we were so shocked—and we never got a chance to talk, tell you how we felt, and how much you meant to Judith."

"Is she feeling better?" asked David.

"Much better, yes," said Mr. Charabi. "I wouldn't say cured, but the new treatments have made a world of difference. She's home again. She's asleep right now, or you could speak to her. I just wanted to say we're grateful you were able to help her turn the corner. We're just sorry we can't do this anymore."

"Me too," said David. He didn't know what to add.

"Judith misses you, and Lisa says hey," said Mr. Charabi. "You know, maybe this summer, when school is out, you could come visit for a couple of weeks. Depending on how things are going. You can swim in the pool and take the horse out for another ride."

"That would be nice," said David. He tried to think of something to say. "Tell Judith and Lisa I said hi."

"I sure will. Take care of yourself now. Bye."

"Bye."

The Iowa winter continued, long and wet. David's sleepwalking life shuffled on, from room to room, from school to home, and back again, from week to week. His sleep was poor. The worst times were the very early mornings, when he lay half awake, hoping the daylight would come but dreading the day it would bring. He found himself unable to imagine another life. As he lay in the dark, listening to the *click* and *whoosh* from the Iowa Monks' furnace, he imagined that the heat exchanger was rusting through and cracking and that a whisper of carbon monoxide was seeping into the house, building up and concentrating until the moment when it slipped into the bedroom to take him away. He wasn't afraid of it.

One night, he had a vivid dream. He was in a place he didn't recognize, a beach, except it wasn't summer, and there were rocks and pebbles instead of sand. It's Dulcedo Lake, he thought. On the other side, he saw two people riding horses along the shoreline. Out in the water he saw Walter, laughing and windmilling his arms, splashing water. *Come on, man,* he was shouting, but it was too cold, and David didn't want to swim in the lake. David shouted back, *No, let's use the pool. It's heated!* But Walter just kept splashing and dunking his head and splashing water high into the air, giddy.

When David woke, he lay still, making himself remember the dream. He wondered what Walter was doing, whether he had caved to his family's wishes and enrolled in that hot-shot engineering college, or did he escape it all and say fuck it. David realized the dream had been about Spain.

The next Saturday, David asked Aunt Chloe if he could make a long-distance call to an old friend back home, and she said, *of course, David,* and didn't even suggest a time limit.

He phoned Walter. His mother picked up. Just like old times, she thought he was Rory Tisdale. "Walter, it's Rory," she called.

Walter knew it was really David, of course.

"Hey, man! How are things wherever the fuck you are?"

"Iowa. I'm so bored I could stick marbles up my nose for fun."

Walter laughed, that sneering, contemptuous laugh he could do so well and that David had missed.

"Well," said Walter, "I have a cure for boredom, and if you don't go for it, you'll regret it till the end of time."

"You're still set on going to Spain?"

"So set, we have a date and a plan. Denise is in, too. She even worked out all the details with a travel agent. Are you ready to talk turkey?"

"I want to go, yes," said David. "What day were you planning?"

"You have a pencil? Write this down. Are you ready?"

There was always a pen and pad of paper next to the Monks' phone.

"Yeah, I'm ready," said David.

"Okay, the graduation ceremony is May 25th. It's a Thursday night. Of course, there'll be a lot of parties that night, and I'm going to be at one of them."

"Which one?"

"It doesn't matter," said Walter. He was speaking quietly, afraid that his mother would overhear. "The point is, I will be out all night and will end up spending the night at the house of a guy who lives way out east of town, you know, so I'll avoid all the drunks on the highway."

David was confused. "Wait … *Whose* house?"

"It doesn't *matter*," said Walter in a stage whisper. "The point is I'll be gone all night and all the next day. That gives me a day to get to … the first destination."

He said something so quietly David couldn't make it out.

"Get to *where?*"

"Saint … Louis," said Walter, barely audible. "Do you understand?"

"Why?" asked David.

"Because that's where we'll catch the you-know-what to you-know-where."

"Where?"

"New … York," Walter whispered.

"And then to Spain?"

"Yes, yes, that would be correct," said Walter in his normal voice. "Are you in?"

"Yeah," said David. "May 25th?"

"May 26th." Walter was whispering again. "First flight is early the next morning, the 27th, and the big one is late that afternoon, out of Kennedy."

At least David was pretty sure he said "Kennedy."

David heard Walter's mother's voice in the background.

Walter continued at a normal volume. "Yeah, thanks, Rory. Hey, give me a number where I can reach you, and I'll call you later, maybe tomorrow."

David read off the number from the center of the phone dial.

"Gotcha. Tomorrow," said Walter.

"Tomorrow," said David.

As it turned out, Walter did not wait for tomorrow. He called midafternoon while David dozed on his bed with a sci-fi paperback open on his chest.

"David, it's for you!" said Chloe, delighted, imagining David making friends.

Walter spoke quickly but at normal volume. "First question, can you come up with three hundred twenty dollars in cash?"

"Uh … yeah. I can."

"Okay, next, you need to mail it to Denise right away. She has a travel agent who's setting everything up … our plane flights, the hotel in Marbella, even the train from Madrid. All you have to do is get yourself to St. Louis by May 26th. Bring your passport and backpack. We'll stay in a motel by the airport and catch the plane to New York at 7 a.m. Can you do that? You can take the Greyhound. That's what I'm doing."

"Okay," said David.

Walter provided Denise's address, and the conversation was over in three minutes.

David did as instructed. He fished out sixteen twenty-dollar bills from the envelope he had pilfered from Dad's floor safe. The envelope was in the inner pocket of his Skyway suitcase, sitting otherwise empty in the bedroom closet, along with his passport. He folded a piece of lined notebook paper around the money, worried that the cash might be obvious. He knew where Uncle Phillip kept envelopes and stamps and tried to make the letter look as flat as possible when he sealed it. He hoped it wouldn't be too heavy for a regular first-class letter.

The next day at lunch, David walked through gray snow the four blocks from school to a post office in a strip center and mailed the bulk of his life savings to a girl in New Hampshire he had never met.

That night he was studying for his world history midterm, half-heartedly reading a passage about Winston Churchill in a larger book on World War II, and he came across a quote from the legendary prime minister. Upon hearing plans for an upcoming British offensive in Africa, Churchill had written: "Here, at last, is something worth doing!"

David counted his remaining savings—one hundred eighty dollars. He would probably need more than that. How much was bus fare to St. Louis? A night in an airport hotel? Food?

The next night at dinner, David asked Phillip and Chloe if it was okay with them if he found a weekend job. Since they constantly worried about David's mood, and since he was an A student, they said yes. Within two days, he had found a grocery store where he could work Saturdays and Sunday afternoons stocking shelves and bagging groceries for two dollars twenty cents an hour, or roughly thirty dollars a week if he got all his hours. It wasn't Resident Healer of Dulcedo Lake Ranch, but it was a job that took him a step closer to Something Worth Doing.

March passed. There was no new snow, but the old snow wouldn't go away. It just got dirtier and piled up in muddy drifts on the curbs. He kept working at Bledsoe Grocery and soon began working after school two days a week, providing a little more money. He put that money into a checking account every two weeks but always got a twenty-dollar bill back with each deposit, which he added to the envelope. He never went anywhere and had no close friends, so he never spent more than the occasional dollar or two for snacks.

Walter called him after work one Saturday in mid-April.

"Everything is set up," he said. "Denise has our plane tickets, and she'll mail the New York ones to me. When you meet me in St. Louis, I'll have yours. Go ahead and get your bus ticket as soon as possible."

"May 26th?"

"That's right. I'm pretty sure the Greyhound from Des Moines goes through KC, so maybe you and I can be on the same bus. When we get there, we can share a cab to the airport."

"Okay," said David. He wondered how much this was going to deplete his meager savings.

Twenty-six dollars and forty cents, it turned out, with one stopover in Kansas City on the Missouri side. The bus left Des Moines at 6:50 a.m. A little over one month away. David was scared. The whole scheme had so many potential pitfalls. When was he going to break the news to Phillip and Chloe, and how? What if they put their feet down and said, "Absolutely not, young man, we are your legal guardians, and this whole plan is crazy?" Officially, David's school year did not end until that Friday, so he'd have to miss the last day of school. He had to plan carefully over the next month to pull this thing off. He felt short of breath.

But ... David felt fully alive and interested in the future for the first time in months. At last, Something Worth Doing.

And then ... Nathan Charabi called. It was the last day of April, a Sunday when David was doing his six-hour shift at Bledsoe grocery. Usually, Aunt Chloe got the messages, but this time, the pad by the phone had Uncle Phillip's scrawled handwriting—half printed, half sloppy cursive:

David – that man you used to work for, Mr. Charabi, called. Asks you to call him back COLLECT. He says don't worry how late it is.

Below that was the number, which he recognized. Chloe was in the kitchen, and Phillip was somewhere else. David had called home collect a couple of times in his life and knew how. He would dread it until he did it, so he dialed 0 first, and then the area code and number asked the operator to make the call collect and gave his name. He heard the phone ring, and then the operator said, *Will you accept a collect call from David?* and Olivia's voice replying, *Yes, we will accept.* He felt a little sick. Please don't let Judith be dead or dying.

"David? This is Olivia. I'll get Mr. C for you."

It wasn't bad news, it was an invitation. In fact, Mr. Charabi sounded very cheerful.

"David," he said, "I have a great idea for you. Why don't you come out here and see us as soon as school is out? In June. Judith misses you. The whole house, really, but especially Miss Judith."

"I ... uh ... have plans for June ... unfortunately," said David. He suddenly became aware that Aunt Chloe could be listening from the other room.

"Really? Are your plans firm? Because it would be a particularly good time for you to come see us."

"Yeah ... I'm sorry. My friend and I are leaving at the end of May."

"How long will you be on this ... uh ... trip?"

Why did David suddenly feel like he was telling a lie when it was as true as anything he'd ever said?

"We're going to be ... a few weeks," said David. "I could come see Judith ... maybe in July?"

"David, I need to be honest with you. Judith is not doing as well as we had hoped. And you always gave her ... reason to think she could get better. And since you left ... I'm not throwing blame, of course. That was just awful—what happened to your family. But since you haven't been seeing her, her condition is ..."

"I'm sorry," said David. "My friend Walter and I are doing this big trip and we've been planning it for a long time. He's graduating. It's his graduation trip."

"Where are you going?" asked Mr. Charabi. "If you don't mind me asking."

David tried to lower his voice without being inaudible and put his hand up around the mouthpiece like people did in spy movies.

"Spain," he said.

"Spain, you say! Gorgeous country. Well, I can't blame you for wanting to do that. When you get back ... give me a call, okay? Collect, of course."

"I will."

"And, David, calling collect can happen any time, any day. We'll always take your call."

"Okay." He didn't know what else to say. Finally, he added, "Tell Judith I hope she's feeling better soon."

"I'll do that."

David packed his Skyway slowly, in stages. Every couple of days, he'd open the case and toss in some more stuff he might need in Europe. Underwear, undershirts, swimming trunks, extra blue jeans, extra shorts. Socks. Finally, he was down to just a few pairs of things that weren't in the suitcase, and he kept putting those in the laundry hamper, and Aunt Chloe kept washing them. Did she wonder why he had so few clothes? Apparently not.

He had to tell them. He couldn't pull the same stunt Walter intended, just vanishing after the last day of school. That would never do.

He broached the subject at dinner.

"My friend Walter, back in Lawrence, his family travels a lot, and they invited me to go with them after school lets out."

Don't mention Spain yet—don't mention that Walter is leaving home because he hates his father and never wants to see him again.

"Yeah," said Phillip. "Okay. That sounds like fun. How exactly would this work?"

"I would catch a bus to Kansas City and meet them as soon as school is over. I figured out the schedule."

"We can take you," said Chloe. "I'd hate for you to have to ride a bus. Those things are nasty. Not the best people take the bus."

"No, really, I don't mind," said David. "Besides, it would be a working day. And I kinda like riding the bus." Not true. But buses weren't *that* bad.

Then David changed the subject, and the tacit approval stayed in the air. At some point, though, Spain would have to be mentioned. *Oh, didn't I tell you?*

Walter was supposed to call when he knew exactly which Greyhound he was taking from KC to St. Louis and when he had the airplane tickets in hand. Every day after school, he checked the message pad, just in case.

Then, one day there was a message, but not from Walter. It was from Nathan Charabi.

In Aunt Chloe's neat calligraphy, it said:

David – Mr. Charabi called, said he is between phones but he needs to talk to you. He will call again tomorrow or next day.

"What is this about?" asked Chloe. A legitimate question, certainly.

"The Charabis want me to come visit them at the ranch this summer after I get back from … the vacation with my friend Walter." He had come within a hair's breadth of saying "Spain."

"Wow," said Chloe. "It looks like you're having a pretty busy summer. That's great."

Mr. Charabi did not call the next day or the day after that. What did he mean, "between phones"?

Then, when David got home from work on Saturday, where he had finally summoned the courage to give his two weeks' notice, there was yet another note taken by Chloe.

David – Mr. Charabi says he is still away from phone, but needs to talk. Will call later or maybe tomorrow.

The next morning was Sunday. Phillip and Chloe went to church, but David didn't. He had gone with them a couple of times to their gray-headed Episcopal church, but once he had the job at Bledsoe's, he begged off, and they didn't insist.

It was the first really nice day of spring, which had been slow to arrive. The sun was bright, and the burr oaks and aspen trees were budding all over town, and flower gardeners were busy spading up newly thawed soil.

Less than two weeks until liftoff. Spain was starting to seem real. He was all packed and had a little extra money saved. When he cashed his last paycheck next week, he'd have even more.

David walked three blocks to a small snacks-and-cigarettes store just to get a nice walk in the sun. He didn't need a jacket. Winter was truly done. He bought a double pack of processed cupcakes and a bottle of apple juice and walked back, letting the sun bathe his face.

There was a black car parked in front of the house. As he approached the grim vehicle, the driver's door opened, and a large man stepped out. It was Roy.

"David," he said. "Miss Judith needs you. Can you come with me?"

"Right now?"

"Yes."

"To the ranch?"

"No, to the airport," said Roy. "She and Mr. Charabi are in Boston. Can you come now? It's very important."

"Okay," said David. "My aunt and uncle are at church. Can we wait till they get back?"

"We need to leave now if we want to catch the flight," said Roy. "Can you write a note? I'm sorry I had to just drop this on you out of the blue."

So, David scribbled a quick note on the phone pad, tore it off, and left it on the kitchen table.

Had to leave for a few days to see Mrs. Charabi. Everything is OK. I will call. – David

He retrieved the packed Skyway from the closet and hefted it outside, where Roy opened the trunk, slid the suitcase inside, and shut the lid in one smooth motion like he had done a thousand times as a professional manservant.

David got into the front seat of the big rental car, and they drove away. Roy never asked David why he had a suitcase packed and ready to go. They hardly spoke a word all the way to Des Moines International Airport.

Searching for the Real Walter

WALLY'S SHIFT AT THE BOOKSTORE ended at 9:00 p.m., but he stuck around because he wanted to use the WATS line. Tonight was the usual weekly Keystone house meeting, but Wally had asked Sherry to run it. She'd keep it short anyway, which the house members appreciated. There was nothing urgent on the agenda.

While the other three employees of University Books were winding things down and getting ready to go home, Wally went into the store's small office. Peggy, the manager on duty today, was taking paperwork and pens off the desk and putting them away. It would be Peggy's job to babysit the store until 10:00, let the cleaning crew in, then stay until midnight before locking everything down for the night.

Peggy looked up as Wally came in.

"Are you clocked out?" she asked. She always asked that, though Wally had never once forgotten to clock out.

"Yeah, I just need to use the phone for a minute," said Wally.

"No problem."

He hoped she would leave, and after a minute, she did. What he wanted to do was technically against company rules, but even if he were caught, he wouldn't get more than a mild reprimand. Every employee, including Peggy, occasionally used the WATS line for personal long-distance calls.

He took out a small phone book, black and worn, from his pocket and found a number penciled on the last page. He picked up the receiver and hit 0-1. The bookstore shared the WATS line with four other companies in the building.

"Operator."

"Hi, Miriam," he said. At night, it was always Miriam. "This is Wally at University Books. Could I get the out-of-state line?"

"Sure, Wally."

CLICK, CLICK. Dial tone.

Denise Mayberry, Walter's one-time girlfriend, was not likely to still be living with her parents. She must have graduated from college by now—moved on with her life. Her family might not be at this number anymore. He looked at his watch. It would be almost 10:30 p.m. in New Hampshire.

But Denise's father picked up.

"Yes?"

"Hi, this is ... David Monk. I'm trying to get hold of Denise Mayberry. I knew her in high school."

"Denise? She's been living in California the past two years."

"Do you have a number?"

"I do, of course, but I'm not sure she'd want me just giving it out to anybody. What is your name again?"

"David Monk. I'm actually trying to track down a mutual friend of ours, Walter Edelstein. I thought she might know how I can get ahold of him."

"Ah yes ... Walter ... I do remember *that* guy. Hang on a minute."

Wally hoped he hadn't blown his chances by dredging up some uncomfortable history, but Denise's father came back on the line and gave him a phone number in San Diego.

Wally called the operator again to reconnect to the WATS line. At least it wasn't so late out in California.

A man answered the phone and then called out, "Denise, it's for you!"

She came on the line. "Hello?"

"Hi, Denise. This is David Monk."

"David Monk? David ... Monk," she repeated. His real name had now been said several times. It was strange to hear.

"I was a friend of Walter Edelstein," he said.

"Of *course*," said Denise. "You're his old friend from Kansas. I just didn't remember the last name."

"I lost touch with Walter years ago. I was hoping you might know how I could get ahold of him. It's been a long, long time."

"It sure has," said Denise. "It's been a while for me, too. I guess the last time ... maybe three or four years ago ... he called me out of the blue. At the time, he was living in Chicago."

"Chicago?"

"Yeah, I don't know what he was doing. I know he wasn't in school. He told me he was sick of the city and the politics, and it was too cold for him anyway, and he was planning to move south. He said he'd call me when he got settled. I never heard from him, though. I was moving myself about that time, and I think we just lost contact."

"Oh ... okay ... thanks."

"Have you tried his parents? I don't know if they're still in Kansas."

"I did ... or somebody I know did ... and they weren't much help. They didn't know where he is."

"Well, that's too bad. I hope you find him. If you do, please tell him I'd love to hear from him."

"I will. Thanks again. It was good to talk to you."

"Hey ... David," said Denise. "I know Walter said some really cruel things to you when you wouldn't go with us to Spain, but he didn't really mean them. He was just angry at everybody, and he took it out on you."

"I know that. It was a weird time for me, too. My parents had died, and I was living with my aunt and uncle."

"I remember," said Denise. "That was awful. I don't understand why he blamed you. It was just supposed to be a fun adventure. We were going to see Spain, ride the train to France maybe, have a blast, then go back home and start college. But for Walter ... it was his great escape, I suppose. I don't think he even meant to come back. He had worked so hard to pull it off, and then you couldn't go. In the end, we never got to go either."

"You didn't?" said Wally. "I thought you guys just went to Europe without me."

"We made it as far as New York, but then Walter had an accident, and the whole scheme fell apart."

"Wow," said Wally. "I never knew. What happened?"

"I was supposed to meet him at Kennedy Airport. His plane from St. Louis was late, and by the time we found each other we had about ten minutes to make it to the Madrid flight. We're running through the airport, lugging our backpacks. We found the gate, but there was this long row of seats, and we were on the wrong side of it. Instead of going around, we decided to jump over this little gap between two seats. I went first and made it—it was only about two feet high—then I hear this huge crash behind me. I turn around and Walter is on the floor moaning. He had caught his foot and come down so hard he broke his thigh."

"Oh, Jesus!"

"That was it for Spain. Walter got taken away by ambulance, and of course, they figured out pretty quick that we were both seventeen and that he was technically a runaway. His parents flew up to get him, but he ended up staying in the hospital a week because they found out he had some kind of nerve condition. That's why he lost his balance."

"I didn't know," said Wally.

"I went up to visit him in the hospital a couple of times, but he was just mad at the world. He was nice enough to me, but he said some horrible things to his dad, which made me uncomfortable, and I wanted nothing to do with it. I just flew back home and went on with my life."

"I can't blame you."

"Well, I just hope he's past all that stuff. Everybody gets mad at their family when they're seventeen. It's a normal part of growing up. I'm sorry to hear he's still estranged from his mom and dad. I know they took it hard when he dropped out of MIT later, especially his dad. Some people just can't let things go. Walter always felt everything ... more intensely than most people."

"Yes, he did," said Wally—long pause. "Well, Denise, thank you for filling me in. I definitely learned some things."

"Good luck finding him," said Denise.

"Thanks. I think I'm beginning to understand. Maybe he doesn't want to be found."

To WALLY'S SURPRISE, the weekly Keystone house meeting was still going on when he arrived back home. Sherry looked exhausted, rubbing her eyes, while two guys talked over each other loudly. Wally hoped she wasn't getting another migraine.

"You have a key!" said Willy. "If you don't want people in your room, lock it. Jeez!"

"I shouldn't fucking have to," said Aaron, a big guy with a mop of tightly curled hair, the house's newest resident. "I can't lock my room every time I go down the hall to take a shower."

"We can't stop people from walking in off the street. It's an open house," said Willy.

Rebecca jumped in: "But it's happening at night, too!"

Wally was the manager, so he had to get involved. "Okay, what's happening?"

"Stuff's getting stolen," said James.

"Wait a minute," said Wally. "Stop talking at once. Exactly what got stolen?"

"I had six dollars in my desk," said Rebecca. "It was there yesterday, and this morning it was gone, just like that. And I was home all night. It had to be somebody who lives here, watching me go in and out of my room. That's just sick!"

"I lost two of my records," said Willy. "But I found them. They were out here." He gestured at the large, common collection of scratched and worn albums on the shelf.

"So, you didn't technically lose them," said Wally.

"Yeah, but somebody got them out of my room without saying a word to me about it. I don't want my records out here. They get treated like shit. So, I'm locking up my room, and everybody else should, too."

"I shouldn't fucking have to," said Aaron. "Especially not when I'm home."

"Aaron, I take it you got something stolen, too?" asked Wally.

"Hell, yeah," said Aaron. "Two of my art books and one poetry book—John Donne. If I catch this jerk, he's getting punched in the face."

"John Donne?" asked Jerry Lewis. Everybody laughed. Jerry looked confused.

"No, the son of a bitch who's stealing my stuff," said Aaron.

"What if it's a chick?" asked somebody else.

"Oh, shut up. You know it's a guy."

"That's sexist," said Rebecca. "Women can be thieves, too."

Everybody was tired, and the meeting collapsed of its own weight.

To Wally (and Sherry), this sounded too familiar. Wally looked around for Nicholas, who never attended house meetings, but he was nowhere to be found. He couldn't be reverting to old, bad behavior, could he? Surely not. Wally would have to ask him about it.

Wally walked to Callie's apartment. He was initially pleased that she had moved out of Keystone—he had been able to find a replacement tenant—but now they seldom saw each other. There was a coolness between them, he thought. She was spending more and more time developing her business, and she talked about the guys—except for one older woman who lived alone in the West Campus area, they were all guys—a lot more than he was comfortable with. He shouldn't let himself be jealous, but it was funny to think that his girlfriend saw other men naked almost every day. Yes, yes, it was all professional. And, except for Dave Diamond, the jazz man, who was probably not yet thirty, they were mostly older men with various infirmities. Would his true love fall for a guy with gimpy legs? That was a mean thought, and Wally wouldn't go there.

Callie was not at her apartment. He should have called. He started walking the three blocks back to Keystone. About halfway home, midway down a street a block over from the co-op, he heard the unmistakable sound of an air-cooled engine. He looked up, and around the corner came the old Type 3 Squareback, which pulled up to the curb and parked thirty feet up the street.

Callie got out of the car, shut the door rather hard, then spotted Wally.

"Hi!" she said. "You'd think I could park at my own damn apartment! But, no!"

"What happened?"

"The usual. A guy downstairs tells his friends they can park at the Frontier every time they come over to drink and watch football. But, of course, there's only six parking spots, and somebody like me is just shit out of luck."

"I'm sorry," said Wally. "Can you call your landlord?"

"I could," said Callie, "except the landlord is a company in Dallas. There's a manager, but he's worthless even when he's home, which he never is."

"That blows," commiserated Wally.

"Yeah, and now I don't have my key with me, so I have to leave the massage table in the car unlocked."

"I'll help you carry it."

"Thanks," she said, "but it's not worth the trouble. Nobody wants my damn table anyway. I'm just irritated."

She walked right over to Wally, stood right in front of him, and kissed him hard on the mouth.

"I've missed you," Callie said. "I want something good to happen."

"You want to go back to your place?" said Wally, hopefully.

"Yes, I do," said Callie. "And I think we should have SEX. I've had my hands all over men's bodies lately, and I have really missed being touched."

"Well, okay," said Wally, his mood lifting like a hot-air balloon. "I can do that."

They held hands and walked back up the street. An old woman they had not seen in the shadows, standing with what may have been most of her earthly positions in a Safeway shopping cart, winked at them comically as they walked past her.

"Have a great time, you two!" she said.

Wally averted his gaze, but Callie replied brightly.

"Thanks! We will."

WALLY HAD WANTED TO STAY THE NIGHT at Callie's, but with the recent theft complaints, he thought he should probably keep an eye on the house of which he was nominally in charge. He walked back to Keystone through the dead-quiet streets.

It was almost 2:00 a.m. The residents had voted to lock the front door after eleven o'clock at night, but of course, the door was not locked. It was not even shut all the way. To his dismay, Wally found that almost every light downstairs was blazing, even the three-row bank of bright fluorescents that lit the dining room like a movie set, and there wasn't a wakeful soul in sight. He walked around downstairs throwing switches.

Somebody was in the kitchen, however. Wally walked in to find large bags of flour, sugar, and rice stacked neatly on the large cutting board and heard somebody thumping around in the walk-in pantry.

It was Nicholas, on kitchen cleanup duty. He had a wet cloth in one hand and a roll of paper towels under his arm.

"Hey, Wally!" he said.

"Nicholas, what are you doing?"

"Cleaning out the pantry, obviously."

"Again?" asked Wally. "The pantry looks pretty clean to me."

"Well, it isn't," said Nicholas. "I've been worried about this place. I found roach droppings on the bottom shelf. Some of the food bags are open and haven't been put in plastic, which is a basic kitchen rule. I also want to make sure there is nothing dangerous being stored back here."

"Like what, exactly?"

"Like things that can become unstable with age. There's a chemical smell in here, somewhere, but I can't locate the source."

Wally looked around at all the stacks of food staples. "I do hope you're planning to put all this stuff back."

"Of course," said Nicholas. "By morning, all will be restored to a clean and safe condition."

"Okay," said Wally, "but deep cleaning like this is beyond the scope of the job. It's more like a once-a-semester project."

"I know it's going beyond normal," said Nicholas, "but us older guys, me and you, even Nixon, we've been around the block a few times. These kids today—I know I'm starting to sound like somebody's dad—but the young people in this house, they're living away from their parents for the first time. You remember how it was. It starts to dawn on you that the life they've been preparing you for consists of a bunch of pseudo games that the world expects you to get good at. Then you forget what's important, and you get all cynical."

"You're starting to sound like an old friend of mine," said Wally. "His parents were smart and rich and spent all their time making sure he'd be smart and rich, too, but in the end, it just made him mad, so he dropped out of college and left it all behind."

"That was kind of my story, too, said Nicholas. "My folks were academics, though they didn't have a lot of money. My dad pulled all kinds of strings to get me into UC Santa Barbara studying chemistry. But after two semesters, I quit and joined the army just to piss him off."

"I didn't know you were in the military," said Wally.

"Well, it didn't go very well," said Nicholas. "But one thing the army taught me was the importance of keeping everything clean and in order. These kids today—there I go again—but these young people like to think deep thoughts about changing their pseudo world, but they live like pigs. Guys like you and me, who know how things work, we have a responsibility to keep these kids safe till they can figure their lives out."

"I don't think there's anything too dangerous in the food pantry," said Wally. "Anyway, don't you have work tomorrow?"

"I don't have to be there till seven," said Nicholas. "Don't worry about me." He turned and resumed wiping down a shelf with long sweeping motions.

Wally gave up and went to bed. How could he not worry about Nicholas? The obsession with cleanliness was strange. Well, at least it was a huge improvement over last year's bearded, naked night wanderer.

He had forgotten to ask Nicholas about the missing books. Oh well.

Something in the Air

LBERT, THE MANAGER OF EAST END BAKERY, sent Nicholas home early. He had been working with his usual energy, but there was something off about his behavior today. For one thing, he was talking to himself more than you'd expect somebody to do when they're absorbed in a routine task. A few times during the day, Albert overheard Nicholas saying odd little phrases like "It's warm in the sun world," or "We must hold this pose," or, strangest of all, "Some have called thee mighty and dreadful." What was *that* about?

Albert was aware of his employee's mental history—Nicholas had been completely up-front about his stay in the Travis State Hospital.

"Nick, have you been getting enough sleep?" Albert asked. "You seem a little whacked out today."

"Oh, I get the sleep I need," said Nicholas. "It's not always eight hours. I guess I was up pretty late last night."

"Hitting the music scene again?"

"No, just doing some work around the house. Once I get started on something, I like to keep going till I finish. That's just how I am."

"Well, tell you what," said Albert. "Go ahead and clock out for today. We have plenty of help, and you need your beauty rest."

"I'm really okay," said Nicholas.

"No, seriously, I need you fresh for tomorrow. Clock out and go home. Get some sleep tonight. I insist."

"Sure thing," said Nicholas.

IT WAS 6:50 WHEN HE LEFT THE BAKERY, early enough that a lot of buses were still running. But he decided to walk home.

It had been a hot fall day, and the streets radiated heat even as the sun set. He took his time, strolling across the north side of campus. The students were back, and the place was bustling. He admired the age and stateliness of the old gray buildings, the thick ivy, the smooth, concave steps worn by thousands of shoes, boots, and bare feet over the decades.

He came to the main west campus street and crossed at the light with a stream of students and staff, then turned south through fraternity row to get away from the crowd. As he reached a smaller street and turned, he heard the bells of the tower clock chime and stopped to listen. He closed his eyes. The bells ... were saying something. There was anxiousness in their tone as if they were afraid. Were they trying to warn him? He waited and counted through the seven low chimes. What were they trying to tell him?

And then he got it. It was the smell. Very faint, more like the memory of a smell than anything he could identify. He looked up and realized he was standing in front of that house—Pi Sigma Rho fraternity—a place he usually avoided. The big iron gates were open, and a van was backed into the driveway. Several boys were there, unloading large square cardboard boxes. A queue of boys was lined up behind the van while two others handed each one a box in turn, which was then carried into the house.

"That's all of them!" shouted one and slammed the rear doors of the van.

The smell came to him again, stronger. He turned and walked, wanting to leave it behind. After a couple of blocks, the thought came to him, like a laser beam right into his brain. He remembered the smell. It was hexogen. RDX.

He stopped in his tracks. That was it! They were unloading boxes of RDX!

But, wait ... he remembered from army training that RDX itself is odorless. The smell is the binder they use to turn RDX into C-4.

He had to go back and warn them. But ... that made no sense. If the Pi Sigma Rho fraternity was storing boxes of C-4, they must know what they're doing. Nobody obtains C-4 without having some specific purpose. He had seen them carrying at least a dozen boxes, maybe twenty inches square. Each of those boxes could contain ... how many ... twenty or twenty-four demolition blocks? Ten of those wired together could destroy a building if they were placed skillfully.

I have to tell someone. Will they think I'm getting schizy again? No, I don't have to tell anybody. I can just keep it to myself.

Being sane is agreeing not to say certain things. But ... those beautiful old buildings. What if the plan is to take out one of those? Bring it down in a thunder of dust and stone, killing dozens or hundreds of people.

If I don't tell, how could I live with myself?

He walked briskly toward Keystone. He could talk to Sherry. She understood him. But then again, she'd asked him yesterday if he'd stopped taking his mellow-real, and he'd told her no, of course not. *I just have it down to one dose per day,* he said. But even that was a lie. The bottle of thioridazine had sat untouched in his top drawer for many days now. He didn't need it anymore, he was quite certain. How could Sherry believe him when he'd already lied to her so many times?

Wally. He's a smart guy, and he gets me. I need to tell Wally about the C-4. He has a gold aura. He'll believe me.

The Youngest Son

AVID SAT IN BRIGHAM AND WOMEN'S HOSPITAL in Boston, waiting to see Judith. They were keeping her here for now, but Mr. Charabi said there were plans to move her to a "chronic care" facility where she could take a longer time getting better. It would have to be somewhere in Boston, he explained, because she was too sick to travel.

David wondered what Phillip and Chloe were thinking. He'd tried to call them from the Des Moines airport, but they still weren't home. They had been kind to him and took him in when his world fell apart. To just leave a short note and disappear …

The waiting room was busy, though it was Sunday night. People came and went while David tried to watch TV. He'd been here over an hour. He thought he could see Judith right away, but Mr. Charabi said there was some sort of problem getting permission. He looked around the room for interesting magazines, but there were none.

Two televisions, one on each end of the room, played different stations at too-low volume. One was showing a travel documentary about South America, and the other was the long-running show *The Wonderful World of Color*, except the hospital TVs were not color. The show started with a segment featuring Walt Disney himself, though the great man had died five months earlier, almost the same time as David's parents.

Walt Disney it would have to be. Just as David stood to turn up the volume, Nathan Charabi came into the waiting room, spotted David, and beckoned. David followed him out into the hallway.

"Okay, they said they'll let you see her," said Mr. Charabi. "But, listen, I had to fib. I told them you were her son. They let some of her friends see her a few days ago, but now they're saying she's too sick, so it's family only. Lisa is with her now, and she says she'll go along with the deception. Is this okay with you?"

"Sure," said David.

They rode a slow elevator to the fifth floor.

"This all came on so suddenly," said Mr. Charabi. "We thought she was getting better. We were making plans to go back to the ranch, and then ... they gave her an MRI and ... there's a new problem. She has a tumor in her brain."

"Oh, no," said David.

"It's very small, but it's deep, on the left side, and they can't get to it with surgery. We might try radiation when she gets stronger, but for now, her doctors say she's too weak, so we just have to wait. If they had just caught it earlier ..."

"I knew something was ..." David began, but then he stopped. He was going to say *something wrong on that side of her head*, but there was no point. The truth was ... he had known a year ago there was something bad going on, that her illness was unbalanced, focused on one side. If he had said something, then maybe ...

The elevator opened, and they stepped out. David followed Mr. Charabi to the desk where there were two older nurses.

"This is our youngest son, David," he announced.

"Hi, David," said the nurse. "You can visit your mom for a little bit, but please keep it short and sweet. She is very, very tired."

"All right," said David.

The room was dark, lit only by a dim lamp in the corner and the glow from the dials on a couple of machines. One of them was pumping oxygen into a mask. An IV drip went into her left arm at the wrist.

Lisa stood up. He hadn't seen her. She had been sitting in a visitor's chair, and David's eyes were not yet adjusted to the low light.

"Hi, brother," she said and smiled weakly. Her eyes were puffy.

"Hi."

Mr. Charabi put his hand on Lisa's shoulder. "Honey, let's stretch our legs and let David visit with Mom. You want to go downstairs and get some dinner at the café?"

"I'm not hungry right now," said Lisa. "I want to just walk around for a while."

Mr. Charabi went to the bed, leaned over, and put his hand on Judith's hair.

"Hey, pretty lady. David's here." He bent down and whispered something to her. Her eyes half opened, then she turned her head slightly toward David and nodded. Maybe she was smiling, but with the oxygen mask, you couldn't tell.

Mr. Charabi came over to David, leaned close, and spoke very low.

"Do what you can do, David," he said. His voice was choked. "I don't know … It's almost like she's giving up. I don't want her to give up. She has to hold on and get stronger."

Mr. Charabi left the room, followed by Lisa, who pulled the door shut behind her.

David was alone with Judith.

Except he wasn't. He looked around the room. He saw no one, but someone else was here, and he could feel it, the way you can sometimes tell a person is sitting quietly behind you. Nobody was visible, but somebody was present.

He turned to Judith on the bed. She was tugging at her oxygen mask, trying to take it off.

"It's okay," David said. "You can leave it on."

But she kept pulling at it with one hand, so he helped her remove it and set it beside her head on the pillow. Her eyes were red and watery, and there were lines on each side of her face where the mask had been pressing.

She smiled softly.

"I'm sorry," she said and closed her eyes.

David began. It had been a very long time since he tried to help Judith or anyone else. He hovered his right hand over her forehead. Judith was there, very quiet, alive. He had to keep his hand very close. He began searching her body for pain to discharge, but there was none. It was as if her spirit were resting quietly on top of her body rather than within. He looked over his shoulder again, but no one was there, and yet someone else was there. Then he recognized it because he had felt it before. It was Death, waiting patiently, showing David respect, letting him finish his work.

David could detect her life energy, but there was nothing to do with it.

"I'm floating," Judith said.

"Why don't you imagine you're riding Bumblebee?" he said.

"Okay," she said.

David's hand hovered. In all his time as Young David, the healer, he never touched anyone on purpose, but now he placed his hand gently on her forehead. Her energy, so tenuous, was there beneath his hand. If he stayed, could he keep her life from slipping away? He would remain here as long as they let him.

"I'm riding," Judith said dreamily. "Where should I go?"

"Ride up the hill," said David. "Go up to where you can see the house and the lake and the river."

"Uphill," said Judith. "I'm riding up."

David's lifted his hand ever so slightly, and it trembled. He held it an inch above her forehead, between her eyes. His shoulder throbbed, but still, he stayed. He felt he was holding Judith by a tether, and he must not let her go, not yet. He concentrated on her breath and his breath. They breathed together.

In breath. Out breath. Breathe. Breathe. Breathe.

The door opened, and a nurse whisked in. David quickly pulled his hand away.

"Why is her mask off?" said the nurse accusingly.

"She took it off herself," said David.

"We'll have to take care of that," said the nurse, looking at David, disbelieving. She put the mask back on Judith's face. "Lift your head a little bit, honey" she said and slipped the strap over her black hair to secure the mask in the back. She turned to David. "Let your mom rest, okay? You can see her later."

"Can I stay with her just a little longer? She can keep her mask on."

"No. She needs to rest. Go now."

And so David, who was of no use to anyone, left Judith alone with the nurse and with Death and walked out into the brilliantly lit hallway.

DAVID MONK RETURNED TO DES MOINES to live with his aunt and uncle.

He called Walter and said he wouldn't be going to Spain after all. There would be no European getaway for David, no Mediterranean beach resort, no Eurail pass.

"Don't be a chickenshit," said Walter. "What did you do? Tell your aunt and uncle? They're not even your real parents. Just go! That was always the plan, to just go and say fuck them all. How can they stop you?"

"I can't go," said David. "It just didn't work out." He couldn't say the real reason—that he did not deserve Spain or any good thing.

"Then you *are* a chickenshit!" said Walter. "A chickenshit and a loser." Walter had started out in a hushed tone, but now he was yelling. "You're just gonna be a good little boy and do what they tell you, do the high school bullshit and the irrelevant college bullshit, and find yourself a nice, safe little job somewhere. Is that your plan? You're worse off than me, and you don't have the balls to do anything about it. God damn it, this is your *chance!*"

"I can't," said David. "I'm sorry. You go."

"What is *wrong* with you?" said Walter. "Is it that old rich lady? You have to keep faith healing?"

"No. It's not that. She died. I just can't go."

"Oh, I get it," said Walter. "You want to find yourself some other rich people who'll pay you for your magic tricks. You can be a kept man and live the lifestyle you're accustomed to. Is that what you want?"

"No," said David.

"Then fuck … you!" His oldest friend hung up on him.

MAY CAME AND WENT, and then summer. David worked at an ice cream shop in Des Moines, then a gardening center, carrying bags of mulch and potting soil to customers' cars. The salary wasn't great, but he sometimes got tips. He made a couple of friends, not confidants or intimates, just some guys who were irreverent and funny and liked to do stuff. Occasionally, he found himself invited to gatherings. He enrolled at Roosevelt High School for his senior year and had his picture taken wearing the top half of a white tuxedo.

In early September, a package addressed to him arrived at the Monk house. It was a big, sturdy box packed with paperback books, mostly old science fiction. There was also a note from Walter.

> *Hey, I'm taking off. I wanted you to have these books, because my mom would just give them away. Maybe you'll appreciate them. – W*

That was it. Nothing more. David took out one book, a title he had never seen. It was a novel called *This Immortal* by Roger Zelazny. He would read this one. The others he left in the box, which he shoved deep into the bedroom closet.

He took off his shoes and lay on the bed, propped up by pillows, and opened the book. He would savor this book, read it slowly, and after that would be another book and then another. And in this way, the time would pass.

The Mission

WALLY GOT A DAMN PARKING TICKET. Last week, he found a decent spot on the street about half a block from Keystone, parked there, and then left his car because the transmission was making more and more noise, and he feared a cataclysmic failure. He had taken the car to Perry's Westside Motors. The mechanic had poked around the car for a bit, drove it around the block, accelerating and decelerating while the transmission growled, then shook his head in commiseration. Wally should take it to a transmission specialist—a mechanic with highly specific skills and who would charge like a neurosurgeon. He topped off the transmission fluid, which was a little low, added a special chemical additive that might give it a few more miles, but the old crash box needed some serious love. That's exactly how he put it: "The old crash box needs some serious love."

He left the Maverick where it was, walked everywhere he could, or took the bus or borrowed Callie's car, putting off the decision that had to be made: Fork over two weeks' wages to fix the car or sell it for junk and get a new one. Or rather, a "new" one, another unreliable steel albatross to bleed his savings.

The ticket was not just a ticket but a big orange sticker on the driver's side window. Move or lose it, buddy. He started the car and drove it up and down streets in an expanding square, gears grinding, until he found a good spot about four blocks away. When he peeled off the orange sticker, he didn't have a razor blade, so he couldn't get all the adhesive off the window. He walked home.

Back at Keystone, there was a commotion in the kitchen. As soon as he walked in the door, somebody said: "Wally's here!"

Oh, shit. What now?

Mike, the cook's assistant, had tried to run the giant Hobart stand mixer plugged into one of the outlets next to the long central cutting board. This was something everybody supposedly knew not to do because the circuit breaker would trip every time, sending one side of the kitchen and half the downstairs into a blackout. Nobody had warned the new sous-chef, who kept muttering that the kitchen needed "some better equipment." Don't we all?

Wally told him to move the Hobart back to the side of the kitchen where the power was reliable and went back into the pantry to find the breaker panel. He struck a kitchen match to see by. He found the tripped breaker, threw the switch, and—*pop*—the lights came back on.

He went back into the brightly lit kitchen, where Jerry Fox Lewis, the cook, and Mike, the sous-chef, scurried to make up for the power delay.

"You guys need anything else, or can I go now?" asked Wally.

"I think we're good," said Jerry. "Let everybody know dinner will be about fifteen minutes late."

Like that's my job, thought Wally. He started to leave the kitchen.

"Wait," said Jerry. "Nicholas was looking for you."

"Where is he?"

"I don't know, but …" Jerry lowered his voice. "I think he's acting a little … you know … coo-coo." Jerry twirled his finger next to his head, the universal sign for insanity. "He's talking strange shit again."

This I don't need, thought Wally.

As he exited the kitchen, Wally heard Mike call: "Jerry! Where's that big chopping knife? The pink one."

Somebody probably washed it and put it away wet, thought Wally as he headed back to his room to fetch a fresh shirt, replace the one he had just sweated up, and then see what was up with Nicholas. *Surely, he hasn't stopped taking his medication. Please.*

Wally found a fresh shirt, then went to the large bathroom and washed his hands and face. Feeling better, he thought maybe a twenty-minute catnap was in order. It was certainly tempting. But, really, he wanted to talk to Nicholas first, find out what was going on.

As he headed back to the common room, he heard a girl shout something and then a male voice.

"Go get Wally!"

Oh no.

Walking into the common room, Wally met Rebecca, who was coming to get him.

"Nicholas is outside!" she said. "He's got a knife! Sherry's trying to talk to him."
Oh shit.

Outside, he found Sherry at the bottom of the porch steps, facing Nicholas, who was standing twenty feet away on the sidewalk, facing the house.

He had the Big Pink Knife. He was holding it with the blade facing down, flat against his chest.

"Just come back inside, please!" Sherry said.

She took a couple of steps toward Nicholas, who backed up. Nicholas spotted Wally standing on the porch.

"Wally!" he shouted. "You have to come with me. It's an emergency."

"What emergency?" said Wally. "Whatever it is, I don't think you need a knife. Come back inside so we can talk."

"There's no time," said Nicholas. "They have packs of C-4. I saw them."

"Nobody has packs of C-4, man," said Wally. "Just come back inside and give me the knife. The cooks need to use it."

People were coming out onto the porch. Nicholas looked left and right, frantic, clutching the pink knife close to his body.

"Everybody, please go back inside," said Wally. "I want to talk to him."

He descended the steps and stood beside Sherry.

"Please, Nicholas, stop," she said. "You're doing so much better now!"

"I'm sorry!" said Nicholas, "but it's way worse than you think, Sherry. People will die if Wally and I don't do something. Listen to me. There are boxes and boxes and boxes of explosives. I saw them. They're planning to blow up a building."

"Who's planning to blow up a building?"

"Those guys at that house!" Nicholas backed up a few more steps. "Wally, if you help me, we can find it."

"There's nothing to find, man," said Wally. "You need to just take a deep breath."

"Give Wally the knife and come back inside," pleaded Sherry. "Please, I'll fix you some tea. You can tell us all about it."

Nicholas hesitated. Sherry tried taking a couple of steps toward him, but he backed up to maintain the distance.

"Should I call the cops?" asked a male resident.

"Wait! No," said Wally. "I just need everybody to mellow out. We don't need …"

Nicholas bolted.

Sherry ran after him for a few feet, then screamed at the top of her lungs. "NICHOLAS!"

He was gone, down the street, his footsteps fading away into the distance.

Wally took off after him. Nicholas was already half a block away and getting farther. He emerged under the light of the corner streetlight and then turned right. A few seconds later, Wally reached the corner and turned, but … he didn't see him. Wally kept running, out of breath, heart racing. Suddenly, he spotted Nicholas, the long knife in hand, half a block distant, almost to the corner.

Man, he's fast.

Nicholas reached the corner, turned right, and disappeared, heading back in the direction of campus. Wally, puffing fiercely, reached the corner and stopped, resting his hands on his knees, sucking wind. Nicholas was almost a block away. This was hopeless. Should he return to Keystone? Maybe it was time to call the cops. But … he has that knife. What if they fucking *shoot* him?

Wally started trotting again, trying to keep Nicholas in sight. A third of the way down the block, he suddenly found himself running past Callie's Volkswagen, which she had parked a block from her apartment.

The door was unlocked, as usual. He could drive it! He flopped into the seat and turned the ignition switch with its broken key jammed inside. The engine cranked and started. Wally slammed it into gear and turned the wheel hard to get out of the tight space. His front right bumper clipped the car parked in front, but he kept going, roared out onto the narrow street, and accelerated.

He had lost Nicholas. At the street corner, Wally paused. *Which way? Left, right, or straight ahead?* One was as good as the other. He turned left and sped down the street, looking left and right in the yards. No sign of a crazy, skinny man with an oversized knife. Where would he be going?

Two blocks farther, Wally turned right and headed back the other way. No Nicholas. He had to get oriented, make a plan. He pulled over to think.

Nicholas had been headed in the general direction of campus. Maybe Wally could go block by block, gradually working his way east. He could have already driven past Nicholas in the dark. Must keep his eyes peeled.

Wally drove more slowly. He fell into a pattern: Go three blocks south, turn the corner, then head three blocks north, then turn again and repeat. Soon, he finally found himself turning onto the main street that paralleled the west side of campus.

He searched for any sign of commotion or turmoil. If people had seen Nicholas with the comically big kitchen knife, they'd react, surely, but all appeared normal.

Wally drove back to Keystone to see if Nicholas had returned.

When he arrived at the house, Sherry, Nixon, Jerry, and several other residents and neighbors were standing in the front yard. Wally pulled up the curb, rolled down the passenger side window, and shouted.

"Have you seen him?!"

Jerry Fox Lewis trotted over to the window, Sherry following.

"He hasn't been back," said Jerry. "Should we call the police?"

"No!" screamed Sherry. "They'll kill him!"

"I don't know what to do!" yelled Wally. "I'm gonna keep looking."

Wally roared off again. He drove north to Twenty-Fourth Street, turned right, and slowed down, scanning both sides of the street.

Suddenly, red and blue lights flashed in his rearview mirror, and he heard a siren. It was a cop car, in full pursuit of somebody or something, coming fast up the narrow street behind him. Wally pulled the car to the curb, and the cop car screamed past him.

Wally pulled back onto the street and tried to follow. Were they responding to a report about Nicholas?

Where is he going? And what the hell was all that babbling about C-4? What did he mean by "those guys at that house?" What house?

Pi Sigma Rho. Of course!

Wally drove on until he reached fraternity row and turned left. Straight ahead, two blocks away, the lights of two cop cars flashed in the middle of the street. Wally looked for a place, any place, to park. There was an illegal space on the corner next to a fire hydrant, and he pulled into it, jumped out of the car, and ran toward the commotion.

In the yard in front of Pi Sigma Rho, a dozen boys were congregating, and others were coming out of adjacent houses. Wally trotted toward the scrum of people, trying to get as close as he could. Nicholas was nowhere to be seen. A cop carrying an enormous flashlight was talking to two boys in the yard. Wally pushed through the growing crowd and approached a young man standing in the yard next door. "What's happening?"

"There was a crazy guy with a knife," he said. "He ran into the Rho house and started yelling about bombs. Those guys chased him out."

Wally pushed past some more people until he was close enough to hear.

"He had this huge knife, almost like a machete!" one guy was saying. "He said he'd cut me if I didn't tell him where the bombs were. I threw a chair at him."

"He tried to get upstairs, but we blocked him," said the other guy. "He ran out the side door."

"Did you see which way he went?" asked the cop.

"I think he went around the back of Lambda House."

Wally ran back to Callie's car. Nicholas hadn't hurt anybody yet. Hopefully not. But there was nothing more Wally could do. He climbed back into the Volkswagen, started it, and U-turned, heading back to the main street. As he drove south toward Twenty-First Street, another cop car zoomed by going the other way, lights ablaze.

It was up to the police now. What would they do if he refused to drop the knife? Kill him, probably. If somebody could just talk to Nicholas, get him to slow down and recognize that the thoughts in his head were not normal.

There is nothing I can do. Literally, nothing. I am no use to anyone.

He had to return Callie's car. Was the same parking place still available? Maybe he should try to find another spot since he had bumped into another car on the way out. He felt bad about that, but ...

In his peripheral vision, Wally caught a glimpse of someone walking quickly on the campus side of the street next to a parking garage. He had driven a hundred feet past before it registered. He slammed on the brakes and looked back.

A man was walking briskly, his right arm clutched to his chest. Was that Nicholas?

Wally tried to put the Volkswagen in reverse but ended up in fourth gear and popped the clutch, killing the engine. A car pulled up behind him and honked. Wally waved them around and restarted the car, then found the reverse gear and backed up the street. He saw the man duck into the stairwell door of the four-story parking garage. It sure looked like Nicholas.

Turning the wheel hard, Wally gunned the engine and crossed all four lanes of the street, and drove into the entrance ramp of the garage. There was no gate, just an empty booth with a sign, Public Parking Top Floor. He stepped on the gas and went up the ramp, working the clutch and grinding the gears.

When he popped out onto the garage's second floor, he hit the brakes and looked around. No Nicholas, though it was hard to tell in the twilight. Since it was the end of the day, there were only a handful of cars parked here and there, and Nicholas could be hiding behind any of them. Wally hesitated, then backed onto the ramp and drove up and around to the third floor. Again, he nosed the car into the parking area and scanned his surroundings. Only two cars were parked on this level, but no Nicholas. He hesitated again, watching the stairwell door, then backed up and continued to the roof, a wide, dark, empty expanse, no cars at all.

There was no place to hide up here. Nicholas was either in the stairwell or back on one of the lower levels. Wally would have to drive back down slowly and check each level again. He motored across the roof, headed for the down ramp.

Then, in the far corner by the stairwell entrance, the door opened, and Nicholas came out. He wasn't running, not even walking fast. He held the kitchen knife in front of him and walked across the width of the roof. Wally's first instinct was to slam the gears into reverse and back over to Nicholas, but he didn't want to spook him. Wally did a careful U-turn, drove slowly across the lot and into a lined parking space. He shut off the engine and got out of the little car.

It was quiet up here. Somewhere blocks away, a car alarm was blaring, but it didn't disturb the peaceful evening. After a few moments, he heard a siren, also far away.

If Nicholas had seen Wally, he hadn't shown any reaction. Nicholas reached the three-foot-high concrete wall that surrounded the roof and stopped, gazing out over the city below. Wally approached him, heart pounding, sweat trickling down his face.

Get his attention. Don't startle him.

"Hey, Nicholas!" he called. "What are you doing up here, man?"

Nicholas looked back.

"Oh, hey, Wally. I screwed up bad, man."

"It's okay. You just got your information wrong. There were no bombs. Now we just need to tell the cops it was all a mistake."

"Wally, the C-4 was there. I smelled it. I just couldn't find it. Maybe they moved it already, or it's hidden really well, or maybe … they've already planted it. Either way, I screwed everything up so bad."

Nicholas gazed out over the city far below, still holding the big pink kitchen knife in his right hand.

"Can I come closer so I don't have to yell?" said Wally.

"Sure, man. Come over here. I want you to see something."

"Can you *please* put down the knife? That thing freaks me out."

Nicholas looked back at Wally, shrugged, and placed the knife gently on the parapet.

Wally took a few steps closer.

"Come look," said Nicholas, pointing out toward the city. "Check it out."

Wally stepped to the edge and looked over. All the remained of sunset was a red glow. To their left, the giant bell tower loomed from behind a smaller building, brilliantly lit and imposing in the fading twilight, while to the right and farther away were the tall downtown buildings, both government and commercial. Closer and down below, city lights were beginning to come on. Red and white car lights moved in slow processions on the streets. Then he leaned over and looked straight down. It was a sheer four-story drop to the sidewalk. His head swam, and he recoiled.

"Beautiful, huh," said Nicholas. "But by tomorrow, one of those buildings will be a smoking crater. People will be dead. I should have stopped it, but I didn't. That's on me." He wiped his forehead with the back of his hand and turned back to the street below. A dark, wet streak glistened on the side of Nicholas's forehead, extending down to his chin.

"Hey, man, are you bleeding?" asked Wally.

"Yeah. The dude threw a chair at me when I tried to check upstairs. I got so mad, I was gonna stab him, but then I didn't. A couple other guys came out. One of them had a baseball bat. What did I do? I chickened out and ran."

"You made the right decision," said Wally. "No harm done. We'll just explain to the cops it was a mistake. Everybody makes mistakes."

"They'll put me back in the hospital," said Nicholas.

"Sure, but it will be okay. The doctors can help you get your medication straight. You can rest, do your yoga. I'll lend you some books to read."

Wally became aware that sirens were drawing closer. He swallowed his fear of heights and peered over the side. Down below, two police cars pulled up in front of the garage. Somebody had seen Nicholas go into the stairwell. One car stayed on the street, its lights whirling in circles across the garage and the buildings on the other side. The other police car backed up and entered the ramp. Wally guessed they would check each level of the garage thoroughly on their way up. He might have a few minutes.

"You took a good whack on the head," said Wally. "Does it hurt? I can help you."

"Like you did with Sherry? It's a different kind of pain. I hurt everywhere. I screwed up so bad."

"Just let me try," said Wally, "before the people get here. It'll just take a second. I won't touch you." Wally stepped closer, just within reach of Nicholas, and extended his right hand so it hovered an inch from the cut on his forehead. "Just relax. Shut your eyes."

Were there ever worse circumstances for healing? A hot summer evening, standing on the edge of a roof, police closing in? But Nicholas closed his eyes, so Wally tried.

The acute pain of the head injury was impossible to miss, and he was able to see it easily. The man's body energy was strong. Wally felt his forehead tingling as he moved his hand up and away from Nicholas's head. There was something deeper down, which the wound was drowning out. Wally tried to sense his way around the distress, find something he could identify and discharge. His hand trembled. He took a step closer and moved his hand over the back of Nicholas's head. He tried to sweep away the bad energy, which was blocking whatever was going on inside.

Nicholas remained still for a long moment, but then he exhaled suddenly and stepped away, turning to face Wally.

"Just let me try," said Wally and reached toward his head again, but Nicholas pushed him away.

"No," he said. "It's too late. They're coming for me."

"Please!" said Wally. "It will be okay. Let me do what I can do."

Far down below on the street, a third vehicle pulled up to the curb, a van with flashing lights. It was a TV news truck.

The roar of the heavy cop car engine echoed from inside the ramp, tires squealing, coming closer. Bright headlights appeared at the top of the ramp exit, and suddenly, the cop car screeched out onto the roof, blue and red lights dazzling. It roared across the lot and stopped short of where Nicholas and Wally stood. Nicholas quickly grabbed the knife from the top of the wall and whirled around, brandishing it like a sword.

Oh, Jesus!

Two cops got out, hands on their sidearms.

"Drop the weapon and get on the ground!" yelled one cop. "Both of you. Down!"

"I'm his friend!" shouted Wally. "I'm trying to talk to him!"

"Then you back away!" ordered the cop.

Wally moved back a few feet.

Nicholas stood facing the two officers, pointing the tip of the blade toward them and moving the knife back and forth like he was waving a wand. Both cops drew their weapons and pointed them at his chest.

"Drop the knife! Now!"

Nicholas glared, defiant. Then he went down on one knee, gently placed the huge knife on the concrete, and slid it toward the police. It skittered a few feet and then sat in place, spinning around on its hilt before stopping.

One officer holstered his gun while the other kept his sidearm pointed low.

Wally sighed. *Oh, thank God.*

But instead of submitting, Nicholas turned, placed both hands on top of the parapet, hopped up, turned around, and stood straight with feet together, facing toward the roof.

"Nicholas. Get down!" said Wally.

The two cops conferred briefly, then one of them climbed back into the patrol car and picked up the radio handset. The other one moved forward and quickly kicked the knife out of the way. He kept his pistol out but pointed down.

"Listen, son," he said. "Just step down from there. Whatever it is you want to talk about, we'll listen."

"Nicholas, just do what he says!" pleaded Wally.

The cop turned to Wally. "Sir, I need you to step back!" said the officer. "I'll handle this."

"I don't want him to jump!" yelled Wally.

"We don't want that either," said the cop. "The best thing you can do is give us room."

"I know what he's worried about," said Wally. "If I could just ..."

"SIR! Step back! Now! Or I'll arrest you."

Reluctantly, Wally moved back a few more feet.

Nicholas appeared calm, but he stayed where he was, hands straight down by his side.

"I have to wait," he announced.

"Tell me what you're thinking, son," said the officer. "Talk to me. What are you waiting for?" No response.

The second cop got out of the car.

"Crisis is on their way. They said ten minutes."

The red and blue lights played across the parking lot. The police radio crackled. They were at a stalemate. Minutes crept by. The officers talked together quietly. Wally sweated in the dark, hearing the beat of his own heart.

Three blocks away, the tower bells began to chime. It was eight o'clock. The bells began to ring their solemn notes—"Westminster Quarters."

Nicholas moved. He pivoted his body around, put his hands together in the prayer attitude, and then stood on one foot, his left leg bent into a triangle: the one-legged prayer pose, two inches from the ledge.

He's waiting for the bell, thought Wally.

"Listen, pal," said the officer. "Stand still. We have some people coming to talk with you in a few minutes. It'll be okay. Just don't move."

"Westminster Quarters" ended, and the hour chimes began. Wally counted them in his head. On the fifth chime, Nickolas looked straight up and raised his arms over his head.

Do something. Now!

Wally leaped. Reaching the wall in a few long strides, he grabbed Nicholas by his leg and pulled back hard. Nicholas came down on one knee, then pitched forward, his body rolling over the ledge, arms flailing. Wally succeeded in grabbing his belt but found himself being pulled forward over the edge. The street loomed far below, and he felt a wave of vertigo. Nicholas grabbed at Wally with one hand as he slipped farther over the parapet, pulling the back of Wally's T-shirt over his head.

Struggling, blinded, Wally hooked his knees against the wall and pulled back with everything he had, dragging Nicholas with him, and they both crashed in a tangled heap on the roof. Immediately, the two policemen were on them, manhandling Nicholas, rolling him over onto his stomach, and snapping handcuffs onto his wrists.

One cop turned on Wally. "That was *stupid*!" he yelled. "You almost knocked him off. We had a suicide specialist on the way."

"He would've jumped," said Wally, picking himself up and pulling his shirt back down. He rubbed his elbow where he had landed hard. He wondered if it was broken.

The cops stood Nicholas up. The expression on his face was of wounded sadness.

"Wally, I wasn't gonna jump," Nicholas said. "I just wanted to hear the bells. They were trying to tell me something."

The officers pushed Nicholas up against the police car and patted him down.

"He has a bad cut on his forehead," said Wally.

One of the cops put his hand on Nicholas's chin. "Lower your head," he commanded. The officer shined his heavy service flashlight onto his forehead and then along the hairline.

"He's okay," said the cop. "Not bleeding. It looks like an old injury to me, mostly healed."

Below on the sidewalk, a local TV cameraman, who had heard the police radio dispatch, had caught the minutes of drama on camera, zoomed in as far as the lens would go: The young man standing precariously on one foot on top of the garage wall, another man appearing suddenly in the frame to grab him, nearly being dragged over the edge himself as they tangled together, then pulling the would-be suicide to safety. Real-life drama and a news cameraman's dream. He radioed the station to send out a reporter. They had some killer footage for the ten o'clock news.

The Healer

WALLY WANTED TO BE LEFT ALONE, but they wouldn't leave him alone.

At first, there was some confusion about the identity of the good Samaritan—that's what they were calling him—but soon it was clarified that the man who had saved Nicholas Symansky was twenty-seven-year-old Walter Edelstein, aka Wally Stein, manager of a housing co-op.

The item on page five of the local city paper was titled 'Police Call Bystander's Actions 'Misguided.''

… "I didn't know what else to do," said Edelstein. "He's my friend, and I was afraid he would jump. I had to stop him."

However, Police Chief MacAskill said Edelstein's reaction to the crisis, while understandable, was misguided.

"The responding officers had the situation in hand and were in communication with the disturbed person. The bystander could have made it much worse by doing what he did. Police are trained to handle these incidents. The public needs to step back and let us do our jobs. We got lucky this time."

The local TV station that first broke the story was more sympathetic. They sent out a reporter and cameraman and got several shots of Wally standing on the porch at Keystone. The quote they used was something Sherry had suggested.

"It's up to all of us to look out for each other," Wally said. "If you think a friend may be suicidal, tell somebody."

They liked that so much that they had him say it again because a car with a loud engine had driven past during the first take.

Then, they drove to the Pi Sigma Rho house to interview some witnesses to the fraternity house invasion. But in the end, they liked the mental health angle best and focused on that.

The most flattering piece ran in the college newspaper. An earnest young female journalism student talked to Wally for half an hour, asking him leading questions about friendship and communal living and what makes somebody a hero. A student photographer got a shot of Wally holding the pink kitchen knife. The story would run on the front page.

WALLY LOCKED HIMSELF IN THE KEYSTONE OFFICE for the afternoon, catching up on bookkeeping and general paperwork, then escaped to Callie's apartment.

It was a stifling day in the early fall. They sat together on Callie's balcony amid ferns and various trailing plants. She brought him a cup of cold hibiscus tea on ice with honey.

"Well, that was your fifteen minutes of fame, I guess," she said, laughing. "For today, at least, everybody in town knows you."

"I don't want it," said Wally. "I didn't ask for it."

"Well, it found you, and I think you handled things pretty well."

"Everybody thinks I'm either a hero or a guy who should have minded his own damn business. I'm leaning to the 'mind your own business' side."

"You saved a man's life. Give yourself some credit."

"I don't know. He told me he wouldn't have jumped, but I'll never know for sure. Maybe the hospital will give him better drugs, and he'll stay on them this time. Assuming the police don't bring charges, maybe he'll just go back to being a normal person, whatever that means. Then he may just stop taking his meds again, and the cycle will start over."

"It's up to him," said Callie. "You already did what you could do."

Wally sipped his tea, eyes closed.

"I can't save anybody," he said.

"Nobody expects you to," said Callie.

"No, you're wrong," said Wally. "I have always been expected to save people. Since I was five years old—ever since the day they found out I could make people feel better—they've been asking me to save them. But I can't save anybody. I don't *want* to save anybody. We're in this alone. Nobody can help."

"That's a miserable way of looking at it."

"It's the truth. We're on our own. It's always been true, but it took me my whole life to admit it. It was worse for me because I was born with this thing I didn't ask for. I wish I could have just had a normal life, kept it secret. But no. Once people know you can do something special, they think it's your duty to do it. The preacher at our church would always tell me, 'You have this gift, young man. This is something God gave you.' So there I would be every Sunday up at the front of the church clutching a Bible in my greasy little hand, waving my other hand over these really miserable people. Then they'd jump up and shout 'Hallelujah!' and everybody would pat me on the back and tell me how special I am, but I could never tell them the truth—I wanted to be left alone, to just be a kid."

"Of course," said Callie. "Everybody needs to be left alone sometimes. It's human nature."

"They would never leave me alone. And when they did, they acted like they were doing me a favor. Eventually, I broke down and told my parents that I wouldn't be a healer at church anymore. They said okay because they didn't really like it either, but I never got to stop. I kept getting asked to help this or that person and I always tried—always—because that's what was expected of me. 'The doctors are giving up. Call young David. That kid can do miracles.' And then they put me in a lab and tried to study me. You know what I did? I blew the test on purpose so they'd leave me alone. But they never would. I couldn't cure anybody, but I still had to keep trying, over and over."

"Hold on, Wally. You actually do help, and you have. Sherry told me what you did for her migraines. That was pure kindness. Nobody made you do it."

"I did help her feel better," said Wally. "Regular old pain I can usually deal with, even if it's pretty bad. But I can't save anybody's life."

"You probably saved Nicholas."

"Would he have jumped? I'm not so sure," said Wally. "Anybody could have done it. But when it really mattered, my superpowers made no difference. I could never save anybody, even when I desperately wanted to—when I really loved somebody. I couldn't save my parents. I couldn't save Judith."

"Wait. Who is Judith?" asked Callie. "Your mother?"

"She's somebody I loved and couldn't help. And I can't stop thinking that I could have saved her if I'd just tried harder. I knew there was something wrong in her brain, but I never said anything. Turns out she had a brain tumor. Maybe the doctors would have used a different treatment. But I'll never know, will I?"

Callie placed her hand on Wally's back but said nothing. She was listening.

"I should have stayed in Des Moines," said Wally. "Nobody knew me there. After I graduated, I didn't even try to go to college. I decided to go back home, but it turns out you can't do that. Even though my parents were dead, people kept finding me and asking for help. Usually, I tried because I was David the Healer. I never found a regular job I could stand, and I was broke most of the time. Well, people had always wanted to give me money to heal them, so after a while, I just set up shop and told them to pay me a hundred bucks. Sometimes, that made them go away, but usually, they paid, and that just made me hate myself. I didn't want to be a healer, but it was money, so I kept doing it."

"You know I do the same thing, Wally," said Callie. "It's a skill I have. I don't feel guilty being paid for it."

"But that's different. You're legitimate. You have training and a license. I was just doing this hustle on the side, off the books. Then, one day, this scary guy from the city showed up at my door and said that I was under investigation for operating an unlicensed medical practice, whatever that means. So I said that's it. I'm done. Never, never, never again. I just quit everything, quit my crappy restaurant job, skipped out on my apartment lease, and disappeared."

"Is that why you moved here?" asked Callie.

"Yeah. I was sick of being me, and I thought I could turn into somebody else, somebody less interesting. And I did, for a while. I met you, and I was happy for the first time in ages. But then, last night, I grabbed a crazy guy by the leg, almost got killed myself, and now I'm a hero again because I saved somebody. I don't want to save anybody else. I just want to be normal, Callie!"

He tried to take a sip of iced tea, but he coughed and sputtered and spilled a little red liquid on his shirt. Callie jumped up and returned with a paper towel. As she wiped his shirt, she saw tears streaming from his closed eyes. She patted his face gently with the towel and kissed his forehead.

"Wally, come inside with me."

He stood up. "I'm sorry, Callie. I'll leave now. I'm an idiot."

"No, you're not," she said. "Come into the bedroom."

She led him inside, where she kept her massage table. With a quick and practiced motion, she opened the table and locked it into position. She then put the face rest into place at one end and adjusted its height. Opening a drawer, she retrieved a clean folded sheet, spread it over the massage table, and tucked it under the edges.

"Get undressed and lie face down," she said.

He obeyed. He took off his clothes, folded them loosely on a chair, and lay down. The headrest cradled his face. Callie, professional and discrete, spread a thin top sheet over the lower part of his body.

"Let it go now," she said. "I'm in charge. Let it all go."

He moved around on the table, finding a comfortable position, then relaxed.

"Okay, Wally, I want you to say, 'I'm letting go now.' Go ahead. I want to hear you say it."

"I'm letting go now."

She placed her hands a couple of inches above his shoulders and slowly moved them together and toward his head in an upward sweeping motion. Then, beginning at the crown of his head, she glided her hands down across the entire length of his body. After a minute, her hands began to tremble, but she continued to move them up and down, inward to outward.

To Wally, everywhere her hands moved, he felt a soft, warm light illuminating the inside of his body. Then, as she worked her way down his spine, the stranded rope that was twisted tight in his core began to release and unwind and dissolve. He floated.

He felt himself to be two parts. The part of him that was in pain, fear, and sorrow was still there, alongside another part that was joy, peace, and freedom from pain. He could see them both objectively, as if from outside. Gradually, imperceptibly, the two parts came together and then merged.

So, this is what it's like, he thought.

Wally breathed in very slowly, then exhaled even more slowly. He had a small revelation, something so ordinary it was hardly worth mentioning. Why had he not seen it before, when he was on the other side of the process?

The secret is surrender. Let someone else do the caring. The healer and the healed are the same.

"Are you doing all right?" Callie asked.

"Yes. I am."

"Good. Let me know if you need some water."

An Evening on Dave's Tab

ALLIE AND WALLY drove in the little Squareback to the far southeast side of the city, almost to the county line. There was a little music club called Fleming's Grill. It was mostly a bar, but it did serve sandwiches and passable burgers to qualify as a restaurant for tax purposes.

They had dinner first, but not at Fleming's. Callie took Wally to the Oilman, a snooty white-tablecloth place on the twentieth floor of a downtown building. Wally wore a secondhand dinner jacket and a borrowed tie for the occasion. They had cocktails and medium-rare steaks and then crème brulee as they looked out over the vast expanse of city lights down below. Callie paid and wouldn't let Wally see the check.

Wally would have been perfectly happy to head back to Callie's apartment and spend a close night with her, but she had other plans. She kept them secret, but Wally guessed.

"We're going to see that lounge singer, aren't we?" said Wally.

Callie rolled her eyes. "Of course."

"You're really getting into this old-fart music lately," said Wally. "You know it's not my thing, right?"

"It wasn't mine either, but it's growing on me, and you'll like it too if you give it a chance. Anyway, I promised."

"So, lucky me, I finally get to hear the Dave Diamond Trio."

"Tonight, I think it's just Dave Diamond and a piano. He says it's a tiny little place. Roll with it. This is my treat to you."

"Okay."

At Fleming's, there were only a few cars in the parking lot. The club was dark inside like they always are. There was a two-dollar cover at the door, and Callie paid. A couple of dozen people sat scattered through the room.

"Sit anywhere you want," said the doorman. "Just not that table up front. It's reserved."

"I think it's reserved for me," said Callie. "The name is Pender."

The doorman checked a clipboard. "Indeed. Pender, party of two. All right, just take a seat. The waitress will be with you in a minute."

They picked their way through the club in the dark and sat at the little round table about eight feet from the stage, which was really just a low platform large enough for a piano and not much else, where Dave Diamond was playing a slow version of the jazz classic "Straight, No Chaser."

Wally sat in his chair and watched. He had to admit Dave Diamond was good. He had full command of the scuffed baby grand piano, with his large hands splayed out over a wide range, working the keys effortlessly. Dave Diamond looked pleased with himself and relaxed. He reminded Wally of ... wait ... No. It couldn't be.

"What would you folks like to drink?" asked the waitress.

Wally looked over at Callie and tried to say something but couldn't quite form words.

"White wine for me," said Callie. "How about you, Wally? Is white wine okay?"

He nodded, then looked back at the virtuoso on the little stage. Dave Diamond finished the song, then turned toward the audience, shading his eyes. His face lit up when he saw them. He pulled the microphone over close to his lips.

"Ladies and gentlemen, good evening. It's great you could all come out on a Tuesday night. Don't you people have jobs? I'm kidding! Hey, we have a couple of important guests tonight. This is my good friend Callie and her special man ... I'm sorry, what was your name?"

Wally was tongue-tied, so Callie called out, "His name's Wally!"

"I was *kidding*. I knew that," said Dave. "Callie and Wally. It's great to have you folks. Hey, Frank! This table is on my tab tonight."

A voice came from the bar, laughing. "Dave, you don't *have* a tab."

"Well, start one and put these fine people on it. Ladies and Gentlemen, before we get back to the music, I have a funny, crazy story to tell. It happened a couple of weeks ago. I'm sure a lot of you saw the news about a guy who almost jumped off a building on the university campus. Okay, that's not the funny part. I hope this poor man gets the help he needs. Fortunately, one of our good local citizens was there on the scene and came to the rescue. He's just one of those regular guys who *could* help, so he did. Anyway, the man sitting up here in front of the stage tonight is him, our hero. Frank, put a spotlight on the cat."

"Dave, you know we don't have a spotlight."

"Well, if you did, it would be pointed right there. Wally, you're the kind of man we need more of in this world. Everyone, let's give Wally a hand."

There were a few scattered claps.

"All right, ladies and gentlemen, *now* I'll tell you the funny part. The day after our hero appeared on the evening news, he was a mystery man. Nobody knew who he was. So, at eight o'clock in the morning—after I'd been up playing a set till 2 a.m., mind you—I wake up to a reporter pounding at my door, asking me if I'm the good Samaritan who jumped to the rescue last night. It was pretty hilarious because, as you all know, I am no great physical specimen. I couldn't rescue a kitten from a low tree. So, I'm standing there at the door with my crutches saying, uh, nope, sorry, not me, I promise. Wrong boy."

A glass of white wine was set in front of Wally. He took a gulp.

"Now, here's the crazy part," said Dave Diamond. "The reason they thought it was me is because this man and I have the same name, first and last. But we're not related. Isn't that wild? Like a lot of people in the music business, I use a stage name. But my birth name is Walter, just like this guy. Even weirder, it turns out that we have a very good mutual friend, and neither of us knew it. Truth is stranger than fiction, ladies and gentlemen, stranger than fiction."

Wally looked at Callie and tried to say something but couldn't quite manage.

Dave Diamond turned back to the piano. "So, I dedicate this next song to all the unlikely heroes in this world. Wally, this one's for you. 'Round Midnight.'"

They couldn't talk easily over the music, but Wally leaned over to Callie and asked, "So you knew?"

"I figured it out." Callie grinned.

So, they listened as Dave Diamond worked his way through piano jazz tunes, famous and obscure, and threw in a few originals. Wally finished his glass of wine, and another appeared almost immediately.

After a raucous version of "Sweet Georgia Brown," Dave said, "Folks, I'm gonna take a short break. If you need another drink, ask Theresa, and tip like you mean it. Frank, don't let the jukebox play too loud—I want to visit with these people."

"Dave, we don't *have* a jukebox."

He stood and took up his crutches, then worked his way slowly to the edge of the platform and carefully down the single step to the floor level. He hobbled over to Wally and Callie's table, grinning. Wally stood and pulled back a chair for him, but Dave leaned his crutches against the table and opened his arms.

"Come here, you old fraud!"

They hugged, and then they kept on hugging. Dave, who was a head shorter than Wally, rested his bushy hair against the taller man's chest and held him tight. The hug went on for so long that Callie finally said, "Don't worry about me, I'm fine!"

Dave laughed and let Wally go, gave Callie a quick kiss on the cheek, then plopped down in the chair. He shook his head. "Wow. Until you walked in, I really thought it might be some crazy-ass coincidence. But, nope, here you are, damn it. Look at you. It's really you."

"How are you, Walter?"

"Pretty damn good, David. How about yourself?"

"Stunned, really. Blown away? Thunderstruck? … I'm running out of words. I didn't see it coming."

"Well, me neither, till Callie told me. And even then, I wasn't sure I believed it."

Wally turned to Callie. "How long have you known?"

"Well, I didn't know for sure until just now," said Callie. "But I guessed. You know how I'm really bad about getting my checks deposited—I wait till I have a bunch before I go to the bank. Last week, I was going through all my checks from clients and filling out the deposit slip, and I found this check for sixty dollars from 'Walter Edelstein.' I thought, 'Why on Earth did Wally write me a check?' Then I remembered. Dave usually pays with cash, but one time, he wrote a check. I never looked at it till later."

The waitress brought a glass of mineral water for Dave. He raised it.

"Here's to old friends and new," he said. His water glass clinked against the two wine glasses.

"You want your name back?" asked Wally.

"No, that's fine. I think 'Wally' suits you," said Dave. "I have a confession to make. When I was first trying to get noticed in the Chicago jazz scene, I went by the stage name 'Dave Monk.' But then everybody thought I was trying to be the next Thelonius Monk. A friend suggested 'Diamond,' which sounded nice and sparkly, so I went with that. Of course, now I get accused of trying to be the next Neil Diamond, but what can you do?"

"Well, if you ever want to switch back again, let me know."

"I'll keep that offer in mind," said Dave. "Or maybe I should just legally change my name to avoid confusion in the future."

He raised his water glass above his head and shouted to the room. "To Wally and Dave, together again!"

"And to the summit, which we will never summit!" said Wally.

Dave burst out laughing. "I'll drink to that."

"You guys are weird," said Callie.

THE END

Acknowledgments

THIS IS A NOVEL ABOUT changeability, and the desire to turn into a different person if who you are isn't working out. It is not about healers and healing per se. But as the story grew, I became more and more interested in healing as an ancient, universal art, what it means, and why it works when it does. And also, who are these people, the healers? What do they think about the practice, and about themselves? While I know there are cynics and scammers who call themselves healers, the ones I'm familiar with are sincere, thoughtful, and care deeply about the welfare of others. For the most part, they don't reject science-based medicine, though many are skeptical of the medical industry. Personally, the older I get, the more in awe of doctors and their skills I have become. (By the way, there is no such thing as Blaine-Fischer disease. The symptoms are based on some real, though rare, genetic disorders.)

Most of the healing in this story involves physical pain. And, yes, there's a lot more to pain than throbbing hips and heads. Psychic disorders, mental anguish, uncontrolled fear, panic, low-level anxiety are also forms of pain, and they cause real suffering. Relief is what people seek from healers of all types, mystical, medical, and everything in between. (Nobody ever went to a Raiki practitioner for a painless nodule on the thyroid.) Has there ever been an effective healer who knew they had a gift but came to resent and reject it? I don't know. Is it plausible? I hope so.

This novel started as a pandemic project because I needed something to do while we were locked down and isolated, and to take my mind off the final slog of a previous book. In February 2020, just a couple of weeks before the S.S. *Normal Life* ran aground, I had a conversation with an old friend, who said, "You remember that co-op in Austin where we lived in the '70s, and all those crazy people we knew there? Write about that."

The house was called "Ramshorn." In an earlier incarnation it had been a Jewish men's co-op, but by the time I got there in 1974 it was a crazy stew of young men and women, teenagers and twenty-somethings, from every imaginable background, all brought together by cheap room and board. Some were students and some were just one step up from vagabonds. There were religious zealots and atheists, radicals and traditionalists, libertines and prudes, every imaginable personality. A few were certifiably insane. For people looking to grow, reinvent themselves, or hide from their past, it was a unique opportunity for radical personal change.

As ALWAYS, there are so many people who have helped me as a writer that I can't begin to name them all, but I will pick out a few.

Grateful thanks go out to: Felix Scardino, for listening to me ramble and encouraging me to be a storyteller; Rosa Glenn Reilly, therapist and writer, for helping hone my ideas about healing, and for giving priceless feedback for this book; Max Regan, an incomparable writing teacher, (nay, writing whisperer) and a great friend over the years; my daughter, Abby Henson, a sharp-eyed and opinionated beta-reader; my cousin Elizabeth Ream, a novelist, who told me what she wanted, as a reader, from the story. (This is very useful information.)

Beyond that, I am thankful to the many, many people who, just by living and being who they were, inspired a big basketful of fictional incidents and characters to draw from. (And thanks to Bill Marshall, who reminded me about the time a disturbed man went on a frantic mission to find an imaginary hidden bomb in Austin's West Campus neighborhood. I heard about the incident at the time, but forgot. Bill was an eyewitness.)

Most of all, I thank my wife Sarah, who has loved and sustained me for decades, and to whom I owe my life, comfort, companionship, and happiness. She is also a very perceptive reader. I love you more than ever, if that is possible.

– Henry D. Terrell, August 2024

HENRY D. TERRELL was born and raised in West Texas and attended the University of Texas at Austin from 1974 to 1978. He is a retired business editor and writer who lives with his wife in Houston.

Other fiction titles by the author:

Salt of the King
Desert Discord
Wait Till I Come Down
Headfirst Off the Caprock

Contact: Books@HenryDTerrell.com

www.ingramcontent.com/pod-product-compliance
Lightning Source LLC
Chambersburg PA
CBHW050518110726
47899CB00005B/1501